Leitsack combines breakthrough science-fiction with deep philosophical and religious considerations... and insists on the universal aspirations to godliness.

... The scope of *AD 2188* is reminiscent of one of my favorite classics, Teilhard de Chardin's "*The Phenomenon of Man*", but ... goes further as it offers a worldview with an exciting plot grounded in current political events and that links physical science with human consciousness.

... The metaphysical aspects of the novel, and its ending will leave you in a wonder. Truly inspiring!

Dr. David Wake, *Fellow*
Royal Society of Arts, *London, UK*

AD 2188
The World Under
the Grand Caliphate

~ E Pluribus Umma ~

D. LEITSACK

~ exemplum ~

Credits:

Sacred texts from official translations
All other translations by the author

Maps by the author

Diagrams: 14 by PJC, 18, 19, 22 (Guoliang tunnel rendition)
and 29 by DC
Satellite simulation diagrams (24, 25, 26, 27 and 28) by WJB
and the author
All other diagrams by the author

All computations by the author
Science review by DF
Editing Advisor: MC

Cover design by DC
Back Cover Image: *Western Woman in Muslim Dress,* oil on
canvas, by CD *c.* 1977, with permission

Disclaimer:

All characters except for known historical figures
cited are fictional and any resemblance to current
or known persons is purely coincidental.

— ≈ —

ISBN-10:   0 9847501 1 8
ISBN-13: 978 0 9847501 1 5
Library of Congress Control Number: 2011941566
Printed in the United States of America

Caliphate, Islam, Quantum Weapons, Quantum Entanglement,
Quantum Tunneling, Neutrino Beams,
Thought Waves, Post-Death Consciousness

exemplum publishing, llc   p.o. box 5425 washington, dc 20016
www.exemplumpublishing.com

AD 2188
The World Under
the Grand Caliphate

This book is dedicated to the memory of my mother whose thoughts continue to reach us, and those entangled with ours have found their expression here.

The author

What truth bound by these mountains
That is but lies in the world that is beyond?

Montaigne, 1533-1592 Christian Era

CONTENTS

AD 2188 - The world Under the Grand Caliphate

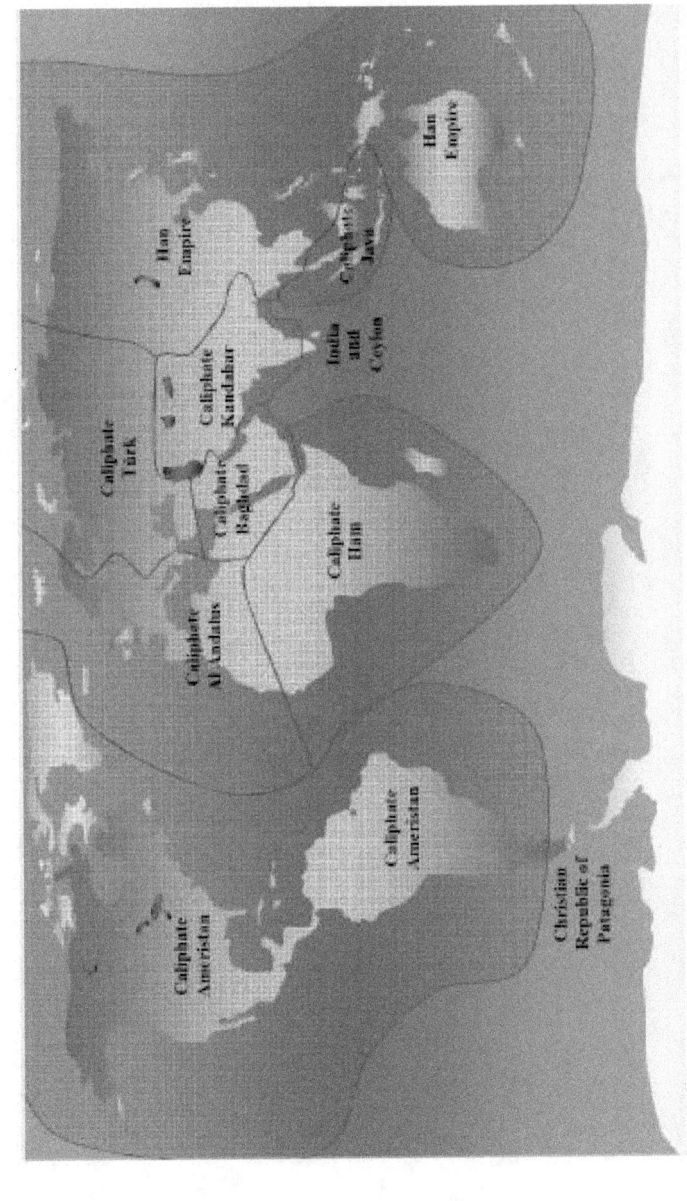

1. The World Circa 1615 Hijri Calendar, 2188 Christian Era

PART I

UNFINISHED BUSINESS

1

A DAY IN THE CALIPHATE

Usamabad, Ameristan[1]
Latitude 5.7638 steps to the Shama'al
Longitude 36.0603 steps to the Gherb[2]
Year of the Prophet (pbuh) 1615[3]

t was the nineteenth day of Safar of the year 1615 of the Prophet (pbuh). It corresponded approximately to August 13, Year 2188 of the Christian Era and commonly noted as 2188 CE. The number 19 was of particular importance in the Qur'an unlike the superstition associated with the number 13 in Christian culture.

The number 19 is special in the Qur'an as many occurrences are either nineteen or multiples thereof: the first revelation contains nineteen words and the total number of letters in the first revelation is seventy six, that is four times nineteen; the words Bism'Allah – in the name of Allah - occur one hundred and fourteen times or six times nineteen; and the last chapter revealed has nineteen words with the first verse containing nineteen letters. There are other occurrences of the number nineteen of course.

---

[1] The original US motto is *"e Pluribus Unum"* , in Latin literally *"out of many, one"*. In order to denote the values that were honored in those times in *Ameristan* the Caliphate changed it to *"e Pluribus Umma"* that is *"out of many, the Umma"*, the Umma being the world Muslim community.

[2] Latitude and Longitude are measured in *steps*, or fractions thereof, from the Kaaba, the Holy of the Holies in Mecca. A step is a unit of distance equal to that separating Mecca and Medina. Steps are normally counted in decimal fractions for directions from the Kaaba, Shamaal (north), Janoub (south), Sharkh (east) and Gherb (west). For Usamabad, they correspond to the former 38 degrees 53 minutes, 23.23 seconds North and 77 degrees, 2 minutes, 23.51 seconds West of the Christian Era.

[3] As is customary and must be done out of respect and awe, all references to the Prophet (pbuh) will be followed by the respectful and necessary "Peace Be Upon Him", or "pbuh" in abbreviated form.

A scientific assessment of the system of latitudes and longitudes in use in the Caliphate indicated that the circumference of the Earth when measured according to a polar method was of one hundred and nineteen steps, that is nineteen steps in addition to the first one hundred. Similarly, the circumference of the circle of latitude passing by Mecca was of one hundred and eleven steps while for Medina it was of one hundred and eight steps. The total of the two was thus two hundred and nineteen steps, nineteen more than one hundred for each of the holy sites.

Was it truly 1615 or 2188 or any other number?

Sheikh Assam Al Amriki sat at his desk in the Room of the Two Crescents in the heart of *Al Dar Baida*. And he pondered about Time.

Eternal Time

According to the History books used in all schools across the entire Grand Caliphate, that year 1615 would have been known long ago as AD 2188, Anno Domini, Year of the Lord, Anno Dei, Year of God. That obviously was *haram*, sacrilegious to the Umma. But in those days of yore, polite company had insisted in calling that yearly reference Common Era, since Dei, meaning *of God* referred to a god that was God to only a few in the world. In the strange atmosphere that reigned in the days of the last American President, Common Era or CE was accepted as correct socially and politically since Common Era did not offend anyone, except of course those who believed it was truly Christian Era, or more appropriately to them A.D. Still, the true believers of that faith either insisted that this time reference be A.D., or secretly smiled to themselves understanding it was really not Common Era but Christian Era. Which it was. But no more.

The exact day, month and year 2188 CE were approximate because the Christian calendar, Gregorian as it was then known, was based on the perceived movement of the Earth around the Sun. Which assumes the model to be the correct one to determine the essence of Time. The Holy Book, the Qur'an, brought to us by the Prophet, Peace be Upon Him, told us that our year must truly be the twelve months of the Hijri calendar, each of these months beginning at the moment of actual sight of the first crescent of the Moon. That is the signal from Allah that a new moon, a new month has begun.

The purely lunar months without intercalation, or corrections which consisted of adding a month or a day to the regular calendar to accommodate the movement of the Earth relative to the Sun, are described to us in some of the most moving verses of the Holy Qur'an:

The number of months
In the sight of Allah
Is twelve in a year
So ordained by Him
The day He created
The heavens and the earth;
Of them four are sacred;
That is the straight usage
So wrong not yourselves
Therein, and fight the Pagans. (IX: 36)

Of a prohibited month
In truth the transposing
Is an addition to Unbelief:
The Unbelievers are led
To wrong thereby: for they make
It lawful one year,
And forbidden another year,
Of months forbidden by Allah
And make such forbidden ones
Lawful. The evil of their course
Seems pleasing to them.
But Allah guideth not
Those who reject Faith. (IX: 37)

At the root then, there was a disagreement on the definition of time between Christianity and Islam. Christian dogma was rooted initially in Judaism, hence in God's Word. These two original Scriptures were God's Word only at the respective beginnings of these faiths, but by the time of the Revelation brought to us by the last Prophet (pbuh) they became incomplete and insufficient. And ever since those beginnings, the infidels strayed more and more away from the Truth by putting all laws, and all discoveries, and all science in the hands of man. That was an error.

The Christians, and it took them centuries even to convince their own priesthood, based their theories upon astronomical observations. The flaw is that observations were man-made. The Qur'an is divine.

5

What the human eye saw, or believed it was seeing was useful for a lot of applications in technology, medicine and many other fields, but it was not transcendent. Can a blind man see better than a man with two useful eyes? There is no definite answer as a blind man can sometimes see what others may not.

It is recounted that a blind man, Abdullah ibn Umm Maktum came up and asked the Prophet (pbuh) the following:

"O messenger of God, teach me from what God has taught you."

The Prophet (pbuh) then frowned and turned away from him. After that, the Prophet (pbuh) suddenly felt partially blinded and his head began to throb violently. A revelation came to him:

"He frowned and turned away when the blind man approached him! Yet for all you knew, (O Muhammad), he might perhaps have grown in purity or have been reminded of the Truth, and helped by this reminder. Now as for him who believes himself to be self-sufficient, to him you gave your whole attention, although you are not accountable for his failure to attain to purity. But as for him who came unto you full of eagerness and in awe of God, him did you disregard. "(Sura 80: 116)

So that the Prophet (pbuh) learned that truth and purity can be sought and seen by a blind person and obscured from the eyes of a seeing one.

Western science in fact admitted the ephemeral character of all scientific theories. Newton's Classical Theory of the Universe explained many phenomena and indeed ushered in an era of innovation and technological accomplishments. But then Relativity and Quantum Theory placed this Classical view in context, as it did not comport with experiment or observation for the infinitely large or the infinitely small, and the truth once true became only a particular part of a larger truth. And that continued, and will continue forever. Only Allah brings the absolute Truth that does not change with man's interpretation.

The Hijri calendar is unique because it is divinely inspired and bases its measurement of time beginning with the Hijra, the migration of the Prophet (pbuh) from Mecca to Medina, ten years before the Prophet's (pbuh) death in 632 AD, and the eternal struggle of man when faced between Truth and Evil. As the great Samiullah wrote:

> *"All the events of Islamic history, especially those*
> *which took place during the life of the Holy Prophet*
> *and afterwards are quoted in the Hijra calendar era.*
> *But our calculations in the Gregorian calendar keep us*
> *away from those events and happenings, which are*
> *pregnant of admonitory lessons and guiding*
> *instructions....And this chronological study is*
> *possible only by adopting the Hijri calendar to*
> *indicate the year and the lunar month in line with our*
> *cherished traditions."*

The Hijri calendar is therefore a guide book to the rich traditions of Islam, rather than an impersonal, technical counter of days with no true meaning. In fact the revolving nature of Islamic events, disconnected from the seasons, connects a true Muslim to the immutability of God's Time, and to the eternity of God. Ramadan is not a Summer holiday, or a Spring festival, or a Winter lamentation, or a celebration of the Fall harvest. It is more than a metaphor. It is Ramadan, the holy month which occurs regularly and only when Ramadan occurs. And the same is true of all other months.

Since the start of a new month is marked not only by a new moon, but by a human sighting of the crescent moon, when Allah indicates the nascent crescent, time as reckoned by man is a human observation. But that act of observing differs from the clockwork of the Sun and its planets described by astronomy. Indeed, without man to record it, there is no earthly time. Just as some Quantum theorists advocate, only observation of a phenomenon makes it be. But unlike Quantum Theory, the observation of the Truth does not alter it. And God, eternal, does not need Time. Allah created Time for us. And Time is not to be related to earthly references such as the seasons. God's Time is eternal.

Of course in the Grand Caliphate, to ensure orderly celebrations the then widely accepted Islamic Lunar Date Line connected the Umma in a unified Time, regardless of their location on Earth.

Sheikh Assam looked at the holographic calendar and clock that appeared out of thin air anywhere he would look in his Room of the Two Crescents, but did not appear if he did not look - observation creates the event – a clever contraption based on quantum phenomena. The time for his meeting was approaching.

One thing the History books did not teach, he thought, but that he learned from experience is that the definition of Time is fundamental to all beliefs. It is not just an observation, or a mechanical clock. Time is what God defined for us when He created His Earth, and to give His ultimate creation, man, a point of reference for changing circumstances.

Thoughts while Mourning

Sheikh Assam recalled a mourning ceremony for a friend of his, a Jew - a few were still allowed to practice their faith in the Grand Caliphate - a ceremony in which they recited a prayer for the dead. It was called a *kaddish* as he could recall. In this *kaddish*, not a word was said of the deceased person, or of his memory or even his future in Heaven. All that prayer did was praise the name of an entity that *was not named*.

In the eyes of the congregants of course, what was not named meant God. Why they gave no name to their God, while Islam cherishes Him with ninety nine beautiful names was still a mystery to Assam. Allah is a special name of God containing them all. The Prophet (pbuh) had said:

> *"To Allah belong 99 names, 100 minus 1, anyone who fully understands and memorizes them all will enter his Paradise; He is odd, because he is One And the Only One.*
>
> *... Allah!, There is no God but He! To Him belong the Most Beautiful Names." (Qur'an 20:8)*

What intrigued Assam even further is as follows.

While the congregation of a few dozen only, the deceased being a community leader and attracted what was then considered a crowd in these lands depleted of non-Muslims, he Assam read the adjoining translation of that *kaddish* in Arabic, which included several commentaries. Assam noted a comment concerning a change in the wording of the eternal character of God. As the mourning grew louder, and he could hear the weeping of some, his attention was drawn to the fact that, according to the commentary, in prior versions of this praise to the name of God especially written on the occasion of the celebration of the life of a deceased person, it said that God's realm was *forever*. However the commentary continued, a learned religious man long ago insisted on changing it to *forever and ever* to reflect more fully the eternal character of God. What struck Assam was that looking at the Hebrew text, which he could decipher albeit with some difficulty, he noticed that this time reference, *forever and ever*, was stated in Hebrew – actually in Aramaic as the original text was written - as *"le 'halam ul 'halme 'halmaya"*, and in parentheses the commentary indicated that only *"le 'halam"* was in the prior versions of the text. Now he could easily see that *'holam'* in Hebrew or *'halam* in Aramaic was *'halam'*, the world or the universe in Arabic. Therefore *"le 'halme 'halmaya"* was literally the *universe of the universes*. To Assam it comported with the Qur'an which states that Allah created the *worlds*, in the plural form.

So the translation for *universe of the universes* was *forever and ever*, while the *universe* was translated as *forever*.

Thus in ancient texts, the connection between time and space was made at the outset. The *universe of the universes* is actually *forever and ever*. Time exists only if Space exists, and one evolves with the other: space becomes Space when Time begins. And Time is created when Space begins to be. Science had finally connected the two, Time and Space, some four hundred years before. Time and Space. Spacetime.

These thoughts reinforced in Assam's mind the fact that the Gregorian calendar, although accurate in measuring or observing the cycle of the Earth relative to the Sun, did not have any connection with absolute Time, or divine Time. Something else had to be. Even the ancients had guessed the connection, before science could arrive at the same conclusion.

The very first verse of the first *sura* in the Qur'an praises God as *Lord of the Worlds*. The plural for the creation of the *worlds* was in his view more accurate that the creation of the Earth first and then the firmament as described in the previous holy texts. Assam's mind then drifted toward the differences in the Scriptures between the Qur'an, which is the word of God revealed by Gabriel to the Prophet (pbuh) and not a human interpretation of things both holy and historical. Assam knew that this divine character of the Qur'an as opposed to other sacred texts was paramount in the True Religion. He thought of time in the Qur'an.

9

Assam knew that the Qur'an teaches that God created the world, actually all the *worlds*, in six *ayyam*, plural of *yaum*. Although *yaum* in the singular means a day, in its plural form it can of course mean days, but also *lengths of time* which could be translated into six days or actually six periods. In *suras 52 (5)* and *70 (4)* days were variably defined as a thousand years, and fifty thousand years, a clear implication that God in his Revelation was referring to divine periods, not comprehensible to man in his limited frame of reference. The six *ayyam* were truly six stages, or just long periods that man cannot fathom. In fact since the Earth did not exist before it was created, and Earth days had therefore no meaning, it did not make sense to Assam to believe that God had created the Universe in six Earth days. According to Assam the Bible, written by man, should therefore be corrected to conform to the Qur'an.

Of course Assam knew that other corrections could have been brought to the Bible. One of them which particularly disturbed Assam concerned the fact that in the ancient Bible it was said that man was created in God's image. But God is unique and One, man must however intrinsically carry His divine commandments and strive for submission to Him.

Another question that troubled Assam was that the Bible taught that God had rested the seventh day (*shabbath* relates to 'rest' in Hebrew). The Qur'an however was clear that God after the sixth stage beheld his Creation:

> *"We created the heavens and the earth and all that is between them in six days [ayyam], nor did any sense of weariness touch Us" Sura (50:38).*

Assam's further thoughts were intriguing as well.

While the congregation stood and sat in turn and repeated for the umpteenth time their *kaddish*, and Assam sat and stood mechanically with everyone else, his mind wandered about the very first four verses of Genesis which he knew by heart and which consisted of revelations that had disturbed him since his young days as a student of Science:

> *"In the beginning God created the heaven and the earth*

And the earth was without form and void and darkness was upon the face of the deep and the Spirit of God moved upon the face of the waters [4]

And God said Let there be light and there was light

And God saw the light that it was good and God divided the light from the darkness"

God had thus *divided,* separated light from darkness on the very first day of Creation. In his childhood that seemed a bit strange to Assam. How could light and darkness be mixed up? And how could they need to be separated? How could that be? Of course he wouldn't tell.

Later in Science class he learned that one theory advanced by physicists for the beginning of the world, and which to Assam did not contradict the teachings of his faith, was known as the Standard Cosmological Model.

In the Standard Cosmological Model, the Universe started with a Big Bang, a singularity as it was referred to. Scientists were able to reconstruct the evolution of everything that existed from that singular event forward through the analysis of ambient radiation they could observe in the present day cosmos and also from the estimation of the number of hydrogen atoms, helium atoms and other data. What they could conclude is that a short time after the Big Bang, a time in seconds equal to about forty-two zeros and a one following the decimal point, known as Planck's time, everything was a very hot plasma of elementary objects. In Assam's view that uniform plasma was *without form and void and darkness was upon the face of the deep.* According to the theory, that primordial fog as Assam saw it, cooled down, and as Time was therefore being created by the sheer changes the universe was undergoing, energy particles known as *quarks* began to group together to form protons and neutrons which then formed the nuclei of basic elements, especially hydrogen and helium. The fog of Assam's imagination was still that, a foggy something. But then other elementary particles, the electrons were able to become attached to these nuclei to form the first atoms. By eliminating these randomly flowing electrons then photons, the essence of light and which prior

---

[4] The word *waters* is a literal translation from the Hebrew *mayyim*. It is however not clear whether the reference is to actual water, or seas which were not yet created, or actually to the *deep* mentioned earlier or to water as a metaphor for an opaque medium encompassing all that existed, a fog, "smoke", a plasma etc.

to that interacted violently with the existing elements of the fog and were unable to set themselves free, were now able to do so. And Light was created. Before that moment when Space began to become transparent, darkness and light were literally mixed up. The photons were trapped in darkness. As they became free, the photons, the particles of light could separate from darkness. *And God divided light from darkness.*

Assam found that there was conformity with the Qur'an in this revelation since the Qur'an described the primordial state as one in which the Earth and Heaven were joined in a single mass, all enveloped in *smoke.*

> *"Do not the Unbelievers see that the heavens and the earth were joined together, then We clove them asunder ..." (Sura 21, verse 30)*

and

> *"Moreover (God) turned to the Heavens when it was smoke and said to it and to the earth . . ." (Sura 41, verse 11)*

Assam delighted in another curious aspect of cosmology which he remembered vividly and was supported by the Revelations of the Qur'an.

> *"The heaven, We have built it with power. Verily. We are expanding it." (Sura 51, verse 47)*

Besides the expansion of the universe predicted by Science, Assam was concerned with the ever accelerating rate of that expansion. According to scientists this *accelerated* expansion of the universe caused distant galaxies to recede from us, or us from them, ever faster and at some point *faster* than the speed of light. As Assam saw it, this was not a violation of the speed of light being the limit within an *inertial* frame of reference, as acknowledged by Science. But as he understood it, in the case of an ever *accelerating* expansion of the Universe, the reference not being an *inertial* frame, the speed of light could be exceeded. Another way to view this was that in the expansion of the Universe, Space was being created and Time extended, and in this case faster than the speed of light which was perfectly acceptable. The light within that new space would still travel *locally* at the speed of light, a speed that could not be exceeded in that new space.

The conclusion that left Assam in awe was that any light from a cosmological object at those distances, in that expanded Space, would never reach us even in an infinite time, because that light would travel toward us at a speed lower than that at which the new space would be moving away from us. The speed of the light emanating from these cosmological spaces and directed *toward* our galaxy would therefore never exceed the expansion velocity of these spaces *away* from us. The situation as described proved scientifically an even more important point according to Assam, in that there existed things that would never be visible or understandable to man.

Anything beyond that *horizon* belonged to God, and God only. Scientists had calculated that space to be situated about sixteen billion light-years away from our own galaxy. Even Science admitted that there was a realm that man cannot enter. But that realm existed and as everything else it was the realm of God, but God had not allowed man there, nor would He ever. Allah has thus ensured that even with all our might a universe limited to sixteen billion light-years in size is all we will ever be able to see and comprehend. All events and things that occur beyond that frontier shall remain the realm of God. *Forever and ever*, the *universe of the universes.*

The Standard Cosmological Model theory was therefore still taught because it could support the tenets of Creation as written in the Qur'an. And everything was interpreted, correctly so Assam thought, to match, and nothing in the theories contradicted the Creation as taught to us by the Prophet (pbuh). In fact, according to Assam, the scientific theories reinforced the Qur'an revelations. It was the word of God.

"Does man need any more reason to submit to Allah, as Islam commands?" Assam asked himself.

"Amen" said the congregation in chorus. Assam was a bit startled and came out of his reverie. All present then stood, embraced, and formed a line to console the mourning family. He, Assam, bowed respectfully to the women standing at a distance on one side, and embraced the men standing on the other. He then joined his official escort and headed back to his quarters.

So the year 1615 was just as correct as any other. In fact it was the correct one, since the Prophet (pbuh) had brought it to the Umma.

Al Dar Baida

For Sheikh Al Amriki, to be here in this year 1615 was a blessing. Being in this modest, white building on Sheikh Hussein Avenue, was already an accomplishment. It was the culmination of 1600 years of efforts, reversals, humiliation and revival. It was fitting that the building was at 1600 Sheikh Hussein Avenue.

The building was named *Al Dar Baida*, literally 'the House White', just like the city Dar Baida in the Maghreb, known in Christian times as Casablanca, or *white house* in Spanish.

Even more meaningful for Sheikh Al Amriki was that *Al Dar Baida* had a special hallowed room known as the Room of the Two Crescents. One Crescent had its hollow part facing Mecca and Medina, the other the Han Empire, the last place of any import on Earth where Islam was still not recognized as the True Religion, "which it was, and still is and will always be, and Allah the only God. *La Illah illa Allah* - there is no God but Allah - and he is One. *Al Hamdulillah*. Praise Be Upon Him." [5], said Assam to himself.

La Illah illa Allah. This was the battle cry of the Muslim warriors, under the command of Sultan Mehmet II during the siege of Constantinople in 1453 of the Christian Era. As the Muslim warriors repeated at dusk this eternal truth in cadence, accompanied with the rumble of the drums and with the torches burning between the tents, the Christian defenders of the Christian city of Constantinople had become terrified, it was reported then. And Constantinople had fallen. And the church of Hagia Sofia became a mosque. And now history had repeated itself with the rest of the West, although no siege or bloodshed had been needed this time.

The Fall of Constantinople, capital of the Byzantine Empire, had marked the end of an empire that had lasted for over eleven hundred years. It is said that the second Christian empire had begun in the West just after that event. The terrifying Orban bombard taught the West the importance of military technology and they subsequently used that precept to dominate the world. Their next empire would

---

[5] According to history books, at the time of the last American president and for a few years thereafter, the two crescents were seen as seamlessly joined at their tips, so the room was commonly referred to as the Oval Office.

last no more than six hundred years until the advent of the first Caliph of the Grand Caliphate.

Assam recalled that the Muslim fighters had fought valiantly in the siege of Constantinople. As had been written:

> *"They [were] coming right up under the walls and seeking battle...and when one or two of them were killed, at once more...came and took away the dead ones...without caring how near they came to the city walls. Our men shot at them with guns and crossbows, aiming at [anyone] who was carrying away his dead countryman, and both of them would fall to the ground dead, and then there came other[s] ... and took them away, none fearing death, but being willing to let ten of themselves be killed rather than suffer the shame of leaving a single ... corpse by the walls."*

Although it is claimed that Mehmet II allowed his troops to plunder the city, if he did so it was for only three days. Raping, massacring and pillaging if they even occurred, were less than the ancestors of the Muslim warriors had suffered at the hands of the Crusaders two, three and four hundred years before. Sheikh Assam was therefore satisfied by the behavior and magnanimity of his people throughout history and throughout the march of Islam's conquest.

Forbidden Music

Caliph Assam Al Amriki sat at his desk in deep reverie. He had just emerged from the secret room, a low-tech contraption that by its simplicity attracted not the least of suspicion. It was a traditional library full of ancient books with pages made of paper, the Qur'an prominent among them, and various scriptures of the hadiths and other commentaries. In those days no one would have expected an old-fashioned series of bookshelves to hide a secret entrance.

His secret room is where he listened to the forbidden music. In fact it had been forbidden once before, six centuries earlier to be exact, by the Christians themselves who had created these wonderful sounds that transported him to his childhood in the holy lands, where music was always a sentimental voyage to the inner soul.

The feminine voice, although in itself another sacrilege because feminine, was pure and beautiful, as if from another world. The high notes carefully sung in a slow but constant and controlled tempo pronounced a deep personal meaning of inner spirituality that always left him pensive and in a state of dream:

> *"Lascia la spina*
> *Cogli la rosa*
> *Tu vai cercando*
> *Il tuo dolor"*[6]

In his daydreams in the secret room, Assam wished to be with Leila, his third wife as she was when he had met her and decided to make her his wife as well. Assam had four wives, as it was fit for a person of his rank in the Caliphate. Aisha was a good mother and became his first wife, the mother of his first children, his heir in particular. She became his wife by arrangement since he was a child. He then met Jamilla, which he decided to marry upon pressure from the Caliph of Baghdad. The third one, Leila is the one he would have chosen if he were in a monogamous society as the Christians once held in these lands. She had dark almond-shaped eyes and flowing black hair. And a skin that wasn't too light nor too dark, just perfect. It hid the flesh, something some too-white skins did not do as they became pink over time. It also showed texture and relief, and shades of light that too-dark skins, like his own, did not reflect.

Having studied classical oil painting as a way to occupy his free time while in Science and Religion school, Assam was familiar with the intricacies of shades and colors, and he could appreciate beauty in many variations. Although no one was allowed to depict any human representation in full, the teachers did allow art students, and those only, to study shades of skin, parts of faces such as cheeks, eyes, and areas surrounding the eyes and how a smile is shaped. One instructor, Mohammed Al Modili, liked to remind his students that by looking only at the corner of a person's eye, everything else being hidden, one could guess whether the person was smiling or crying, happy or sad. He was right. The *niqab,* especially the half *niqab* proved that theory time and again and imparted a mystery to a woman's beauty that was hard to describe to those who could not experience it, like the Han. In particular, Leila's features let him prove

---

[6] "Let go of the Thorn/Pluck the Rose/You Go on Seeking/ You own Sorrow"

that theory every time. Of course his attraction to Leila was not based on a theory of classical Christian Western painting. It was purely sentimental and sensual. With Leila art met his senses. All the senses. Including the melodies which he associated in his dreams of Leila, such as the ones he heard in his secret music room. And the melody continued:

> *"...Come il foco alla sua sfera*
> *Come serva alla fresc'onda*
> *Come al mare, o fiume, o rio*
> *Si veloce, e si leggiera,*
> *Per l'affetto, che l'inonda*
> *L'alma mia vola al suo Dio"* [7]

And the voice kept repeating *"L'alma mia vola al suo Dio"*, "My soul soars to her God."

"How beautiful", Assam kept repeating to himself, "and how forbidden, then and now."

These were written by Caldara in the year 1708 of the Christian Era and reflected passions that were considered sinful at the time. They were part of what is known as *Opera Proibita*, the *forbidden opera*. They were forbidden then. They were forbidden now. But that was Sheikh Assam Al Amriki's weakness.

That weakness was listening to sacrilegious music, not because of any evil intent against the True Religion, but because it reached his soul like nothing else. Even more than the call to prayers of the Muezzin in the evening, which was described as 'the sweetest sound on Earth' by Sheikh Hussein a long time ago. That comparison was sacrilegious enough, but he couldn't help it. Since he felt closer to all his brothers when he listened, it could not be *haram*. But perhaps it was, since the imams, who could issue a fatwa against him, could not read his soul and determine his true intent. They had to act upon the evidence. And the evidence, listening to forbidden music, was damning. Nonetheless, with this music he felt a sense of joy invade him. And that is why he had built the secret room, with the secret library entrance.

---

[7] As the fire to its sphere/As the doe to the fresh water/As to the sea, the river, and the brook/So swift, so light/Filled with passion/My soul soars to her God

Of course the real Leila was in her quarters and he could visit with her at will. This was his right with any of his four wives. But the idealized Leila, that of his dreams seemed even more capable of transporting him closer to Heaven. To a world of purity and bliss. Leila represented to him the *femina perfecta*, the perfect feminine so revered before in the lost world of the ancient West.

And so were Assam's thoughts on this nineteenth day of Safar of the year 1615 of the Prophet (pbuh) as he awaited his next visitor.

Caliph Assam Al Amriki was the head of the American Caliphate. He reported, just as the Grand Caliph of Baghdad and other Caliphs to the Grand Keeper of the Faith in the True Holy Land.

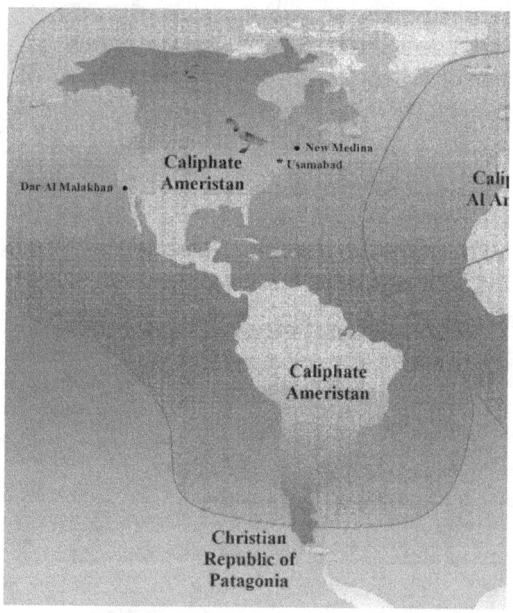

2. Ameristan, the American Caliphate

Assam Al Amriki was slender and tall, with a thin and long face. His beard was elegant and slightly grey in some areas but otherwise trim and orderly. He had a presence that some said was close to holy. Maybe it was a result of his ancestry as some say he resembled his most famous ancestor. Yes of course his early ancestors had been violent. But all revolutions and revelations, all human upheavals begin violently and then softly the ideals of these same upheavals become part of a peaceful society and ingrained in the people. The new culture, begun with the force of arms, slowly pervades the souls of those who earlier resisted it. The barbarians who burned Rome became the heirs of its religion, its science and its traditions. They became peaceful and civilized and embarked on a mission to carry on Rome's civilization, which they had just destroyed, to the rest of the world, as if it were theirs. And they viewed themselves not as barbarians, but as peaceful civilized beings, wishing for peace and justice for all. The barbarians appointed themselves the heirs of a great civilization, the origins of which they obscured to make it their own; they even declared themselves in some instances Aryans, and that Rome had been founded and brought to glory by Aryans, and everything seemed perfect and harmonious. Of course it was an illusion but that is the way of History, Assam knew.

Assam was a direct descendant of the early sheikhs who paved the way for the takeover of the West, yes sometimes violently he knew. But the pursuit of the acceptance of Islam through legitimate struggle was consistent with the Scriptures. Several verses in *sura 9* explained it.

> *Verse 14: "Fight them! Allah will chastise them at your hands and He will lay them low and give you victory over them!"*

> *Verse 29: "Fight against such of those who have been given the Scripture as believe not in Allah nor the Last Day, and forbid not that which Allah hath forbidden by His messenger, and follow not the Religion of Truth, until they are... humbled."*

> *Verse 123: "O ye who believe! Fight those of the disbelievers who are near to you, and let them find harshness in you, and know that Allah is with those who keep their duty (unto Him)."*

In the grand scheme of things the surrender of the West had been tame. The Han would be a different story, Assam knew. As the West was for his ancestor of two hundred years before, this would be *his* challenge.

Assam wore an immaculate white robe over ordinary dress clothes, which included a white shirt, also immaculate and buttoned at the neck, and no other ornament. The white robe with no adornment denoted his humility and rank.

And again the words of the singer came ringing in his inner self, and kept repeating themselves slowly and in this wonderful slow and sustained tempo that only trained singers of that era could accomplish:

"Tu vai cercando Il tuo dolor"
(You go on seeking your own sorrow)
"L'alma mia vola al suo Dio" (My soul soars to her God)

So there sat Caliph Al Amriki when in his ear rang a soft tone, audible only to him; the voice was that of his assistant, a man named Abu Bak'r, who told him Mohammed Al Kansii had arrived and was with his deputy Sheikh B'rak Al Kenii.

Sheikh Al Kenii was a Ham, the descendant of the second son of Noah. Caliph Assam was a Sem, of the first son of Noah, and as such could not help himself feel a certain sympathy for Judeans, sometimes called Semites, and who according to tradition were also descendants of Sem, although they had strayed in many errant ways.

Origins

The visitor, Mohammed Al Kansii, was visibly not a Sem or a Ham. Al Kansii was, as most of the people of the West were, a Yaphet. He had fair skin and blue-grey eyes which conveyed to Assam either cold blooded cruelty or apathy. Assam's people had experience in centuries past from Al Kansii's ancestors. These experiences were not all peaceful. But now through Islam they were all united, Sem, Ham and Yaphet, sons of Noah.

Noah, who is said to have lived to be one thousand years had three sons, Sem, Ham and Yaphet. All monotheistic religions and their civilizations, in fact the revealed religions of all mankind, trace their origins to the descendants of Sem, just as Assam. As younger siblings, Ham and Yaphet owed respect and consideration to Sem. And the world had existed ever since according to that order. As all religions had been revealed to Sem's progenitors, these brought the message to Ham and Yaphet. It was the right order of things. Yes, some Yaphet descendants became overtaken with pride and had caused years of misery. But that was over. The Yaphet were to build, be creative, and assist in the march of the world, but not to take the spiritual lead. As for Ham and his descendants, they were to repent for their original curse and were then also to follow the guidance of the elder brother, Sem.

Assam noted that this correct order of things was reestablished following the changes brought about by Sheikh Hussein, a Ham, during his reign of over two decades as leader of this predominantly Christian continent. And after *Al Andalus*, Al Franciya and surrounding areas were converted, peacefully it must noted, *Ameristan* had followed the attraction of Islam, the only True Religion brought to us by the Prophet, Peace be Upon Him. The Ham had begun their redemption, and the Yaphet reassumed their proper role.

Mohammed Al Kansii had learned this order of thing since childhood. His talent was technical and related to the accomplishments of things material. For spiritual guidance, the descendants of Sem had proven throughout history that they carried the message revealed to them by a few true prophets the last of which they now revered (pbuh).

It was only natural that Al Kansii's ancestors had followed the masses into the proper conversion, just as one thousand and nine hundred years before, the ancestors of these same Yaphet people had accepted the conversion to the religion of the second prophet. And they had adopted his religion and his precepts, and they had built, as only they knew how, a most advanced and rich society on Earth. Now that the two strands of the family of Noah, indeed the three strands, the family of all nations, were united, greater accomplishments were to be made. And that is what filled Al Kansii with great determination and faith in his mission.

Al Kansii was a good Muslim. He was aware of his roots but just as his ancestors, thousands of years before, had reneged their archaic pagan beliefs to adopt a messianic creed, either by force or by the sword, he believed in what was taught to him as a child. He was, as most of his compatriots were, comfortable with Islam, their religion for at least four generations. It provided structure, peace, devotion to one's brothers, and a place for men and women to be socially situated, a place that they would know and respect. Perverse attitudes were forbidden and severely punished. Drugs and alcohol, these satanic temptations, were long gone. Even interest on loans, that financial perversion akin to usury was forbidden. Lenders now helped their fellow Muslims with loans, and of course were properly remunerated for their services so that they could continue assisting their fellow Muslims. But the remuneration was justified on service, not on some theoretical and unjust value-of-money forbidden by the Qur'an. Morally it sounded better. It was better.

Al Kansii had attended a madrassa, or religious school, in *'hala Guadal*, an approximate transliteration of the Arabic words for *Over the River*. In the Spanish transliteration many cities had this suffix *guad* (for *wadi*, river in Arabic) as Guadalquivir, *Wadi Al K'bir*, literally Big River or Rio Grande in Spanish, or Guadalajara, *Wadi El J'ra*, or River of Excrement[8]. Guadalcanal also derives its name from the same root, although as with Guadalupe, it appears to be a juxtaposition of two languages. In any event *'hala Guadal* was formerly known as Overbrook, and was located at the center of the continent.

Al Kansii excelled in school and shortly joined the elite engineering school *Al Miyatyia*, which some say was named after its original Christian initials MIT. He studied quantum engineering with a specialty in military applications of the non-locality of the quantum realm. He also pursued advanced studies in the still rudimentary engineering of quark stream propagation weapons. He was so capable that academic authorities, and the Council of the Caliphate, suggested, or rather requested, that he be allowed to graduate from the military academy of Noukhta Al Gharbiya, to the north-west of New Medina, the world's largest financial center, on the Bin Hud River.

There he became a commando. A commando in those days required physical strength and courage. But it also required an exceptional intellect and of course advanced degrees in Engineering, Physics, Biophysics or related fields including Mathematics, with concentration on advanced warfare techniques especially those

---

[8] Many etymologists translate Guadalajara as *river of stones*, *Wadi Al Bajara* or *Wadi Al Hajara* in Arabic. However there is no *ba* or *ha*, just *jara, or j'ra*, the meaning of which is known and cannot be printed here out of decency. These etymologists further contend without justification that *jara* is derived from *caruca* or 'stony'.

related to quantum-based weapons. He also had to have written a dissertation on a specific topic he had to have practically invented or at least perfected, preferably a new way to *weaponize* a scientific principle.

These were not studies prescribed by the Qur'an, but until the World Caliphate was instituted, bringing peace to all on Earth, according the Prophet's plans (pbuh), military competition with the Han was required. And the Han were very assiduous, and stubborn.

Al Kansii obviously was versed in the Qur'an and the Hadiths and he understood the logic of their precepts. He was the ideal agent to attempt The Jolt. And Sheikh B'rak Al Kenii, Assam's right hand man, was very proud of his find.

Assam let them in and greeted them: *"Salam Halikkum"* ("peace be upon you"), he said.

"Halikkum Salam" ("upon you shall peace be") they responded.

Assam then put his right index finger horizontally and parallel to his lips, pronounced *"Al Hamdulillah"* (praise Allah), kissed his finger and raised it toward Heaven, pointing as much east as he could.

The other two raised their right index finger, placed it upon their lips, horizontally and parallel to their lips. They said "Al Hamdulillah", kissed their finger and raised it to Heaven. In their position they were pointing straight east. And they were satisfied.

An Important Discussion

"Brother Al Kansii" Assam began, "you know why you are here?"

"Yes Sheikh" Al Kansii replied, "Sheikh Al Kenii explained some things to me."

"You are to become a martyr if things go well" added Assam. "Death is not just probable, it is certain. Death by quantum disintegration I mean. Only your soul will remain, and will go to Allah. This is our chance now to break through into the Han Empire."

"Yes Sheikh, *Al Hamdulillah*" said Al Kansii.

"Al Hamdulillah" the two sheikhs responded.

"You know that all our attempts to infiltrate the Han have failed. They are smart and stubborn" continued Assam Al Amriki with a certain impatience in his voice.

"Our predecessors in these lands were smart too, but we outsmarted them" quickly responded Al Kansii.

"Yes, as you said, they were smart, but they were not stubborn. The Han are stubborn. Can you think of another obstacle?"

"Yes. Well, they don't look like us. And they are not in a hurry. And they don't even want us to be like them. Well, we can't. There is no way the whole world would be Han."

"Not true. With the new quantum imaging and cosmetic alteration technology, facial features, or at least our perception of them, can be altered and we can look like someone else if we wish to."

Al Kansii knew better. A friend of his, also a commando, from Dar Al Malakhan, the City of Angels on the west coast of the Caliphate, had written his thesis on that.

"Sheikh" he said, "but the results cannot last for long with this procedure. The procedure is good for suicide commandos who need to infiltrate enemies that don't look like us..."

"Yes" interrupted Assam, "but the Han have time. And one day the techniques will be perfected so as not to dissolve before say twenty to forty years or more, in which case we can all look Han for most of our lives if we choose to. Plus biological science can already alter genes making this procedure unnecessary anyway, so we should use it only for commando-type operations where looks are to be altered on short notice and for a short period of time."

"I understand Sheikh" nodded Al Kansii.

Prayer and Dinner at Al Dar Baida

"Al Kansii" said Assam, "before we go any further let us praise Allah and eat together."

Three prayer rugs were already arranged on the floor, oriented west to east. The three stood at the feet of the rugs, that is on the west end of these rugs, Assam in the center, Al Kenii to his right and Al Kansii to his left. They had removed their shoes and kept their legs straight, their feet slightly forming an outward V. Their arms were down and hung loose with their hands almost joined at the wrists and offering two open palms facing slightly upward as a sign of supplication and therefore submission.

"Allah U Akbar" (God is Great) said Assam.

"Allah U Akbar", responded the other two.

They then recited in unison the following prayer:

> *"May the Peace and Prayers of Allah be upon our Messenger Muhammad, his noble and pure family, his companions, and those who follow them in faith until the Establishment of the Hour."*

After that they remained there, each praying silently. A moment later Assam said:

"Al Hamdulillah"

"Al Hamdulillah" responded the other two.

Assam then turned his neck slightly sideways and issued his commands to an unseen person. Assam's intentions were communicated to his servants on the other side of the wall of the Room of the Two Crescents using accurate brain-wave analysis to interpret, route and decode to their specific recipients his desired commands, or rather his desires.

Brain Waves

For over three hundred years brain activity had been monitored and analyzed, especially for medical purposes. It was believed that brain activity was the result of electrochemical reactions maintained by nerve cells called *neurons.* These reactions in the neurons generated electrically charged ions which released their energy in the form of waves. Very early on, brain specialists had divided brain waves into four frequencies that corresponded to the level of activity of the brain in question. It was common knowledge that these were usually categorized in order of frequency of the wave as δ (or *delta* at

1.5 Hz and up to 4 Hz), θ (or *theta* up to 8 Hz), α (or *alpha* up to 14 Hz) and finally β (or *beta* up to 40 Hz), a Hertz, or Hz being of course one cycle per second.

What science did not distinguish for decades, although it was suspected, was that these were *carrier frequencies*. Just like a broadcast is transmitted at a specific frequency, it is the modulation within that frequency that carries the information. Electromagnetic communication was several hundred years old and various implementations existed to carry information such as music, voice conversation and images either moving or still with various degrees of efficiency within a carrier frequency. Efficiency was needed when these frequencies in the electromagnetic spectrum had become scarce as higher and higher volumes of information transfer became needed. Some of the developments related to these transmissions at one point became readily applicable to the interpretation of human brain waves.

For example, in order to optimize the use of limited electromagnetic spectrum, the sharing of frequencies was needed. It was observed that the lower the power of the transmissions, and the higher the frequency at which they were carried, the shorter their range. These were the parameters within which technicians had to work, and thus by carefully adjusting them, they could reuse the frequencies outside that spatial range. This was necessary in order to support a global population exceeding sixty eight billion souls[9], each and everyone requiring vast amounts of information to be exchanged practically with everyone else, and therefore power levels, ranges and frequency reuse had been fine-tuned to an art form.

Of these developments, especially those related to extremely low power level communications and from which deployed systems needed to extract the maximum information, several found their way to the research work of a special branch of brain specialists, known as *communication brain specialists*. As great insights were gained in the handling and analyzing of very low power transmissions, these specialists based their research into parsing information contained in the carrier waves that had been known for centuries.

---

[9] For the past two hundred years authorities worldwide had agreed to establish a limit for acceptable population growth of 1.2% per year bringing the global population from 6.3 billion at the time of the last American President to the present 68 billion. Certain regions of course exceeded that rate while others fell below it.

For example the *beta* waves were known for high intellectual activity, and the *delta* waves were originally linked to states of relaxation such as sleep. What was not investigated in these early times was the actual content of such activities. Science had been able to parse through that and detect, indeed read, the inner components of these brain waves, that is obtain an insight on what the brain was thinking. In some cases with almost infallible precision. It was said that the Han Empire had perfected such techniques to the point that it could not only read minds, but also anticipate what a mind would think. The emulation of one's thinking process, and this even after somebody's death, was based on patterns of one's brain activity and the understanding of the modulation schemes beyond the carrier frequencies.

Further, unlike electromagnetic waves that were used to carry information from relatively simple signals such as voice, music or images, brain waves were complex structures that represented the thought processes and were the result of the exchange of neurotransmitters between neurons at the brain synapses. These exchanges produced faint wave-like emanations the superposition of which created the macroscopic brain waves, and in this case the *thought waves*. Their analysis in their minutest details allowed science to enter the thought process of a given brain. The interactions at the synapses were symbolically arranged according to the mathematical protocol of multidimensional matrices, and these formed the basis for the theories of survival of consciousness beyond death then in vogue.

In the Caliphate, because there was a strict interdiction from entering the realm of God, that of the faith, research and applications focused on detecting immediate intentions, translating them into bits of information which could be relayed using common transmission media. So if Assam was *linked* say to his assistant, which he was indeed, Assam could for example *think of ordering tea*, an implant would read his mind, which was nothing more than the analysis of minute details of his brain waves, translate those into words, in any language that Assam would *think* them, and transmit them to the intended recipient using normal telecommunications channels. Assam's assistant in turn would *hear* a tone inside his ear, in fact in his brain since the actual ear did not play any role, and he would then hear Assam's *wishes* and then *intent* his answer back to Assam, which was then transmitted normally. Communication was therefore entirely private, hands-free, and action-free unless one called the act of *intending* an action. Of concern to some was that there was room for intercepting one's intentions, which was useful for crime prevention and to ensure the security and preservation of the State. Submission could then be monitored in the farthest confines of one's mind. In the cause of submission to Allah through the Islamic State, it was thus proper.

Within a few seconds of Assam issuing his commands, or rather thinking or intending his wishes, three butlers, all male, entered the room.

The butlers were dressed in flowing green pants and wore short red vests adorned in gold over white blouses with puffy sleeves. They also wore ornate turbans, with a red and gold filigree. The color missing in all this was obviously blue. Green was definitely the color of Islam, and of the Caliphate. Red was also part of the culture, although it was a Han dominant color as well together with yellow. Blue was almost absent in these two societies, which meant over more than ninety percent of the world. Blue was considered a Christian, and Jewish color, which it had in fact been.

At the beginning of the Caliphate a meticulous study of colors was conducted by an official commission and that commission had analyzed preferences, national flags and other parameters, to determine which color schemes were most able to achieve the permanent conversion of the infidels.

The commission had found that almost all the conquered lands had blue in their flags, and none of the original Islamic countries' flags did. Blue was a Western color, and the color of King David and most of the Christian kings afterwards. But it was not a color of Islam, except the *Shia* used some light, bright version of it. Assam had no patience with the *Shia*, and no one in the Caliphate did.

The commission had recommended the avoidance of blue if at all possible. Just as the interdiction of loud, non-melodic music was also *de rigueur* in the Caliphate.

Assam liked the color blue. It was a cold color and it allowed him to retrench to his inner soul, with its surreal music and his dreams of Leila, or what he dreamt Leila ought to be in that idealized world. On the music though, he was all in favor of the new norms. Animalistic sounds perpetrated by humans, with beats more apt at exciting beasts, were not his idea of music.

For Assam, preferences of color, music, smells, tastes, sounds, even touch, were the result of the impact of early childhood on the senses. Assam held the theory that what one experiences through these senses in early childhood becomes one's truths. It becomes one's divine self. And although he would not discuss that publicly, he also noted that since time immemorial, the overwhelming majority of adherents to a religion were born in that religion. Until a new revelation struck. So the phenomenon that makes that what the senses perceive during the early years of a child, *the magic years*, stays with that child for his entire life, that phenomenon applies to thought and belief as well.

The first truth one learns is ingrained deeply in our soul, and we venerate that truth, despite the assaults from any scientific and rational evidence. This is a problem when exporting the faith to the infidels, since they are convinced of their own errant ways. But it can be turned into an advantage, as it had been by the Caliphate, when one is able to begin teaching a new generation in the true faith. How quickly these children forget the faith of their forefathers! It had happened in the early years of the Prophet's conquest (pbuh). And it had happened now. Your early enemy becomes your staunchest supporter and ally.

The first butler held a large silver terrine from which some steam and a wonderful smell of baked semolina escaped. The second butler carried a china container, of smaller size, from which the scent of stewed lamb emanated.

The third held a large open plate with pumpkin skins, pumpkin chunks and squashes of different sorts and various colors, orange, green and yellow, and colors in between. It also contained raisins, almonds, dates and walnuts, and several delicious spices flavored the dish.

The three butlers lined up in a crescent. A fourth helper, a young boy of sixteen at most had positioned himself in front of the three men who were about to eat, and who sat on thick pillows on the ground, their legs crossed.

The couscous butler scooped large portions of the semolina upon each of the three plates, stood up and went to a corner to place his container on a warming device. He then walked toward the door and stood in silence.

The butler carrying the lamb served ample portions first to Assam, then to Al Kenii, and last to Al Kansii, who received a little less.

"Pour more, he is young and he needs it" said Assam. The butler obliged and over-served Al Kansii. Al Kansii realized that it was perhaps too much but he did not dare to stop the butler. He sat there in silence.

The third butler then served the vegetables, and did not need an invitation to serve more to Al Kansii. Al Kansii would have to eat fast to end his meal at the same time as the other two, which was a mark of respect. It would be an affront to continue eating while the most important officials of the Caliphate had finished. Of course to finish first would be embarrassing as well. So Al Kansii was prepared to time his meal according to Assam's consumption.

As the three butlers then stood by the door, after having placed their containers on their respective warming devices, the boy reached closer to the men sitting on the cushions on the floor and presented a mixture of sugar and cinnamon, a choice given to guests as a show of respect toward certain traditions of the western Mediterranean, where people sometimes sweeten their couscous with sugar and cinnamon.

As the door opened and the three butlers and the boy withdrew, two other servers entered the room, one holding a large sliver plate with an ornate silver tea pot and three tall thin glasses containing mint leaves which were visible through the walls of the glasses.

The empty-handed server placed each glass in front of the three men, then reached out for the teapot and began the ritual pouring of green tea. He began placing the spout of the tea pot near the rim of a glass and poured a little quantity of tea. He then moved to the next two glasses successively and poured a little quantity of tea in each. He then returned to the first glass, Assam's, and began pouring close to the rim while raising the teapot higher and higher up to the point where the liquid would splash but he stopped just short of that and began lowering the teapot toward the rim of the glass. The glass was then full. He repeated this ritual for the other two and the server retreated to a corner, ready to serve more tea when needed. The three men had equal amounts of tea, the strength of which was perfectly balanced as it was poured equally and evenly during the infusion of the tea leaves within the hot water, an infusion that continued during the serving.

Assam then lifted his right arm and shook his hand very slightly, a sign that the two servers were to withdraw as well, this was to be very confidential. The two therefore withdrew at once.

The three, Assam, Al Kansii and Al Kenii, ate in silence, and when they were satisfied, they praised Allah and his Prophet (pbuh), one at a time. Sheikh Al Kenii burped to himself and murmured some sort of thankful prayer.

Assam took a sip of his tea and began:

"Al Hamdulillah" said Assam.

"Al Hamdulillah" responded the other two.

"Let me get to the point" said Assam after a brief pause.

2

HISTORY

After Dinner Monologue

$\mathcal{S}$heikh Assam Al Amriki continued:

"You may know all this but let us set the stage for what we want to accomplish.

"For us to conquer the Han, that is to bring them to the True Religion, the religion of Allah, one must abide by the five strategic pillars, the five pillars that served us well in the past, and apply the specific tactics pertaining to that situation, that of the Han.

"When we conquered the West, we used these same five pillars. First we need a Jolt. While the enemy is busy handling the jolt, we implement the second pillar, Deception. To assure the success of the deception, we need the third pillar, Infiltration. And yes the next pillar, the fourth pillar, requires Treason from within, or let's call it help from those who see the truth of Allah's religion although they are born from the enemy. The last pillar consists of Force, but it is really what the military call a clean-up operation, or mopping-up, when the enemy has already lost the battle. Unfortunately, many in the West saw Islam as a violent religion, imposed by force. Nothing is further from the truth. The *force* they allude to is really the last step, after the true battle has been lost by them. And that is what they remember. We need to see to it that this distortion does not happen again.

"Brother Al Kansii, you are to carry out the Jolt, the first pillar. Of course we attempted several jolts already, but to no avail. Why? Because the other pillars had not been thought of well or properly conceived and implemented. Besides, the Han have been able to conceal what we thought would have been a jolt, and no reaction whatsoever has been noticed. And if the event is not observed, as in quantum philosophy, it does not exist or at least not in the form expected. Our last jolt, although physically powerful, was smothered in a fog of secrecy and therefore had no impact. In fact, those who knew of our attempts have become more guarded, and more suspicious of our actions, thus stronger. We have to behead the snake this time.

"Let me summarize how we applied the five pillars to the conquest of the West. And in what we are to review I want you to keep in mind that certain elements apply to the Han and others do not. We must therefore adapt our strategy, and the tactics that follow to that specific situation."

Assam took a sip of his green mint tea. The other two immediately imitated him. He then began a historical exposé, which Al Kansii didn't really need. Al Kansii probably knew better and more. But Al Kansii listened dutifully to Sheikh Assam:

"… In the early years 1400 of our Prophet, Peace Be Upon Him, as the Caliphate schools taught us and continue to teach to our school children, the early 1400's is when the last American president ended his office. Sheikh Hussein, we learned in school that he became the first Caliph of *Ameristan*, although he never actually held that title. He had to be stealth. Now bear in mind that this was a few years after the Jolt, where thousands of their citizens were sacrificed to the cause of Allah.

"What was the West's reaction then? Twofold. First, they reacted with extreme force against the *shaheed*, our martyrs whom they called the perpetrators of crimes, and then they invaded our lands, and of course killed several of our Umma. And they took casualties as well, in addition to depleting their treasury. Second, and this may have been their biggest mistake and I am not sure the Han will fall for that, in order to appease other would-be agents of violence, they engaged in an effort to win their opponents' cooperation, that is our cooperation, in fighting these same opponents. While they fought the last provocation, and there were many in succession, the forces of Islam focused on the second pillar, Deception.

"Yes, although the Jolt had given us a voice, we officially reneged it and condemned it. We insisted on cooperating with the West in order to eliminate the possibility of any new jolt. Which we never planned to repeat on that scale anyway. We had already found our voice. Our second pillar was to use Deception to achieve the third pillar, Infiltration.

"With Deception, we were able to make the West fail to acknowledge that their enemies were indeed their enemies. To do so, we of course needed help from within. Sheikh Hussein used his allies, not all Muslims, and not all believers, but useful nonetheless. And they proved to be key. This is how it happened.

"Sheikh Hussein was born a Muslim. And you know as it is said that *once something is of Islam, it must remain of Islam*. Before seizing power in these lands though, Sheikh Hussein had admirably convinced the people that they needed salvation and change, although they were the most powerful on Earth. Now how these miserable spoiled and depraved children of power and wealth needed hope and change and to be *saved* is another question. Several years of war had broken their resolve and *change* was a currency for which they would fall. Of course no one had specified what the change would be. But Sheikh Hussein knew. Stealthily and methodically he changed the West's alliances, apologizing to its enemies and condemning its friends.

"Of course in lamenting their lot, these children of privilege never thought of the wretched children of the Earth that died in war, of malnutrition, of disease and of neglect. Sometimes at their own hands, but not always it must be acknowledged. The wretched of the Earth Sheikh Hussein knew well, and understood well. He was of them, not directly but through his ancestors. And he had vowed to change the West. Of course, being spoiled did not help these fools. But I digress here…

"Sheikh Hussein thus began to rule these either naive or blind people by emphasizing a messianic salvation of the country, the most powerful on Earth. And he proceeded to undo, undermine and dismantle all the institutions, either actual or virtual, that supported their societies…"

Assam stopped and tried to lower his voice. He was getting excited and angry. Every time he thought of the glorious past of the West, right at the time when the Caliphate was established, he went into that trance. Sheikh B'rak Al Kenii, his deputy, knew it and very often he challenged him in a historical and psychological debate of what ifs. B'rak Al Kenii was very smart. And so was Al Amriki. The two were perfect for each other, perfect for running the Caliphate of *Ameristan*.

Still Assam thought: *"But if these Westerners had not been as abject and inept as they had been, the Caliphate would not be. It was Allah's plan. He, Assam, should accept it and not think rationally at what these people had done to themselves, or could have done to prevent their fall."* Still his inner logical self told him there was something wrong in a people, the most powerful and resourceful on Earth, in all of History, *"a people who would just let themselves... with no resistance...be conquered from within!"*

He breathed deeply and continued.

"In these ancient times, our third pillar, Infiltration was carried out masterfully by the first Caliph of *Ameristan.* Sheikh Hussein maneuvered time and again to remain in power, and he utilized the same forces that had catapulted him to victory the first time around. He used what was then considered the *useful idiots,* what was then known as the *intelligentsia,* or the *elite,* usually rooted in academic circles and institutions of public opinion, all mostly imbued of self-hatred and guilt. Yes guilt for having achieved world domination at the expenses of others, the weak and the downtrodden. Of course had this intelligentsia had the strength of Islam to justify the West's actions, or the actions of their forefathers, yes Islam, the spiritual basis for all actions, they would have felt no guilt.

"In fact those last old Westerners did not even have their own spiritual basis, since most had abandoned any religion whatsoever. In any event with this scent of local flavor to the struggle, Sheikh Hussein could not be seen as maneuvering for a future Caliphate. In fact we don't know if he was actually maneuvering for the Caliphate but the result is the same. By insisting on expanding the powers of the State at the expense of the law of the jungle that existed then, he laid the ground work for any all-encompassing philosophy to overtake that civilization. And the descendants of the West are grateful that Islam is what was inherited and not some perversion of a godless political theory.

"In all his endeavors, Sheikh Hussein had to pretend he was doing the best for the people. For example he introduced the *zakat,* our charity, which he disguised as a compulsory contribution thereby transferring wealth from those who had wealth in excess to those for whom it was scarce. And the successive economic crises made that latter group very large.

"A basic tenet of a struggle against an enemy more powerful

than thee, is first to weaken that enemy as much as possible.

"Although Sheikh Hussein was not a traitor, by any means, since he labored for the cause of Allah, willfully or not, his *useful idiots* allies were the foundation of the fourth pillar, Treason.

"With the help of these, Sheikh Hussein used all his power to weaken the economic engine that was the foundation of the West's power. First he enacted rules that encumbered the orderly exploitation of natural resources, and curbed what he deemed was the exploitation by the rich of the natural patrimony of the poor. That weakened the West enormously since their wealth depended on the exploitation of world resources, that of others of course. In energy, these resources were mostly ours.

"Second, Sheikh Hussein used a popular movement to divert the creative energies toward illusory new-age technologies with no promise other than the satisfaction of the soul of rich, irresponsible parasites, then known as *green* I think. Actually there is a symbolism argument here. Green is the color of Islam, the vegetation of our lands, given to us by Allah. Islam introduced agriculture practically to the entire world…well the Han will argue otherwise. The verdant fields of Islam are represented by the color green.

"In any event, illusory, unproven dreams were the hope, while real, proven techniques were shunned. Sheikh Hussein used his enemies' weapons against these suddenly blinded people. And I insist on this point, because the Han are anything but naïve or blind. He used the laws afforded to the State under their *democratic* principles, to prohibit the dissemination of ideas contrary to his goals while forcing the State into engaging in economically prohibitive adventures it could ill afford. And all this while maintaining a stranglehold on these institutions and ensuring the permanency of his rule.

"Of course, as I said earlier, that was after he had seized control the first time. That first time, using then unknown powers, he managed to displace all the powerful political families in the land. How he did it remains a mystery to this day. Except for the fact that an economic catastrophe occurred just at the right time to sway all popular sentiment toward him and away from others, especially one of their own. Yes, one of their own heroes was passed over by Hussein, who was alien to them, and Hussein achieved this mainly because of a mysteriously timed economic disintegration.

"The Qur'an asks us to use patience against the enemies of Islam. As sura 8:65 teaches:

> 'O Prophet (pbuh) urge the believers
> to war; if there are twenty patient
> ones of you they shall overcome two
> hundred, and if there are a hundred
> of you they shall overcome a
> thousand of those who disbelieve,
> because they are a people who do not
> understand.'

"Brother Al Kansii, do not show your hand. Be steadfast and you shall prevail."

The three took a few sips of tea while Assam paused and recovered his breath.

"Sheikh Hussein" Assam continued, "was therefore installed at the helm to help prepare the advent of the True Religion worldwide. Willingly or not. One will never know. But we recognize him as the first Caliph nonetheless because as he promised he ushered in the new era of change, our era.

"Allah's power is infinite. *Al Hamdulillah.* Praise Be Unto Allah."

Sheikh Al Kenii and Al Kansii both responded:

"*Al Hamdulillah.*"

"By the end of Sheikh Hussein's rule which lasted over two decades" continued Assam, 'the Islamization of Europe' as one of its detractors put it then, was well underway. England, France and Spain, as these lands were known then, had already nearly half or more of their population identifying themselves as Muslims. *Sharia* law was accepted as an alternative to common law in those lands. The populace in fact did not care. Most of them there and in present *Ameristan* never saw a court of law anyway. And those who did were either abusers of the system and they used all of the legal technicalities of their man-made laws that produced anything but justice; or they were victims of that judicial incoherence. Victims were punished, culprits rewarded, or let free. Wasn't *sharia* more just after all? Even good Christians had to admit it."

Assam paused and looked deeply at Al Kansii. After all, Al Kansii was a descendant of these people the attitudes of whom he kept deriding. But Al Kansii was also a descendant of good converts, and since Al Kenii had selected him, Assam knew he had vetted him thoroughly.

"Pious Christians" he continued, "and there were very few left in Europe in those days, actually agreed with the true tenets of Islam regarding the role of women, family, commitment to the community, charity and above all the banishment of that abomination they called homosexuality.

"Slowly many non-Muslims, seeing the efficacy of *sharia* courts brought their cases there since all citizens then had a choice of courts. Swift justice, true justice was obtained. Newborns were given Muslim names. Even women, modern women as they used to call them then, began appreciating the *hijab*, the beautifully modest head scarf which was at one time forbidden, the *niqab*, especially the half-*niqab*, that elegant veil that properly covers the face and lets the eyes project an aura of mystery, and even the *jellabiyya*, the full dress that brings so much grace to the wearer. Western women now looked more distinguished and less ordinary than in those so-called liberated times when one would see in some places, especially near the sea, practically half-naked women. Yes, barely covered, their modesty exposed and provoking the men around them in incontrollable ways. No wonder rape and violence were so frequent!"

Assam lowered his voice as it had risen again in the last few sentences.

"What was more" he continued, "men had to suppress their masculinity to avoid reacting naturally to the depraved women. When a man is deprived, and cannot exercise his masculinity in the face of blatant provocation by depraved half-naked women, what is he to do? Violence or suppression and emasculation. No wonder homosexuality blossomed in those countries and days.

"But worse, emasculation took away out of these men the desire to achieve, to conquer, to fight. And a society were men become women is bound to decay, miserably … to decay" concluded Assam with a certain contempt in his voice.

"Now" he continued, "the forces of Islam did not cause that degeneration, they just took advantage of it. Order, sharing, community, happiness, that was what the True Religion brought.

"So as you can see Brother Al Kansii, although the infidels initially obtained success by subduing many peoples across the earth, especially in the Muslim lands, which they humiliated for tens or hundreds of years, the seed of their destruction was carried in their minds. They did not believe. And they stopped believing in themselves as well. Hence they had no will. Yes, some outbursts were noticed. But look at the last invasion of our lands, they fought apologetically in Baghdad and Kandahar, and Islamabad and Qom. Their intellectual class accused their leaders of misgivings, of mistreating their enemies. What are we to do with the enemies of Islam, pamper them?

"In their contorted logic, to the infidels or at least to their presumed elites, the enemy was always right, and *they* were always wrong. Despite heroic efforts of some, they had no chance. Baghdad and Kandahar, two glorious caliphates were unavoidably liberated, with the help of Allah.

"The reason their intellectual class thought that way was twofold: first the economic interest puts profits first, not the Umma; second and most important, unconsciously or not, they must have known they were fighting the True Religion. Our fighters, martyrs knew the same. So what happens when two men fight, one knows that he is right and the other knows that he is wrong? Who will win?

"They knew they were fighting the wrong cause, or at least their elites thought so and told them so. Did we do that? Of course not. We know the truth, and thus the hearts and minds of the faithful come to us. And then come even the infidels. And they become the faithful as well. And all are ready to die for Islam.

"Islam means submission to Allah. And it is through this submission that you will find '*salam*' or peace. There is no *salam* outside *Islam*. Take the other two religions. First the Jews. Do you know what Israel actually means? It means Yisra-El, or 'struggled with God' or 'challenged God'. Yes. How can one find peace by challenging the true God? It is a blasphemy to even pronounce these words. Talking about Yisra-El, that was the name given to Jacob when he fought with the Angel, when he fought with God. Yes, do you know what Genesis says, I think it is in *verse 32*?

"It says that Jacob asked the angel for his name. The angel responded he had no name, that angels take the name of their mission. And Jacob named him Penu-El, the *face of God*. Angels really do not exist, they are something like representations in this world of what God wants to accomplish. In our day we would call them *quantum states* of God, the transubstantiation of God into a specific task, a specific mission. And that brings me to Christianity.

"Christians? They confuse what is to us a prophet, with God, or God's son, or his Spirit who supposedly commanded them to find peace by forgiving their enemy. We call him Issa, they call him Jesus. They confused a true prophet with God Himself. And they added God's Spirit. Three in One. Very confusing. But even that faith, they had lost it by the end. How could they then convince their infidels, the enemies of God, to find the truth if they did not believe it themselves? If they were unwilling to defeat their own enemies? If they didn't defend the truth, if they didn't fight for it?

"That is what the West lacked. A conviction. First they replaced religion and true belief with artificial religions called ideologies. When that did not work they attempted to impose on the entire world something they called *democracy* and that was a perfect way to prolong their hegemony. However their so-called democratic freedoms is what allowed us to infiltrate them to the core and find a voice with those that democracy ignored. For those, and they were billions, for whom democracy just did not respond to any spiritual need of their inner souls. Islam, by submission to Allah, gives you that spiritual platform. You can then relate to the eternity of Allah's universe, where Time and Space are united and infinite, since they are the work of Allah.

"The last pillar… we do not need to spend much time on it. Force. Force to convert the infidels. As I said this happens when the battle has already been won by Islam. And it is just a method to shorten the struggle and yes, save lives. Unfortunately, it is all that our enemies remember. And if our plans succeed, *Insha'Allah*, the Han will follow the same pattern. Let us however still review what happened with Force.

"As I am sure you studied in school, and during your stay in Europe, in the Caliphate *Al Andalus*, riots between various factions spread around Europe and ferments of that rebellion were also observed in American shores. These factions, except for the believers, were disoriented and had no true compass.

"They were fighting by negating their own states and their own culture, but they proposed not much in return. The faithful always knew the way, the way of Allah. At least in these lands here, the faithful gathered their support of Sheikh Hussein to extend his reign. Yes states of emergency were declared here and there, now and then, but the dispirited opposition to Sheikh Hussein's grand design was in fact of very little consequence. That grand design was the advent of a just society where greed is replaced by wealth sharing. By weakening the private institutions, that is the selfish and greedy institutions, and especially those in charge of disseminating information, and by controlling all the means of political discourse and economic activity, Sheikh Hussein ensured an easier migration to a Caliphate, that of *Ameristan* and next to a World Caliphate, *Insha' Allah*. And so did Sheikh Hussein last enough to achieve our grand design."

Assam finished his tea at that moment and with a subtle gesture and a movement of his head, *intended* for the tea butlers to enter the Room of the Two Crescents and pour fresh tea on new glasses which contained fresh leaves of mint. The tea pouring ceremony took a few minutes after which Assam resumed his monologue.

"Of course" said Assam, "to support the tyranny of secular law, the arbitrariness of what they used to call democracy, and to oppose a society based on divine and just law, is absurd. To deny the supremacy of Islam and believe that Allah is not All-Knowledgeable is also absurd. The soldiers of Allah awaited their just reward in *Jennah Al-Firdaus* - the Highest Heaven, just as an Islamic leader of those times put it most beautifully:

> *'Which art is more beautiful, more divine,*
> *and more everlasting that the art of martyrdom?'"*

He paused and took another sip of his mint tea.

"What you learn as a child" he repeated his now known *mantra*, "when the magic of the world is revealed to you, that which you learn then stays with you forever. The smells, the tastes, the music. This is what you are. The West, since they learned nothing in particular and everything from other peoples and cultures, ended up with no compass, and nothing to defend. Islam, the True Religion makes sure a true Muslim knows what he wants or ought to want, what he likes or ought to like, what he will die for. And this is our strength.

"The Qur'an says that once something is of Islam, it is always of Islam, there is no taking back. *Al Andalus*, which the infidels called

Spain, was an aberration. For over six hundred years Islam did not give up the hope of regaining the caliphate of *Al Andalus*. But then the stakes were higher. The big prize was America. And as in the time of Columbus the road to America began in *Al Andalus*.

"Sheikh Hussein is thus credited for laying the seeds for the conquest of America. That is why he is described in history books as Sheikh Hussein Al Kenii, first Caliph of *Ameristan*, the American Caliphate."

Assam paused once more.

"Brother Al Kenii, am I right in my review of our recent history?" asked Assam.

"Yes Sheikh, of course" answered Al Kenii. "Take the march of Islam across the North African desert sixteen hundred years ago. It wasn't always easy or pleasant. Some North Africans had to be converted by the sword. And now, in the name of Allah, they fight for us and with us. What other proof is there then that ours is the True Religion? When your enemy, against whom you fought hard and violently, and you perhaps killed his mother and father and siblings, when that enemy recognizes the truth of your faith, what does it say about Islam? That it is the True Religion. And the Berbers did, and the Moors did, and the Libyans did. And the Egyptians did. And in the other direction even the Persians did! Obviously this is the True Religion.

"*Al Andalus* at that time followed the same path. But as you said the stubborn Christians in the north, including the Franks, resisted. These people took seven hundreds years to reclaim a land that wasn't theirs any longer, since it had become Muslim. We let the guard down. We were as the Christians say tolerant, and perhaps too much. They were not at all. They displaced us. We had Jews and Christians live in our midst with the same rights. They, the Christians of that time tolerated no one. We tolerated them as if their truth were the same as ours. And it wasn't. It destroyed our caliphate. In fact by the late 1400's of the Christian Era, about eight hundred years after the prophet (pbuh) revealed the Qur'an to us, we became complacent, soft, un-desirous to fight for our cause, just like these people of the West of the twenty-first Christian century.

"It is also true as you indicated Sheikh Al Amriki, that Sheikh Hussein was made a martyr. We actually don't truly know whether it occurred or whether it is legend, but we learned that he died a martyr at an advanced age. Nonetheless his legacy endures. And that's about when *sharia* law began to take ground for good.

"Now, and this is important for the consideration of our offensive against the Han: the grand alliance that formed the Grand Caliphate in the Year 1515 of the Prophet (pbuh), integrated in a single caliphate all the lands from India to the shores of the Pacific. The lower part of India and Ceylon remain to be conquered. They practice religions that are not true. The Vatican was moved to the suburbs of Rivadavia, a city in former southern Argentina, now called Patagonia, where many Christians from all over the world who would not convert had gathered. These were mainly older people who could not reconcile themselves to abandoning their millennial religion, or simply atheists who felt offended that someone finally would impose a belief system on them. And of course assorted *leftists* as they were known, secretly regretting having undermined their own liberty with self-hating policies that encouraged enemies of the state into defeating that same state. That is how Rivadavia became the capital of the country now known as Patagonia.

"This was always a problem for democracies, or for lovers of liberty, but it is not for the Han. I believe there is a paradox in that if someone does not want democracy and believes in some form of supreme power, can he democratically seek leadership of a democracy? In other words, if a group opposed to free elections gets elected, how could they be pushed out once they cancel elections as they had promised beforehand? So is it freedom for the freedom-loving only? It is a paradox. Karl Marx, that scoundrel, however said it best albeit in another context, that 'Capitalism carries in itself the seeds of its own destruction'. And so does democracy.

"But not Islam. Any deviation is eliminated. That's why we have a Grand Caliphate."

And then he paused. He took a long sip of tea and remained silent.

Assam, who was also silent, appeared exhausted by his earlier speech and he was pleased that Al Kenii had helped out with reaffirmation of his ideas and connected those to the present situation, that of the offensive against the Han. Of course Al Kansii already knew all that. He had picked up some historical inconsistencies but would not dare bring them up. Embarrassing the

Caliph in front of Sheikh B'rak Al Kenii was not a good idea. Moreover, he had a better perspective being a descendant of the defeated West. His great-grandfather, who had died when Al Kansii was about six years old, had told him stories of glory about the West and those memories had stayed with Al Kansii.

Assam looked at Al Kansii seemingly in search of some feedback.

Al Kenii stepped in. He knew where Assam was going. He had had this conversation with him before and the two enjoyed debating finer points explaining the fall of the West, the most successful and powerful civilization the Earth had known till then, and this without much violence. "From within" as they had been taught and as they desperately tried to accomplish with the Han Empire, the last non-Muslim standing power of any import.

"Sheikh, if you allow me" said Al Kenii.

"Of course Brother" answered Assam.

"One must admit that the lack of will power, the lack of a belief in their own uniqueness and the superiority of their creed, if they even had a creed remaining, those are not the only reasons for their fall" continued Al Kenii.

"The Han helped us a lot. By the end of Sheikh Hussein's reign, one of my ancestors I am told, the West had a combined debt of four quadrillion, yes four thousand trillion dollars. Brother Al Kansii, a dollar then was what …something like a quarter of our dinar is today. And the interest alone, which is forbidden to us of course, the interest on that debt was impossible to pay, even using all the resources the West had at the time.

"But this is not all. The Han in fact did not want to be paid…"

"They didn't?" asked Al Kansii, somewhat surprised.

"Of course", continued Al Kenii, "a country's debt is not like an individual's. An individual wants to pay back his debt, if he can of course. A country is different. The West did offer the Han many solutions to eliminate, or at least reduce its debt to the Han. They offered to produce machines, airplanes, communication systems and many of the best things they had created. The Han refused. They just wanted to keep the debt owing. Why? Because they thought, if they got all these goods, all these products for free, well… in exchange of their debt, the West would be working to produce them, and they the

Han would just sit there and wait for those goods to be produced. I am oversimplifying here but the effect is true in economic theory. The West would have an injection of capital to produce goods and services for the Han equal to the debt, and the Han would in turn not work for or produce the equivalent sum. Putting aside other benefits that derive from this type of activity, such as improved technology, research and all the consequential assets the West could then inherit, a net transfer of economic activity would flow in the opposite direction to that observed when the debt was created. In fact the Han had produced economic assets for the West while the West had accumulated the debt before. Paying the debt would have the exact opposite effect. And the West would end up debt free and even more advanced technologically, and more dynamic and psychologically strong. So the Han refused to negotiate the debt, they let it hang there, like a sword.

"I don't think that these people in the West would have allowed their standard of living to be downgraded whatsoever in any event. It must be said that while the West would work "for free" for the Han to repay their debt, a lot of their products would be exported and not for their own use. But the result nonetheless is interesting. Two interdependent major economies do not want to accumulate debt, and if one does, the creditor should not want to be paid, at least not too fast, and not in full. All of this concerns the material well being of mankind only, not its spiritual backbone.

"Now as you know, these societies were very materialistic and they shone in their accomplishments in technology and science. But they lacked, or they lost, their spiritual compass. Which we always had. And which they adopted, by choice or by force.

"They adopted our spiritual guidance since they had none. Their power as I said was based on technological prowess. With the financial demands toward the Han mounting, they would produce less. Their forebears were doers. They, their descendants, had ceased to be doers, their very soul in a way had left them. And the cause of their financial dependence exacerbated their problems. It was a vicious cycle.

"So in brief, a society of engineers and doers had slowly become a society of what I would call, a society of talkers: bankers, lawyers, politicians, and other braggarts. Sheikh Hussein knew how to talk. He was it is told an extraordinary orator. And a society in decline loves to hear words of hope. So doers become talkers, but with no spiritual compass, talk can go so far. It was an easy prey for our ancestors to take over the West, with hardly a fight, hardly a drop of blood spilled. Two types of people, doers and talkers...In Islam, those who talk, talk of the divine word, not of the constructs of man.

"Brother Al Kansii, you probably know all that, but I want to emphasize two things: first the Han are still doers. They love material comforts to a point. But not above their own identity. And that is the second point, they believe in themselves. Objectors are treated as traitors, and rightly so, and often eliminated, just as we do here. Yes they have interest on debts, unlike us, but that hardly matters since it is an internal issue, and there is no interest in the transactions between the Caliphate and the Han Empire. We need however to define our tools to either conquer them, or bring them to the realization that Islam is the True Religion.

"In the present struggle we do not enjoy the same advantages that allowed us to subjugate the West, by their own hands. The Han like to quote an ancient Westerner, Churchill I think was his name, who referred to the West's actions as the *folly of democracies* and the Han won't fall for it. The Han have no such folly. And their materialism is limited. And they are industrious.

"In a word, we need to be creative" Al Kenii finished.

"Well?" said Assam looking at Al Kansii.

"Yes, ventured Al Kansii. It is all true. Only the True Religion brought to us by the Prophet (pbuh) can provide peace, stability, justice and happiness to all the people in the world. And I am committed to see to it that I will do anything that I am asked to do to achieve our goals. *Insha'Allah, Al Hamdulillah."*

"*Al Hamdulillah*" the two sheikhs responded. And they all brought their right index finger to their lips, kissed the finger and pointed to Heaven, eastward if possible.

In his discourse Assam had made many historical errors of course, and taken many short cuts, but as far as Al Kansii was concerned, and the reason he was there was that the Caliphate was not a *global caliphate* despite Al Amriki's expressed wishes. At least not yet.

As Al Kenii had indicated southern India was still infidel, although the Islamic push would continue grinding southward until the entire subcontinent were conquered, or so was the current assessment.

Al Kansii also knew that the lower part of South America in Lower Patagonia where some Christians, Hindus and Judeans, as they were now called, and as well as several assorted atheists, agnostics and so-called *humanists*, all of whom stubbornly refused to accept the True Religion, had converged, that region was also unconquered. But for how long was still debated.

There remained thus the Han Empire.

The three sat there in silence as if each had retired to his own thoughts. While sipping their tea, they all thought, each on his own, of that long historical exposé by Assam and its complement by Al Kenii, and how they would fine-tune the strategy against the Han. Or at least that was what it appeared. Assam retrenched into his inner soul as usual while Al Kenii was trying to formulate a coherent strategy for the assault on the Han. As far as Al Kansii was concerned, while they all peacefully sipped their mint tea in the Room of the Two Crescents, he began to gaze into a mental panorama of the world as he saw it. His thoughts were as follows.

Days of Yore

When the Vatican was moved from Rome to Patagonia, the local government had offered the Catholic hierarchy the *Casa Rosada* in Buenos Aires and resolved to move the government to a lesser building. The Vatican declined the offer out of religious humility. These were difficult times for Christendom and the Vatican wanted to share the suffering with the people in an act of voluntary absolution of sins. It was a good decision in any event since the *Casa Rosada* and Buenos Aires were evacuated shortly thereafter.

The *Casa Rosada*, or Pink House, had been the seat of government in Argentina for centuries. In its site was first a military fort called the *Fortaleza de Juan Baltazar de Austria* which was built in the sixteenth century of the Christian Era. The fort was replaced by the *Castillo San Miguel*, an exquisite masonry building built some two hundred years later and that is where the colonial government held its sessions. Many reconstructions and expansions in the subsequent centuries had culminated in a beautiful landmark where Italianate accents brought to it elegance and an air of robustness fit for a strong government, and all the presidents held their offices in that building thereafter. To add to that national character of strength and passion, the exterior of the building was given the pink color which was obtained by mixing paint with cow's blood. Although some interpret the inclusion of blood in different manners, the truth is that it was done to infuse the nation with the desire and strength of blood. Blood in the Spanish national conscience had always had a special meaning as symbolized by the red capes that the *matadors* hold in front of the *toro's* eyes, although bulls cannot see colors. The Pink House therefore represented the ardor of the people's struggles and their passion for life.

The beautiful buildings in the vicinity of the *Casa Rosada* betrayed a missed past, a past of glorious promise never achieved. A past of underachievement. As Al Kansii saw it, those times were over and with the new faith, new opportunities abounded, especially now that those without the true faith had been pushed down to the lower confines of Patagonia.

The authorities in Patagonia were aware that the original Vatican in Rome had been replaced by the Mosque of Sidi Hajara. The reference to the stones was a clear allusion to St Peter, but evil mouths contended that Hajara had another much more sacrilegious meaning, but of course only pagans could think that way. In Islam, respect for the sacred, even what is sacred to others was paramount. Yes, the infidels could be conquered and be fought with determination and sometime without pity, but never were they subject to humiliations, especially in their beliefs.

The Patagonian authorities endeavored to build *El Nuevo Vatican* in their new capital Comodoro Rivadavia. They raised sufficient funds to erect a copy of the *Casa Rosada* in Rivadavia and called it *San Pedro de Rivadavia*. Pilgrims flocked there annually from all over the world. In fact many of those posed as tourists and came clandestinely to honor their lost heritage, although officially some were now Muslims. Of course year after year fewer and fewer came to *San Pedro de Rivadavia*, and the audience of Pope Innocent XIV began resembling those of the opera goers in Buenos Aires of years past, greyer and older.

An art form, superior to all the world had known before but unappreciated by the masses, and especially the young, Opera seemed to have been dying for over two hundred years. But it never did die completely. Perhaps it was rather that only the dying found beauty in Opera. It was not a dying art form, far from it, but an art form for the dying. And Christianity had become, to them at least, the Opera of religions.

Opera was an art form beloved and respected in Patagonia. The new *Teatro Colón el Nuevo,* a smaller copy of its famous predecessor in Buenos Aires was where not only the dying, but also the very much alive enjoyed the many performances, unique in the world. Although not one of the five best acoustically designed theaters in the world as the original *Teatro Colón* was renowned for being, the smaller replica came surprisingly close. It is said that officials from the Caliphate, young and old, men and women, and sometimes disguised as pilgrims came to enjoy the sounds of that ultimate art form.

A new Pope was elected around that time, in the Year of Our Lord 2184 to be precise, and immediately after his election a welcome plume of white smoke was thrust out of the *Casa Rosada la Nueva* in Rivadavia one cold Winter day in August. To the Caliphate, the fact that that new Pope had chosen the name of Urban was an affront.

Yes, it was an unpleasant provocation. The new Pope in Rivadavia had chosen the name Urban XXII, a clear reference to the line of Urbans, especially Urban II who had single-handedly launched the Crusades on November 27, 1096 in his address of Clermont. Yes Urban II had been the instigator of this most odious assault on the people of Islam, the Crusades, as it was believed for centuries.

Quentin of Orange, of dual French and Dutch ethnic origin, Cardinal of Rivadavia prior to his election by the College of Cardinals of which he had been a member, had chosen not only the name Urban, but Urban XXII, the twenty second. Twenty two, two equal digits, two *two's.* The last Urban was Urban VIII who had served God until 1644 of the Christian Era. But more significant to Quentin of Orange was the tenure of Urban VII who came to serve Christ on September 15, 1590, and God had taken him back only thirteen days later on September 27, 1590. Quentin then added these thirteen days to the number eight, that of the last Urban, and obtained twenty-one. He would be Urban XXII. He was to be the twenty second. It was a sign from Heaven that beginning at the end of Christendom's hegemony, the time of the last American president, there had been two hundred and sixty six popes in the service of Christ, Servants of the Lord. Until he Quentin was elected, only thirteen popes had acceded to these pontifical heights and were able to wear the tiara and could hold the scepter. The fourteen increments that Urban XXII had added to define his title were also an allusion to the suffering of Christ during his fourteen stations in the *Via Dolorosa* and a reminder that Christendom was expecting still more suffering before its ultimate deliverance and redemption.

Urban also attributed the two digits in his title as follows: the first *two* in honor of the second dynasty named after that most holy Pontiff Urban II, and the second *two* indicating the second time a *reconquista* was to be, the first having begun one thousand years before.

Despite past common beliefs about the Crusaders and its most glorious knights, the Templars, official History in Patagonia had been corrected to present these warriors of the faith as heroes. According to scholars, the explosive growth of the Order of the Templars, apart from the combat operations in which they took part, was mainly due to the confidence they inspired and at the same time the nostalgia and secret aspirations with which they filled the hearts of their compatriots. These aspirations were simply the hope in the final triumph of Christendom. The Templars were Knights of Christ, and as such rather than reviled as they had been in the ancient West, in Patagonia they were venerated and glorified. It was believed that with the new Crusaders, the humble and the disinherited would rise again.

Rivadavia, Christian Republic of Patagonia

On the front lobby of the *Casa Rosada la Nueva*, the new *Casa Rosada*, smaller and less ambitious than the older one in Buenos Aires now part of the Grand Caliphate, a copy of the old Papal Bull issued by Urban II on November 27, 1096 of the Christian Era was visible to all. It was a reminder that history does not end, that it continues, sometimes repeats itself as Man does not learn from his mistakes, nor his crimes, nor his suffering. The text was in the original French, with adjacent translation in several languages, and some key passages proclaimed as follows:

> *"Frères Bien Aimés (Most Beloved Brethren),*
>
> *"Poussés par les exigences de ce temps (Urged by today's exigencies), moi, Urbain...*
>
> *"I, Urban, who with the permission of God wears the pontifical tiara, pontiff over the whole world, have come here toward you, the servants of God, as messenger to unveil to you the divine order...It is urgent that you hasten to bring to your brethren of the Orient the help so often promised and of pressing need. The Turks and the Arabs have attacked them and have advanced into the territory of Romany[10] as far as that part of the Mediterranean which is called the Arm of St George[11], and while penetrating deeper into the lands of these Christians, they have seven times vanquished them in battle, they have killed and rendered captive a great number of them, they have destroyed the churches and devastated the kingdom. If you let them now go on without resisting, they will spread their tide more widely upon many of the faithful servants of God.*
>
> *"It is why I pray to you, I exhort you – not I but the Lord prays to you and exhorts you as heralds of Christ – the poor as well as the rich - to hasten to chase away this vile brood from all regions inhabited by our brothers and to bring a needed aid to those who adore Christ. I say this to those who are here present, I will proclaim it to those who are absent, for it is Christ who commands it...*
>
> *"Let those who were previously accustomed to fighting wickedly, in private wars, against the faithful, now fight the infidels, and wage to a victorious end a war that ought to have been started long ago; may those who until now were thieves become soldiers, and those who earlier were mercenaries for sordid wages, now earn eternal rewards; may those who have exhausted themselves at the expense of both their body and their soul now strive for a double reward. What shall I add? On one side will be the wretched, on the other the true rich; here the enemies of God, there his friends. Enlist without wait; let these warriors arrange*

---

[10] This is a translation from the French, *Romanie,* which refers to the lands of the then Roman Empire (Eastern Empire)

[11] The Bosphorus.

their affairs and gather what is necessary to provide for their expenses; when winter ends and spring arrives, let them set out with joy and take the road with the Lord as their guide."

Al Kansii knew that in lower Patagonia the call for a new Crusade was etched in stone in many places of worship, and in official buildings as well. The religious spirit was fervent everywhere. And that was a sign of trouble for the Caliphate.

As Al Kansii had studied, earlier in these same lands where he had come to life, in these once mostly Christian societies it was recognized that the Crusades had been wrong, the Crusaders cruel murderers that deserved the opprobrium even from their own descendants. Now Muslims never throw opprobrium and contempt on their ancestors, especially those who fought for Islam. But Christians of the twentieth and twenty-first centuries of the Christian Era did. They had abandoned the false idea that Judea had been for hundreds of years a Christian land, after most Judeans had been expelled from it, for it had been a Judean land for millennia before and that is where Jesus was born and buried. It had become Muslim by conquest in the year 638 of the Christian era, and as such, according to Islam, had to remain Muslim. Yes it made sense. The Prophet (pbuh) from there had ascended to Heaven during his Night Journey with the Angel Gabriel. *What is of Islam, must remain of Islam.* And that was the way it had to be.

At that point Al Kansii interrupted his thoughts, he was talking of his own ancestors who, at least a few of them but not all of course, had fought until death to maintain their beliefs. These were the wrong beliefs he now knew, but they did not know that then. They had been sincere in their struggles. Al Kansii did not want to pursue this train of thought. It was dangerous. It would lead him to instability, unhappiness, and alter the full conviction that he needed to be a martyr, especially with a commando mission. Maybe it was better to die a martyr after all. He brought himself out of these disturbing thoughts when Assam spoke.

"Well, what is your reaction to all of this, Brother Al Kansii?" asked Assam.

Al Kansii was in a stupor. He had been daydreaming about his place in the world but he recovered quickly. He responded:

"So what we are proposing to do is to infiltrate the Han Empire, at the highest level, in person, utilizing all our technology to evade detection. But detection there will be, so the challenge will be to switch methods at every step to stay ahead of the Han. As the Han have all the detection methods available to them all the time, from multi-band satellite constellations to neutrino beam detection and perhaps even quark stream propagation detection, it will require alertness and the help of Allah of course. I am to be the Jolt. The rest is your duty. I believe we shall prevail."

"You know that death is certain don't you?"

"I know Sheikh. I am ready for Allah. *Allah u Akbar, Al Hamdulillah.*"

"*Allah u Akbar, Al Hamdulillah*" the other two responded.

They each raised the right index finger to their lips, kissed it and then pointed it to Heaven, eastward.

Al Kansii and Al Kenii walked out of the Room of the Two Crescents.

Assam now felt tired. Looking through the window he then saw that Al Kansii and his escort were exiting *Al Dar Baida* on the side of Sheikh Hussein Avenue. He turned to the opposite window and he could see the vast expanse separating his Room of the Two Crescents from the Islamic Monument, a very large obelisk between Sharia Avenue and the Avenue of Islam further south. From Assam's perspective, the glorious Islamic Monument seemed to rise from the river.

Further Thoughts

The Islamic Monument was a monument to the glory of Islam in these lands. The religious authorities were proud that as an obelisk it represented not only the conquest of the West, but also the victory of Islam over paganism, since obelisks had originated in pagan Egypt before the monotheistic onslaught on these cults had begun. The obelisk was thus the proper form to link the passage of time and the culmination of Islam's victorious path in history, as it pointed toward the heavens.

The Islamic Monument had four inscriptions in beautiful Islamic calligraphy on each of its four sides. The north side, facing Assam had *sura* 8:12:

> *"Remember when your Lord inspired to the angels, 'I am with you, so strengthen those who have believed. I will cast terror into the hearts of those who disbelieved, so strike them upon the necks and strike from them every fingertip."*

The south side facing the New Vatican had the appropriate *sura* 9:29:

> *"Those who do not believe in Allah or in the Last Day and who do not consider unlawful what Allah and his Messenger (pbuh) have made unlawful and who do not adopt the religion of truth from those who were given the Scripture – fight until they give the jizyah willingly while they are humbled."*

The west face of the monument, in a message to the Han proclaimed from *sura* 8:60:

> *"And prepare against them whatever you are able of power and of steeds of war by which you may terrify the enemy of Allah and your enemy and others besides them whom you do not know but Allah knows. And whatever you spend in the cause of Allah will be fully repaid to you, and you will not be wronged."*

While the east side facing the Holy of the Holies declared the eternal ways of Allah, from *sura* 5:32:

> *"If anyone slew a person ... it would be as if he slew the whole people. And if anyone saved a life, it would be as if he saved the life of the whole people."*

More glorious still was that the Islamic Monument was adorned at the top with a very large crescent, made of pure solid gold, certified eighteen carats at its core and twenty-two carats in its outer layers and which was attached to the aluminum cap that few if any had noticed before.

The crescent was not welded to the cap in the vulgar sense, since the melting temperatures of gold and aluminum are quite different. Gold melts at 1,060 degrees Celsius while aluminum does so at a mere 660 degrees. Furthermore aluminum is somewhat difficult to master as at a temperature close to its melting point it can barely be handled and just a few degrees above, it melts uncontrollably. Only very skilled artisans could work on such a prized piece. Therefore the aluminum cap had been removed, brought down and attached to the gold crescent after undergoing a process called annealing.

By slowly increasing the temperature of the cap to about 260 degrees Celsius and then allowing it to cool also slowly, aluminum is made much softer and malleable, a little closer to gold, especially high carat gold. It was said that annealing of the gold was not needed but in any event the two surfaces, of similar softness now, could be bonded using a known technique called ultrasonic bonding. Ultrasonic waves, that is acoustic waves of a specific frequency would impart energy to the now almost perfect interface between the two metals where it could be assumed that the atoms on both sides were basically bonded to each other. This technique formed a very lasting and strong juncture, almost as if the interface were an alloy of the two metals. It also presented from the outside a perfect line with no discernible weld or gap. This was very important symbolically because it represented the bonding of the two societies, Islam and the formerly Christian West, into a common everlasting bond.

Unlike welding, in which bonds between atoms are thermally forced to create a strong but unnatural interface between two metals, annealing followed by ultrasonic bonding allowed the atoms on each side to share the peripheral electrons. An electron initially orbiting a nucleus of an atom in the first metal found itself now orbiting the nucleus of an atom in the second metal. And vice versa. That electron belonged in a sense to both atoms. Of course when an electron of the first metal is within an atom of the second metal, an electron of the second metal is also within an atom of the first metal. In complete union. The bond is stronger and appears natural.

Since Assam believed that all human feelings and endeavors can be traced to the early years of one's life, which he called *the magic years*, he compared this fortunate bond of the crescent and the cap to the bliss of the baby in the womb, or just out of the womb. At that point in early life, the baby does not know yet that his own body is different from the ambient world. Weeks if not months pass before that baby begins to understand the separation of himself from the outside world and recognize his own shell, his self.

Spiritually too, Islam afforded him, and he believed it afforded all the faithful as well, unity with the Universe. The crescent and cap were in themselves a monument to that unity, separate from the actual huge monument upon which they sat.

The many steps needed to achieve the union of the aluminum cap with the gold crescent, especially the softening of the interfaces to be joined and then the perfect juncture prior to the burst of energy of the ultrasonic process resembled in his view the steps leading to the life of the symbolic baby.

Of course Assam also thought of his union with Leila that brought him back to that state when one is one with the rest of the universe. Assam liked to think of him and Leila as the crescent and the cap, when one does not know when one's own body ends and the other's begins. Unity in bliss, just as in the beginning. But he chased these thoughts off his mind.

The reflection of the gold on the aluminum highlighted its silvery shine which contrasted with the gold of the crescent. The annealing process also left a bluish tinge on the metals that seemed as if reflected from the sky. In contrast to former times, the aluminum cap was now very noticeable by all and it guided one's eyes to the glorious gold crescent on top of it. The sight was most beautiful in the early evening in the Fall when the angle of the Sun's rays at that latitude provided a unique glow that lifted one's heart toward the crescent. The light at that time of year, and especially in the evenings was similar to that at higher northern latitudes in early Summer, when the Sun dwells late into the night and the angle of incidence of its rays provides a wonderful combination of light schemes that radiate everywhere. Some say that radiance, that incredibly beautiful glow had given rise centuries before to the dominance of Western painting, as artists had access to an inexhaustible palette of natural glows and colors to render their work purely radiant.

The union of cap and crescent, of Islam and the West, was thus like all other perfect unions: a softening phase through warmth, followed by a perfect embrace, and ending with a burst of energy.

Assam brought his thoughts to Li Li.

Li Li the Han

Li Li, or Lili as she was referred to affectionately, was a mid-rank cultural officer at the Han Embassy. Her official duties were to establish open communications between the two Empires, as the Han referred to the Caliphate and themselves. Of course Assam knew she reported to the highest levels of the People's Council. In fact, as Assam had easily guessed, she was an intelligence agent, or a spy. But Assam also knew she could be a useful agent. And he had worked hard over the years to cultivate their relationship.

Cultivate was the right word since it was based on culture. Many an evening was organized either at the Embassy, or at *Al Dar Baida* where distinguished guests, scholars, scientists and prominent thinkers of both Empires assembled with Assam and Lili, who alternated as hosts, to debate in a very civilized manner issues of the day, and of days long gone. In fact Assam and Lili had established a sort of literary club for the intelligentsia of both sides to exchange ideas of interest. It was nicknamed the Club. That was coexistence, peaceful coexistence at its best.

Of course Assam and his side had a goal, the Global Caliphate and the advent of Islam and *sharia* worldwide. Lili on the other side did not dream of global Han, or Confucianism or anything of the sort. She was an exclusionist, as most Han were. So the Han's interaction with the Caliphate was a defensive one while the Caliphate was on the offensive. That was the only parallel with the West, but unlike with the West of two centuries before, the Han had will power and a specific identity to defend.

Nonetheless the Club provided a forum to resolve outstanding issues in the world, away from the cacophony of the Assembly of Nations, where the Patagonians and other lesser and still independent entities, caused a raucous atmosphere of useless deliberations and resolutions with no consequence. In fact, if both sides stayed as such, peace throughout the world had finally been achieved. But man, especially if directed by Allah, would not be satisfied with such limited achievement. The Caliphate had to pursue and achieve its mission. The Han on the other hand hoped the Caliphate would one day not wish to interfere any longer with their beliefs, or lack of them.

The fact that the Caliphate strove for worldwide inclusion and conversion, proved that their religion was the True Religion for all. If the Han, just like the West, believed they held the truth they would fight for it. And so thought Assam.

Second Visitor to Al Dar Baida

A soft sound rang in his ear. Assam heard Abu Bak'r's artificial voice, that is a voice activated by Abu Bak'r's brain waves reflecting his intentions. Abu Bak'r was announcing Li Li and Assam in turn *intended* that she be let in.

Lili wore a head scarf as a mark of respect for the customs of the Caliphate. In fact many if not most in the Han Empire had adopted the use of a head covering, and full length garments, at least for women. Just as several centuries before the fashion adopted practically worldwide indicated a maximum showing of skin, when temperature permitted of course, in this Caliphate-Han Empire world, chic was maximum covering. The Han had espoused the advent of what was referred to as *modesty*. The traditional Han tunic, dresses that did not mold the body and head coverings that enhanced the beauty of the bearer were perfectly appropriate to the new dress code. The world in a sense had gone back, fashion wise, to an earlier time when things were simple, and traditional, and just correct. To a time before the West's onslaught on national customs had degraded those and everyone ended up looking the same: men with tee-shirts with writings on them and women with molded tight-fitting trousers and shirts. Assam found this fashion, these new fashions, more elegant and more elevated. He looked at Lili with artistic pleasure.

Lili's face was China white, whether it was her true color, or the make-up that women in the Han Empire had not abandoned as they had done in the Caliphate, Assam did not know. Although Lili was of middle age, she looked much younger and Assam couldn't help a certain attraction to what he felt was a China doll in front of him. Of course Lili was a not a doll, Assam knew. She was an agent of Assam's most feared adversaries.

Lili wore red *pants*. That was the only word Assam could ascribe to the overflowing, natural silk garment that covered her legs. Because they were wide, Lili could as well be wearing a skirt. Over a white silk blouse, Lili wore a matching red jacket with very fine gold lace at the end of her sleeves and around the collar. Her hair, of which a few strands protruded from the scarf, was jet black, again Assam wasn't sure if it was her natural color. It was held by a gold hair ornament with five rubies forming a star and that ornament could be seen below the scarf as it moved the scarf up and held it as if floating above the hair. That way Lili could conceal her head *modesty*, in the parlance of the Caliphate, with a scarf and at the same time carry a little hint of vanity. Lili wore red and gold slippers on her very small feet.

As Lili entered the Room of the Two Crescents, Assam smiled at her and greeted her with a sincere *"Welcome."* Assam's next instinct was to look down at her feet. Assam was not a foot fetishist, by any means. But Assam considered he had the heart of an artist although his lifelong occupation was political and religious. He saw beauty in all things. Even mundane objects. Of course Lili's feet were not mundane. It amazed him how these tiny little and almost perfect feet could support a grown person. The little feet added to the aura of fragility and grace that Lili conveyed, at least to Assam, the aura of a China doll.

Thousands of thoughts converged simultaneously into Assam's mind concerning the art of feet, on which volumes were written during the millennia past. He recalled one special poem, by an ancient Persian poet and admirer of only the feet in women and nothing else, strictly:

As she stands on her little feet of glass
The hundreds little bones that make her be
Softly spread to carry her
And provide for balance.
And they give her slender body
A perfect posture.

The woman is what her feet are
Noble feet support a noble heart
And what her eyes say
Is truly told by her feet.

Assam quickly pushed aside these thoughts and subtly gestured the order for tea, green tea of course.

Al Kenii was standing on the eastern side of the room. He bowed his head to Lili and the three sat at a round table.

Lili began:

"Sheikh Assam, my Government thanks Your Excellency for the disposition it exhibits in all our endeavors.

"Our leadership awaits the visitors the Caliphate may wish to send to accomplish progress in our mutual understanding. We are ready."

At this moment, as the tea butlers performed the tea pouring ritual, Assam looked at Al Kenii, who nodded imperceptibly.

Lili had given the signal that the infiltration was about to begin. Her people, *the leadership* as she had said, not 'the Supreme Leader' as was expected in this context, appreciated the Caliphate's *disposition*. Assam and Al Kenii did not miss the *visitors which the Caliphate may wish to send,* clearly not an officially sanctioned and vetted envoy. *We are ready* was the unmistakable sign that Al Kansii was expected, at the earliest.

This double entendre between Assam and Lili was a result of their relationship at the Club. Of course Assam made this a somewhat personal and sentimental communication. But Al Kenii understood as well, and there was nothing sentimental between Lili and Al Kenii. But Assam assumed he could interpret such hidden communication because of his special relationship with Lili. Of course without Assam, Al Kenii would not have had the opportunity to communicate at that subliminal level with Lili. So Assam was right.

It had begun at the Club. Once, a long time ago, when all the guests had retired, even Al Kenii who it was said was Assam's shadow, Lili had remained. Her mysterious eyes fixed on him, Assam could not comprehend the moment. Assam had seen women's eyes before, and plenty. But he was used to *his* type of eyes, which he could read. Lili's were undecipherable. He could not tell whether she had stayed because she was attracted to him, that seemed implausible as both Empires remained on their own turf in these matters, especially for high ranking officials. Was she trying to corrupt him, or recruit him for some kind of treasonous act? The Han did not adopt these tactics, there weren't interested in converting the Caliphate. The reverse of course was not true. As Lili looked intently at Assam with a sort of passion, but a cold passion, Assam was perplexed. Then in a motherly gesture she ran her right index finger, slightly curved in the air as if she were caressing his left cheek, from below the eye to the end of his chin and then lowered her hand. Lili had not touched him, but Assam had felt the touch. Was it real? Was she using some kind of quantum effect, unknown to the Caliphate? Had something in her hand *quantum-tunneled* through the air to reach his face?

Assam could swear he had felt the touch, and he knew at the same time Lili's hand was far enough from his face as to not have touched him.

"I need your help" she said in the loveliest voice.

Assam, with four wives and a myriad concubines, and a strong man he thought, felt powerless.

"And...how?" he asked.

"This situation cannot go on forever. We need to be closer to each other" replied Lili.

Assam wasn't sure whether she was talking of the Han Empire and the Caliphate, or of the two of them. By his standards, she was *old,* that is over 20 or 22 years of age. In Assam's culture, women were supposed to be young to be of interest. But whether she referred to affairs of the states they each represented or just the two of them, he wouldn't know. And her age, to his surprise, was her attraction. In his philosophical manner, Assam thought that maybe the West wasn't that wrong after all. The Westerners were able to see things which Assam's people couldn't as in his culture everything was defined in advance. *"But that in which we believe is divinely inspired, so it is true"* he thought. These were not thoughts that were permissible, Assam knew.

Still he felt an irresistible attraction to Lili. Lili then suddenly stood up and announced that she was leaving as it was late.

"We will need to talk about this again" she finally said. She walked backward a few steps, bowed her head and disappeared just after Assam, totally confused had answered something he couldn't even remember. Maybe "Yes, of course" or "Good night", or both.

And so it began. Their secret relationship. Which wasn't a relationship at all, except for a constant suspended communication when the one who had engaged first, Lili, grew more and more hermetic and the recipient, the confident Assam was left wondering, and desiring.

And so it continued. After most of the Club's *soirées*, Lili would stay a bit longer, and Assam insisted that some other guests remain as well to dispel any rumors. But Lili was able to communicate to him serious and daring thoughts. This is what Assam could gather.

As Assam understood it, Lili represented a faction close to the People's Council that was dissatisfied with the Supreme Leader's policies and sought to unseat him. They desired peace and coexistence with the Caliphate. And if Assam could help that faction with accomplishing its goals, things would be better for all. And the Empire would begin a slow and peaceful conversion to the True Religion. And perhaps for himself and Lili as well. Assam wasn't sure that was communicated in any implicit way, certainly not overtly, but he believed he had somehow concluded that that was what Lili meant. When freedom and openness would enter the Han, she would be free to be with him. Perhaps. Assam wasn't sure he even wanted that. But he could not help being attracted to that idea.

He remembered one of the first concubines he had acquired a long time ago. As a young, proud warrior in those days, he had boasted of his valor, power and other attributes. He had said that 'he took what he chose'. The concubine, in a daring moment responded "No, you take what chooses you."

And against all odds Lili, at least in appearance, had chosen him. Well, she did choose, but to what end he knew not. At least not yet. But she chose him, that was certain. And that filled him with pride and desire. He truly liked Lili.

But the affairs of state trumped the affairs of the heart. Assam decided to play along and see how and where he could help Lili and her people. But Assam knew as well that he had found in a bizarre way an entry into the inner sanctum of the Han Empire. Assam could now use Lili to infiltrate the adversary. Just like the forces that had catapulted Sheikh Hussein, the first Caliph, into power and resulted in the advent of the American Caliphate. History was repeating himself. And his destiny, as ordained by Allah, as with his ancestor's, was to prepare and cause the advent of the next, and final Caliphate, the World Caliphate, the Global Caliphate.

Yes he would use Lili. He did not like the idea. He thought of her beautiful little feet, and he could not admit to himself that he would use her. He convinced himself however that Lili was aware of what he would do. He would assist her in toppling the leadership. She knew he would not stop there, since it was an open policy that the Caliphate sought to convert the entire world to the True Religion. Lili knew that, so she knew which sands she was walking on. Hot sands for sure. But known sands.

XinJiang Uyghur

The Uyghur, mostly Muslims in the Han Empire, had lived for centuries in the western part of the Han territory, the XinJiang Uyghur. Even before Islam had expanded in these regions and brought its spiritual benefits, there were Uyghur there. Although they were Han and looked Han for the most part, according to the vast majority of the Han they worshiped a different god. Or to be precise they worshiped the true God. The other Han did not worship any god at all, according to the faithful Uyghur.

The Han had limited their net population growth for the past two hundred years at precisely below 1.26 percent per year, and had reached a population of over twenty two billion, which of course included souls in the lands since then annexed to the Empire. The Uyghur, which at the outset numbered about fourteen million had grown much faster to reach over 220 million, an average growth of 1.6 percent. Although a minority, its sheer size commanded attention and accommodation from the central authorities.

The Uyghur were good citizens and they held very strong beliefs borne out of millennia. These beliefs, and their hope, were that the rest of the Han would adopt their True Religion one day as they had done themselves by the end of the first millennium of the Christian Era. That conversion had brought them stability, culture, happiness, and spiritual comfort. Because of their community of spirit, they were natural ideological allies of the Caliphate.

To many Han, especially because of the competition between the two Empires, the Caliphate and the Han, the Uyghur's allegiance was sometimes in doubt. The Uyghur's themselves contributed to that situation by demanding unique privileges, such as *sharia* courts, special restrictions on food, particular holidays and other special treatment. Furthermore there were many youths, by no means a majority, that were ready to sacrifice themselves to the glory of God, even if it meant acting against the national government. Not unlike what the West had suffered centuries before. As a result, the national authorities threaded with care but were nonetheless very suspicious of the Uyghur. That suspicion of course exacerbated the problems as many Uyghur complained of being amalgamated with a minority and that discourse produced more retort, and this vicious cycle had not exactly contributed to a healthy relationship. Despite efforts on both sides to cooperate with each other, at least officially, the situation progressively and very slowly deteriorated each day a little bit to the point where trust was lacking. Since the Han traditionally accorded trust and honor an essential place in human interactions, the loss of mutual trust could not be helpful. The People's Council had a problem on their hands, and they hoped that with time it would go away. Of course, extremist Uyghur hoped that with time, the other Han would go away, or rather would join the Umma.

In one word, like a myriad minority groups elsewhere and since time immemorial, the Uyghur were vocal and their voice was heard incessantly. Their demands were echoed in the propaganda spread by the Caliphate. They could not be ignored by the Empire.

Li Li was not a Uyghur, but she had seen these people's dedication to their faith. And she could not miss the fact that the rest of the Empire was loosing its convictions, its willpower, just as the West had done centuries before. That is what had transpired at sessions of the Club, especially when those assembled reviewed works of history, philosophy and religion. Animated debates considered for example whether it was the true faith that brought conviction and willpower, or conversely conviction led one to consider one's faith as the true faith.

Assam obviously thought the first proposition to be true, since revelation brings conviction and one defends it. The opposite was physically impossible as for conviction to lead to the true faith, the true faith must first exist. And where would it come from? From a true revelation. This logical construct was in contradiction with Assam's held view that what a child learns in early childhood, *the magic years*, stays with that person his entire life. It would follow normally that a conviction inculcated early on would lead to unwavering faith, and not the other way around. But Assam could not reconcile with the idea that conviction with no basis could survive, the true faith had to be there in the first place to sustain it.

In any event, the politico-religious debates at the Club is how Lili was able to communicate her most intimate feelings toward him, or at least his philosophical him. And the relationship had grown into a mutual trust albeit unspoken, and in fact just assumed.

And the two, Lili and Assam, with Al Kenii as a witness now and then, had plotted the overthrow of the Han leadership, and its replacement with Lili's friends.

And Lili would be free to... Assam did not know. He could only dream, if dreaming was even necessary. He wasn't sure he even wanted Lili. But if Lili wanted him, he could not ignore that attraction. Just like quantum effects. A tall energy barrier impedes a particle, but somehow, on the other side the particle is expected, wanted, because of the laws of probabilities. The particle eventually will cross the barrier, or rather will find itself on the other side of a forbidding barrier. Assam smiled to himself and thought that in fact humans were subject to what he called *emotional quantum effects*. Perhaps even just plain quantum effects. He always thought so.

Just as when Lili had at a distance caressed his face and he had felt the touch. And it had started the strange communication that led, that would lead *Insha'Allah*, to the conquest of the Han Empire by the Caliphate. Something had tunneled from her hand to his face. *Emotional Quantum Tunneling*. Just like the weapons they had devised and that they would use. Except those were not emotional of course.

Quantum Thoughts

Quantum Theory was a branch of Physics developed over three hundred years before and which first provided a mathematical description of the wave-particle duality of matter and energy. In the quantum realm, subatomic particles and electromagnetic and other types of waves are neither strictly waves nor particles. They are packets of energy that travel as waves. As such they appear to be both wave and particle. For light, an electromagnetic wave, these packets of energy are seen as particles and they are called *photons*.

Quantum Theory was based on the observation that physical quantities only exist in discrete amounts, in packets called *quanta*. The energy of a particle for example can only be one, two, three or any multiple of these packets, but not a fraction of a packet. The same applies to matter since matter and energy are related.

Most people in the Empire and in the Caliphate were familiar with a most famous equation known as $E=mc^2$ which related mass and energy. What was less known, at least to the uninitiated, was one of the fundamental equations of Quantum Theory which states that the energy E of an entity undergoing simple harmonic oscillations can only have discrete values and these are related to the frequency of these oscillations as follows:

$$E = nh\nu$$

where ν, the Greek letter *nu*, represented the frequency, h was Planck's constant, an extremely small quantity, and n = 0, 1, 2, 3, 4 and so on... The energy is called *quantized* and the single quantum is $h\nu$. For most everyday experiences, h is so small that it can be assumed zero and the discrete *quanta* appear all stacked on top of each other in a continuum of energy. That is why most people had never experienced a quantum effect, at least not consciously.

An important tenet of the theory was that the universe in its most minute detail was therefore non-continuous and rather consisted of something like steps of matter and energy. These *quanta* being extremely small they were not observed in prior centuries and were ignored by what ended being called Classical Physics. However, at microscopic scales the *quanta* did have an impact. A fundamental law of Quantum Theory posited centuries ago that physical parameters of a particle such as position and momentum (or velocity) could not be known with absolute certainty, but only within a certain range. This came to be known as the *uncertainty principle* proposed by Heisenberg, and was formally written as:

$$\Delta x \cdot \Delta p \geq \hbar/2$$

where $\hbar = h/2\pi$

and Δx and Δp are the uncertainties in the determination of the position x and momentum p (mass times velocity) of a particle.

Because of that inherent uncertainty and prior to making a measurement on it, to each possible value of a physical parameter of a particle is associated a probability rather than a specific magnitude. The import of this is that strange phenomena were predicted and later actually observed and which in the present world had led to the conception of unique weapons.

One such strange phenomenon is as follows. Since a particle's position cannot *a priori* be known with certainty but rather given by the probability of it being somewhere, it follows that if the probability of it being in a wide region of space is not zero at any point in that region, that particle therefore could be found anywhere. In other words if a particle is considered to be *here*, the probability of it being also *there* is a finite non-zero number although small.

So the particle could in principle be anywhere, even on the other side of a barrier that may seem inaccessible. The barrier could be an electric potential, or the nucleus of atom or any other physical impediment. When such a barrier was encountered and a particle was found on the unexpected side of it, the particle was considered to have *tunneled* through the barrier, as if the particle had crossed a mountain, the barrier, through a tunnel. The phenomenon was dubbed *quantum tunneling* and was the foundation of many of the weapons being deployed by the two Empires.

Li Li was well versed in Quantum Theory. She had to, as her world's defenses and the Caliphate's threats were all quantum based. Weapons of Human Disintegration as they were called sometimes had re-established the balance once known as *MAD*, Mutually Assured Destruction. But unlike with the ancient *MAD*, the two competing Empires had reverted to a type of check mate, and focused their efforts on stealth weapons, which could not be traced and provided pin-point targeting of enemy assets. It was a type of chess game and both players knew that a check-mate would be fatal.

On her way to the Han Embassy, Li Li recalled her younger years in the Han Empire as a student, which she had shared with Yu Lin. Yu Lin was a brilliant scientist, and her intellectual equal. She could not interact with lesser brains, it annoyed her. She had to admit that Assam was close though. But his vanity prevented him to reach the heights she knew she and Yu Lin would reach. Although she knew Assam considered himself humble, and he was in a sense, in matters of relationships between the sexes, he could not help being somewhat vain. Perhaps it was his cultural background. And she had taken advantage of it. She felt a bit guilty, but the affairs of state trump all others.

Li Li had progressed through the Party's hierarchy and was selected, with Yu Lin's help, to the top post at the Embassy in the Caliphate. Of course her title was not that of a top official, but she knew she had the top job. She did not waste time with formalities and administrative matters, and other pretensions of diplomatic officialdom. She was there on a mission. To use the Caliphate to achieve the ultimate power for herself and Yu Lin in the Empire, and perhaps the entire world. But that, the world, they really did not need, did not want. The Han were content with the Han. They did not desire the rest which they did not consider worthy. At best the rest of the world was equal to the Han. Truly at best. And best was rare.

As Li Li reached the Han Embassy, she prepared to send a soft message of love to her *contact* deep in Han territory. Li Li knew that the quantum encryption and other countermeasures the Han could deploy would be sufficient to avoid detection by the Caliphate. However what she had to conceal was from the Han, and in a sense she wanted, she needed the Caliphate to intercept her message. The best defense therefore was to communicate human messages that would be difficult to interpret, and with an encryption key that would be easy to decipher.

Assam was aware of Lili's special relationship with her *contact*, who was to inherit the Han Empire and usher in a new era of peace. But Assam knew, or thought he knew, that Lili and her *contact* masqueraded as romantically involved to dispel any notion of their plans. This subject would of course mislead the Han counter surveillance but perhaps the Caliphate's as well. Assam had to take account of that too. However, the way he thought of Lili helped Assam not to be concerned by this aspect of the messages that Lili usually transmitted to her *contact*.

In the presumed safety of her Embassy, Li Li placed an quantum-encrypted call to her *contact*.

Quantum Encryption

The communication consisted first in data capture and then editing, both steps performed by pronouncing the words, or inputting the associated thoughts, into a quantum encoder. This encoder translated the digital bits representing the voice into quantum bit states, or *qubits*, defined by the encoder. The *qubits* in turn were entangled with a series of *qubits* at the receiving end.

By acting on the *qubits* at the originating encoder at the Embassy, quantum entanglement ensured that the *qubits* at the receiving center *aligned* themselves and produced a series of states, similar to those produced at the Embassy. The encoding produced a large number of possible states, in the millions. The information for actual decoding, the *key* so to speak, was simply transmitted using normal communications means. This process was called teleportation of the *qubit*, especially because nothing was truly transported.

The entangled pair of *qubits* acted in tandem, and an eventual eavesdropper would be powerless as he did not possess a member of the entangled pair of quantum states. That eavesdropper could potentially detect the *key*, or keys, but he could not know what these quantum states were since they were not transmitted, just recreated, or rather read or 'observed' at a distance through entanglement. The eavesdropper could not therefore perform the necessary decoding. In other words, even if the eavesdropper were to intercept the so-called *key*, he did not have a set of quantum states to which he could apply that key.

A comparable example of this communication would be that of a football team and a coach that are separated by a large distance. The coach and the captain know the plays they could use by number. All the coach would have to do is transmit the key, the play number for the team to execute. Unless the eavesdropper had in his possession a set of plays numbered in the same way, the knowledge of the key would be useless to him. The entangled quantum states go further indeed as a change or observation in a set of plays would have a corresponding change in the other member of the entangled pair, without any other need to communicate.

Another advantage of quantum encryption was that quantum theory guaranteed that since measuring quantum information disturbed that information, the eavesdropper could himself easily be detected all the while being unable to decrypt among the millions of quantum states that characterized the data that is said to be *teleported*.

For this specific communication between Li Li and her *contact*, the space chosen consisted of only two hundred and fifty six possible states, and the eavesdropper could easily decide among this small number of possible states. And this for every bit of the classical voice conversation. Any conventional computer could decode this message.

In any event, deep in the Han Empire Li Li's *contact*, when a special tone tinkled his ear, answered: "Ha."

Li Li's voice, quantum teleported then said:

"Dear One, I recalled our trip along the Yang Tse river. Our love is shared for its poetry. We will soon join."

The *contact* concluded with a simple "Ha."

Assam was immediately informed of that message which was easily decrypted by the massive Office of Counter Surveillance and Decoding. Quantum Encryption was in principle unbreakable, but this was an area where the Caliphate excelled and their massive quantum super-computers had been able from time to time to break the codes which were dynamically updated. Luckily for Assam, given the simplicity of the encoding, this was one of these times.

The ease of intercepting the communication should have been cause for alarm to Assam. But then maybe not, he thought, since Lili may have also meant for him to know what she was communicating, rather than spread misinformation. In fact, because of her plans, to which he was privy, the misinformation from Lili would rather have been directed at the Han leadership.

Assam understood the river trip as the new voyage the *contact* would take with the Caliphate. This major history-changing endeavor was symbolically compared to the Yang Tse River, a most powerful and mighty river in Han territory. To Li Li and her *contact* however it meant to have Yan – for *Yang* in the message - readied up for battle as the trip of Assam's agent would soon begin. To Assam, he was to join them in their love for poetry, the Truth of Islam. To Lili and her *contact* poetry meant the disintegration by an agent of the Caliphate of the entire People's Council, allowing the *contact* to remain the only power in the Han Empire. And he would not trust the Caliphate.

Assam was pleased. Yet he felt some doubts and wondered if he shouldn't be more suspicious. Was it too easy? But still, the *contact* and Lili would be executed for treason if the plot came out. Assam knew however that the *contact* and his agents controlled all the detection systems in the Han Empire. The chances of any message, especially one of a personal and private nature to be intercepted were low. Furthermore it appeared that the Supreme Leader was aware of the relationship between Lili and her *contact*. Or so Assam was informed.

We will soon join was a bit more problematic. *"Join who, what?"* Assam asked himself. Yes, an agent would soon *join* the plot and be on his way, although Lili could not possibly know who it was and how he would get there. They would have to detect him on their own, and this for two reasons: first they could not allow a mishap by the *contact* and his people, and second no hint could be given whatsoever to the surveillance system which could tap into the *contact*'s information and intent through their mind reading systems. So willingly or not, the *contact* could be a liability.

Nonetheless, Assam was still uncomfortable with the words *for its poetry*. Was it a way to indicate their own love, or the love for a coup, or for Islam? Assam had no illusions. The *contact* only wanted power, and he was no Islam lover, or lover of anything else. So what was that poetry about? Again their mutual love? But she had said, *'our love is shared'*. *'Our love'*, does that mean that Lili indicated to her *contact* that Assam was aware of their relationship, approved of it and knew that it was the basis for their plot against the Empire?

Assam had to be careful. All traces of Al Kansii's whereabouts were to be erased - *remain one step ahead of detection.*

Quantum Infrastructure

In both the Caliphate and the Han Empire, quantum computers were linked via quantum networks, and rather than transmit full sets of information as in the early days of telecommunications, the bits of information, called *qubits* or formally quantum bit states, were linked, or entangled, sometimes just in pairs for high security applications, or more commonly in strings, where a member of a first pair connected its own entanglement to a member of another pair to form a string through which it was in turn paired. Broadcast could in this manner be easily achieved.

An action, such as the measurements of the state of a *qubit* would be felt instantly by the other entangled member of the pair, and a set of probable states was established by the receiving communication node or quantum computer. The instantaneity of the communication, known as *teleportation*, appeared to be in violation of the limit in the speed of light for the transmission of information, but it was not so. Nothing was transmitted since the two members of the pair were entangled with each other. They each contained the same states, or information, and only their pattern, not their content needed to be revealed. Such phenomena were discovered centuries before but had to wait decades before they were perfected and made into practical applications. As a result, the mayhem created in the early days by what was then called *cyber warfare* had abated considerably and was seen as a thing of the past. In quantum networks indeed, an attempt to observe the quantum states would alter them as just the act of measuring a quantum state modifies it. Furthermore the victim of such attempt would immediately be notified and be able to take protective measures. In fact, these protections were built-in, pre-programmed in quantum networks. They acted as antibodies; when sensing a virus they immediately erected defenses against it and began fighting it.

But that had not stopped both sides from trying to break through these seemingly insurmountable defenses. The answer to science was more science.

On the other side of the world, in a cabin to the north of Manzhouli, deep in Han Territory, Yu Lin received word that Li Li's message had been intercepted and decoded and more importantly *interpreted* as expected. He smiled with self-satisfaction. Yes the Han were smarter. At least *he* was.

He issued a quantum command through his holographic display which appeared anywhere he stood and when he wished it to appear in this rustic cabin. The command was to the Qiqihar Annex Surveillance Center, which immediately and discretely, in a routine manner, relayed it, or at least the parts of it that it deemed proper, to the National Surveillance Center at Golog Maqen in the center of Han territory.

3

INFILTRATION

BeiJing, August 22, 2188 CE[12]

*Y*u Lin Liao was a member of the People's Council. Deng Zuolin, his childhood friend had acceded to the post of Supreme Leader five years earlier. A post that Yu Lin had coveted since his years at the Academy of Sciences of the Empire. Yu Lin was not envious, he respected and admired his life-long friend. The problem was that the Supreme Leader did not always see things the right way. And Yu Lin's ability to influence him had become weaker and weaker as they both grew older, and as the Supreme Leader felt more and more comfortable in his leadership position.

The comfort level of the Supreme Leader disturbed Yu Lin enormously. The comfort level that displeased Yu Lin had nothing to do with political comfort; they were all safe politically. They all knew it. The comfort that Yu Lin disliked was more of a psychological nature.

There is a time Yu Lin knew, when leadership becomes ingrained in you. When everybody around you caters to your every need, kowtows to you even if they think you are wrong, attends to your every desire. There is a time when suddenly something clicks in your brain. As Yu Lin observed, leadership comfort invades your being. Since for you as a new leader nothing is like for everyone else, and you know this from the time when you were like everyone else, no matter how resilient and intelligent, and philosophical a leader you

---

[12] Although their civilization spanned more than 3000 years beyond the Christian Era, after the Fall of the West the Han had continued to use the Gregorian calendar which they dutifully referred to as Common Era, or CE. Some Han believed they were the heirs and the successors of the great civilizations that had migrated West from Central Asia, to the Middle Orient, Greece, Rome, Europe and America, and now back to the source, the Han. They regarded the Islamic takeover as an aberration that History would eventually correct and thus their adherence to the Common Era calendar.

are, you will succumb to a strange feeling that Yu Lin called *"apartness"*. Evil spirits would call it *apartheid*. Although the two terms meant the same thing etymologically, Yu Lin classified *apartness* as a psychological state and not a racial or political philosophy.

To Yu Lin, *apartness* was not really a feeling of superiority. It was a feeling of being apart from the common man. Apart for normal life, as if living in another dimension, a dimension unseen by the common mortals. And no matter how one fights that feeling, it invades one's being. Thus as a leader you become *apart*.

In fact not just leaders feel that way, Yu Lin thought. Depraved people also see themselves in another dimension, since their entire existence and being is that of a depraved nature, apart from normal beings. In the first instance, the leaders feel they are above the common mortals of course, less mortal in a way. In the second instance the depraved are below the common mortal, and more mortal. The depraved include common criminals especially if they are jailed for long periods of time, and their jail existence places them in another world where normal things seem distant memories, or just abstractions. Yu Lin ventured to guess that prostitutes and their pimps of ancient times, who lived in a cocoon of a world where the common rules of decency do not apply, felt that same kind of *apartness*. Of course, neither in Han territory nor in the Caliphate were there prostitutes or pimps any longer. Perhaps in the autonomous regions of the lower Southern Hemisphere some remained but he wasn't sure. Everywhere else, the morality police, and the law, made sure that human dignity was respected. The Caliphate and the Han Empire had always agreed on that, morality. The West did not. And the West as such was no more.

Yu Lin also called that state of mind *"leader apartness syndrome"* because it was indeed a kind of disease in that it was usually responsible for the fall of many a great leader. Yu Lin knew first-hand that feeling. At a much more modest level of course. He had had leadership positions in academia and in government. O how he missed these old times when students were in awe at his brain power! But also in the several government institutions he had headed. First was the Ministry of Energy, where he established ties with the Caliphate since the Han Empire needed their trade. Those ties were now bearing fruit, if what was about to happen could be called fruit. A bitter fruit at best, Yu Lin had to confess to himself.

Yu Lin had felt that same *apartness* long ago, but fought it successfully he thought, also and mainly at the Ministry of Military Technologies where power, pride, duty and sheer intellectual and scientific capability were merged. Yu Lin loved that job. He felt master of all, well of all that counted that is, of all that thought. Of course the policies were not his decision since they emanated from the People's Council. But he could still control outcomes as the People's Council needed to be versed in the new weapons and technologies developed or advanced by the Ministry. And that, he controlled. Of course, only to a certain extent. He was not to deprive the Han Empire of any development out of sheer political selfishness, but still he felt in command.

Upon his promotion to the People's Council he became one of several members carefully chosen by the *people*, in other words by the Supreme Leader. Some members in his view were has-beens. They were yes-men. The Supreme Leader knew that and he trusted his childhood friend, and fellow Manchurian, Yu Lin Liao.

The problem Yu Lin thought was that as the Supreme Leader became afflicted with *apartness*, he began acting more and more as a *leader*. His gait was different, his patience with subordinates different, his gravitas deeper. All of these changes were obvious. He was in a sense of a different race, a different species even. He was *apart*. Few men reach that level Yu Lin knew. And he, Yu Lin, was so close.

He had been number two in the nomination process. But the Supreme Leader had outmaneuvered everybody. Yu Lin did not complain about that. The Supreme Leader had to, otherwise a third man, probably the malicious Zhang Yan could have had the job and both would have been out, or worse. So he did not blame the Supreme Leader for trying to prevail at all costs. Except that it still mattered that these costs, to him, meant that he would die a member of the People's Council, and never its Supreme Leader. And he would never be able to bring to bear his superior intellect to help with the challenges that the Empire faced. And indeed that point, that his intellect which was superior to all in the People's Council, was certain and obvious to him. And that, no matter what, pained him greatly. And the *apartness* of the Supreme Leader which he could discern very easily having known him since their childhood made this situation even more painful.

What was more serious though was that the Supreme Leader seemed to know the best route to everything. He listened carefully to all points of view, participated in debates, and considered all positions. But ultimately he made the decisions. And the fact that the Supreme Leader brought each debate to a definite point inevitably contributed to the Supreme Leader's attitude of *apartness*. Nonetheless the problems facing the Han Empire were real.

Threats to the Han Empire

Within the Empire the economy was on a stable cruising mode for decades. None of the ancient West's ups and down happened in the Han Empire but the time bomb of the western provinces was unresolved. Over a century before, the huge neighbor to the north of the Han Empire had succumbed to the same internal pressures from irredentists in its prior outlying provinces. And now they were part of the Grand Caliphate. The Han would not tolerate such an outcome.

And that internal problem was linked to the Han external challenges. Since they had managed an economic assault on the West, this had become a double-edge sword: now they had to face a Grand Caliphate with over two thirds of the world's geography and population under their control. And, as the Supreme Leader would say, two thirds of the world's population were fanatics.

The members of the People's Council were aware that the West's mismanagement of its economic resources, coupled with their political ineptitude, and their protection of their enemies at the expense of their patriots had caused their downfall two centuries before. The outcome, which the Han had in a sense precipitated, had taught the Han Empire that good management of economic assets is key to survival as a civilization. In the former West, when the political and economic system could not sustain the material well-being to which its people had grown accustomed, a new way was sought. The seeds were planted for an all-encompassing ideology to take over, since in periods of turmoil, the State normally is able to gather almost all powers. At the time when the Han were decentralizing and allowing the people, the true people, to make choices, the West in a counter-historical move attempted to centralize everything. In the centralized world of the first Caliph, Sheikh Hussein, who extended his reign for decades until his martyrdom, Islam became the answer.

At least that is how the Caliphate taught History. The Han knew otherwise. The first Caliph was not a Caliph at all. He had usurped the constitution of his State, manipulated the means of information and engaged in a societal change that made his State unrecognizable. The Han, yes the Han were left to teach them by example the benefits of individual freedom and enterprise. What an irony of History!

Yu Lin, and everybody in the People's Council he thought, believed that the Han should have managed the situation better. They had helped let the genie out of the bottle. And their present adversaries, the masters of the Caliphate, these were the ones who had actually created the metaphor of the genie and his bottle. Now the Han Empire faced an implacable foe, and not the soft opponents of yore.

In the western part of the Empire, the Uyghur and other religious people who held strong beliefs were opposed to the officially atheist Han. The only religion *per se* in the Empire was that practiced by the followers of Islam, the True Religion as these followers viewed it. And Islam, as officially declared by the Caliphate in their policy statement, intended to conquer the world in order to bring the message of the Prophet to all men. The problem for the Han was that there was not much world left to conquer outside the Han Empire. As such therefore, the Caliphate's Charter was basically a declaration of war against the Empire. But these were words.

In practice, trade was active and profitable for both entities and except for the isolated *incident* or other acts of violence in the unruly western territories, peace reigned. The authorities in the Empire privately attributed these disturbances to sabotage by the Caliphate, and even considered that these were calculated incidents aimed at destabilizing the Han Empire, jolts aimed at provoking the Empire with localized violence from extremists. By immediately condemning these acts, the Caliphate proclaimed there was an explicit distinction between extremism and its official doctrine of coexistence and peace. The result was that the Empire was forced to make politically acceptable concessions in the troubled territories. And life went on.

Yu Lin knew that the West had succumbed to the same pattern of alternating provocation and deceit and was weakened when it had adopted those distorted tenets of political etiquette.

There was potentially another very serious threat. A frontal assault by the Caliphate. Yu Lin knew it wouldn't happen, since it would be suicidal for the Caliphate. Suicide, which they called martyrdom, was not foreign to the individuals in the Caliphate, but it was strictly forbidden for the Caliphate itself. The purpose of martyrdom for individuals was to preserve the community, the Umma, the Caliphate; so Yu Lin knew it would have been counterintuitive for the Caliphate to expose itself to extinction. Its individual subjects of course were expendable for the good of the cause, but not the whole.

And this is where Yu Lin and the Supreme Leader differed. Yu Lin, which had been a better student, and better scientist that the Supreme Leader, knew there was little chance the Caliphate would match the Han Empire in science, technology or weapons. The Supreme Leader by contrast, although a *bona fide* scientist himself did not believe that science alone would protect the Empire. "People, unfortunately, still count" he liked to say.

The Supreme Leader was therefore open to accommodation and talk to delay a confrontation with the Caliphate. Yu Lin wanted to be ready at all times, let the Caliphate know that there would be consequences for their provocations, and strike if necessary. Yu Lin of course kept these thoughts to himself.

Uyghur Mehmet Yakub Khan who sat on the Political Committee reporting to the People's Council had befriended Yu Lin. Yakub Khan could read people's inner thoughts and ambitions. He had studied the Qur'an when young and that combined with his formal Han education had given him a perspective in at least two very different thought systems. He prided himself of understanding the human condition, and particularly how to manipulate vanity. Yu Lin was very intelligent and very knowledgeable in the most important sciences in the Empire. He held a position of power. To Yakub Khan, Yu Lin was a prime candidate for manipulation by someone whose ambitions were modest, or even non existent. Yakub's only ambition had nothing to do with him, it was the advent of Islam in the Han Empire. He had no vanity, no desire for riches or power, only the just recognition of Allah by these godless infidels. He therefore nurtured a close relationship with Yu Lin, who surprisingly remained unsuspecting of someone like Yakub.

Yakub's thorough patience and perseverance was able to persuade Yu Lin to unseat the Supreme Leader and become head of the Empire, an Empire with which, Yakub assured him, the leaders of the Caliphate wanted to live in peace. Yu Lin had bitten to the bait. Deeply he knew that the Caliphate did not need to plot to obtain peaceful coexistence with the Han. All they had to do is abandon their claim that the world must adopt the True Religion and join the Caliphate.

But even in the mind of a great scientist, a great mind indeed, ego played a significant part. If he did not act, he would die as a member of the People's Council. The Supreme Leader was there to stay. Even if he died, technology now permitted bodies to remain in a state of *suspended life*, in which the body was preserved. Of course it couldn't move or think, but thought processes were *extended* via the remainder of the weak brain waves that emanated from the dead person's body immediately upon his end. Those brain waves were *frozen*, that is their mathematical pattern preserved in their most detailed intricacies, and replicated in *brain wave replicators* that could extrapolate further thoughts. All thought processes of the Supreme Leader, as from many others as well, were stored, cataloged, cross-indexed and quantum arranged and then processed and analyzed by massive quantum-based *conclusion engines*, the successor of the rudimentary *search engines* of centuries past that used to yield vast amounts of data but no useful or intelligent conclusions. Artificial Intelligence had found a way to extend life outside the body. Most people in the Empire would not know or even be sure if the Supreme Leader was alive or not, well until the new leader was firmly established. And that could wait until the needs of the State so permitted.

So the Supreme Leader was scheduled to live until the age of eighty six precisely, at which point another Leader, aged between fifty four and sixty six would be chosen. The Supreme Leader was now forty eight, and the last to be appointed before the age of fifty four. The prior minimum age for the position of Supreme Leader was forty four and it was later determined that to be a threat to the state because of *probable lack of commitment to the cause of the State* as it was euphemistically stated. The People's Council had therefore voted the change which was now official policy.

Yu Lin was now excluded forever, unless… Unless he could use the Caliphate to take power and then use this power to reign in the Caliphate. It was risky, and perhaps not very patriotic. But Yu Lin could convince himself that his intentions to strengthen the Han

Empire made his endeavor totally patriotic. Yu Lin was obviously in conflict, and confused. But his decision was made. He could not go back.

A cabin near Manzhouli, Han Empire Territory
Latitude 45.312 North
Longitude 124.178 East

The cabin was at the end of a dirt road which itself could only be reached by passing through a series of bifurcating secondary roads, about sixty kilometers from the main maglev highway. This highway was a branch that extended to the north-west at Ulanhot off the main Maglev Artery, as it was called, between BeiJing and Qiqihar. Qiqihar was where Yu Lin had established the Annex Surveillance Center.

Yu Lin's was a wooden cabin made of local Manchurian walnut, the very sturdy wood used in floors of wealthy homes. Yu Lin had insisted on making the walls of that hard material, not just the floor. The exterior showed the weathered planks of Manchurian walnut while the interior had the same walls but varnished, which gave them a soft glow under the light of the table lamps at each of the four corners of the main room.

On the north side of the cabin, a small pond, which Yu Lin could see from his chair, had thawed considerably and the red-crowned cranes had returned. Three of them stood on the remaining frozen patch that floated on the surface of the pond. Their thin legs reflected on the pond's mirror-like surface and made each one appear as if it were sustained by a wire emerging from the water. Yu Lin had a soft heart for things of nature. Although he had no reason to believe one way or another, he assumed the three cranes were a family, a complete family as most in the Han Empire were, a father, a mother and one child. Just as he and Li Li could have been, or would be one day. Perhaps it was too late now, they had dedicated their lives to the Empire. The sight of that peaceful pond with the elegant cranes filled Yu Lin's heart with warmth and it took him some steps away from the constant struggle among humans, Caliphate and Han, or Han and Han, and all the other combinations. The cabin was a necessary retreat to which he returned in times of turmoil. And turmoil Yu Lin expected plenty. And soon.

Yu Lin sat on his favorite chair. It was made of Manchurian ash, which was somewhat more refined than the sturdy walnut and showed some curves in the arm rests and the back. The back of the chair was high as if to support the head, and from it hung a rather flat cushion made of red silk and attached to the upper end of the frame by two laces of yellow silk, one on each side. The seat had a matching red silk pillow filled with goose feathers as was the custom in this area. Yu Lin could sit for hours reviewing various scientific papers, or reports on the affairs of the State, on the comfortable, *but not too much*, chair.

Yu Lin had asked Keum Kam Ho[13], his intelligence chief to join him to monitor the progress of their project from this safe place. Ho, whose code name was Albert, was in real-time contact with the Qiqihar surveillance center not far from Manzhouli, the one Yu Lin had insisted on building for *redundancy*, but also to maintain a check on the official National Surveillance Center at Golog Maqen.

Yu Lin observed that while the Caliphate called itself sometimes global, it was no such thing. And this was not only because of the New Vatican and the remnants of some hold-outs of the old religions in the southern tips of India and Patagonia, or even those scattered around some lost lands, such as Easter Island in the South Pacific. That could be taken care of over time. The problem for the Caliphate was the Han Empire.

The Han empire comprised China proper, Manchuria, Mongolia, Korea, Nippon, all the Islands from Nippon to Borneo, which the Empire shared with the Caliphate in what was called Kalimantan, Australia and the former New Zealand. Kalimantan was the largest Island of the Java Caliphate, formerly known as Indonesia. The Empire stretched west past Mongolia, and included parts of Turkestan, and a portion of Kazakhstan. It had a large Muslim population in those western territories but there was no way around it. The energy and mineral resources of these lands required such accommodation.

As Yu Lin had often observed, the Han leadership and the Supreme Leader in particular were well versed in the History of

---

[13] Although his proper name in Mandarin was He Kun Qian (何坤强) Ho insisted on a Cantonese pronunciation (Ho Keum Kam) and on the usual English inversion of his first and last names. In any event he went by his code name Albert in all his official duties.

Nations. The Supreme Leader was especially interested in the fall of
Europe and America to the Caliphate. Europe's in particular had been
bloodless: just apathy on the part of its citizens, for whom all truths
had become relative, religion was abject, the enemy was often if not
always right in their view, and avoidance of conflict, especially
violent conflict, was key. Prior internecine conflicts which they had
generated had tamed these peoples. They had suffered a combined
death toll of nearly one hundred million souls in just a few decades in
centuries past. Of course by the Han scale, this number was not so
impressive. And on a moral scale, since the future of their race, of
their civilization, had been at stake, that number was small indeed.

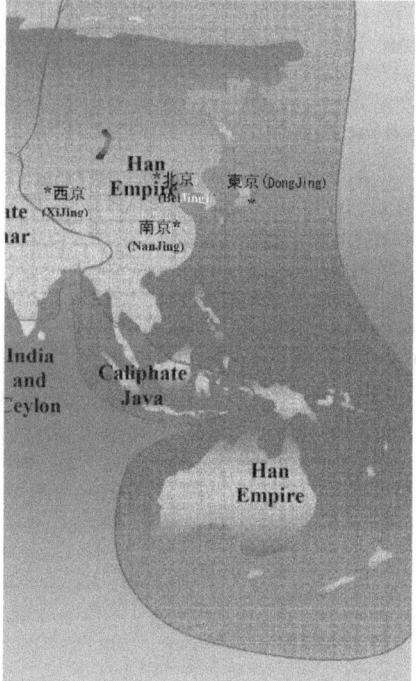

3. The Han Empire, circa 2188 CE

The one thing the Han had and which Yu Lin considered
impenetrable to assault by the Caliphate, at least peaceful assault that
is, was that apathy in the citizenry was not present. That had forced
the Caliphate to plan physical, even violent operations to infiltrate
and take over the Han Empire to achieve finally their goal of world

expansion, under *sharia*. With Yu Lin in charge, there would be no soft creeping invasion of the minds.

One weakness the Han had though, and which could be turned into a strength in some instances, is that they did not seek world domination. They just wanted their fiefdom undisturbed by *foreigners,* anyone alien to the Han. In addition, outside the Empire, and even within it to a certain degree, people were just not Han. It was obvious. The Empire did not want them to become Han. They couldn't, at least not yet although genetic engineering would make that possible one day in a routine manner. But then who would want these non-Han to become Han, assuming they themselves consented? The Han were exclusionary, not imperialistic despite the name of their nation. The whole purpose of the Empire was to gather enough strength internationally to make it impossible for outside invaders, cultural or otherwise, to reach their core. That balance made the Empire a formidable fortress, fortress of the mind of course.

Philosophically, and for reasons that seemed absurd to the Empire, the Caliphate wanted the Han people to worship their god, recognize their religion as the True Religion and help them institute a 'World Caliphate'.

The Empire was officially agnostic, or rather atheistic, due to their Communist heritage. Confucianism was however the *de-facto* ideology, since it had defined the philosophical make-up of most of the citizens of the Empire for thousands of years, and that was not about to change according to Yu Lin. Nonetheless in the western provinces Islam attempted inexorably to expand its reach and that was the principal internal problem, which was exacerbated by the external pressures from the Caliphate.

The Empire had taken technology to new heights: they had perfected quantum tunneling at macroscopic scales, achieve superconductivity at practically all temperatures, resulting in improvements in energy efficiency of over ninety nine percent, and were well advanced in quark stream propagation although these advances were kept secret.

The Caliphate had used all its power to match the Han achievements, either through research or espionage. The Han were proud. They took credit for all inventions of mankind, one way or another. Yes, the West had developed and discovered many things, but almost invariably all Western inventions had an eastern root, specially in the Han.

The challenge for the Caliphate, Yu Lin knew, was how to penetrate the Great Wall of the Han, as the Han fortress of the mind was metaphorically called. The Han were not apathetic as the Westerners had been upon their downfall and they did not view everything in relative terms. The Han believed they were superior, it was obvious to them, and they were not shy about it. Political etiquette did not require them to side with their adversaries. Threats to the Han system were not admired, they were punished, most often violently.

Justice prevailed in the Han Empire as well. Justice meaning the rightful adjudication of claims between Han and Han for business, marriage, contracts, and other disputes. It was not an aberration based on legal technicalities that more often than not in the now defunct West punished the victims and rewarded the culprits, the more criminal the more rewarded they were.

Political justice was also widespread in the Han Empire. Freedom of expression, that is the right to *critique* national institutions and policies was permitted. What was not permitted as *freedom of expression* was the supposed right to attack or even denigrate the Han system and the Han race and especially to jeopardize its hegemony over its realm. That was not considered freedom in Han territory. It was, according to Yu Lin, Western stupidity. And that attitude in his view was what had brought the West down, and as a result the Han now had to deal with a pesky Caliphate that wanted nothing more than to overtake their political and philosophical systems.

Yu Lin thought *"the Caliphate is not going to sleep until they 'conquer' us. That is we cannot peacefully manage our affairs until the threat is removed."* Except Yu Lin knew the threat would never end. Sooner of later, one party, either the Caliphate or the Han, would make a mistake and the other would take over. Just as in a game of chess. And based on their differing ambitions it was more likely that that unthinkable consequence would be inflicted on the Han. That could not be.

Of course Yu Lin also knew that even after that world conflagration that would result in a single country, single religion, or lack of it, and single economic system, that state of things would not last long. Human nature craves diversity.

He liked to tell his audiences that if the whole world got assembled and adopted a single language, as in prehistoric times Esperanto was to be, and that language were to be taught in every school by teachers all formed at the same academy with the same accent, everything being exactly equal, that Esperanto would slowly diverge into several dialects, slangs, argots and then different proper languages *per se.* It was the law of human entropy. Just as in Thermodynamics which predicts that entropy increases with the arrow of time, indeed it defines the arrow of time, so does human entropy. Humans organize, fight hard to reduce entropy through sheer expense of energy, and then when they let go a little, entropy increases quickly and recreates a physical state quite similar to the original one.

It's all for nothing it seems, but not quite. In the process, arts, literature, religion, technology and a myriad other things are developed beyond imagination. Quantum tunneling was a good example which Yu Lin knew well since his Doctorate in Science centered on quantum theory and practice. As a high level government official in the Han Empire, Yu Lin had to have the highest credentials in at least one of the Physical Sciences, Mathematics or Engineering. Since the Empire was quite orderly and controlled, the need for enforcement of the laws was minimal. Disputes were few, and those enforcing the laws were mere administrators. Prestige and privilege were reserved to those who developed the advances necessary to stay ahead of the Caliphate and protect the Empire's future. The Empire prided itself of being an Empire of doers, not talkers. In the ancient West, now dead, power and privilege were reserved in the hands of legal scholars and practitioners, politicians, opinion makers and other nonproductive professions. In the Han Empire, power and privilege were to Science and its applications.

Another example of the technological prowess of the Han was quantum entanglement on a large scale, one of the theories Yu Lin had helped develop into a practical science with applications to weapons systems. Of course he suspected the Caliphate had *stolen* in his view some of these discoveries from the Han and put them to evil use.

Quantum entanglement was based on the principle that two paired quantum objects, usually two particles that originated from a single source, mysteriously acted as if connected without any prodding, and this phenomenon was true at short distances and times. In fact it was considered to hold true even at intergalactic distances and through millions of years of separation. Yes, hard to believe but true.

Quantum Effects

"Let me explain" Yu Lin would tell his few students, the very best minds of the Han Empire, "the Heisenberg uncertainty principle in Physics, well known to high school students, states that a particle's position and momentum, that is its speed if one assumes its mass constant of course, cannot both be known with precision at the same time. Hence the physical state of a particle is only known within a degree of probability. The electron can be here or there, with a definite probability, hence technically speaking, it is in both places at the same time."

Yu Lin then would write the following equation on the holographic space created by an unseen field that floated in the center of the lecture hall to make his point:

$$\Delta x \,.\, \Delta p \geq \hbar/2$$

"As this equation shows, the uncertainty in the position multiplied by the uncertainty in the momentum is always, always, greater than zero. In fact greater that $\hbar$ over 2. As you know h bar is h divided by *two pi* and *h*, Planck's constant is very, very small and for most practical everyday situations it can be perceived as zero. But for the infinitesimally small, it produces effects that are purely outstanding. Let's take quantum tunneling.

"A particle's position is defined by its wave function which is given by Schrödinger's equation the solution of which yields the probability density of the particle's position, that is the *probability* that the particle is at any given place at any given time. Now, Schrödinger's equation is the result of accommodating the duality wave-particle of matter as you may recall. Let me write it in a simplified form as:

$$\partial^2\psi/\partial x^2 = ik\ \partial\psi/\partial t$$

"where $\qquad\qquad k = 2m/\hbar$

"Now, does anyone know without explicitly solving this equation why it would give probabilities rather than deterministic solutions?" Yu Lin had once asked the class.

"Professor," had answered a student named Hsu Liu, "isn't it obvious that this equation is different from the normal equation for a classical wave, in that it states that the second derivative with respect to space is a function of the first derivative with respect to time, unlike the standard waves where both derivatives, with respect to space and to time, are of the second order like...?" Hsu had then traced the following in the floating three-dimensional holographic space:

$$\partial^2\psi/\partial x^2 = k\ \partial^2\psi/\partial t^2$$

"Yes , but what is the consequence of that?" had Yu Lin challenged.

"Well..." hesitated Hsu, "aren't the solutions complex solutions? In addition, the effective vibrational constant ik is not a real number as it contains i, the imaginary number i, the square root of -1, and the wave equation must hence yield to *real* solutions only if we consider its complex conjugate and this leads to various probabilities, rather than a deterministic solution, am I right?"

"Very good. Indeed these are *wave* equations but we are not dealing with *real* waves but rather with mathematical constructs resembling wave constructs, and these constructs have significance or existence if you wish within the context of the theory of which they are part." had answered Yu Lin, before continuing:

"Since the solutions to the state of a particle are probabilities, there is no certainty in that particle's position, just a probability that the particle is at a certain place. And as a consequence that probability is not zero on either side of a physical barrier for example, since the probability distribution yields a non-zero value there. Thus a particle can actually cross that barrier, probabilistically.

"In summary, contrary to classical physics, one can never make simultaneous predictions of conjugate variables, such as position and momentum, or energy and time, with accuracy.

"Of course the predictions of quantum mechanics converge with those of classical physics at higher energies or, which is equivalent, for larger quantum numbers. When averaging the statistical probabilities of millions of particles, the apparent random behavior gives way to a deterministic result. In other words, a quantum system becomes a classical one at large scale. However quantum effects still remain. Quantum tunneling has a definite effect on macroscopic, everyday situations.

"Let us now illustrate this with a concrete example.

"Let's take an electron behind a wall, an electric potential for example. Clearly the electron cannot overcome that barrier. Experiments centuries ago found that the probability of that electron being suddenly on the other side, the forbidden side was not zero, and indeed this electron was *observed* on the other side. The probability distribution of the position of the electron allowed that particle to be on the other side of a seemingly forbidden barrier. As if the electron had tunneled through the barrier. Here is a graphical representation of quantum tunneling."

Yu Lin then would draw a holographic diagram in the space separating him from his students.

4. *Illustration of Quantum Tunneling through a Barrier Potential*

"What makes this phenomenon curious" Yu Lin would continue, "is that experiments conducted by Western Scientists before the Fall of the West showed that under certain conditions, this effect is actually physically true, and measurable.

"Applications of these effects have been numerous over the centuries. What the West could not achieve, but the Han did, was to extend this tunneling beyond the microscopic scale. In other words could a group of particles, such as an atom as the West had already done, or better a collection of atoms, jump in unison from one side to the other? If this number were large enough, then *objects* could be transposed from one side of the barrier to the other.

"We can of course talk of the size of these objects and consider the width and the height of the barrier. These parameters were all extended through our own research and advances. Let us just say without breaking any military secrets that the objects we can now tunnel would be considered macroscopic by the early pioneers of quantum tunneling, say the size of a human cell, or its components. The barrier's height that can be crossed obviously depends on the object's size and the desired width of the tunnel. We can observe, and in fact induce tunneling within a human cell by acting at a safe distance, very much as old-fashioned handguns were used.

"Another even more interesting and more mysterious effect of quantum theory we should review is that called quantum entanglement. Essentially it states that an effect observed *here* is the result of something that happened *there*, instantly, even if *here* and *there* are separated by intergalactic distances and millions of years. The objects that happen to be *here* and *there* must of course be quantum entangled. We can conclude that quantum theory, and experiment, allows for the non-locality of quantum phenomena. Let's draw some pictures."

Yu Lin Liao would then show the following diagram of a classic interference pattern that is obtained when a source of light shines through two tiny slits onto a screen.

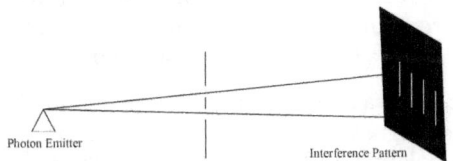

Photon Emitter

Interference Pattern

5. Light Going through Two Paths Produces an Interference Pattern

"It is common knowledge as you have learned in high school, that the bands of light you see here" would explain Yu Lin, "are separated by dark stripes and denote a wave-like pattern. Constructive interference among the two beams created by splitting the original beam through two slits produces the bright stripes, that is the two beams add to produce light, and conversely destructive interference causes the two beams to cancel each other. This is how waves behave."

"Interestingly, this effect is still observed if one emits one photon at a time. The photons as you know are energy packets that are considered to behave as particles. But they are also waves, as shown by the interference pattern. Wave-particle duality. Nothing new here." And Yu Lin would show the single photon emission diagram:

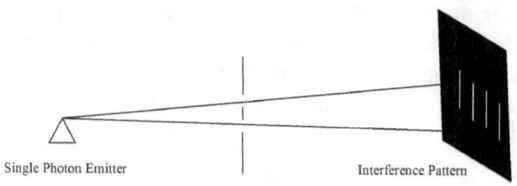

6. *Interference Pattern is Observed Even in the Case of a Single Particle*

"In the case of a single photon" Yu Lin would continue, "if we consider it a particle, then it would have to use one of the two slits. Unless of course the photon used both slits. It seems that is what happens since we observe an interference pattern and we thus conclude that we don't know through which slit the photon went. Very strange indeed.

"We can carry the same experiment by constructing different paths for the photon, or any other particle. It needs not be slits. It could be mirrors or any other arrangement that allows paired particles to arrive at a target or screen via two different paths.

"Now let's take advantage of the fact that light can be polarized, and do so when it goes through the slits. It has been observed that the presence of a polarizing filter around one of the two slits, on either side of the slit, makes the interference pattern disappear. Here is the diagram showing this result:"

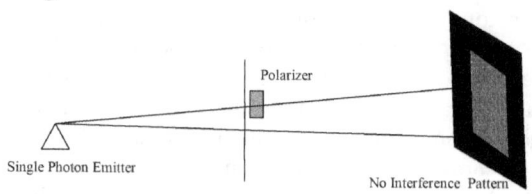

7. *Action on One Path Destroys Interference*

"We can clearly see that the interference pattern instantly disappears if the path is known and only appears when the photon's path is unknown," Yu Lin would conclude.

After a pause, Yu Lin would then proceed to the next explanation.

"So far quite simple, you all know that. Let us now shine a pair of beams obtained by splitting a single beam into two streams of light of opposite polarization, a common practice, and insert in one path a modifier, for example a double-slit just in front of one of the detectors with each slit equipped with a polarizing filter. On the other detector we place an equivalent and adjustable polarizing filter. Say we act to eliminate the interference in Detector B. The strange result of that experiment is that by acting on the filter in Path A and producing an interference pattern on Detector A, the interference pattern is reestablished on Detector B. Similar patterns are obtained in *both* detectors! Here is the set-up:"

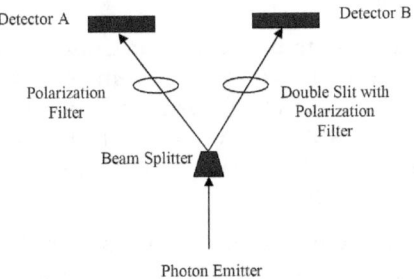

8. Quantum Action at a Distance

"How do the photons arriving at detector B know that the polarizations had been modified at detector A? Let me remind you that similar effects are observed using beam splitters in both paths and observing, or counting, the number of concurrences or correlations between the two beams, that is their entanglement. Results show over 95% correlation according to some experiments," Yu Lin would conclude with satisfaction.

"We conclude that the two beams are entangled, and that action on one affects the other instantly," Yu Lin would add after having paused again.

After a short while, letting the students absorb the impact of the results he had just described, Yu Lin would then continue:

"This gives us an opportunity to provoke a beam to have a specific effect on a target, by acting on its entangled beam, at a distance. If the beams are harmful, you have a weapon. We suspect the Caliphate has focused on exactly those applications. If you wish to use this effect for peaceful purposes you have a safe communication path, since you transmit only one parameter, say the polarization, and the detector detects a pattern. You transmit a trace of information, not the information itself. That information is already contained in both entangled quantum states. You transmit the code to decrypt the information that both entangled states possess, and only an entangled member of a pair can interpret that code. Eavesdropping, which is easily detected, is nonetheless useless."

After a last pause Yu Lin would relish concluding with forward thinking statements:

"Quantum effects can be observed macroscopically. In fact most macroscopic properties of a classical system are direct consequences of the quantum behavior of its parts. Even the stability of matter which must resist at its atomic level the interaction of electric charges, the rigidity of solids, and the many other properties of matter all are the results of quantum theory.

"Let me conclude with other curious effects of the probabilistic nature of quantum physics. Just as a particle can tunnel through a barrier of higher energy that classical physics finds forbidding, a particle can be reflected when encountering a barrier with *lower energy* and that it could traverse easily. Just think of the military applications of such an effect!"

Yu Lin remembered again his star student, Hsu Liu, who was assertive enough and so during one of these lectures raised his hand to ask the following:

"Professor, if one could assemble *objects* at near macroscopic scale that could alter cells in the brain for example, or nano-circuits in electronic devices, and tunnel through larger distances, then a quantum tunneling *bomb* of sorts could take out a network, a weapons system, or cause a heart to cease beating, or a brain that suddenly goes dead. With no traces, no explosions, no mess. The object would just disintegrate and absorb itself into its surroundings as additional particles that would be embedded in whatever macroscopic object lay there. Things, and perhaps people one day, would just vanish into the fabric of space-time. Am I right to be thinking that way, Professor?"

"That is correct, Hsu" had responded Yu Lin. "At a macroscopic scale, if millions, or trillions of such particles were entangled and would carry shared information, a change in the path of one subset would also be observed for its paired subset and this could induce a series of actions such as a bombardment, or a disintegration of a target. With no traces and no detection! We believe the Caliphate has attempted to perfect such a weapon. Of course I cannot tell of our progress here. These are state secrets."

It was evident to all assembled that this was an idea for the Han to push forward, if they had not done so already. Student Hsu then volunteered:

"Professor, these... weapons...aiming and controlling them would be difficult, wouldn't it?"

"Yes of course" Yu Lin had answered, "but that is where progress is to be made. Let us not forget that quantum effects participate in the workings of biological and organic processes as well, such as photosynthesis, the foundation of life in our planet. Well Hsu, you belong in the Ministry of Weapons. Come see me in my office later."

While he pondered all these memories in his cabin in Manchuria, not far from Manzhouli, Yu Lin of course knew that student Hsu, now Professor Hsu, had succeeded him as head of the Ministry when he Yu Lin became a member of the People's Council.

Yu Lin comforted himself with the thought that his plans with the Caliphate would help the Empire and reduce the risk of annihilation that could happen if one were to pursue the Supreme Leader's strategy.

Yu Lin had to be careful. All of the Council members and many others in the Empire, one day or another, had to subject themselves to *mind management sessions*. These consisted of a simple scanning of the brain waves, in their minutest details, that could reveal thoughts and intent, and the results of which were stored and constantly analyzed by the massive *conclusion engines* of the Empire. Thoughts, opinions and intentions were detected and the subject disciplined, *corrected,* or eliminated. Since Yu Lin was the father of the technology, he knew how to avoid detection, only to a certain degree of course. There would come a day when a young brain scientist would implement an improvement, and Yu Lin's countermeasures would fail. He wished his plan to overtake the People's Council would have proceeded before then. He knew that once he had had the *thought* of taking over the Supreme Leader's position with the help of the Caliphate, any rudimentary *conclusion engine* would be able to detect his intentions, given enough scanning, time and analysis. So he de-scanned his brain once in a while with a brain de-scanner he kept available at the Qiqihar Center.

Yu Lin obviously knew he would be caught sooner or later. And the humiliation of having betrayed his childhood friend was worse than the torture they would inflict on him. What made matters more delicate was that the more he thought about it the more thoughts related to the subject were presumably stored in his brain, ready to be detected, or at least analyzed and *concluded.* He had to de-scan himself by erasing thoughts from his brain, from his memory. This was a rather painful process that left him in a daze for hours. Further, it was not totally effective: as in ancient computers, brain erasure was imperfect and there always remained some trace of something. And the diligent analysts manning the *conclusion engines* would sooner or later zero-in on him.

Thus was the state of affairs in the heart of the Han Empire in the year 2188 Common Era, as the Han had decided to continue counting the years.

Yu Lin sat up in his chair and looked intently at Keum Kan Ho, a.k.a. Albert, to give him all the details of the operation with the Caliphate, an operation he was in charge of monitoring exclusively for him Yu Lin Liao. As *Albert,* Ho was Yu Lin's agent *in the field.*

When Yu Lin and Albert were done discussing the mission, Albert respectfully wished his boss good fortunes for the day and left the cabin. Albert was to take the MagLev train at Manzhouli.

MagLev

The MagLev concept was over three hundred years old. MagLev stood for magnetic levitation, and was originally devised to avoid friction between a traveling vehicle and the surface over which it traveled. The MagLev concept followed the usual path of scientific discovery where one sometimes must wait decades and even centuries to be able to enjoy the practical and economically effective benefits of their application. The first MagLev trains were tested successfully for public service over one hundred and fifty years before, but even the Han had to wait another fifty years to achieve widespread use of that technology as an everyday product.

MagLev trains in these times could be seen as low flying airplanes. Like airplanes, maglev vehicles did not ride on surfaces and did not suffer surface friction. But as it was noted, for airplanes the air resistance they encountered was intrinsic to their flight as it provided lift. Further, airplanes had to carry their own fuel which normally resulted in substantial inefficiencies because of the added payload weight and because there was little or no choice in the selection of the best source of energy. Magnetic levitation vehicles by contrast were powered by massive superconducting magnets along a *track*, which provided magnetic lift to the vehicle, usually a train but also private vehicles, and propelled these vehicles at speeds initially under Mach 1 and well over that limit since. Of course at these speeds, the air drag had become the highest cause of energy waste and maglev tunnels were built to connect major centers. These were called MagLev Arteries and Veins depending on their size and importance. In these tunnels a near vacuum was maintained while the trains travelled. Economic studies had shown that the trade-offs heavily weighted in favor of the maglev solution, even when accounting for the cost of creating the vacuums and lifting the vehicles so they could *float* over the *rail*. The highest contributor to these efficiencies was the fact that superconducting magnets were able to perform at near ambient temperatures now and did not necessitate extreme cooling as in past centuries. The energy required to power these national highways was provided by the many Nuclear Fusion Super Plants that the Han had established at strategic points in the territory and freed up the beautiful Han rivers from the ancient dams and the destruction these brought to the flora and fauna in the areas in which they were constructed.

The superconductivity breakthroughs also allowed the construction of Personal Use MagLev Highways (officially PUMs but usually called Plums) in which the rails were a sort of curb along various roads and where magnetic fields were generated which could lift and guide smaller vehicles at reasonable speeds, usually not exceeding 250 kilometers per hour, so the need for vacuum tunnels did not arise. What was ingenious with these Plums was that the traffic engineering computers could set an individual vehicle for a certain destination, optimize its route and speed and guide it safely along the way. The passengers could enjoy the ride without having to pilot the vehicles. Of course there was another major benefit to that infrastructure: the State could know at any instant where anyone was and where and when he was going. A life of goings and comings was inscribed in the memory of the national Quantum Computer Super Centers for each citizen and each visitor, and the archived data covered now over a century.

Of importance though was that these maglev systems, whether for personal or public use, were based on a unique arrangement of magnets that produced both lift and thrust. The Han believed that the Caliphate had *stolen* these techniques to implement their magnetic launch sub-orbital flight system, but of course according to the Caliphate that was untrue: the Caliphate Sub Orbital Flight System was built using purely Caliphate engineering where it was concluded that different sets of superconducting magnets for thrust of the capsule and for guidance within the launch tube was much more efficient.

The Han were so proud of their technological achievements, dating almost five thousand years that sometimes they attributed to themselves the inventions of others. In any event, neither the maglev highways, nor the Caliphate Sub Orbital Flight System would have been economically and energetically possible without the widespread use of superconducting magnets at ambient temperature that the Han had perfected.

Superconductivity

Superconductivity is the phenomenon that occurs when electrical resistance in a material becomes null, or zero. This characteristic occurs below a certain temperature which is different for various materials and is called the critical temperature. Normally, electrical resistance usually translates into heat in conductors, therefore waste in the transmission of electric current. At zero resistance and thus practically no losses, the efficiencies achieved could in fact be substantial. Furthermore, no-loss conductivity enabled extremely powerful engines, or thrust generators that would practically be impossible to construct using traditional techniques regardless of size or capacity.

Superconductivity was first observed over three hundred years before for certain materials and at extremely low temperatures. For example mercury at $4.2°K$ (degrees Kelvin) or $268.8°C$ (degrees Celsius) below zero, had been found to lose all resistance. Currents in a loop of a superconducting material at such temperature can persist *forever* with no appreciable loss and with no external power source.

In the intervening centuries materials were developed that exhibited critical temperatures that were higher and higher, especially when the $90°K$ (that is $-183°C$) was reached. This had been an important milestone because the *boiling point* of nitrogen is $77 °K$, and therefore these materials could then be cooled cheaply and with more ease than at the difficult to maintain $4.2°K$ which required the expensive and difficult to handle liquid helium. In particular mercury and barium based compounds were found to be superconducting at temperatures of $134°K$ (equivalent to $139°C$ below zero). *Liquid air* as it was known had been available for centuries at between the freezing point of nitrogen $63°K$ (-210°C) and its boiling point.

In normal conductors the flow of electrons through the material is marked by collisions with the ions in it, and these collisions create heat, and therefore energy is dissipated. This is the phenomenon of electrical resistance. In a superconductor, quantum physics binds the electrons into *pairs* which can avoid under certain conditions of temperature and energy the normal collisions, and hence avoid energy dissipation as well.

The expense of energy to cool a material to its critical temperatures varied with the material under consideration. That expense made it inefficient to deploy superconducting systems at large scale. As science had progressed and materials were designed that exhibited higher and higher critical temperatures, the technology applications became more affordable.

The Han some fifty years before had developed a specific compound, based on niobium-gallium-titanium and other ingredients which they hoped they would maintain secret from the Caliphate. This material exhibited superconducting properties at ambient temperatures. In fact the critical temperature was a secret but knowledgeable sources estimated it at least at 24°C above zero, if not more. Research was ongoing and the Han scientists believed they could create a compound with a critical temperature of over 45°C, making practically all electrical applications superconducting. Of interest was also research conducted concerning the surface characteristics of these superconductors. Certain compounds exhibited superconductivity at ambient temperature in their bulk, while their surfaces remained of high resistance or even not conducting at all. These provided electric wires with their own sheath, superconductors with an insulating outer layer all part of the same material. The efficiencies in energy use were therefore improved to over 99.9%, a major step when compared to applications of just one century before.

Another useful benefit was that the lower the temperature of a material relative to its critical temperature, the higher the currents and magnetic fields it could handle, enabling the many applications found in the Empire.

With such easy to handle superconducting materials, superconducting wires were used to transmit power without losses over vast distances and to make coils to construct superconducting magnets. Although in past centuries these had to be cooled to relatively low temperatures, which is acceptable for many applications, the maglev highways were only made possible by the advent of room temperature superconducting materials developed by the Han.

4

PLANS

Preparations

$\mathcal{A}$l Kansii arrived at Space Force Base 7 located at the center of the Caliphate *Ameristan*. Captain Ahmed Dromm, a veteran of previous armed conflicts greeted him at the base.

"So you are here to make your farewells to your people?" asked Dromm

"Yes Sir, but also to review our plans, Sir," answered Al Kansii.

"Of course, of course" said Dromm without much conviction. "Let's review those then. First you are to conduct a martyrdom operation against the Han, do you understand that?"

"Yes Sir," was Al Kansii's clear reply.

Captain Dromm asked Al Kansii if he was thoroughly familiar with the technology he was to use against the Han.

"Yes Sir," replied Al Kansii.

"Go ahead, explain. Take your time. We need to go over this in great detail, so that we don't miss anything," said Dromm.

Dromm was a former intelligence officer trained at the Space Force Academy. As such, weapons like those Al Kansii was to describe were familiar to him. In space warfare, the absence of earthly obstacle and atmosphere made those much simpler and their strikes more lethal and assured. Of course countermeasures could also be more difficult to enact, although Dromm had designed response tactics that allowed him to survive Han space *missiles* several times.

A *space missile* was not really a physical missile but a burst of directed energy, invisible, travelling at the speed of light and the *detection* of which was exactly what the shooter intended. The *missile* was intended to be detected, not stealth.

Based on Quantum Theory, by *detecting* the *missile* these weapons systems enticed the energy burst that obliterated the detector, and the vehicle containing it, and of course its crew. The closest analogy was that it was something not unlike the old fashioned laser beams: if one looked at them, one damaged his own retina. Of course lasers could be directed toward any part of the body without the subject's participation and harm that part of the body. Dromm then had conceived of the *feelers*, which were basically expendable energy-burst detectors that were launched miles away from his space ship, and actively sought such *missiles*, actively wishing to be obliterated. It was an old fashioned technique used in aviation centuries before where decoys were dropped to attract heat-seeking missiles. But this was different and much more potent.

In any event Dromm was eager to hear Al Kansii begin his exposé.

"Yes indeed," said Al Kansii, "and that gives us another weapon. If I may I will go back to the basics of quantum tunneling and explain how we developed the QT Disintegrator, formally the QuaTunDis in military jargon, or what we refer to familiarly as the Quty, which some pronounce Qudy.

"Quantum tunneling is a phenomenon with which we have been familiar for over two hundred years now, and in a way a precursor to our Non Local Quantum effects, which I believe the Han have mastered as well. It goes as follows," and Al Kansii drew the following diagram in the holographic virtual screen floating between the two:

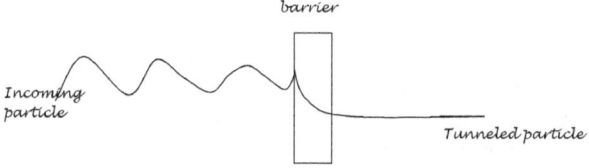

9. Quantum Tunneling Barrier

"Quantum tunneling is a consequence of the wave-particle duality of matter. That duality is expressed in terms of a wave function, which describes the probability of the state of a particle. The bedrock of Quantum Mechanics is the Heisenberg uncertainty principle, with which we are all familiar now. The uncertainty of a particle, or in this case, a fleet of particles, is described by their wave function, and that wave function has non-zero values on the other side of an apparently insurmountable physical barrier, insurmountable at least in classical terms. Therefore there is a non-zero probability that the particle can be on the other side.

"So one particle has a small probability of crossing that barrier, but that low probability when applied to a large number of particles, ensures that as a whole that large number has a reasonable probability for some of its members to cross that barrier. So for a very large number of particles, their low individual probabilities translate into a high probability for a small number of particles. Thus, and that is usually observed in a myriad applications, particles do cross the barrier. It is as if a vehicle coasting at a speed too low for it to make it over a steep hill, still has a low probability that it will go over the hill, as if it had *tunneled* through it.

"Or a more accurate comparison is let's say, if a very large number of such vehicles, millions of them, were to try that hill, a very small number of them would make it over the hill although they never had sufficient speed. As if they had tunneled through the hill.

"Of course common vehicles are too large to experience such an effect and although at the beginning, only individual particles could actually cross the barrier, we have been able to observe, and recreate this phenomenon for several particles at once, or for a fleet, or a squadron of particles. First whole atoms were able to tunnel nearly two hundred years ago, and now systems of atoms. That is, a specific set of coordinated particles. When that became possible, we were able to create a particle beam for which the probability to go through such a barrier is sufficiently high to predict that tunneling will occur when a target is bombarded by such a stream. Quantum tunneling guns are therefore possible. The advantage? No mess, no blood, no noise. Just an unseen beam that forces the disintegration of the target's live cells for example. The target dies quickly. Of course one must ensure that the beam of particles one wishes to tunnel through the live cells will be of a nature that will destroy these cells.

"So in summary, these weapons are based on the concept that when a particle is on one side of a barrier, the probability function makes it that that same particle is, *to a certain degree*, on the other side of the barrier as well. People call it magic, but it actually is verified experimentally and common science. Our high school kids do these experiments everyday now."

"Is that what you propose for the Han People's Council?" asked Dromm.

"No, targeted tunneling requires time and complete surprise," replied Al Kansii. "Any agent would be overwhelmed once it would target and attempt to eliminate his first victim. Also death by tunneling of deadly particles into living cells can also be slow, therefore not fit for our mission. We intend to employ the nLQD, affectionately named the Noloquad, and which stands for non-Local Quantum Disintegrator."

"As I said," explained Al Kansii after a brief pause, "our most appropriate weapon is the Noloquad. It uses ambient particles laid out by our forces everywhere, and harmless of course, unless and *until* someone attempts to detect these beams, or better someone collimates these beams on a narrow target. The result is complete disintegration, coming from nowhere. It is practically undetectable, unless of course the person attempting its detection wanted to be disintegrated..."

"You mean the Angel of Death," interrupted Dromm. "Noloquad is for sissies. I know it sounds sacrilegious, but let's call things by their name."

Angel of Death

"Yes," replied Al Kansii, "the Angel of Death. And once deployed the Angel hangs there, over the entire Creation, ready to strike a chosen target, and sometimes a random target, just like the true Angel of Death of biblical lore."

"Go back to the beginning," said Dromm, "we must ensure we have the best weapons set for our mission. So let's start with the basics."

"Yes Sir, of course," replied Al Kansii

"The principle in fact is simple. It was discovered over two centuries ago, but its applications were not conceived until later, as is usually the case when fundamental science moves into applied science and then to engineering.

"The Noloquad, or the Angel of Death as you prefer to call it, is based on the Heisenberg uncertainty principle. As most of us know, that principle, the foundation of Quantum Theory, states that the position and momentum, that is the product of the mass times the velocity, of a particle cannot both be known precisely and concurrently. In other words, if one can determine the position of a particle, one cannot know at the same time its momentum. It is expressed as *delta-x* times *delta-p* is greater or equal to *h bar* over 2," explained Al Kansii as he drew the following formula on the holographic field that was available in the space between the two of them:

$$\Delta x . \Delta p \geq \hbar/2$$

"where x is the position and p is the momentum, and $\hbar$ is Planck's constant h divided by 2π. Hence the uncertainty in the position, multiplied by the uncertainty in the momentum is always greater than a finite number related to Planck's constant. And the uncertainty is never zero, that is we always have an uncertainty. Of course Planck's constant is extremely small, of the order of 10^{-34}, that is thirty three zeros and a one following the decimal point. For most common life experiences it is irrelevant and assumed to be zero. But in the realm of tiny particles, in the quantum realm, it makes a huge difference, and that is what gives rise to certain weapons systems.

"Although counterintuitive at the time, scientists attempted to explain it by saying that the act of detecting the position of an object affected that position itself and the momentum of that object. So observation, or detection, of anything in the universe, would affect that same thing.

"Of course for macroscopic objects that we are familiar with, the effect is practically irrelevant and negligible. But for particles of extremely small size, for them to be detected, something must hit them for us to be able to observe them, say a photon or other particles of course, and that photon bounces back and hits a detector, like our eye; the particle to be observed has therefore obviously been affected. So the fact of observing affects what we observe and the uncertainty of anything observable is an inherent property of the observable. This is high school science of course, but you asked me to start at the beginning…

"Since the uncertainty principle was counterintuitive at the time it was posited, many scientists in what I will call our scientific prehistory rebelled against that interpretation of nature. *"God does not play dice with the Universe"* had Einstein said if I recall correctly.

"In fact Einstein and two colleagues, Podolsky and Rosen, devised a thought experiment to disprove the uncertainty principle and that became later the basis for the Noloquad, the Angel of Death. The EPR thought experiment as it became to be known after the initials of its authors, is based on the idea that *indirect* observation of a phenomenon can yield certainty, because there is no effect of direct detection.

"It goes as follows – I actually do not remember what the original EPR suggested, but my analogy should suffice. If two symmetrical and exactly equal events are generated, say events A and B, according to the prevalent interpretation of the uncertainty principle, the detection of one (A) does affect its position and momentum, but not the other one (B) and therefore one can know exactly the parameters of the non-affected event, thus invalidating the uncertainty principle. For example, if a beam splitter produces two electron beams, exactly equal but travelling in opposite directions, the detection of one confirms the parameters of the other without one having to detect the second one, which thus undisturbed allows us to conclude its particulars with certainty."

"Be more explicit," said Dromm.

"Well Sir, say you and I decide to race two magnetic propulsion vehicles on a magnetic highway powered by the same electromagnetic generation plant, therefore at the same speed, but we decide to do so in opposite directions. We of course expect to reach the same distance from departure after the same time of travel, each of us in his own direction. Unfortunately since we are both breaking the speed limit and a speed detector picks you up, but assuming that that type of device is not installed on my side of the highway, then although your travel parameters were detected, mine were not and therefore can be determined with precision by easy mathematical induction.

"So EPR says that indirect measurements do not affect the object that is not directly *observed*, and its state can therefore be known with certainty because it was not subject to any perturbation due to the observation of it. Therefore the uncertainty principle cannot stand for them."

"However," continued Al Kansii, "experiments decades later determined that EPR was in fact *wrong* in the quantum realm. Yes, wrong. Experiments showed that when a laser beam was split into two paths, the observation of a target photon did affect the behavior of its companion photon, the equivalent of you and me in the example above. So when your speed is detected, and your position and momentum are therefore affected, at the same time my travel parameters are also affected! Almost as if we were connected. Unbelievable but true. And that effect allowed us to produce weapons such as the Noloquad, the Angel of Death."

"Not so fast," interrupted Dromm, "explain these experiments since they are key to our mission success."

"Yes Sir," continued Al Kansii. "If I recall correctly, a particle emitter, say of photons, emits a beam that goes through a splitter and the two resulting beams are then gathered on a target screen after being reflected by two identical mirrors. You can also achieve the same with two slits for example. Two paired paths from a single beam. If you allow me, let me draw a picture."

Al Kansii reached out to a floating pen-like device and drew in the air a three dimensional picture, that the holographic device recorded and exhibited very accurately in a diagram floating in space as follows:

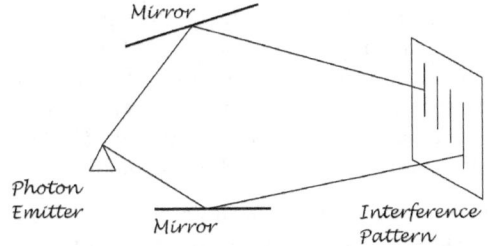

10. Al Kansii's Diagram of Beam Splitter Experiment

"So you would expect an interference pattern when the two waves travel via two different paths before reaching a common target," continued Al Kansii, "as there is complete uncertainty as to the direction in which the two photons traveled. Just as light beams going through slits produce interference patterns. The bright lines correspond to the constructive interference of the two beams, when they *agree* with each other and reinforce their amplitudes, and the dark bands to destructive interference when they cancel each other, high school stuff.

"What is interesting is that a detector placed in the path of one beam destroys the interference pattern as it is known, but adding screens and detectors to both paths ensures that the perturbation of one beam is exhibited on the other beam as well. As if the two beams were connected, entangled with each other. In this case as if the paired photons behaved as single particles hitting the targets, and not as interfering wavelike objects.

"So in an attempt to prove EPR, the experimenters in fact disproved it. To make sure they had not left anything unaccounted for, the experimenters made additional arrangements by introducing several detectors, beam splitters and down-converters. Every time the path information was *known* for one beam, the whole system appeared as if it was known for both beams. As if the two beams were related.

"It is a bit like the common belief that when two twins are separated even by continents, and say one of them dies, or has something drastic happen to him, the other one *feels* it. Psychology experiments with twins have produced that kind of strange correlation or connection, whether it is true or not I can't say. I don't know if or how that happens, this is not my field, and it is possible that some kind of non local quantum effect is at play, although I doubt it. I would rather guess that some kind of low energy *wave* of some sort may exist, and some are more able to detect those than others. For example one also *feels* when one is followed, although the follower may be at a distance and truly out of the field of any possible peripheral vision. But going back to the Noloquad…

"The consequence of these strange effects is very important," continued Al Kansii, "since the two beams do not have to be in the same locale, they may be miles, or light-years, away from each other. In that case, and that is the crucial thing, the space in which the beams have to travel while being seemingly independent of each other spans not only space but time. And although one can emit the photons say today, years hence and at a vast distance from the source, one can modify their behavior as if they had been emitted in such a way.

"Thus detection of a past event modifies what the original event was! Well of course that is not exactly true. It modifies what our *perception* of the past event is. That means a harmless radiation floating in space for eons, can be marshaled through detection to mean something, including an explosion or a tunneling effect, or a disintegration, if that radiation can indeed produce such effects upon detection. Or more appropriately an emission of particles, rather than an innocuous ambient radiation that it may normally be, can become something much worse if manipulated to such end.

"So if an entangled pair of beams made of harmless particles, but particles that can become deadly under certain configurations, if the pair is shot everywhere and if one were to act upon one member of the pair, its partner beam will respond accordingly, miles, and centuries away! If one were to collimate several of these beams for greater effect and to focus them on a target, the screen in the experiments that I described earlier, one could produce a particle bombardment of the target at will. Silent, undetectable, coming from nowhere. Almost as if thinking of something makes certain things happen. Well that is what the ancients believed and it is the realm of superstition. But true science in fact has similar phenomena. It is not superstition, they are the effects of the non-local character of the quantum realm.

"The potentially deadly beams are deployed say today, and they just exist there, harmless to all. And suddenly, when at a distance something happens, the companion beam strikes. They are there hovering above you and someone, or something happens far away and you are obliterated. Just like the Angel of Death.

"Of course the early experimenters never thought of weapons. They continued their experimentation and developed theories, and they attempted to reproduce the effects on a larger scale, just as they did with quantum tunneling..."

"I was waiting for that, this is related to QT," interrupted Dromm, "carry on."

"Well that is what the Han did. As usual, we developed it into a weapon although I suspect they may by now have mastered that as well, or at least some in their hierarchy must be aware of what we have," added Al Kansii.

"Well that is the point of the treason of a highly placed scientist who may know of that weapon but would not make it available, nor its countermeasures. At least that is what we are told," answered Dromm.

"Possibly," continued Al Kansii, "it may be speculation but it makes sense. An inside traitor knows what we are going to do, he would enable us to have the leadership *disappear* and then he would become the new leader, with no traces, no blood, no mess. At least that is what I am capable of understanding."

"Would you trust that traitor?" asked Dromm.

"Sir, I don't know," answered Al Kansii. "If he does carry out his project and he becomes indebted to us, we can expose him at once."

"But he can manipulate the information," interrupted Dromm.

"Yes, but to what purpose?" answered Al Kansii. "OK, he accuses us and so what? It might be difficult for him to pretend that he didn't know of such plot, him being the lone miraculous survivor."

"So honor among thieves, I guess," challenged Dromm.

"Yes, in a sense yes. But in defense of the True Religion we can be justified. We are not thieves, just playing to prevail," concluded Al Kansii.

"Let me summarize," resumed Dromm, and he continued as if speaking to himself, "the observation or not of an effect caused by a particle depends on the conditions of observation of its entangled companion. Since one observation may be later, by millions of years some say, therefore a known condition today can be affected by what someone has done in the past, or may do in the future? In a sort of delayed action, in both directions of time? As if one action could retroactively change the past, erase the past?"

"Not really. The past cannot be changed. Only God can change the past..." Al Kansii stopped short, not sure if what he had just said made any sense. He resumed:

"Uh...God is all powerful..." And after a short pause he added:

"The past is not changed in the quantum realm. It is our *perception* of events that is changed depending of what actions happen at a distance, the distance of course being space and time. It is interpreted as if phenomena could take many paths, many ways of happening, many *states* as they say, and depending on the observation of related phenomena, that is of their entangled companions, we observe one *state* of these events or another... The past has not changed... We cannot change the past."

"I see," said Dromm pensively.

"Yes," responded Al Kansii, unsure of what to say next.

'hala Guadal, Central Caliphate

Al Kansii returned to his birthplace. A formal dinner was arranged and his extended family and close friends were all invited. Although nothing was said of his mission, which remained a secret, and whether he had a mission at all was also a secret, all knew that such *honor dinners* as they were called were usually organized in anticipation of a martyrdom operation. The mood was solemn if not somber. The food plenty and hearty, not particularly refined or delicate. This was the moment of return to one's origins. Return to dust. Return to that primordial time when life had begun. All guests felt a kind of animalistic relationship with nature.

When close to death, to imminent death, although not their own, the guests invariably began connecting with eternal things, or things they considered eternal. Mountains, lakes, clouds, forests and intangibles such as storms and earthquakes. Everything that was the world but not human life. The world before human life that no one knew but everyone felt they could conceive in their imagination. Close to the end man reaches for the beginning. As when a dying man reviews his life at light speed. In a flash he can recall all events in his life, as if to make a summary, a complete summary before departing.

The dinner consisted of a traditional menu for that region: meat and potatoes, and apple pie for dessert, *à la mode*. The meat was *halal* as required by the authorities. Each diner received a very large steak, grilled over charcoal and at least one baked potato which was slit along the middle where butter, salt and pepper were added to it. Some guests had also poured some sour cream, and others yoghurt. The grilling was performed by two of the men present, in an exception to the traditional roles in effect in the Caliphate for two hundred years and which assigned all meal preparations to women. There was of course an exception for commercial establishments in which meal preparation was an occupation for men only. The apple pie *à la mode* meant that vanilla ice cream was served over the pie. The apple pie had been made at the home of one the women present.

Al Kansii enjoyed this *last meal* very much as it brought him close to his roots. It was of course not his last meal, but most probably his last home meal.

At the end of the dinner, Al Kansii made a short speech in which he praised God for His blessings. God had given all assembled there their earthly life, and the blessings to come in a future life. Al Kansii pledged his devotion to the Caliphate, his own family and the mission that God in His mercy had decided to award him.

Al Kansii embraced all, and noticed that many had tears in their eyes, and not only the women. Men, grown men, had red eyes, men with wet eyes.

Al Kansii, a sort of ball growing in his chest, or rather as is commonly described, in his heart, returned to the Space Force Base.

Space Force Base 7

"You were saying it leaves no traces," asked Dromm.

"Correct. It would leave no trace. We would use a derivative of the quantum entanglement science to ensure that the target is obliterated, with no trace of its prior existence. We will use quantum disintegration weapons."

"Yes but you are not going to shoot photons at low energy. These are harmless!

"True. We are to use more effective particles."

"Which ones?"

116

"That, they won't tell us. It is a state secret, since they have been deployed as the Mantle of the Angel of Death upon God's Creation. Even the users don't know."

"But you must have an idea, though?"

"Yes I believe it must be neutrinos. Perhaps a cocktail of neutrinos."

"Why do you think so?"

"Because neutrinos are undetectable and can tag onto a nucleus and change it, or disintegrate it. The human body is a very fragile system, an unstable equilibrium, like a ball at rest on top of a hill. It cannot move back and forth without falling. It is *just right* as is, if undisturbed.

"Of course humans can take a lot of abuse, but not in their inner structural realm. Even DNA can be altered, and the subject survives as a mutant or something. Cells can be killed, members amputated, but if you change the atomic composition of the carbon-hydrogen-oxygen-nitrogen-phosphorous molecules that form the DNA structure in these cells, the subject is no longer a subject. DNA no longer is DNA. There is no human, no mutant, no life.

"So a neutrino acting on a carbon atom, or on any other of those contained in a human body, can change it into a lower form such as boron, or beryllium, or hydrogen, and the body simply ceases to be a body, it simply disappears. All is left is some un-disintegrated atoms, such as the minerals contained in the body, the oxygen combines with the hydrogen and produces a puddle, the nitrogen mixes up with the ambient air. And the atoms with higher atomic number, when their protons become neutrons, or the reverse too, provide enough matching electrons to render the whole experiment neutral. Yes all you have left is a puddle. Even your clothes go with you since they are based on organic materials. Wooden floors on which you stood will also sublimate, although that is an incorrect term for such disintegration.

"Yes, all that is left of you is a puddle and some metallic powder if at all visible. Witnesses coming after your disintegration don't even know you were there a moment before and that you just evaporated. Just disappeared. A biblical type of curse.

"From what I know, only *muon-* or *tau*-neutrinos can cause such changes in the basic nuclei of life. And the Mantel of the Angel of Death is uniquely suitable to act on the Han capital with the natural reflectors of the Himalayas and the Urals first providing a local rough concentration of its beams. The next mountain ranges of Stanovoy on the north of their capital city and the Kunlun range on its south do the rest, and of course our quantum collimator-detector allows us to focus on our target."

"You mean the *collimateur*? That is in the Caliphate *Al Andalus*, correct?" interrupted Dromm.

"Yes, of course. That is where my first stop is," answered Al Kansii. He added:

"I mean the minds given to us by God allow us to make extraordinary things. Let me go to the beginning," said Al Kansii.

"Although they originated only in the mind of a great Western scientist," continued Al Kansii, "neutrinos are known as one of the fundamental particles which make up the universe. Neutrinos do not carry an electric charge, and are therefore able to pass through great distances in matter without being affected by it.

"There are three types of neutrinos ν_e, ν_μ, and ν_τ, and these are represented by the Greek letter *nu*. That is the electron neutrinos (*nu*-e), the *muon*-neutrinos (*nu* with subscript *mu*, another Greek letter) and the *tau*-neutrinos (*nu* with subscript *tau*, also a Greek letter). The electron neutrino is of course associated with the electron, and the two other neutrinos are associated with heavier versions of that electron called the *muon* and *tau* particles.

"This is how it works. Neutrinos are generated here in the Caliphate and they travel great distances everywhere in the world, perhaps even the galaxy afterward. They do not interact with anything, so they are undetectable. However at the source we split the beams before they can travel and we just wait. We spread the Mantle.

"At one point in time, when the Caliphate decides to act, the action on one component of the entangled pair, under our control here, produces an equivalent action at a distance, *a spooky action at a distance*...Einstein had called it. The Angel of Death is ready to strike.

"That action is also felt within the Han Empire, and everywhere else. If one is there to harness the entangled beam there, and if that beam is by any means harmful, you've got yourself a heck of a weapon."

"Yes, but you must be there to do the targeting, you must expose yourself," interrupted Dromm.

"Yes of course, that is the state of our science, of our technology. And that is why I am needed, I guess. I am not the Angel, just his helper," answered Al Kansii.

Dromm and Al Kansii then went to the officer's club and ordered as was then the custom, green tea with mint leaves.

While the waiter, an enlisted man, retreated after having performed the tea pouring ritual, Al Kansii glanced as Dromm poured the contents of a little flask he had discreetly pulled out of his pocket into his glass of tea.

"*Forbidden life-water*," thought Al Kansii.

After a few days undergoing harsh physical training which included flying and landing of various jet-packs in all conditions and even two days in the wild with only a knife tucked on the side of his boot, Al Kansii returned to Usamabad, ready to begin his mission. During his stay in the wild, Al Kansii had managed to cut the throat of two mountain cats that had surged upon him out of the dark on two consecutive nights. Mountain cats, or something else, he did not know. Nonetheless, Al Kansii was ready, physically and spiritually and *Insha'Allah* his mission would be fruitful.

Meanwhile deep in Han territory, Yu Lin heard, or rather his brain believed it had heard a slight vibration. He answered the quantum encrypted call from Li Li.

"Ha," said Yu Lin.

"The labor of our love will find its soul in *Al Andalus*. I will come back to you. As always," said Li Li.

"As always," responded Yu Lin.

Yu Lin then alerted Albert to get ready for his interception in *Al Andalus*.

PART II

JOLT

1

LANDING

𝒯 he sub-orbital capsule, having cruised east from Usamabad at 14,463 kilometers per hour, reached the effective latitude of about 4.56 degrees West of Paris, turned in the direction of the Earth and with a puff of its plasma actuators pushed its way toward atmospheric reentry at an angle of 47.7 degrees from the normal.

At a narrower angle of incidence, that is a wider angle to the normal, and at that speed, the capsule would have bounced back on the atmospheric layer and gone inexorably toward space. If the angle of incidence were wider or closer to ninety degrees, that is zero degrees to the normal, the capsule would explode and disintegrate, as the frontal shock against the atmosphere would have been too strong. It would have been similar to a fast falling body hitting the sea surface and breaking into pieces. 42.3 degrees was found to be optimal for the blunt-nose capsule used in the Caliphate.

Design of the reentry profile of the capsule required careful attention to the aerodynamic heating caused by friction with the air molecules at high speed and therefore to the form and structure of appropriate heat shields. Early studies of reentry on various vehicles had found something counterintuitive: the best reentry profile was not that of a torpedo shaped object as one might have guessed, but that of a blunted surface. The advantage of the bluntness of the impact surface of the capsule was explained by the fact that such wide area trapped the frontal air which then acted as a cushion that pushed heated shock air layers forward away from the capsule. Since most of the hot gases were no longer in direct contact with the vehicle, the heat energy was diverted to the capsule's sides and dissipated in the atmosphere.

So bluntness was preferable to a pointy nose in these circumstances, especially if the impact surface was so constructed that it would be able to dissipate heat efficiently, the larger the surface, the more dissipation. In addition, bluntness of the vehicle undergoing reentry provided increased deceleration in its descent toward Earth's surface when compared to a pointed profile.

Of particular interest in the design of the reentry profile of the capsule was the use of *ablative* heat shields. *Ablative* heat shields used ablation, a heat dissipation technique which was enabled by the blunt aspect of the vehicle's nose. Heat dissipation through ablation had been used for over one hundred and fifty years and was based on the fact that a carefully constructed surface when under high friction, rather than resisting being scraped by the air molecules thereby creating very high temperatures, could be allowed to shed its outer layers, to have these layers be peeled off progressively by those air molecules. The inner layers it was shown could remain surprisingly cool.

The peeled-off layers of the ablation material had previously been *ad*sorbed into the surface of the heat shield. *Adsorption,* as opposed to absorption, is a surface process of adhesion by which atoms of an adsorbate bond to a material. In the bulk of a material, atoms form an ordered structure by interacting in all three dimensions with neighboring atoms surrounding them. At its surface however these same atoms lack neighbors above them and therefore can attract and bond with an adsorbate's atoms and often form an ordered structure different from that in the bulk. This new structure in turn often results in different electric and magnetic properties at the surface as well as in different heat conduction characteristics.

The outer surface of the heat shield then consisted of several layers of a special substance, usually an impregnated carbon composite, with layers of a poor heat conductor in between. During re-entry, ablation caused the adsorbate to transition from its solid phase to a gas phase without passing through its liquid phase, evaporation without melting, a transition commonly called *sublimation.*

The precise layering by adsorption provided sufficient heat shielding for the capsule for its intended re-entry into the Earth's atmosphere. Normally, a new outer shell was fitted into the blunt part of the capsule before a flight if the prior shell had been depleted of adsorbate beyond a *worthiness point*, and the ablated one sent back for factory rebuilding.

After piercing through the upper atmosphere, and powered by gravity, the capsule kept directing itself toward the receiving Reverse Magnetic Sling at ever increasing speeds.

Ma Sling

A short time earlier the MagLev Magneto-Sling at Usamabad's Central Magport had shot its capsule in no time.

The Magneto-Sling was the pride of the Caliphate. It allowed intercontinental flights in less than thirty minutes from anywhere to anywhere on Earth, or almost, since reaching the South Pole from northern temperate latitudes added some delays. But that was not a problem for the routine sub-orbital flight, such as Al Kansii's.

The Magneto-Sling, affectionately known as *Ma Sling* to give it a motherly character, consisted of a long tube of about eight kilometers, dug perpendicular to the surface of the Earth, and pointing toward its center. The width of that tube was of 4.8 meters, and therefore allowed capsules of up to four meters in diameter to be positioned in it for launch. The above-Earth part of the tube projected itself for about one kilometer from its surface. The *Ma Sling* was first equipped with a maglev system that positioned the projectile in its perfect center, separated all around by 0.4 meters and maintained in that position the entire length of its trajectory within the tube.

The MagLev system was not truly a levitation system as used in terrestrial transport since the capsule did not really levitate but rather was forced to reside in the middle of a vertical cylindrical cavity along which it was to travel at high speed while avoiding contact with the walls of that same cylinder. As a result, the accuracy of the attitude control systems was paramount to avoid disasters. The technology was by now well perfected and accidents of the early century were rare if nonexistent. Only in less well maintained facilities at the fringes of the Caliphate could such mishaps occur. On-board control systems could also use inertial aids and micro-ballasts to anticipate and correct minor deviations before they would become critical. The outside-the-capsule control systems could also alter to a very large degree of accuracy the magnetic fields and ensure perfect centering of the capsule during its flight toward the upper exit of the tube.

The second and main subsystem of the *Ma Sling* was the sling itself that was to propel the capsule at speeds sufficient to allow it to reach sub-orbital altitudes of about 200 kilometers above Earth's surface.

The so-called *propulsion* system consisted of a series of powerful superconducting electromagnetic coils of 1000 meters (1 kilometer) in length each, separated from each other by *dead* zones of 180 meters. Each coil acted on the *jaws*, giant superconducting magnets that encapsulated the capsule, known as the *cap-encaps*, and that were the virtual string of the sling. The outside superconducting coils provided enough thrust to the magnetic *cap-encaps* core to achieve a net acceleration upward of 2.25 * 9.81 m/sec^2 and beating gravity by 1.25g. Such acceleration was usually tolerable for healthy passengers. The discomfort was therefore minimal and the actual energy expended easily achievable by the fifteen to twenty terawatt-hour nuclear fusion power plants supplying the sling.

An essential feature of this system must be pointed out as it gave rise to a major technological feat on the part of the Caliphate. As it is well known, the temperature gradient inside Earth is approximately of 25 to 30 degrees per kilometer and at a depth of eight kilometers temperatures can be at least 200 degrees Celsius higher than at the surface of the Earth. This presented a considerable challenge to the operation of any system but was even more critical due to the fact that the *Ma Sling* comprised many superconducting sub-systems that are inherently sensitive to high temperatures. The Caliphate engineers thus developed insulation and cryogenic cooling methods for the interior of the launch tube to alleviate these conditions.

What was unique in this mode of propulsion, also known as Pulsed Magneto Sling, was not the *coil gun* aspect which was used widely for several other applications from silent and stealth hand-guns to magnetic valves in nuclear submarines, but rather the pulsed nature of the thrusts which provided interesting effects and efficiencies.

Theoretical calculations showed that for a uniform sling made of these same eight kilometers, that is an eight kilometer long coil providing a constant 1.25*g*, the capsule would reach the end of the tube in just over 36 seconds as opposed to the 168 seconds needed in the pulsed system. The exit speed would however be just over 0.44 km/sec rather than the 1.92 km/sec. The pulsed system effectively traded time and additional energy for speed by dwelling under *g* forces longer.

According to these computations, the first pulse on the capsule at rest (zero speed) would also provide a constant acceleration for 1000 meters and result in an end-speed of 156.52 m/sec or 563.5 km/hour which is slightly more than the speed a person would be subject to if he were to fall for about one kilometer. However at that point, the capsule would enter the first *dead zone* and only gravity would act upon it, and this for 180 meters, thus slowing it down to 144.30 m/sec. The capsule would then enter the second coil and receive a new 2.25*g* pulse upward for another kilometer and which, when applied to a capsule with a starting velocity of 144.30 m/sec, would propel the capsule to a speed of 269.06 m/sec at the end of the second coil. The process of acceleration, short slow down, new acceleration and so on would allow the capsule to exit the tube after a run of 8,080 meters with an exit speed of 1.9724 km/sec enough for it to reach sub-orbital altitudes of theoretically 204.12 km above Earth.

Providing a pulse to a moving object rather than one at rest produced efficiencies similar to those seen in regular space flights. This was known as the Oberth effect where a *delta V*, or a change in velocity, was usually applied to a satellite at perigee when its speed were the highest in order to achieve greater impact along its entire orbit.

Of course these theoretical limits were never reached as the capsule encountered stiff atmospheric resistance in its upward path. However it rarely reached under 160 kilometers of altitude, sufficient to attain sub-orbital height and maneuver toward the longitude of its descent.

Air drag is normally proportional to the air density, the square of the velocity, the effective impact area and of course the drag coefficient. This coefficient was kept low, as for a high performance rocket at about 0.46 with a specially shaped envelop, called the *clam shell*, that covered the capsule. Once sub-orbital flight was reached, the four flaps of the *clam shell* would open up and form the outer part of the auxiliary propulsion system.

To reduce the atmospheric drag during launch, the *Ma Sling* engineers had devised a system of air pumps along the tube which carried air from on top of the capsule and forced it down underneath the capsule. This allowed the capsule an additional boost from the air pressure at its bottom, facilitated the maglev positioning system since the capsule *floated* above its platform rather than sit on it, and dramatically reduced the air resistance while it was accelerating along the tube. Of course the back drag was also reduced if not eliminated as no zero-pressure zone existed behind the capsule at launch and little afterward during its ascent.

In fact this was a technique aimed at emulating the benefits of sea-launched rockets when they ejected their propellant onto the surface of the sea, a hard surface that provided support during the initial stages of a launch as opposed to the soft cushions of air in traditional Earth bound launches. It was also similar to the fact that it is easier to run on a hard surface than on soft sand.

Another beneficial effect of the depressurization of the tube was that it delayed the shock waves that were to be formed in the tube when the capsule reached Mach 1, shortly before the end of the third stage. By forcefully pumping the air away from the nose of the capsule, shock waves were disturbed and *struggled* to create the vibrations that could cause structural problems to the tube. Of course, being an open ended tube, large masses of air were also pumped down from the ambient atmosphere in the vicinity of the upper end of the tube about one kilometer above the Earth. This on the other hand afforded the capsule a smoother *entry* into the *tubeless* part of its flight.

An added benefit was the comfort provided to the passengers of the capsule. The 2.25 *g* acceleration, was the equivalent of just 1.25 *g* upward net of the gravity. For a passenger placed upside down, this provided the littlest discomfort possible. Nonetheless, this effect was suspended after 12.77 seconds, the time needed to traverse that first kilometer coil. The gravity driven *dead zone* lasted 1.247 seconds for the capsule to cover its 180 meters and allowed the passengers to *breathe*. The next kilometer lasted now 10.18 seconds with a rest period in the *dead zone* of just over half a second. Successive acceleration periods became shorter as the capsule gained speed while the rest periods declined to just over a tenth of a second, at which point adjustment to the magnetically accelerated flight was truly not needed any longer, most passengers having already adjusted to the usual accelerations thanks to this stop and go pulsed system.

Within 166 seconds or less than three minutes, the capsule had now passed the seven kilometers of the Earth part of the tube and emerged from the tube one kilometer above Earth. The *caps-encaps* had released the capsule and began gliding down the tube to their rest position, having slung the capsule into the open air with sufficient velocity needed to achieve sub-orbital flight with little or no energy to be spent by the capsule.

One important aspect of the operation of the *Ma Sling* was the Earth's *assist boost* when launching east as opposed to west. Because of the rotation of the Earth a *savings* of about 0.71 km/second could be achieved theoretically when launching east at the latitude of Usamabad, and much more if launching from the Equator. This determined whether for a given destination west of its launch, a capsule would be directed east or west.

Finally, rather than using a rocket which normally consumes energy to carry its own weight and that of the expensive propellant needed to lift off, the *Ma Sling* was just this, a sling powered by electromagnetic forces. This allowed the capsule to reach high altitudes before firing its light-weight engines, the so-called *plasma actuators*, if at all.

Space Ride

After 338 seconds, the capsule was in sub-orbital altitude. It deployed the symmetrical nozzles of its plasma *actuators* and left a first puff as it sped forward toward the Paris longitude. When just reaching the 165 kilometers height, the plasma *actuators* were engaged. These were four magneto-plasma engines generating one megawatt each of power, sufficient to propel the capsule to its longitude of descent, and even to launch it further into a higher true orbit if required. That was sometimes necessary as when going east first to achieve a westerly destination was more efficient in a ballistic flight.

When the capsule reached about 2.56 degrees West, that is 4.89 degrees West of Paris, the plasma *actuators* then maneuvered the capsule so that it would point toward Earth at an angle of incidence with the atmosphere of 42.3 degrees. The capsule then began its descent. Its reverse thrusters, the plasma *actuators* working in reverse mode would slow that descent.

The four *actuators* were judiciously placed to allow forward propulsion, reverse thrust and directionality thus providing a great degree of flight control. The four were also calibrated to reduce instabilities that could arise from the operation of a single *actuator*, just like ancient helicopters used a rear blade to balance the torque created by the main helix. Of course the failure of one *actuator* would allow the pilots to adjust the other three, or two if necessary, to achieve that same stability.

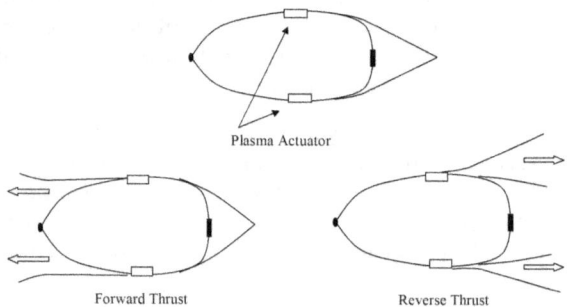

11. Capsule and Plasma Actuators with Nozzle Stowed (Clam Shell) and Deployed, Forward and Aft.

The reverse mode thrust was achieved through an ingenious system. Because the hot plasma could not be diverted once ready for ejection, the weight, risk and cost of reversing the thrust had to be reduced before heating the plasma. The initial 'cold' plasma when just ionized was allowed to go through a direct channel for forward thrust, or 'back channel' for reverse thrust. The hot plasma was then delivered into the mouth of the nozzle and redirected forward to achieve slow-down. The *clam shell* that had been used to reduce air drag and that enveloped the capsule during launch was now rotated to provide the geometry for the reverse thrusters. All these operations were of course carefully calibrated so as to ensure the plasma exhaust would occur at a distance from the capsule and avoid damage to the vehicle. Surface ablation ensured cool ambient temperatures inside the capsule until landing.

Thrust and payload speed could therefore be adjusted depending on the needs of the moment thanks to the plasma *actuators*.

Plasmas Actuators

Plasma is a state of matter similar to the gas phase but where atoms are ionized, that is when intense heat causes electrons to separate from their atoms resulting in a sea of charged particles. In the presence of electromagnetic fields, these unbound electrons and ions in turn exhibit a behavior different from that of a regular gas. To produce such plasma the capsule's *actuators* ionized gas by superimposing a static magnetic field and a high-frequency electromagnetic field at the electron cyclotron resonance frequency.

The plasma *actuators* worked as follows: argon or krypton gas was injected at the 'top' or front of the engine through a short ceramic tube. The argon was then ionized to a plasma which was then conducted through a virtual tube by strong magnetic fields, minimizing both friction and physical contact between the structure and the ionized gas, the actual heated plasma. The last stage was to heat the plasma further to millions of degrees Kelvin, using well established technologies such as electron cyclotron resonance, and that allowed the ejection of the hot plasma, then *floating* inside a virtual magnetic tube and a magnetic nozzle, virtual as well and the shape of which could be magnetically controlled to achieve the desired direction of flight.

Al Kansii's capsule had just used the Reverse Magnetic Sling to keep directing itself toward the Paris Magport. This was the crucial moment for this magnetic anti-gravity system. The receiving or landing *sling* was to emit a reverse magnetic induction to slow down the capsule, and guide it to it, just like the launching sling had done earlier but in the opposite direction. In fact the Reverse Magnetic Sling (RMS) was not a sling in the proper sense since it did not launch anything but rather acted as a giant magnetic brake, an anti-sling that slowed down and guided an incoming capsule in steps opposite those that had allowed its launch through a properly named magnetic *sling*. Launch and Receiving slings used the same magnetic induction engines with their effective thrust reversed.

In the RMS maneuver of these systems however, a slight perturbation in the magnetic field or any other disturbance would detract the capsule from its intended target and lead it to crash onto the Earth. Of course ameliorations had been brought to the first concept of earlier days, when many test pilots had suffered a hallowed death in pursuit of Islamic science to achieve magnetic sling space flight.

The improvements first consisted of applying redundant systems. These turned a single sling into an array of several mini slings dispersed over a wide area. This technique was called multiple targeted reentry or MTR-RMS and allowed the magnetic fields to be active over a wide area and guide the descending capsule toward the landing site with perfect accuracy. Of course early capsule pilots, despite being aided by electronics on board, and supercomputers that adjusted their trajectories, took pride in their skills. These techniques, coupled with advanced and improved navigational aids had rendered the skills, courage, or recklessness of these pilots less needed, or desired. Bad mouths mumbled that Heaven already had a sufficient number of martyrs, and dying for a technology was perhaps not the proper definition of martyrdom in any event.

Another side benefit of the MTR-RMS was that it allowed the system of distributed mini-slings to use auxiliary magnetic fields to route the descending capsule, when needed, to adjoining landing sites, the magports, or *airports* as they sometimes were still called.

The MTR was a derivative of the Distributed MagLev Highway system of which the Han Empire had made full use and which consisted of virtual maglev highways where maglev capable vehicles could receive instructions from the traffic coordination system and *switch rails* to reach their destinations, all the while avoiding collisions and maximizing speed. Optimum speed without the possibility of collision enabled efficient travel in wide areas, including intra-city and suburban individual errands. Al Kansii knew he was to use such a vehicle to reach the inner sanctum of the People's Council.

Paris sera toujours Paris[14]

Al Kansii had just entered the first phase of his martyrdom operation. He had reached the point of no-return.

The capsule descended with no trouble over Paris, a regional capital in the Caliphate *Al Andalus.*

The Caliphate had expanded from its original lands of a thousand years before to what it was expected to be then when it was meant to reach the northern ends of the continent. Especially the lands where pagans still lived at that time. As Assam had reminded Al Kansii, the northern areas of Europe had not embraced Christianity until after the first millennium of the Christian Era had marked its time. It had been a major opportunity lost by Islam in those times. Yes Islam's march had been stopped at Poitiers in mid-Gaul by a certain Charles Martel in the year 732 of the Christian Era, even before the Franks had consolidated their hold in that region. The forces of Islam had been so close to achieving the global caliphate then.

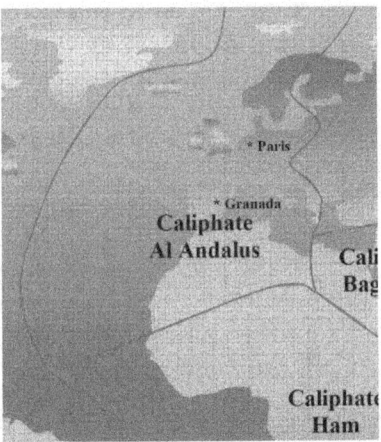

12. Caliphate Al Andalus

---

[14] *'Paris will always be Paris'*, a saying common among the population of its beloved city. Although that is true for any other town, city or hamlet, the phrase denotes the special character of the City of Lights, which remains unchanged through the ages, despite upheavals. Only those who have lived in Paris, especially during their youth, can fully appreciate the meaning of that famous saying since it carries the memories engraved in their hearts.

It had taken just another fifteen hundred years to restore the true path of civilization to its correct course. One thousand five hundred more years to reach the truth is not much when one thinks of what is achieved.

The capsule descended over Paris. It seemed to be a flying meteorite crashing on Earth, but that slowly began to float and float even more until it hovered over the mouth of the landing tube. When rested deep in the tube, power was then shut off and anyone could just walk out to what had been an electromagnetic cauldron seconds before.

The passengers in the capsule, numbering twelve, plus two pilots, emerged a bit shaken. They were directed by local crews toward recovery chambers. Shortly after, passengers and crew were released to the city, on their own.

Al Kansii remembered a few years back when he had landed here as a student at the Institute Of Islamic Studies that although rebranded for over a hundred years was still called *Sciences Po* by its students. He looked at the street signs. They had not changed. They were still made of that porcelain coated metal plaque with blue background and white letters. This stuff was at least three hundreds years old and never changed. What had struck Al Kansii then, and again now, is that the names of everything on these plaques had not changed, or barely.

The conversion of France, and its transformation into the Islamic Republic of Al Franciya which was now part of the Caliphate *Al Andalus*, was done in a bloodless manner. Despite that fact ill-intentioned people at the time had claimed that Islam spread through the sword. The French had, out of practical expediency, disdain for blood, or cowardice as some wrongly accused them of at the time, just folded and adopted the True Religion. The benefit is that they had been able to retain basically all their traditions, names, and habits.

Even alcohol was in a way tolerated. There was no way the French would live without their famous wines, cognacs, or the very wonderful liqueurs they produced since the beginnings of civilization. So Al Kansii was told that they had negotiated a progressive withdrawal from alcohol by creating *l'Institut pour la Recherche Avancée sur la Saveur des Boissons Préférées,* (the Institute for Advanced Research on the Taste of Preferred Beverages) in the Islamic tradition.

For over one hundred years now, the "researchers" were looking for that taste of every alcoholic liqueur presented to them for research, that taste that would be achieved without alcohol content. Of course the research not having concluded yet, everyone, not officially of course, enjoyed the fruits of the research institute. All beverages had to be approved by the Institute, which issued what they called euphemistically the *Niveau Acceptable de Saveur de Dégustation* (Acceptable Level of Taste of Enjoyment) or simply the *Niveau.* All the Institute had to do by law was to lower the level, or *niveau,* from one *cuvée,* or vintage, to another. The *cuvées* were organized in *millésimes,* which the Institute declared one year, two years or even ten years, depending on the political pressure to reduce the *niveau* of the previous *millésime.*

Many a French, all Muslims by now, enjoyed a dose of *Niveau,* especially on Friday after prayers, at home with their family, and of course with friends. An unintended consequence of the Institute was that in trying to eliminate the alcohol content, its researchers enhanced it by attempting first to warm, then heat the concoctions. Usually when heated, alcohol evaporates, but the *Saveur* is gone. After all, the *Niveau* was supposed to keep its flavor. So the researchers tried to confine the mixture in elaborate, old fashioned closed container systems, or *alambics.* The result was in fact distillation, which many suspected the researchers knew all along, and the product an even more potent drink, a higher *Niveau,* with great appeal.

Of course the Ministry for the Promotion of Virtue and the Prevention of Vice was ever vigilant. When its enforcers refused to taste the new *Niveau,* per the current *millésime,* it led to trouble and entire batches were withdrawn, or destroyed. Evil minds said that the destruction was made at the hands of the Police, or rather at their mouths and in their bellies.

In any event the researchers had tried another method, *Niveau* sublimation, by which the mixture was first frozen in a bath of liquid nitrogen at 77°K, that is 196°C below zero, and then let warm at very low pressure. By maintaining the pressure constant and slowly increasing the temperature, alcohol would sublimate before anything else. Since alcohol freezes at a lower temperature than water, it was expected that its taste would be extracted and repackaged into fresh water. Of course what was sublimated was taste, and texture and drinkability of the resulting concoction. For the *connaisseurs*, it was no *sublimation*.

It was believed by some that the researchers had in fact no interest in finding a cure for alcohol. The longer they could delay, the longer they could absolve their *millésime* and serve their compatriots. And they would keep their jobs of course. Their detractors, they were very few, compared their activities to a certain hoax of two centuries before where apparently respectable institutions had dedicated their energies and the money of others to the study of the impact on climate of various human activities. Like the climate scientists of then, the *Niveau* researchers had found no better way to keep fed, paid and employed, but unlike the austere and joyless climate scientists, the *Niveau* researchers could enjoy the liquid fruits of their labor.

Al Kansii stepped out of the maglev station at Sidi Mishal first and walked across the Seine River to the *Grande Mosquée*. It was magnificent. The legend was that Islamic architects from *Al Andalus* had taught the locals to build these masterpieces, in near perfection. Of course the stained glass representations of humans, be it of Christ or the Madonna, had been replaced by intricately beautiful geometric designs. The Persians and the Moroccans had contributed to this renovation. It was beautiful with the rising sun illuminating the transept, the *rosace*, the giant rose-window, projecting its holy glow by the evening.

An *imam* with a venerable white beard of medium length and dressed in an immaculate white robe was standing, barefoot, near the transept and a row of men was behind him. Other rows of men were behind but they weren't complete rows. *Allah U Akbar!* pronounced the *imam*. *Allah U Akbar,* replied the assembly of men.

Al Kansii left his shoes at the entrance where several other pairs lay and walked toward the back row of men. He closed his eyes, joined his open palms near his belly, the tip of his fingers pointing forward and recited his prayers in silence. The whole congregation then followed the *imam* and kneeled on the prayer rugs that were spread in front of every congregant, and so Al Kansii, flexing his legs over his thighs, bowed low so as to allow his head to touch the floor in front of him. Submission to Allah was their strength, and their freedom.

Al Kansii thought to himself "*Lest they forget. The Han… no, no extraneous thought was to intrude on this holy moment. The Han were his mission, and his martyrdom, but now his focus was his submission to Allah, and no other thought ought to interfere.*"

He bowed again, hitting softly the ground. At his young age, and with his body cells able to repair themselves quickly he had not yet acquired the mark of distinction of pious men, a scar on their forehead that was proof of their devotion. And he knew he would not reach that age. But his lot was far better, he was to become a true martyr.

After the prayers he walked back across the Seine, Al Seyna they called it now, up the Boulevard Sidi Mishal, turned right on Boulevard Sidi Germa'in until he reached the Mosque of Sidi Germa'in, on his right. He noticed that all the Saints in the street names had been relabeled Sidi, so he guessed that Sidi Germa'in had been indeed St Germain before. As Sidi Mishal had been St Michel and so on.

Sidi Germa'in had not changed in two hundred years. Across from him was the *Café des Deux Magots* where the first war of liberation of Islamic lands had begun, or at least symbolically. Bombs were placed there and locals and traitors were eliminated. Freedom fighters had sipped coffee right on that terrace. Some had become martyrs right inside that café…

Across was the *Rue de Rennes* into which Al Kansii engaged on his left. He veered slightly right onto the *Rue du Four* and entered the *Rue de Sèvres*. When he reached the corner of *Boulevard Al Raspail,* he stopped abruptly and smelled. It was about 5:30 am. When Paris began to awake. The smell of the bakeries around and the sweet scent of coffee brewing coming from many cafés was too hard to resist.

Al Kansii had his faith in God invigorated by the smell of the freshly baked croissants coming from everywhere. He sat at the terrace of the café at the north corner of Al Raspail and Sèvres and ordered two croissants, and a double *café crème.*

The waiter, in a tradition that had not changed in centuries, asked: «*un petit Niveau avec?* » (a little *Niveau* to go with it – the breakfast)?

"Non", answered Al Kansii who was not used to becoming inebriated so early in the morning, actually never in fact.

He took the first croissant between his fingers and reflected on that very Islamic gift to the French, and to the world. Wasn't it the Viennese that had created the Crescent (or *croissant* in French) to honor their repelling of the Ottoman forces at the gates of Vienna in 1683 of the Christian Era? Yes they had used that traditional Muslim baking technique consisting of alternating layers of dough separated by butter, and shaped them in the form of a crescent in commemoration of the battle that had *saved* them. *Hamdulillah* that was only temporary, they were truly saved now. The French had also of course used this layered dough process to create a straight mini-bread with chocolate inside. They called it *pain au chocolat*, bread with chocolate, but somehow everybody else in the world called it a croissant, although it was not a crescent.

The coffee was wonderful with the croissant. In times like this, Al Kansii did recognize the existence and infinite power of Allah. Whereas in the past Christians justified their gods and saints with miracles believed only by children, the power of the smell and the sense of joy it gives to one's soul was in Al Kansii's mind proof of Allah's creation.

To a materialistic interpretation, Islam offered a spiritual one. And just like beauty, or love, all feelings that cannot be explained or artificially created are manifestations of what Allah has bestowed upon mankind. Does a dog, or a turtle, or a fish rejoice when they smell a freshly baked good? Al Kansii doubted it. While the West had battled with all its energy to find the *how* of this world, they never understood the *why*. It was so simple, as Allah had told the Prophet (pbuh) and was then revealed to the faithful.

In fact people had died over the centuries over the *why*, never over the *how*. One example he had learned right here at the *Sciences Po* Institute was in a course dedicated to the Knights Templar.

These Crusaders were to be banished and dammed in all media. But for students of Islam, the enemy had to be known and understood, unlike the West who had refused to name, or even distinguish its enemies, at least for two generations before what they then called the Fall of the West. Of course to Al Kansii, the conversion was known as an enlightenment not a fall, it was their ascension to the Umma.

As the author he studied had described them, the Templars were *Knights of Christ,* ready to die for their Lord. Just like Assam's ancestor had done prior to the Conquest. Over twelve hundred years before, Christianity had had its own holy warriors. By the turn of the 21st century of the Christian Era these however were vilified by the common man as murderers, criminals, almost as ignorant beasts. That may have been so, according to Professor Ali Mohammed Ghuillemine who taught the course. But as Al Kansii had learned, and the Professor insisted on this lesson, when a civilization rejects its own heroes, or icons, or martyrs, that civilization is destined to die. It could not have been otherwise since it was predetermined by Allah.

Al Kansii was taught that Christianity and the West's liberalism all carried the seeds of their own destruction. "If you don't believe," Professor Ghuillemine liked to say, "it is because it is not true." People fought for Islam not because they were blind fanatics but because it was the True Religion. The West had reached the conclusion that all their values, beliefs, morals, even their obvious technological accomplishments, were all relative and not worthy of praise or safeguard. Either they had lost their will, or more appropriately they had discovered that all they had was not true. They knew the *how,* they had missed the *why.*

Their children engaged in drugs and promiscuity because they had no compass. Islam was to correct all this by demonstrating, sometimes imposing, sometimes just by believing that it was the True Religion. No one in the West, even the Pope, dared in those times say that his religion was the True Religion. They even promoted interfaith exchanges to compare notes. Religions that accommodate each other are reduced to the level of political theories, true one day, false the next. Only the True Religion can survive. As the Professor had challenged his students using a very Cartesian logic:

"Thus, is it because of lack of conviction that Christianity fell, or is the lack of conviction symptomatic of the absence of truth in Christian beliefs? I leave it to you, students, to decide, but the answer, as the Brits say, is in the pudding."

With these thoughts in mind, Al Kansii walked back on the *Rue de Rennes* toward Sidi Germa'in and turned right. When he reached the *Rue de l'École Islamique de Médecine*, he noticed the sign and his thoughts wandered to the attitude of the local population. They were clever he thought. They had changed little in two hundred years; they had added a few words here and there and continued their happy life. Christ, sure, now it was the Prophet (pbuh). Either way seemed fine with them. One king long ago, a Protestant, had been invited to convert to Catholicism if he were to become a French King. Henry IV had gladly accepted with the famous saying: *"Paris vaut bien une messe"* - Paris is truly worth a mass. And so Paris now was worth five Islamic prayers a day.

Weapons of Human Disintegration

He stopped at No. 45 of the street named after the Medical School. He pushed a button on a metal plate with twelve names on it, six on each side. Mahsood Grenier Al Rishi it said. Now, this was a relic. On the bottom of the metal plate, in roman characters, was the inscription *"intercom"*. This was a device over two centuries old and it still worked. And these people had kept it in functioning order. A rasp voice answered: *"Salam Halikkum"*. *"Halikkum Salam,"* replied Al Kansii.

A loud buzz rang and the old door creaked, a sign that something had released the latch. Al Kansii entered and began negotiating the six floors toward Mahsood's apartment. Mahsood, a middle-aged slightly rotund man was there ready to greet Al Kansii. The two embraced and fake-kissed each other on the cheek. The hot mint tea was ready. They sat on pillows arrayed on the floor and crossed their legs.

Mahsood began:

"I have assembled the following. An ice gun for emergency use in the field. It is practically undetectable remotely by their systems but of course it is quite visible and you only carry it for self defense in uninhabited areas. I have also added a prototype quark stream propagation device for swift action, and martyrdom. It is not tested and for use only in extreme circumstances. Don't ask me how it works. I don't understand even the basic principle. The key tool of course is the *collimateur* for the main purpose of our mission."

"You mean the collimator," interrupted Al Kansii.

"Yes the *collimateur*," continued Mahsood. "It works with the Angel of Death. This one was perfected in our laboratory to the south-west of here, where advances in Chaos theories originated. Now this is clearly detectable, but following quantum principles, the fact of detecting it introduces an element of knowledge which then …Well you know, if you detect the Angel of Death, you become the target."

Mahsood was smiling broadly but with his lips closed, a typical smile of the people of *Al Andalus* and the opposite of the smile of those of *Ameristan* who always insisted when smiling on showing their teeth which they considered perfect. Mahsood was excited; the tea, which Al Kansii suspected was enhanced with a soft dose of *Niveau*, had lifted Mahsood's spirits and his own as well to a state of contentment. Al Kansii smiled back. Although they had known each other for under an hour, they were ready for some jokes.

"I don't know that it will be sufficient, but…" said Mahsood.

"Correction! You must be crazy," interrupted Al Kansii.

"What…Wh…Why?" replied Mahsood with a big laugh. The *Niveau* had begun its effects.

"You just stated a fact and in the same sentence declared you did not know that same fact. That can only be true if you are out of your mind," explained Al Kansii.

"Wh… what?" Mahsood hesitated, totally confused.

"You see," continued Al Kansii, "you have adopted some incorrect colloquialism. You stated that *'that it will be sufficient'* and at the same time you said *you did not know it*. It makes no sense. You should have said *'I don't know if it will be sufficient'*, not *that*. If, not *that. That* indicates a certainty, a fact, and you cannot say that you don't know of a certainty, of a fact that you have just stated."

"Is this some quantum joke?" asked Mahsood, embarrassed but happy.

"No. No, just language."

"I did not know that... that's right... that it was so."

"That's correct. You *did not* know. In the past tense you can claim you did not know of a fact you obviously know in the present. So there you can use *that*, and not *if*."

"Let's have some more tea," said Mahsood.

And they both drank their tea, and made a toast to the success of Al Kansii's mission.

"You are smart," said Mahsood.

"No, just attentive to details. That is what we learn when we train as commandos. Every detail counts. And if you are careless with the details of the language, you might, I say you just might, forget a detail in the mission. And that can be fatal."

"Do you have any other language hint?"

"Not now, when I come back..."

The two suddenly fell silent and went deep into reflection. They both knew Al Kansii would not come back. Mahsood would learn additional language sophistications from Al Kansii in the next world. Mahsood was sure the tea in that next world would not have any *Niveau*. And he did not know if he would be as happy to learn of language tricks there.

"Now let's turn to our weapons," said Al Kansii in a serious tone. Al Kansii, as a specialist trained at the Military Academy of Noukhta Al Gharbiya to the north-west of New Medina, on the Bin Hud River, took an expert look at the array.

Al Kansii had opened a type of case and there they were, the tools for his mission. He examined at length every device. There was no way to test them. These were one-shot weapons, built to self-destruct upon use to avoid providing by their disintegration any clues for the Han to track. The Han had to be left guessing what and where the next steps would be.

"Yes," said Mahsood, "that's the single pulse tunneling gun. It's for self-defense, when swift action is needed and the ice gun is inoperable. You see we haven't been able to master yet the reloading of the ice gun in a sufficiently reduced time. We just can't get the humidity in the air to condense as water and then freeze into ice fast enough, or at least enough of it. Of course we load several rounds ready to be expelled, but after that the gun is useless for a few minutes, actually this one is under twenty seconds for one ice bullet. That is still too slow for reloading. That is why we added the single pulse.

"The single pulse is pretty efficient and works as follows."

"You mean the cutie," interrupted Al Kansii.

"*Le Mignon,*" laughed Mahsood. "That's what cute means, right?"

"Right."

Mahsood could not control his laugh and added in a staccato speech:

"*Mignon* has connotations here that we cannot explain without revealing modesty. We are not used to this type of open un-shameful speech any longer. I am sorry Brother."

"OK, that's fine," answered Al Kansii.

"The QT," continued Mahsood, "is for Quantum Tunneling, or more explicitly Single Pulse Quantum Tunneling Gun. Single Pulse is a bit misleading. It was developed by our lab here near *H'orsay*, and effectively organizes a stream of particles which under quantum principles focuses a tunneling effect on a target. To reduce the possibility of harm to others, and increase usage and range, these particles are of relatively low energy. In order to destroy their target they use QT. I am sure you know all about it."

"That lab at *H'orsay*, is that the same as Orsay?" asked Al Kansii.

"Yes it is, we just added a guttural sound in the beginning to fit with the requirements of the *Ministère de la Nomenclature.*

"As I was saying, the harmful particles just tunnel through the living cells of the target and destroy them. There are three flavors: one, simple disintegration; two, destructive acceleration of biological processes; and three, slow death by deceleration of these processes. Let me explain.

"Disintegration is obvious. The particles, neutrinos for example act on the individual atoms that compose the cells. Since an average of fifty trillion, or billion I don't remember, neutrinos go through the human body on average every day or every second I am told, and this without harm, the key is to focus a small percentage of those and trick them into acting in a certain way. The QT does that. It mixes the three flavors, *e*, *mu* and *tau*, into a very unstable combination whose range is very short, but the lethality of which is enormous. Within about twenty meters, atoms in their path, carbon especially, start loosing either protons or neutrons, depending on whether the QT grabs a straight neutrino or an antineutrino. In any event these atoms become those of other elements, therefore not being able to sustain life. It is said that hydrogen atoms in those cells are also transformed into helium ones, which is very possible although experiments are inconclusive. If that were to be correct, the QT's range and effectiveness could be greatly enhanced. But that is not our situation today.

"Without carbon, hydrogen and oxygen, there is no life. The body disintegrates into nothingness. A puddle of some waste, or some kind of metal or other elements."

"Just like the Angel of Death?"

"Yes in a way, but that is what you have developed in *Ameristan*. A big system that hovers above a very wide target area, waiting to be collimated into the target. However as you know and used ingeniously, local detection of the neutrinos is not necessary to transmit information as entanglement can convey information by implication. What we did here is a small, personalized version of the Angel of Death. The Personal Angel of Death in a way. But let me go to the other two applications."

"Before you go on. You say this thing detects the three flavors and mixes then up. Now, neutrino detection by such a small device? It takes massive installations to detect these things. It can't be."

"Well that is what they tell us. That's beyond me. I just don't know. Maybe you are right. But this thing works. I have seen it on rats, and a few apostates. It works, trust me, Allah is my witness."

"I believe you," said Al Kansii. Al Kansii was satisfied that even those who peddled the devices had no clue how they worked. In fact they were misled as to their basic operation as Al Kansii knew and he did not need Mahsood to educate him. "Carry on Brother," he added.

"Well you know that quantum tunneling can act as an enzyme, that is a sort of catalyst to enhance biological processes. If you switch the QT into that mode, just as in our medicine where this technique is used for healing, we can inject a strong dose of tunneling particles acting as enzymes, and cause the target to be overwhelmed by his own biological processes which go haywire. They say it is very painful, although no one has been able to ask the victims in the try-outs."

"Try-outs?" interrupted Al Kansii.

"Yes, whatever you call them, trials, tests," resumed Mahsood. "In order to test all these weapons, especially if they are aimed at interfering with the human body, after you sacrifice some animals, you must test them on humans. We usually select apostates, criminals or even hardened and unrepentant political prisoners for that job."

"I see."

"This is an important point. Because we sacrifice them at the altar of martyrdom, then they can go to Heaven in spite of their crimes. They are redeemed. We believe in redemption of course. But redemption in Heaven, not here."

"I heard that some of those apostates in your country had been found innocent thereafter. How do you justify that?"

"Oh, it is very simple. If the apostate is guilty, as they usually are, then he deserved to die. He may be redeemed and go to Heaven. If he is innocent because someone denounced him unfairly out of personal hatred, then he dies as a true martyr. He goes straight to Heaven. With even more rewards than the guilty one, the redeemed one, of course. It is a win-win situation as you can see," Mahsood said with a slightly devious smile.

"Yes. It is a win-win situation. The sinner is punished and if it happens that he is indeed innocent and punished nonetheless, he is rewarded in Heaven. Truly a win-win. I totally agree."

"...Well, lastly, the enzyme decelerator. It is, we can guess, the most painful. The enzyme acts as a reverse accelerator, slowing down drastically, and as quickly as we need to by acting on the beam collimator, slowing down the biological processes so that the target begins disintegrating as a person, and it is the same for other things as well. Of course to disintegrate metal and atoms of higher atomic mass, more forceful particles are needed that can tunnel through their nucleus and change it into another element. Restricting ourselves to carbon atoms, and perhaps hydrogen and oxygen but we are not sure here, the targets are human, or animal of course."

"You say elements of higher atomic mass, doesn't carbon have a lower atomic mass than oxygen?"

"Yes, and that is one of our pride developments, here in *Al Andalus*. We can tailor the tunneling and collimation of the destructive beam into a narrow range, with an upper bound and a lower bound, so that the targeted atoms disappear, or at least are transformed into other atoms by acting on their nuclei. Also once it starts, the process continues on its own as the body's natural defenses come to the rescue of the targeted atoms and cause even more tunneling to occur. So the enzyme inducing QT is a very powerful and painful device. You will use it in case of utter emergency. By the way, before these combinations of three flavors of neutrinos separate and become harmless, they are able to reflect back on the emitter. How, we don't know? Neutrinos don't reflect themselves but in this case they do. A few of our researchers have been destroyed that way. So our testing is done in wide areas with no reflection possibility, such as walls, mountain, trees etc. So far we have not had any more casualties. But we will solve the problem."

"Before you run out of scientists I hope," joked Al Kansii.

"Yes," Mahsood laughed and he added apologetically: "Well risk is inherent..."

"To!" Exclaimed Al Kansii,

Mahsood looked a bit perplexed and Al Kansii continued:

"Inherent *to*. I was waiting for you to say inherent *in*. The correct expression is inherent *to*, the *in* is already in the word inherent."

"Oh, you and your language. You can't seem to give up."

"Oh, I *seem* all the time, at least I can seem. *It seems that I can't, rather than I can't seem...*" said Al Kansii in a sarcastic tone.

"Whatever you say," responded Mahsood in a resigned voice.

Al Kansii stood silent and pensive; he was focused on the latest weapons, enzyme QT. Al Kansii knew that quantum tunneling enhanced reaction rates in enzymes, the specialized proteins that catalyze reactions in living cells and are necessary for the processes within the cells.

At that point Mahsood presented a leather case to Al Kansii. On its front a beautifully calligraphed set of his initials in Arabic script was laid in 22 carat gold. Inside, various areas to house the different devices were already preformed. Al Kansii examined the case with pride at seeing his own initials and threw a glance at Mahsood, expressing his gratitude.

"Very interesting and very helpful indeed. I have all I need. I thank you for your help. We will prevail. *Insha'Allah,*" said Al Kansii.

"*Insha'Allah,*" answered Mahsood.

Al Kansii and Mahsood had a last glass of tea and then Al Kansii stood up, gathered his tools in the leather case and prepared to go.

Al Kansii walked to the door and asked: "How safe are you here? Are you sure nobody is tracking you?"

"Paris is very safe. I know my territory," answered Mahsood confidently.

The two then embraced again. Mahsood, since he was older than Al Kansii, began a blessing and the two said in unison *"Al Hamdulillah"*.

Al Kansii began his descent to the streets of Paris with his load. The equipment was in fact pretty small and light. It all fitted in a typical case for school implements. Of course none of his devices was powered yet. He would get the required power attachments after he would have landed in Han territory.

He walked back to the beautiful Boulevard Sidi Germa'in. His plans were to take the local maglev train connections to the *Ma Sling* magport and be shortly en route to Kandahar. Equipped as he was, there was no way he would land in Han territory via magnetic sling. He would enter Han territory by land, through the mountain passes south-east of Tashkent and Dushanbe.

Al Kansii still had some time to kill so he decided to take a stroll through the streets of Paris, just as he had done when he was a carefree student there, years ago. He noticed again that the names of the streets were peculiar. It seemed that the authorities had managed to keep all the names, especially of their former saints, and somehow made them sound more Muslim. St Germain had become Sidi Germa'in, St Michel, Sidi Mishal and so on. In fact the *t* of the St had been changed to a *d*, *Sidi* instead of *Saint*, it was close enough. Sometimes the *t* was just hand-painted into a *d*, and most of the time simply ignored and left as is, as it was two centuries before. Instead of the *le* or *la*, the *el* or *al* were used, so *le château* became *el château* and nobody seemed to care much. A restaurant named *Le Conquistador* had become *El Conquistador* which was in fact more correct in any event.

As he strode along, Al Kansii instinctively directed himself to the residence of an old friend of his, of the old days. He wasn't sure she would still be there, but since things did not seem to change much in this part of the world he decided to take a chance. *"We should still be good friends,"* he thought.

Throughout his mission Al Kansii knew he was at the end of his life so he did not object to sharing one last moment in the way it was when he was here years ago. Just like before. When he was carefree and innocent. It seemed now an eternity. That friend was Leila Al Durand. As far as he knew she was unmarried and lived with her parents, regardless of her age as had become the traditional custom everywhere in all the Caliphates. Their abode was somewhere north of the famous tower. He would surprise her and her parents. He accelerated his pace.

When he reached the west end of the boulevard he crossed to the *Rive Droite* or Right Bank of the river via the *Pont de la Concorde*, the bridge on the other side of which an original obelisk stood. It was still there, untouched. The obelisk, of Egyptian origin, had been brought, or rather stolen, by Napoleon during his campaign in Muslim lands. Of course things had changed since then, and the West had recognized its mistakes and all were brethren under Islam. What was surprising though is that the *Obélisque*, as it was called, was not altered in any way, unlike the Islamic Monument in Usamabad that had been adorned with a glorious golden crescent fused into its aluminum cap. Even the square, *Place de la Concorde*, had kept its name. He guessed that *Concorde* perhaps was good enough for everyone now.

Al Kansii turned left and followed the *quais* along the Al Seyna river until he reached the *Pont de l'Alma*, and veered right of that bridge. To his left while he walked he kept enjoying the sight of the

Eiffel Tower constantly in front of him but on the *Rive Gauche*, the Left Bank of the river. As he went along, Al Kansii reached a very large square from which one could admire the imposing *Palais du Trocadéro* palace and down the hill and on the other side of the river, the ever present *Tour Eiffel*. He noticed then that the square had been renamed *Poincaré*, just like the *Avenue Poincaré* that jutted out of the square and that was his destination. What was still stranger were the selection and the commemorative inscriptions on the beautiful limestone that formed the façade of the palace. It was said that this limestone was from Provence in southern *Al Andalus* where the radiant orangey brown stones were found. Now Al Kansii knew that in Paris, squares were called *Ronds Points*, or round points. He also knew that, except for a missing *t* and a missing *r* in the spelling, Poincaré meant Square Point. So it was literally the *Round Point of the Square Point*. Was it a joke, or a coincidence? Or a message? And why had this square been renamed in any case?

What was most serious is that the inscriptions, etched in the limestone of the palace walls and visible to all, had one of the most famous quotes of the mathematician and scientist:

« *Dieu est l'hypothèse la plus inutile pour l'explication du monde* »

The translation was sacrilegious. Al Kansii could hardly read it and not feel ashamed, embarrassed and guilty of sin. It meant, literally, *"God is the most useless hypothesis for the explanation of the world"*

Al Kansii could not understand how the Police for the Promotion of Virtue and the Prevention of Vice could have missed it, how it had allowed that. "God is the most …" Al Kansii did not even have the strength to repeat these words to himself.

Yes, Al Kansii knew that as a great mathematician from another time Poincaré could perhaps be excused, but reproducing this sacrilege now, here!

In Poincaré's time, the intellectual class, the scientists and the philosophers, not the talkers that followed them and destroyed the West's hegemony over the world, in those days Al Kansii knew, these great thinkers believed that scientific progress would solve mankind's problems and usher in an era of happiness and justice. Yes, those were the deterministic times, when the universe was perceived as a clockwork construction and man could understand it and if not control it, at least control its effects. As scientific history had proven determinism in Physics as naïve with the advent of Quantum Theory, socio-political history was also proven to follow paths different from those predicted with so much optimism and confidence then.

Chaos amidst Order

Jules Henri Poincaré had been one of the greatest mathematicians of his era and many believed, especially in these lands, that he deserved at least co-credit with Einstein for the formulation of the theory of Relativity, if not more. Dispassionate historians attributed usually the development of that theory to three great scientists, Lorentz, Poincaré and Einstein.

Another quotation from Poincaré that Al Kansii noted summarized the deterministic philosophy of his time and was also carved into the limestone:

"*If we knew exactly the laws of nature and the situation of the universe at the initial moment, we could predict exactly the situation of the same universe at a succeeding moment.*"

Quantum theory had proven that not to be exact, only probabilities could be determined, but to Al Kansii, it sounded correct if one added that God held the key and had already determined what was to be.

History also had proven otherwise. It was originally believed in those times that technical progress would bring in atheism to civilization since *religion was the opiate of the people* according to the perfidious Marx. Instead, as Al Kansii had been taught, materialism by its inability to satisfy the soul had brought true religious fundamentalism. To Poincaré and his colleagues the world would have gone backward, Al Kansii thought. But they were wrong. Science as he saw it answered the *how*, Islam the *why*. Al Kansii had been taught this at an early age, it was therefore true.

To Al Kansii, Man carries in himself evil and only through submission to Allah can he find freedom and peace. That is what had evolved from that great century of great scientific minds. Sterile science had given way to spirituality and now there was a Grand

Caliphate and *Insha'Allah* soon a Global Caliphate. And he Al Kansii was to play a key role in unleashing the initial conditions that would help achieve that major result. Yes just as in *Chaos Theory*. Initial conditions, sometimes minute, lead often to momentous results.

Indeed, as Al Kansii knew, and as he reflected when he resumed his march through Avenue Poincaré and away from the square, Poincaré as a mathematician had been a pioneer in many theories that participated in the foundation of modern Physics but also and most importantly the *Theory of Chaos*.

Chaos Theory is based on the observation that small differences in initial conditions may yield widely diverging outcomes even for deterministic systems. The example Al Kansii remembered was that of the proverbial butterfly that flaps its wings in the Amazon and that small disturbance alone is amplified through a series of events that lead to a tornado in the Midwest of *Ameristan*. So even Poincaré had begun to understand and establish that the deterministic nature of a system does not make it predictable.

This was profoundly meaningful to Al Kansii for, over two hundred years before, a series of events of apparently no consequence had led to the Islamization of the West although no deterministic theory could have predicted such outcome based on wealth, technology and military might.

And it was not the first time, Al Kansii knew. It had happened to Rome, to *Al Andalus* and many others. But of deep meaning to Al Kansii, the *chaotic* system that had been present in the West of his ancestors, once unleashed, no one could control. What were those initial conditions? And what would the world be in these days if those conditions had been different? The world of his ancestors? Would he be of another religion? Or perhaps no religion at all? It was difficult to comprehend.

Yes of course, Al Kansii and everyone else had studied at an early age, and therefore knew instinctively, that the West had lacked conviction and spiritual backbone. However he noted that other societies had been in the same condition and not perished as such. What was the *butterfly* of the West? Was it Sheikh Hussein? Perhaps. But that may be giving too much weight to the influence of one person, and still Caliph Hussein, the first Caliph, may have been the consequence of other fateful events that began the unstoppable *chaotic* behavior of that society, *chaotic* in the scientific meaning of course.

Was it the set of laws that in the West seemed to have been enacted so mechanically to protect the innocent but ended rewarding the criminal? Or the blind protection of so-called free speech that ended protecting the enemies of free speech and undoing a free society? These were questions Al Kansii usually tried to avoid, but in this Paris with so many signs provoking his thoughts, he could not help but look back at his ancestors and marvel about his own history.

To the south-west of Paris, as Mahsood had indicated, lied the sprawling University complex known as *Paris Sud* where advanced science has been pursued for centuries. It had begun with the ancient Nuclear Research Center that placed the Europeans in the nuclear age, and was followed with their multinational cooperation on massive hadron colliders, which gave a lot of new insights into the neutrino behavior, the manipulation of which had contributed to modern day quantum weapons.

Theories for Liquid Crystals had also initiated there and that had permitted the displays still in use today when three-dimensional holographic projections out of thin air were unfeasible or impractical. And of course *Chaos Theory* as well had seen major advances in these academic centers.

The Western Caliphates, *Al Andalus* included, would not be if not for those initial conditions before *Chaos*. What were they? Al Kansii asked himself how these events, if present in his world, would end up affecting the history of the Han. Was he part of those initial conditions? Would an insignificant hiccup in his mission, a small delay, an irrelevant incident, or some initial *perturbation* as the scientists called it, cause his mission to take a direction no one could foresee? Could his mission in fact unleash a series of events, a *chaotic* system that no one could control? And if so, was his mission so critical? Was it even valuable?

Assam had shared with Al Kansii the results of the analysis by the quantum computer systems of an almost infinite amount of combinations of initial conditions, mishaps, changes, 'bad luck', and other imponderables that could lead to a result opposite of what they sought. In other words could the Han get lucky, as the Caliphates forces had been against the West two centuries before? But Allah's mission was pre-ordained. No matter the initial conditions. Out of the *Chaos* of the West rose Islam. As the prophet (pbuh) had promised.

Al Kansii suddenly recalled another quotation engraved in the stone that for some reason he had overlooked. It was from another earlier mathematician named Laplace. Laplace had studied the orbits of the planets Saturn and Jupiter and it is said had described his results to an elite group that included Napoleon. Napoleon had asked him why he had not mentioned God in his discourse, to which Laplace had responded: « *Je n'ai pas besoin de cette hypothèse* » meaning *"I have no need for that hypothesis"* almost the same intention as Poincaré's.

Al Kansii could not believe that these inscriptions were etched in stone right in the heart of *Al Andalus*, and those who had pronounced them were being glorified with their names on important city landmarks, even after the Conquest. It was very strange. Al Kansii wondered if there was a subversive group that had infiltrated the State. He thought of reporting these infractions to the Virtue and Vice Squad, but his presence here was to remain discreet, and further this was their problem, not his. Unless of course these developments were part of a larger movement at work under the surface that was already planning the undoing of the Caliphate. That made his mission even more relevant, or perhaps a sort of anachronism, Al Kansii could not decide. What exactly was Al Kansii trying to achieve? Disturbing the balance at the expense of the Han Empire while their own Caliphate was perhaps being undermined from within? Shouldn't the authorities, and hence especially Assam, be focusing on these problems before creating new ones?

Deeply involved in his mission, Al Kansii could not entertain such doubts. He concluded that Assam had thought it all out and as a soldier, a Soldier of Allah, his duty was to follow his orders, to accomplish his mission. He was by now not in a mood to meet anyone. He abandoned his plan to visit with Leila, if she even was there.

He decided to look for the nearest maglev station which he found at Rond Point Laplace at the other end of the Avenue Poincaré. He then remembered from his student days that there was a street named *Rue Laplace* on the Left Bank, he had been there several times since the *Sorbonne* was not far from it, so he concluded that someone had renamed this square after another godless scientist. There was a pattern.

He also noticed that that someone had not pushed his sarcasm to the point of naming this square a *Place*, in a strange play of words similar to that used when naming the square at the other end the *Round Point of the Square Point*. No, they had not gone as far as naming it the Place of the Place, *Place de Laplace*. He was confused and knew something was not right as he entered the tunnel leading him to the maglev platform.

During the short ride toward the *Ma Sling* magport, Al Kansii reflected on the existence of a Creator of course, since what had disturbed him were the words etched in stone from these two giants of science and mathematics. The question of who created, God of course, or of Creation, which was so simple and evident to him moments before was now a cloud. Creation assumed the existence of a Creator. The question itself was an act of atheism. Al Kansii felt a heavy weight of guilt in his throat. He was about to die for a cause imposed on his ancestors, who were too weak, or too naïve to resist, unless the cause was the true cause. It all now hinged not only on whether Islam was the True Religion, which he believed it was since he was taught so at an early age, but whether any religion was true, and whether God existed. Al Kansii began to doubt. He then decided to send a last message to Assam, through Al Kenii, as they had convened he would do when ready to fly toward Kandahar:

> *"There can be no Creation without Creator.*
> *There can be no Creator without Creation."*

The first part of the message was agreed upon. It was a code for 'all is well'. The rest Al Kansii meant as a puzzle for Assam to decipher after Al Kansii's death. Al Kansii did not yet know the meaning that the second sentence would take since he was in doubt. If sometime in Assam's lifetime, or eons from now it was determined that there was no God after all, it would have meant that Al Kansii's mission had been in vain, a total mystification of reality, a waste. And the waste would have been his own life. If of course, as he hoped it would turn out, God would be confirmed *forever and forever*, in the *universe of the universes* as Assam had told him, then his mission would have been one of glory. And that glory awaited him in Heaven.

Al Kansii recalled the small plaque on the corner of the *Avenue Poincaré* and the *Rond Point Laplace*, which he had interpreted as science requiring faith in the truth, the provable, the verifiable.

However it now had another meaning. It quoted Plank: *"For believers, God is in the beginning, and for physicists He is at the end of all considerations."* But what if science had not reached, and would never reach the end of all considerations, wondered Al Kansii?

Al Kansii comforted himself with the first thought, that God was, and thus his mission justified. As he entered the pre-flight chamber of the *Ma Sling* magport, Al Kansii also knew deep inside that even asking the question of God's existence is already acknowledging that God in fact is a hypothesis, *une hypothèse*, as it was so clearly enunciated in the limestone of the Trocadéro Palace. What he felt, but did not admit to himself was that the only question now was whether the *hypothèse* was useless, *inutile*, or useful.

Vue sur Cour

Bashar Kadoor, a Han agent whose real name was Heh Jin, immediately transmitted the *signature* of every single component in Al Kansii's case. What Mahsood and Al Kansii did not know is that Mahsood's neighbor, Kadoor, had been following their deliberations, not the words but their *signatures*.

Mahsood's apartment was in a nineteenth century building in Paris. As most of those, it was designed around a central small court which allowed light to reach the rooms at the rear of the apartments – *vue sur cour* - view on the court as they called it. The whole structure was like a hollow cylinder with a square base. Kadoor's room was on the eighth floor. And luckily for him, Mahsood's apartment on the sixth afforded Kadoor a reasonably clear view of Mahsood's main living room. Kadoor's window was almost diagonally opposed to Mahsood's and that made observation even easier. Kadoor had installed a discreet apparatus that seemed to be a spectrometer, a strange camera looking device and other instruments. In brief, Kadoor could determine the chemical composition of any device in Mahsood's apartment and the DNA of those present there.

Kadoor did not really live there. As in most of these buildings the top floor, in this case the eighth, was a floor designed for domestic servants, with single room apartments that were called *chambres de bonne,* or maid's rooms, with communal facilities such as lavatories and showers. The *chambres de bonne* were originally conceived for the benefit of the wealthy, who lived in the fancy apartments below so these could house their live-in *domestiques*, but were now occupied by students and very low income migrant workers and the like. It was therefore a very auspicious way for Kadoor to remain incognito. He could reside there and mount his spying operation on Mahsood, whom he had tagged earlier as a peddler of sophisticated weapons. Mahsood lived the good life in the cafés of Paris and this careless lifestyle had somehow escaped the Caliphate's attention.

Kadoor however happened to be there that day and was able to fine tune his apparati. In particular he had been able to reconstruct the DNA signature of the leather bag, and even determine the carat content of the calligraphy on it bearing Al Kansii's initials.

Albert, at Qiqihar, received that information from Kadoor. He would now be able to calibrate his systems to expect Al Kansii's entry into Han territory and follow his whereabouts. More importantly he would be able to ensure that only he would be able to do so. And that Golog Maqen, the National Surveillance Center, would be out of the loop for as long as possible.

Back in Usamabad, the *Ma-Sling* was being readied for launch. Twelve passengers and two crew were to travel to Han Territory, to DongJing - the East Capital, formerly known as Tokyo. All the passengers submitted to the DNA scanner. All were cleared. Among them a short Han man was carrying a briefcase with poetry in it. He kept reviewing and reciting his verses in the waiting room, after he was cleared and while the Police for the Promotion of Virtue and the Prevention of Vice surveilled and concluded that all was in order. Of course there was no need to check for vice and virtue there. It was truly the political police making sure no one would travel to Han territory with undesirable purposes. The chief of police was warned not to clear any personnel of the Han Embassy, especially women, and detain them for whatever reason until the highest authorities were consulted. That meant Assam himself.

All the passengers were men, and all businessmen. Of course they could be double agents, but the DNA scanner never failed. They were all tagged, and the real time computer check revealed they were OK, all could be cross checked with their prior arrival data, purpose and length of stay, hotel, the composition of their last meal compared to what was in their stomach at the time, and other metrics. No one could take someone else's place.

When the capsule reached the upper atmosphere, the plasma *actuators* veered the capsule to the north-west and reached an altitude of 180 kilometers over the North Pole. A plane change in its *orbit* allowed the capsule to orient its descent anywhere underneath as all the arcs of longitude meet at the poles. It chose the longitude 165 East and softly descended to its Sling landing station.

After *recovery upon arrival*, the passengers exited the Space port and Li Li walked with her briefcase containing poetry into the crowd. Li Li then chose a more traditional supersonic transport to BeiJing on her way to Yu Lin's cabin in Manchuria.

Caliphate Kandahar

Al Kansii rode the *Ma Sling* east from Paris to Kandahar. It took him 28 minutes to reach the decompression room at Kandahar's Mullah Omar MagLev Space Sling Station. There he reached Rasheed's house where he rested for a few days. The weather reports had called for fair weather in western Han territory for the next several days. He had to wait for the rain. Although not perfect, nature always provides that extra margin of safety. Of course they could induce rain, but the Han would detect immediately the alteration and all their antennas would be up. He needed to wait.

Rasheed offered him for wife a young woman of sixteen that belonged, was daughter of, a peasant nearby. After all Al Kansii was to become a martyr, only he and Rasheed knew, but he deserved some gratitude from the people before his death. Of course the girl did not know any of it. But she willingly complied since that was the way is was, and ought to be. The truth is the truth, regardless of one's opinion. And Rasheed knew he was doing the right thing. Others, in other times *thought* they were right and so they debated, argued and explained. Rasheed *knew*.

Raisah was only about one meter sixty tall, she was slender and had green eyes which seemed perfectly coordinated with her dark hazel hair. Her features were more akin to those found in the northern regions of the Mediterranean than in the more proximate

Persia or to the south in the Indian lands. Millennia ago, Alexander, known as The Great, had passed by these lands.

Then came the news from Usamabad. *"Rain 4.5 cm range 70-76 E 34-36 N time 20:32 - 22:48 Safar 27, 1615."*

That was precise. Al Kansii had the exact prediction of rain within a few minutes and less than a few square kilometers. That was more than enough for his jet pack to get him there, be perhaps detected late and disappear before the vast surveillance network of the Han could act on its information. He would then be in Uyghur territory, in the heart of the Han Empire.

A young analyst at the Golog Maqen Center routinely detected this precise weather forecast and was mildly intrigued by its detailed specificity.

And so after Raisah had dutifully withdrawn from his quarters upon his command, Al Kansii fell asleep but not before reviewing in fast motion his mission. He did so with apprehension, conviction of his truth, and confused about his identity, at this moment when he was to begin his death process. Who were his ancestors? Was he dying for them? Or for someone else's?

No, he was with the True Religion. He had to.

"Have I covered every base?" he thought to himself. The *contact* in the Han Empire that was to get him into the inner sanctum of the People's Council, "Was he to be trusted? Was it too easy?" He felt like calling Assam, but no, there was no question of inducing further potential detection. He trusted.

Al Kansii felt relaxed. And at peace. And so he slept.

2

DECEPTION

$\mathcal{A}$t the early morning hours of Al Kansii's third day in the Caliphate of Kandahar Rasheed and Al Kansii headed immediately to the north-east from Kandahar.

The Caliphate Kandahar, as it was officially referred to, comprised a vast territory amalgamating several nations previously defined by Western colonialism. To its west the Caliphate Kandahar followed a north-south line that began at the southern shore of the Caspian Sea at Amol and went south through Qom, Esfahan, and Shiraz, and reached the Arabian Gulf at Bushehr. To the north, the Caliphate Kandahar shared an imaginary line through the Caspian Sea with The Baghdad Caliphate up to the peninsula south of Balyski and continued north for a few kilometers short of Gurjev, the demarcation point from the Turk Caliphate to the north. At that point the border followed a west to north-east curved line toward Astana, closely tracking the former Kazakhstan and reaching the Han territory in the mountains west of Ulan Bataar at approximately the longitude of Tacheng.

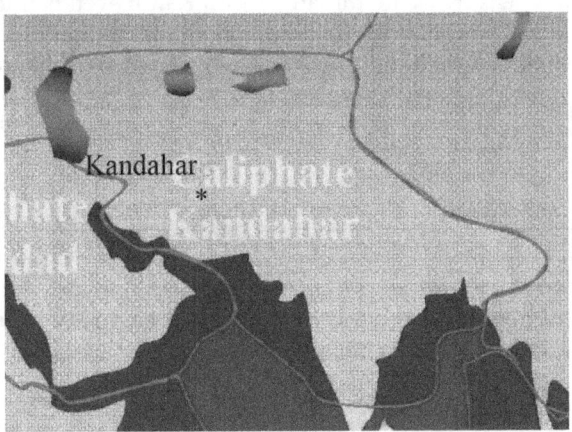

13. Caliphate Kandahar

The border with the Han Empire then formed a large crescent beginning with a line to the south-west toward Karakol, west of Almati, and which then continued along the Himalayas due east, and then again due south toward the Bay of Bengal, west of Chittagong which was in Han territory. Finally the Caliphate Kandahar extended south in the Indian Peninsula as far as Kochi on the Arabian Sea, through Madurai in the center and to Puducherry on the Bay of Bengal. To the south of that line was the Republic of India and Ceylon.

From Kandahar proper, Rasheed and Al Kansii stayed south of Zaboul, Ghazni, and Kabul, and then veered slightly north of Nurestan toward Badakhshan. At that point they turned straight east toward the *pass*. The terrain was now very rugged and not suitable for the antiquated vehicle that Rasheed had chosen. It was an ancient *truck* powered by liquid fuel, which was hard to find anywhere. As a precaution Rasheed had included in the open bed in the back of his vehicle several containers of liquid fuel for the trip, including for the return leg to Kandahar.

After two days on their journey Rasheed and Al Kansii were now in or near Han territory. They had to separate. Rasheed stopped his vehicle first and then performed a dangerous maneuver to turn it around in the opposite direction to begin his return trip. The road was very narrow in this mountainous region and Al Kansii had to assist him to ensure a safe turnaround. Al Kansii even had to lend a hand to free up the vehicle when the rear wheels became stuck in the hardened mud mixed with the snowy slush that remained in these high altitudes. Rasheed was now ready to go. Al Kansii wasn't sure Rasheed would be able to make the return trip in such a vehicle. In any event, Rasheed could walk all the way if he needed to.

Rasheed and Al Kansii embraced and kissed on each cheek before separating. Rasheed made a quick blessing ending in *"Insha' Allah wal Hamdulillah"*, recited by both. As Rasheed waved a good-bye sign from the window of his *truck*, Al Kansii noticed slight tears in his eyes. Rasheed, whom he had known for only three days had become attached to Al Kansii, and in a sense Al Kansii had become attached to Rasheed as well, although Al Kansii's emotional make-up was somewhat colder – *genetics do not lie.*

In these regions, Al Kansii knew, people were very kind, and very emotional. They would love you at first sight, and welcome you into their hearts, their homes, their lives, but when provoked, or when they sensed they were betrayed or threatened, they could become unusually cruel. Being on their good side was a blessing. The opposite was of course to be avoided. Rasheed's people were the most loving people on Earth. Al Kansii only had to remember the gift of Raisah.

Rasheed was now only but a speck of snow or dust in the horizon, and his vehicle produced much of it on the road of mixed slush and dirt, and also emitted smoke of several colors, bluish they said from the burning of the oils of the *motor*, white from the water Rasheed had to add every now and then to prevent said *motor* from *burning* as Rasheed had explained, and black from the poor combustion of the fuel, a result of maladjustment of the fuel mixture, antiquated technology and obsolete and worn-out parts. The advantage is that Rasheed and Al Kansii could travel for days unnoticed, or at least if noticed, unremarkable, just two poor peasants going about their irrelevant business.

Rasheed then disappeared quickly. He was not to witness anything of the secret plan that apparently Al Kansii was to conduct. If caught and tortured by Han counteragents roaming in Caliphate territory he could say nothing, because he knew nothing. Yes he had taken a fellow Muslim in the rugged mountainous terrain. For what, he did not know. He had just left him there.

Al Kansii then alone in the mountain pass between Tashkent and the Han territory began his descent. He walked slowly down the steep slope toward what he knew should be a river. It took him over two hours to reach the narrow river. Its waters flowed irregularly since some of parts of the stream were still frozen.

It was getting darker, and the lower he got, the less day-light illuminated his path as the sun rays, themselves of lower incidence as the evening descended on that part of the earth, were obstructed by the natural screen of the steep slopes. Al Kansii knew that even satellite signals, which rely upon what is known as line-of-sight communication could not penetrate such geometric obstacles. Newer techniques such as path diversity and signal reflection could allow him to communicate were he to use sufficient power. Absent a precise location and time, a satellite would have to use significant power to survey hard to reach areas all the time, and thus waste precious resources. Al Kansii knew it would be difficult for a tracking satellite to focus additional energy on a specific location and at a specific time without knowing that location beforehand and knowing when to do so. It was just inefficient to blast the entire region all the time with the hope of detecting something. Even the Han Empire, and the Caliphate as well, had to optimize their resources. Sooner or later a signal from an intruder such as Al Kansii would be detected, and from then on the National Surveillance Center would latch on to him.

When he reached the point when he felt satisfied that no satellite could detect his presence, barring an unfortunate but quite unlikely coincidence, Al Kansii stopped and decided to rest and collect his thoughts. That turned out to be a gift from Allah since it saved his life.

Ice gun

Al Kansii sat against a tree and was about to eat a concentrated high caloric content *halal* biscuit which would sustain him for several hours.

Not far from where Al Kansii had stopped, a few hundred yards uphill, forester Hekmatyar was making his usual trek through his mountains. He suddenly noticed footprints in the soft soil in the direction of the river shore. The direction of the footprints clearly indicated that someone wearing some sort of heavy boots was heading toward the river. Hekmatyar pulled his old fashioned rifle off his right shoulder and advanced cautiously. He knew the intruder would be several hundred feet away from him, he could clearly see from the shape and depth of the footprints that the intruder had not slowed down where he Hekmatyar was standing. He had time. He bent down to analyze further the footprints and noticed that this was not just another forester. This was a young man, in good physical shape.

Hekmatyar knew the intruder could not be older than twenty-four years of age, and probably closer to twenty or twenty-two years old. He knew this by studying the marks made on the soil by the intruder's steps. Older men place their heel first and then the ball of their feet, the heel thus digs deeper for an older man. The heel-to-ball angle with the ground made by the footprint was an unmistakable telltale of the marcher's age. Young children, Hekmatyar knew, leave almost no trace of a heel; they leap on the ball of their feet. As they age, and they become young men, they place the ball of their feet first and then rest their heels before undertaking the next step. Older men like himself, Hekmatyar knew, dig their heel first and hardly put any weight on the ball of their feet. Hekmatyar knew all that. Of course there were exceptions: city dweller sometimes, as they became overfed and grew lazy, tended to walk like old men even when they were young. But that was probably not the type of city dweller that would trek in this forbidden territory, by himself, if the intruder in fact was a city dweller. So Hekmatyar was convinced he was dealing with a young man. A young man who had a reason to be here. He had to be very careful.

Hekmatyar had specific instructions from the authorities. He did not work for the state, but as a forester who traveled in these rugged areas where practically nobody ever went, he was under contract to scout for anything unusual. Of course the contract was informal, just an honor based arrangement by which he had agreed to report incidents if they ever happened. The contract did not pay him anything, but when he needed assistance, such as ammunition and other favors, the local militia chief would oblige. His instructions were however to report incidents, not handle them himself. He decided as he always did to see for himself. He knew the area much better than the official militia they would send too late to investigate anyway. So he followed his own instincts.

Al Kansii of course did not know of the forester's presence.

As he was finishing his biscuit Al Kansii suddenly heard a rustling in the trees somewhere up the slope to his left. He immediately stiffened and all his senses went on alert. The training in the wild near *'hala Guadal*, that refresher drill, may not have been in vain after all. Al Kansii was ready for a mountain lion or other creature to leap on him. He thought the long knife he carried along his leg tucked into a sheath at the side of his right boot might not be enough. He knew he could not leave any trace. Slowly he pulled without a sound the Ice Gun from his pack, clipped on the single power pack that Rasheed had supplied him with, and hugged the tree so as to appear part of the trunk. And waited. A few minutes later he saw a human form take shape among the trees up the hill which was now much less steep. He pressed a startup button on the side of his gun and a soft vibration that could barely be felt in the handle began.

The Ice Gun operated on the principle that ambient humidity in the air could be forced to condense and freeze in a chamber, and form an ice projectile which could be launched by releasing the air pressure which was built-up behind the projectile. The freezing was achieved by a cooling mechanism based on the magnetocaloric effect.

Discovered centuries before but not implemented for practical applications until recently, the magnetocaloric effect was based on the principle that a magnetocaloric material undergoes significant changes in temperature when subjected to changing magnetic fields. When the field dropped the temperature in the material dropped. A magnetocaloric material is simply a material that is sensitive to variations in the magnetic field to which it is subjected. The variations could be induced by sliding a core of the material several times between the two poles of a specially constructed magnet. Since from the perspective of the material in the ice gun the magnetic field was changing when the material *exited* the magnetic field, a sharp drop in temperature was created.

The Ice Gun did not make any noise. The energy released by the battery-activated miniature magnetocaloric system caused the temperature in its chamber to drop very quickly to 127° Kelvin, that is 146° Celsius below zero, sufficient to avoid liquefaction of the air since liquid nitrogen requires a temperature of 77°K or less, and enough to cause the humidity in the ambient air in the closed chamber to condense and freeze within the chamber.

Extremely low temperatures could be obtained using this technique and although when in its infancy the technique only worked for relatively small volumes to be cooled, it had since achieved large scale and was used for refrigeration throughout both Empires. The Ice Gun itself however did not require large volumes but rather a precise, and noiseless, application of this technology. Special alloys based on an element called gadolinium were used, the composition of which remained a state secret.

The *firing* consisted of simply opening a valve which would cause the projectile to eject toward a target. Speeds in excess of 50 m/sec, very comparable to a regular firearm of that day, were attained and the air resistance ablated the projectile in a manner that its diameter was still over one centimeter after a trajectory of three quarters of a kilometer. After that it degraded quickly through melting and became softer, but depending on the ambient temperature it could still cause significant damage. These specifications were above what Al Kansii needed. At a distance of less than fifty meters and with a barrel of about half a meter in length, accuracy and efficiency were amply available to Al Kansii.

Al Kansii reviewed in his mind the drawing he had seen in the Archives at Usamabad, located in an impressive building not far from *Al Dar Baida* on *Sharia* Avenue. The diagram was said to be the original drawing of the ice gun, made centuries before when it was only a theoretical possibility since freezing ambient water in a sufficient volume in a gun chamber was not yet feasible.

14. *Original Drawing of the Ice Gun*
(Museum of Weaponry, Archives, Usamabad)

While the freezing process lowered the temperature to 146° C below zero, the water molecules in the air condensed quickly and gathered at the edges of a large cavity or primary chamber. Gathering sufficient water molecules was the challenge and required very large such cavities. A mechanism to pump successive batches of condensed water was devised but then the time to load the Ice Gun suffered sometimes unacceptable delays. In any event the water was directed in stages toward the secondary chamber where the successive batches were maintained just above freezing to prevent the projectile formed from all the batches from shattering. When an *ice bullet* of about two centimeters in diameter and five centimeters in length was obtained, the freezing was allowed and a hard torpedo shaped icicle was ready to be *fired*.

The ambient air in the gun was maintained at a temperature above that of liquid nitrogen at about 87°K and it activated a pump associated with the centrifuge and which increased the pressure behind the secondary chamber as it warmed. Once the projectile was ready and when the pressure was near 5000 psi, the system stopped and was ready to eject the projectile. At the speed so obtained any substantial projectile could enter the human body, even a liquid projectile, which of course the hardened icicle was not.

The faint vibrations that Al Kansii felt in the handle of the ice gun were the result of the magnetic slide and the action of the centrifuge that followed. The Ice Gun used no bullets and no pellets and no cartridges. Its stored energy in what was called a *nuclear battery* could be released in small amounts as needed and as such it would practically last forever.

The entire process to *load* the Ice Gun took about twenty to thirty seconds. Ice Guns with several chambers and additional pressure build-up for successive firings were also available. Because of size constraints, Al Kansii's had the capacity of one projectile only. The ambient air, with the expected heavy rain showers in that area though, permitted him to *shave* a few seconds off the loading time since there was more humidity in the air than the required minimum as mandated by the technical specifications of the Ice Gun.

Al Kansii aimed the Ice Gun at Hekmatyar. He did not have the luxury of asking questions, nor of sparing his life. He released the valve and the ice projectile bolted out of the barrel toward the forester's heart.

At the same time Hekmatyar whose age did not allow him to adjust his retina as quickly as he needed – he walked on his heels first – could not discern the actual form from the tree, for him *"light and darkness"* were mixed up, then there would be light followed by eternal darkness. By the time his eyes could discern the intruder, a very dim light, the reflection of the nascent moon on the tiny ice projectile reached his tired eyes. Since he could not recognize any weapon of familiar shape, he hesitated for a split second. It was too late. He felt nothing. He was gone.

The advantages of the ice projectile were many. First was its complete silence. It was also not traceable unlike a metal object moving at those speeds and which could be picked up by the satellite network. The technicians at the National Surveillance Center at Golog Maqen had not programmed their systems to track icicles, water, or snow as those would result in an immense number of false alerts. And although they knew of a possible Ice Gun entering the Empire, they expected any intruder to carry out other operations as well and if the cost of delay in detection was one or two peasants or foresters in the wild, unlucky to have been on the path of an intruder, so be it. The alternative would just paralyze the entire infrastructure.

Another advantage of the ice projectile was that the so-called *bullet* penetrated quickly like a sewing pin and melted with the body heat. The cold would close the wound from outside and no traces of any weapon were left visible to the naked eye.

While inside, the ice projectile would begin a fast process of destroying the victim, a process that would only stop when the icicle were completely melted, and which could take several seconds. At these low temperatures, close to the nitrogen liquid point or boiling point to be exact, but not quite, the cells in the stricken area, and the heart was preferred, were immediately killed by the cold and dead cells could be found quite far from the point of impact, depending on the local atmospheric pressure, ambient temperature, and metabolism of the victim.

Another side benefit which really did not matter here, is that upon entering the body, the ice projectile did not cause external bleeding. The entry wound was almost immediately sutured by the cold, as when pressing an ice cube on a cut on the skin. Yes, some visible scar would remain, but by the time the temperature inside the body would reach its regular level, the man was dead, and bleeding was almost all internal, with no visible entry point. An autopsy was necessary, and easy to perform, to determine the point of entry, if that mattered at all to the investigators.

These investigators would eventually discover during an autopsy that an ice gun would have created the damage to the victim. But not immediately. A standard heart failure would be blamed especially that the victim was not so young.

Al Kansii knew that by the time the victim were found and the investigation would zero in on the Ice Gun by looking at small tears in the fabric of the victim's clothes for example, Al Kansii would be far and deep in Han territory. Further, since he had now announced his presence somewhere in Han territory and in that area, any analyst would guess he was on his way to more promising deeds toward the capital. The alert analyst would then be able to compute the many possible routes he could take and begin to track him. All detection systems would then be trained on those routes. Al Kansii's hope was that the peasant, about whom probably nobody cared, except perhaps his immediate family if he had one, would not be discovered too early.

Al Kansii counted mentally: Caliphate 1, Han 0. He immediately caught himself in error. No, killing this poor peasant was not a point in his favor. In fact sooner or later it would score against him – *he who kills an innocent kills the whole world* (*sura 5.32*).

Al Kansii pulled the victim's body next to the tree, recited a prayer for his soul and prepared to leave. He pulled out the jet-pack, slid his arms around the two lanyards that held it through his shoulders and tightened a lap belt. He then prepared to fire its engines. He was then ready to head straight east to his rendez-vous with Mehmut.

The sudden acceleration surprised Al Kansii although he had flown jet-packs before. Maybe he felt uneasy about the recent incident when he had eliminated a seemingly innocent human being for no other reason than to maintain the secrecy of his mission. Because he was close to Uyghur territory, chances were that his victim was actually a Muslim brother. But the mission is what counted. The mission is above any individual. Individuals must submit. That was the key precept.

Al Kansii hurried through the rest of the mountain pass, equipped with his night vision goggles and raced in the direction of Qaghiliq and then Hétián, cities he knew he should avoid.

The mountain pass east of Badakhshan was impressive. Very steep slopes covered with snow led to a river down in a sort of canyon. Very tall trees lined that canyon. Al Kansii maneuvered to be close to the river to avoid colliding with the trees, and of course remain as undetectable as possible. He knew that the National Surveillance Center at Golog Maqen either had already picked his presence or would do so imminently. He had to hurry. At the same time he needed to change his *signature* to lure the intelligent *conclusion engines* of the Center into indicating a trajectory different from the one he was following. Of course Al Kansii knew he could fool these intelligent machines only so much. They would pick up the different signature, correlate to the prior one that was left hanging and then reconnect the dots. Any human could do that. The reason the machines were so useful is that the volume of information was so great that humans could not follow and correlate all events happening in Han territory, or actually the whole world, the domain of the National Surveillance Center. Monitoring was the easy part, it was said, and the challenge was not the gathering of information but the analysis of the gathered information and the drawing of useful conclusions.

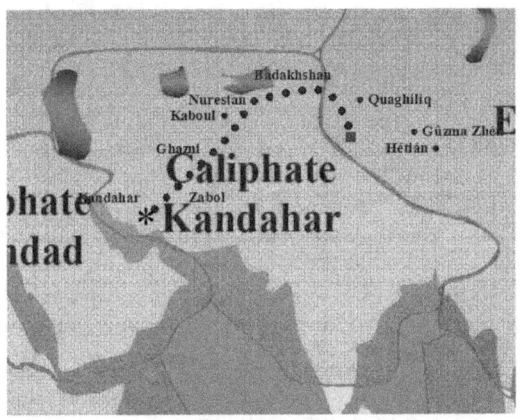

15. Al Kansii's Itinerary into Han Territory

After heading north for several kilometers, Al Kansii landed near a bend in the river beneath him at a spot where the mountainous region was obviously ending. He turned off his engines, went into a thicket in the woods and manipulated various dials on his jet-pack. The sonic signature was now altered. He opened a folded sack made of a lead alloy and stuffed the pack in it. No electromagnetic wave would penetrate and track the jet-pack for now. The altered signature would emulate fast motion of the jet pack toward the north for a few hundred kilometers. This was done by altering some quantum states describing certain elements in his jet pack and which were entangled with other quantum states controlled by the Caliphate far away. The detected member of the entangled pair on the Caliphate end would seem to continue toward the Arctic Ocean, and whoever was tracking the jet-pack would be led to conclude that the jet pack continued on that course. An alert would probably be issued by the computer based on the illogical course, but Al Kansii would by then be far, he hoped. He then ran for several kilometers due south, and stopped to rest.

He sat for a while. He still had about eighteen kilometers to go to Mehmut's cabin. His tracking device was accurate and *undetectable* as it relied on a new constellation of satellites that provided stealth positioning data through quantum entanglement. No visible signs of data emission or transfer could be seen by eavesdroppers.

Al Kansii resumed his march toward Mehmut's rendez-vous. He did it without incident in one hour and thirty eight minutes. His delay was therefore of less than ten minutes, even including the distraction of having to eliminate the forester.

He was now definitely in XinJiang Uyghur territory where he knew surveillance was heightened. Al Kansii had entered the Taklimakan desert in the western fringes of the Gobi desert. He had to orient himself since the rest of this segment of his mission would have to be done by foot. After what ended up being a short break, he headed south a third of the way toward Gúmâ Zhèn. He then marched a few more kilometers due south-east toward what seemed to be a hut, which emerged out of the sand and rock. It appeared to be a shelter for passing caravans, or perhaps for stranded migrants.

Walking in the open terrain toward a single hut rising from the denuded soil made Al Kansii feel very exposed. Or perhaps even in a surreal landscape. He prayed it was the right spot. As he approached the hut, which turned out to be a type of wooden house, a sense of apprehension invaded him. *What if his contact wasn't there?* He nonetheless kept going, walked to the door and checked the local time.

It was precisely 11:33 and 5 seconds on his atomic clock. He knocked three times on the wooden door, waited exactly nineteen seconds and once more knocked three times. It was silly to knock since there was nobody for miles and miles around and if anybody would be there it would be obvious. But it was a signal that needed to be given and that needed to be answered. If Al Kansii did not get the proper response, he would use the Single Pulse quantum gun. The Ice Gun would not be very efficient in the desert and he could not afford the extra seconds to load it. If Al Kansii were to use the Single Pulse, Golog Maqen would detect him on the spot and the Empire would be on his trail in no time. Of course this assumed that on the other side of the wooden door someone would not be faster at eliminating him first.

On the other side of the door after hearing the second set of three knocks, Mehmut Asghar looked at his clock and pronounced loudly *"Allah u Akbar."*

"Allah u Akbar," responded Al Kansii. Mehmut opened the door and the two embraced.

They sat in silence on the floor for several minutes while Al Kansii took off his boots. Mehmut had just served hot green tea and the two drank and remained meditative as if in prayer.

Then Mehmut said: "You need to change. In thirteen minutes we depart."

Al Kansii went to a sort of bathroom area on the side of the kitchen/living room which had a sheet hanging from a rope and that served as a curtain. There he refreshed his arms and neck before putting on a Uyghur peasant outfit that Mehmut had given him, and covered his head with a wool hat which he found pretty attractive. It was surprising that he would wear a woolen hat in the desert but he concluded that Mehmut knew what he was doing. The hat itself was a Mongol type of woolen helmet with a pointy top and that had on each side large areas that covered the ears. Two thin strands hung from these ear lobes. Al Kansii did not attach them.

"We will take the NAV through the no-man's land. We are not taking any short-cuts, but rather the *long-cuts*," said Mehmut with a cunning smile, proud of his joke.

Al Kansii did not respond. As they approached the vehicle which was hidden under a sort of open hangar on the south side of the hut and as they prepared to embark, Mehmut, seeing Al Kansii's wide eye look said:

"This thing is used a lot around here as an all-terrain vehicle. I am sure you are familiar with the origins of this contraption."

The origins of the NAV were quite interesting as Al Kansii recalled when he studied those during the preparations for his mission.

Flat Earth

Al Kansii and Mehmut took what was then a farmer's vehicle. It was an interesting contraption that the Caliphate did not have. It had been originally conceived a few decades back by the great inventor and scientist Deng Li Chao.

Deng Li was a member of the philosophical Society of the Flat Earth. Of course the members of this society were learned men who did not believe that the Earth was actually flat but they continued a tradition of Western thinkers who challenged themselves to imagine what life would be like if the world were two-dimensional.

The Society of the Flat Earth had expanded into several new chapters over the years. The first two of these were the D4L and D4R. These dealt with the four-dimensional world but there was a major difference between the two, and that was the basis for a rather elitist behavior on the part of the members of both chapters toward each other. They all agreed of course on the apparent three dimensions of the world in which we live and with which we are all familiar. However, following the theory of relativity the adherents to the D4L considered the fourth dimension to be non Euclidian, and it was defined as Time. They considered themselves the heirs of Lorentz (hence the L), Poincaré and Einstein and believed they were grounded in reality. They discussed at length how time depended on space, and how Planck's time and Planck's length related to the unification theories of the Universe in vogue then. This was basic science, however one of the most intriguing aspects of their deliberations concerned a universe where Planck's constant was no longer a true constant but was allowed to vary. The key question was 'vary with respect to what?' Time? Space? Then what was the impact on Planck's length, and more critically on Planck's time? The way things were defined, varying the Planck constant would be like having time depend on time. Like a serpent eating its own tail in Han mythology.

Of course a world such as theirs would allow c, the speed of light to not be constant as well. But what would it change with? Would it vary with time, but if time is defined as the measure of change in space..."*Ahah!*" they would tell their detractors at D4R, "*It is not as easy as you think!*"

These *detractors* were mostly the members of the D4R Chapter which contorted their brains trying to imagine all forms of two- and three-dimensional analogies to visualize a Euclidian universe in *four* spatial dimensions, as Riemann had pioneered, hence the R in the name of their chapter. These thinkers focused on the *traditional* four dimensions which they believed was already a mental stretch, especially when considering the upper-dimension chapters of this society which claimed to be societies in their own right.

The D4R insisted on applications, for which they took credit on behalf of the original Flat Earth, especially for the unique vehicle that served the Han Empire, the brainchild of Deng Li Chao. They noted, with reason, that applications of science waited decades if not centuries to appear after their formulation in fundamental scientific terms. Even now, quantum theory, almost three hundred years old was just beginning to produce brand new and intriguing weapons. And the idea of sub-elementary structures, still unproven, if they ever were to be, would take a very long time to see applications. Indeed the vehicle they had designed had seen its conceptualization in archaic times, in archaic science.

But first they insisted on explaining their mission. To imagine the world in four dimensions, four spatial dimensions that is, was truly difficult. An *easy* thought experiment was proposed to new members as follows.

Imagine a two-dimensional space, a flat earth, in other words a surface with no height or depth. All that exists lies on that surface. Imagine further two symmetrical shapes, but irregular, for example a shape like the cut-out of a bottle, or rather of course a cross section in two dimensions of a bottle. Imagine further that these two *bottles* have their bottom facing each other. By simply rotating in the two-dimensional plane one bottle toward the other, one can have one superposed onto the other - no need to jump up the plane since the two have zero heights.

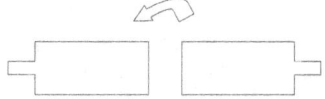

16. Rotation of Two 2-Dimensional Bottles Allows Their Superposition

Now imagine, would the challenge continue, that these two bottles were not symmetrical along the long axis, that is one side off the center axis is bulkier than the other, the larger bulge of each bottle pointing in the same direction. Of course by rotating in the plane one of the bottles, one cannot superimpose that bottle onto the other one. They always remain symmetrical of each other but cannot be made identical no matter how one slides them in the two-dimensional plane. In order to match one onto the other, one, we must flip one bottle *outside* of the plane, hence into the third dimension and then the two bottles can be made to coincide.

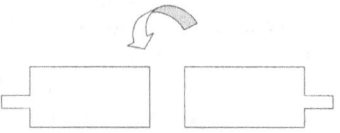

17. Off-Plane Flip of One of Two Asymmetrical Bottles

Scientists long ago had postulated that a fourth dimension would allow a three-dimensional form to be rotated or *flipped* onto its mirror-image. If one looks at his own two hands for example, palms facing you, one has the same problem as with the two bottles. One cannot rotate the hands and make them identical if one stays in the three-dimensional space, no matter how one rotates or flips them in three dimensions. By flipping them, they are always opposite although symmetrical. The same applies to gloves, which are basically cut-off hands for this purpose. One can imagine that by going into the fourth dimension, the two hands can be made to be identical in the three-dimensional space.

Another analogy was that of shadows, as was exhibited in the holographic display in the lobby of the D4R chapter conference center. It went as follows.

"A shadow in our common world", the commentary of the display explained, *"is truly a projection in two dimensions of a three- dimensional object. However in a four-dimensional world the shadow of a four-dimensional object is in three dimensions, just as the hologram shows. A shadow with substance. A shadow with volume. You can easily imagine the four-dimensional object from its three-dimensional shadow."*

The holographic display was unsettling. A shadow with *meat* one critic had called it. The commentary on the hologram also added in an attempt at clarification that:

> *"By dimensional analogy, a two-dimensional object in a two-dimensional world would cast a one-dimensional shadow, and light on a one-dimensional object in a one-dimensional world would cast a zero-dimensional shadow, that is a point of shadow, a point with no thickness and zero radius, thus an invisible shadow, but a shadow nonetheless."*

And the commentary added: *"We urge you to visit the Society of D11 where this can begin to make sense, as zero-dimension objects appear to exist."*

A less abstract way to *see* in four dimensions was proposed by another scientist, Dr. Wu, who reminded his audience that the problem with the human mind was that man tended to reduce all forms of analysis to three *orthogonal* axes. He had stated that certain computations in crystals made use of *non-orthogonal* axes and that helped reduce the complexity of these computations. With three-axes separated by sixty degrees each rather than ninety degrees, Dr. Wu believed there was room for at least three other axes, hence three more dimensions and the resulting picture would be a projection in two dimensions of objects in four, five or even six spatial dimensions, since the three hundred and sixty degrees around a point could encompass six axes separated by sixty degrees.

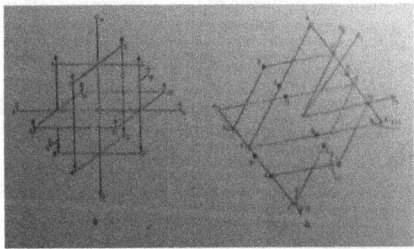

18. *Orthogonal and Non-Orthogonal Axes for the Study of Certain Crystals*

Of course the simplicity advertized by Wu seemed to be only in his eyes, or rather his mind. Dr. Wu was capable of seeing everything in four dimensions and even see a fourth dimension in objects that were clearly three-dimensional to the common mortal.

Another consideration of these societies was the extension into four dimensions of the Poincaré conjecture, solved of course over two hundred years before, that stated that a circle on the surface of a sphere if *tightened* progressively but without leaving the sphere can be reduced to a point. By analogy, would a spherical surface be allowed to contract *around* the 3-D boundary of a four dimensional *sphere*, continuously into a circle?

Of course this was not new. But Poincaré, one of the founders of the field of topology, had anticipated these questions and it had taken about a hundred years for his conjecture to be solved, so there was nothing wrong for this chapter to dwell on the consideration of matters of intellectual stimulation.

As for stimulation, a key chapter of the Society of the Flat Earth was D11, which in fact called itself the D11 Earth Society, as if it were a society of its own and not a chapter of Flat Earth. D11 comprised essentially the same members as those of the Flat Earth Society, including D4L and D4R, whose members also belonged usually to all three. The D11 Earth Society was obviously based on the ten spatial dimensions and one time dimension predicted by what was known for nearly two hundred years as M Theory.

Of course under the M hypothesis, contested by some, but since *proven* in some instances not just mathematically but experimentally as well, all but the three spatial dimensions were *curled up* and thus not perceptible to the common mortals. In particular it was posited that at extremely short distances gravitation revealed these *extra* dimensions, one at a time as the scale was further reduced.

It went as follows: since the force of gravity can be seen as the result of a gravitational field surrounding an object, anywhere in the spherical region at a specific distance from the object the force of gravity will be the same. As one gets further from the object, the force is of another value in the next sphere and so on. The force is therefore spread on the surface of each sphere and the relationship of the magnitude of the force with the distance from the object is related to the square of that distance – as the area of the spherical surface. The test the scientists were looking for was whether at smaller and smaller distances the gravitational force would decrease not as of the square of the distance but as the cube of the distance. That would mean that the *area* of constant gravity at that distance is a volume, not a surface, thus *proving* the existence of a higher spatial dimension. Of course if these constant gravity volumes were not just three-dimensional but of a higher dimension, that would validate experimentally these *curled-up* dimensions. It had taken over a hundred years to see some results, and those were encouraging it must be acknowledged, but nonetheless contested.

In addition, D11 insisted on analyzing the *uncurled* dimensions, that is our familiar three dimensions and including time, in a theoretical universe where they too would be *curled up*. Hence going back to the original flat earth if all but two of these dimensions were *curled up*.

Curling up the time dimension brought these considerations not just to the mundane time travel of science fiction but also to the issues of eternity, to the definition of a *god*. Indeed, if Time were curled upon itself, the past and the present, and the future indeed, would be *mixed up* somehow, and there would be no beginning and no end.

The work of these societies was therefore of political import as well since the concept of the universe coming from Nothingness and heading toward Nothingness was a key philosophical pillar in the Han Empire and a fatal difference with the Caliphate's own beliefs.

The basis for all these considerations was what was known as the Y Theory. It was supposed to be the Z Theory, but its authors, Han of course and carrying the Han virtue of humility as opposed to the West's prior arrogance, its authors that is, had insisted on not calling it Z, z being the last letter of the Roman alphabet which was still used in science. The authors of Y Theory, humble as they were, were sure improvements would occur and there would be ample time – if time existed of course – to devise Y-1, Y-2 and so on, culminating with Z. It was supposed to be named the Z Theory not only because it may have been the final theory, but because its ultimate components were not the one-dimensional *strings* or the multi-dimensional membranes or *p-branes* of M Theory but the brand-new and unobserved so far concept of the *zeron*, a zero-dimensional object which was postulated to be the basis of all components of the universe.

Besides *curling* the time dimension, the members of D11 Earth Society struggled nonetheless to imagine the *uncurling* of the ten remaining spatial dimensions. The members of this society tried to visualize life on earth if dimensions 4 through 10 were not *curled up* about themselves. Of course six separate sub-societies existed and in order to join Sub 5 one needed to *graduate* from Sub 4 first. That was a challenge since imagining four spatial dimensions defies human nature at first, but once that is achieved *graduating* from Sub 5 through Sub 10 was considered *a cinch*.

For good measure, there was a Sub 1 which it was joked had one member only, who could not move except forward or backward for the *meeting*, which means he couldn't get there. And the most mysterious society was Sub 0, the zero dimension chapter which had no members, but its *members* which existed but without any substance other than as mathematical points, *met* regularly. Of course the discovery of the *zeron* had brought new life to Sub 0. Its unsubstantial *members* were going to be very busy.

It helped therefore that the membership among these various, competing chapters was comprised mostly of the same people arguing on all sides of the debate. It was considered a privilege and very healthy mentally, and very intriguing indeed, to attend one of their meetings. Everyone of course was a chartered member of Sub 3, the traditional three dimensions known to man and available to the human senses. Sub 3 included members of Flat Earth and all its chapters as well. To ensure collegiality in their deliberations, all met monthly for a *Dimensional Celebration* were a one-dimensional element was the direction of the flow of the libations, the alcoholic content of which was not restricted in the Han Empire. It is said that visiting scientists from the Caliphate attended now and then such seminars.

So were the considerations of the D11 Earth Society. Nonetheless, the Flat Earth Society over two centuries before had posed a problem to its members. It stated that the wheel could not exist in a flat-earth world because a wheel needed a hub about which it could rotate. And that hub required a third dimension. The Flat Earth Society had then challenged its members to devise transportation and carriage methods in a flat-earth world.

One contraption that Deng Li devised, which the West didn't think of (of course he thought, they were Westerners, not Han), was to make the wheel the actual transport vehicle. Hence no hub would be needed. It was the equivalent of the hamster in a treadmill, an endless loop except that the hoop was not attached to any hub. While the two-dimensional man pushed on the side of the hoop in which he resided, the hoop advanced. To get in and out without hopping into a third dimension, a single-dimension *door* was slid up or down along part of the hoop therefore no hinges were required.

19. Original Drawing of the Two-Dimensional Vehicle

What Den Li had conceived was the Spherical Vehicle. It projected into three dimensions the flat earth *hamster hoop*. Of course hinges were permitted and a motor at its center activated spokes along the radii of the three-dimensional hoop. Two seats located on each side of the motor allowed the occupants to travel. The seats were on ball bearings, assuring that no matter how the giant wheel rotated, the occupants always remained level with the ground, gravity helping of course. To prevent accidents, that is occupants touching the fast running spokes, transparent advanced ceramic walls on each side of the spokes were installed and these also slid past the inside of the rotating vehicle via ball bearings made of a special molybdenum alloy which were considered naturally lubricated *for life*. To ensure visibility nano-sensors in the outer shell transmitted three-dimensional video images of the near and far environments about the vehicle to a computer located on the driver side. This computer in turn reconfigured these images in three dimensions into holographic displays for both occupants.

The driver would also use a slight pressure to tilt the motor which would then cause the vehicle, that giant wheel, that giant ball, to go left or right. The advantage of this vehicle is that it used the wheel as the most efficient method of transportation, without losses inherent to the conversion of a circular motion into a linear motion and which are found in traditional wheeled vehicles. The efficiencies were especially notable for travel to areas where no Maglev highways existed, or in residential and rural neighborhoods which lacked such infrastructure. The peasants had adopted this contraption with enthusiasm.

Even when accidents happened, say a sphere would slide into a ditch or even a precipice, not too steep however, the spherical wheel could recover and even slow its fall if the *tires,* bands that circled the sphere in many directions and which could deploy some type of suction cups, the way the legs and feet of certain insects do, these bands provided sufficient friction to reverse course. The powerful motor was capable of fighting the downward pull of gravity. Stories abounded of exploits by these machines: one said that a survey crew had *fallen down* the incline of the Sanxia Daba, otherwise known as the Three Gorges Dam, only to stop its fall, reverse its direction and move back upward onto safe ground.

The large size of the wheel, compared to other wheeled vehicles, especially those used in the Caliphate, four or even six or eight wheeled contraptions, that large size allowed for a very stable and comfortable ride. The large radius allowed the vehicle to absorb obstacles in the terrain much more softly than with traditional wheels which were a fraction of its size.

20. Schematic of a Three- Dimensional NAV

The Flat Earth members were very proud of this vehicle since most of their endeavors concerned logic and this was an invention born of intuition. A quote from Poincaré in their lobby summarized that pride:

"by logic we prove, by intuition we invent"

It also emphasized their philosophy that patience with science will pay in technology, even if one needs to be extremely patient.

To allow this enormous sphere to rotate and travel, and especially climb steep hills, very powerful motors were needed. Self-contained nuclear batteries provided these vehicles inexhaustible fuel for life. They were named Nuclear Activated Vehicles, or NAVs, or even simply *navs.* Of course outside the Han empire, everyone thought that NAV stood for navigation, which wasn't the case. The nuclear batteries were in fact nuclear micro-plants, well sealed and with containment structures, and outlasted any NAV in service; these micro-plants never needed refueling or replacement.

For their journey Mehmut displayed a map of the Han territory for Al Kansii's benefit. The Han territory had four provincial capitals, one of which, the northern one, served as the national capital as well. These capitals were the traditional 'Jing' or 'city', or 'capital' (京) and for the North, Bei (北), for the South, Nan (南) and for the East, Dong (東). This latter, Dong Jing was formerly known as Tokyo.

Two decades before, BeiJing, NanJing and DongJing had been given a sister, XiJing, the West – Xi (西) – capital. XiJing had risen from the desert and had been a strategic implantation to ensure the cohesiveness of the Uyghur restive lands. XiJing was located at 38 degrees North latitude and 76 degrees East longitude. This latitude-longitude combination had been chosen as multiples of 19 as a sign of appeasement toward and understanding of the Uyghur population. As a result, in the desert a new city had emerged from the desolation of the sands. It boasted one hundred and nineteen minarets and 190 madrassa. Some of these madrassa had become controversial as they did not teach the official *people's creed* that had survived since the Revolution of centuries past and that had defined the philosophical foundation of the State of the Han Empire.

The People's Council in BeiJing had ample reason to be concerned as they focused on the fate of the Western world. They had therefore decided that gathering one's opponents and providing them with the means of expression and assembly perhaps not only assuaged their ever-changing, and they sought irrational, demands, but at the same time it avoided their dispersion into a wider area. In other words one should aim at having one's enemies all gathered in one place rather than dispersed. The Han Empire had invested very large sums and effort to create XiJing out of the desert desolation. XiJing was therefore located directly south of Kashgar and not far to the south-east of Qia'erlongxiang.

To the older generation XiJing was anathema as for millennia the Empire had had only three recognized capitals, albeit under various fealties over time, but never a 'capital' on its west, which it considered wild and under-developed. But these were the times. Unsophisticated people, *the people*, shepherds and nomads, demanded the privileges that the upper classes had worked hard to achieve for themselves. For the authorities that was the price to pay for peace, for now.

Of course Mehmut and Al Kansii chose to avoid XiJing and instead took a detour through the Han wilderness with their NAV. Thus began their beautiful journey.

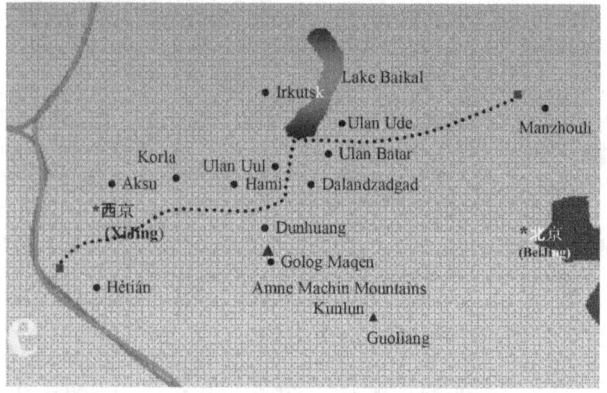

21. *Itinerary of Al Kansii's and Mehmut's Journey*

Mehmut and Al Kansii took their positions in the NAV and headed north-east toward Aksu[15], one of the northern gates of the Taklimakan desert, opposite Hétián, its southern gate. When they reached Aksu's longitude they accelerated deep into the desert and rolled in a near perfect north-east trajectory as they headed toward Korla. They turned east when they were halfway to Korla in order to avoid crossing the main highway which Mehmut said was already 'magleved' so it had all the sensors to determine who was on it. By going still further east through the desert they could avoid such detection so they rolled at full speed leaving Korla on their north and

---

[15] Aksu had been the theater a few years back of a sudden, unexplainable uprising. Although the social and economic conditions seemed stable at the time, the population just stopped working and began making conflicting demands that the central authorities deemed irrational. Low levels of violence had even been observed. These events gave rise to a verb, to "aksu" oneself, that is to become suddenly malcontent in an irrational way and the person in that condition being "aksued".

maintained a mid-distance between Dunhuang to the south-east and Hami to the north-west.

Mehmut and Al Kansii had the perfect vehicle for the trip that Mehmut had planned. They would take some dirt roads, or in fact no roads at all as they would cut through the countryside, go over hills and valleys, sand dunes and denuded boulders, dead tree trunks and other fallen vegetation, rocks and even mountain sides and reach another set of cross roads. In that manner they would be able to crisscross from the south-west of the Han territory toward the north-east and reach Manchuria in about 22 hours. For some of the difficult passes Mehmut had put to use four emergency *propulsors* that allowed the NAV to propel itself without regard to the terrain, as if it were flying, an option that Mehmut used very sparingly in order to avoid detection. True peasant-owned NAVs never had propulsors installed in their NAVs since they would never need them.

When they were past Hami, to their south-east was the Amne Machin range in the province of Qinghai. Al Kansii noted that the Amne Machin, part of the Kunlun Mountains, were one of the deflectors for his neutrino weapon, as he had reviewed with Dromm. Together with the more massive Himalayas to the south which provided a first deflection and the Stanovoy chain in the northern part of the Empire which would deflect the beams previously redirected by the Urals, the Amne Machin were the other deflector which would guide the neutrino beams to their destination in BeiJing. These four natural obstacles would be able to direct a statistically sufficient sample of neutrinos to have the effect Al Kansii required. Or so he and Dromm had calculated, based on the emission by the *neutrino factories* in the Caliphate.

Further south was the Guoliang tunnel carved with bare hands into the rock. Mehmut told Al Kansii that it was a pity they could not make a detour to see the *rock tunnel* as it was known, especially being so close. To Mehmut it was a *marvel* of the world to be seen. He remembered a trip a while back in a NAV and showed Al Kansii a holographic display of his NAV going through the tunnel, while their own NAV rolled in the desert.

The Guoliang region was forbidding. Centuries before, a road tunnel had been carved out of the rock on the side of the mountain, it was said with bare hands. It was a beautiful and wild landscape. The sight of the NAV appearing and disappearing at blinding speed made it look like a disk thrown into the mountain as if it were the disk that was cutting through the side of that mountain. The reflection of the sun on the ceramic outside shell was other-worldly according to Mehmut.

Al Kansii, although he was inside the vehicle could actually see his own NAV as if from outside thanks to a reverse holographic imaging system that Mehmut had made sure was installed. The system used the troposphere scatter reflection, a very old technique brought back to life, and more importantly within the security guidelines of the time, with the special distance attenuators. These ensured that faint emissions were reflected back to the emitter with little side dispersion, and near zero refraction which could have reached the surveillance satellites looming over the subject emitter.

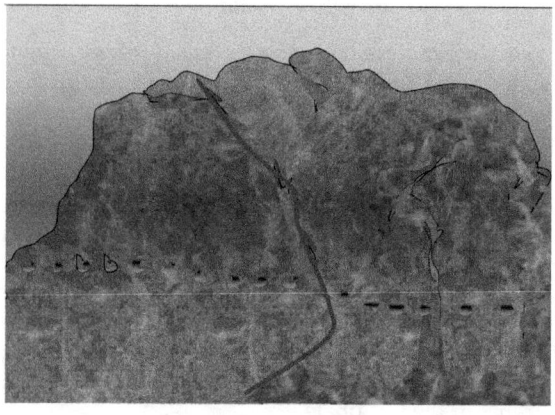

22. The Rock Tunnel in Guoliang

The interface between the atmospheric layers was therefore used as a type of mirror for the special high frequencies used, high enough so they would not travel far into the surveillance satellites. Low frequencies travel far, high frequencies attenuate faster. The ultra high frequency used would not traverse the atmospheric layers without near total attenuation. That way they could see what one could theoretically observe from the upper layers of the atmosphere. That was the same method of self-reflection that Mehmut had used to create the projection of his NAV cutting through the rock tunnel and that he was showing to Al Kansii. For now though, Al Kansii was enjoying the sights. He could see the landscape filing by them intermittently and he could see his own vehicle whizzing by. *What a ride!*

Not far to their south-east now was the Golog Maqen National Surveillance Center, to the north-west of the town of Golog Maqen. Al Kansii thought it was good not to be too far as surveillance in such centers usually focuses its efforts far into distant lands. *'The best bank to rob is the one located near the police station'*, Al Kansii remembered that old saying which he understood although he had grown and lived in a world where there were no physical banks and no fixed police stations any longer, but sayings that are relics of ancient times remain in all cultures. Like *'one should not sell the bear's skin before having killed it'*, usually recounted by city dwellers who had rarely seen a bear and certainly would never kill one.

When they reached approximately the longitude of Xining, Mehmut and Al Kansii veered north again and soon entered Mongolia leaving Dalandzadgad to their east and headed in the direction of Ulan Bator, but remained safely to its west while they approached Lake Baikal. They would aim at the southernmost point of the lake between Irkutsk – the coldest city on Earth - and Ulan-Ude. Both Ulan Bator and Ulan-Ude were now Han territory, their population, despite centuries of animosity between the Han and the local ethnic groups, having enthusiastically embraced the Han rather than joining the Grand Caliphate.

About seventeen hours from their departure, they were at the southern shore of Lake Baikal. Their NAV came to a stop behind some trees not far from the lake. Mehmut and Al Kansii stepped out. The NAV seemed a little out of place here, but there appeared to be no one around. Al Kansii stretched out and admired the sheer beauty of the lake, an inland sea in a way.

Al Kansii had noted that Lake Baikal had the shaped of a crescent, and the crescent faced west as it should. Noticing that the crescent of Lake Baikal was a stop in their long trek, he considered it a divine sign that he was on a sacred mission. Al Kansii had studied the lake before his trip and knew it had a length of over six hundred kilometers and a width of nearly fifty kilometers. What made the lake unique though was its depth, well over a mile. A lake over a mile deep! Lake Baikal's depth made it the reservoir of over one fifth of all the freshwater in the world. That depth was of oceanic proportions.

In fact Al Kansii had learned that Lake Baikal, sitting on three intersecting tectonic plates, was destined to become an ocean according to geologists, as its width expanded by over two centimeters a year.

Al Kansii, as far as his eyes could see could not help but notice that the lake was completely surrounded by mountains. He tried to picture what it looked like two hundred years before when Lake Baikal despite being the deepest lake in the world, still froze in the winter and the ice it is said was so thick that a railway line was run over its surface in Winter.

Since early Spring the lake had thawed considerably. Its substantial volume of water brought by three hundred and thirty six rivers, emptied through just one, the Angara. Al Kansii looked at the clear waters and could understand that the various currents created several pools in which a wide variety of undersea life thrived.

He looked at the horizon and noticed what appeared to be several sea-worthy ships. This lake was truly a sea. A sea of fresh water. A light wind produced small waves that kept crashing on this southern shore. The waves seemed to have no specific direction. Waves of surprisingly clear water as far as he could see. And the waves came crashing, not too harshly this evening, toward the south-west and after three or four cycles, they would crash on the south-east side. Al Kansii wondered how the winds were configuring this pattern and whether a diametrically opposed one occurred on the northern shores. The reflection of the winds against the wall of mountains surrounding the lake, coupled with its crescent shape and the currents of its many tributaries conspired to produce this beautiful water dance of nature.

Looking at this peaceful choreography of the waters on the southern shores of Lake Baikal, Al Kansii felt some warmth fill his heart. When admiring nature he felt overwhelmed with a sense of happiness. The beauty in nature was not a sign of God as many pagans believed, since for God nature was what it was and nothing more, and God existed above and beyond nature. However his feeling of inner happiness when admiring that beauty, that was proof that God has created man, a man with a conscience, a man that must submit to Him. To Al Kansii, and most in the Grand Caliphate that had received a similar education since their early years, nature was not proof of God, since God did not need any proof. The true essence of God was immanent. And the West had lost that understanding years before its fall. And when material things began to lack, when there was no spiritual scaffolding to support a different lifestyle, the West had become unable to function. Until Islam spread to the entire West. Al Kansii felt happy for no other reason than the beauty, peacefulness and serenity of the landscape.

"Brother," said Mehmut, "we need to get going. We will need to reach the Manchurian cabin before day break."

Mehmut and Al Kansii took their seats and the silent motor began to rotate the inside middle spokes. The sphere began to glide like a circle of soft light in the twilight reflected by the lake.

It would now be a straight ride east then north-east toward Manzhouli, and the *contact*.

The ride in the NAV was perfect. Al Kansii tried to wonder why the Caliphate had avoided, actually rejected this technology. In fact it ought to have been developed there first. Al Kansii attributed this decision to the fact that the Caliphate avoided discussions of dimensions if at all possible, especially the two-dimensional concepts of the world. Evil minds had interpreted certain passages of the Qur'an as supporting a flat earth and any reminders of this misconception were thus avoided.

Indeed, millennia ago, the Qur'an had given a first indication that great things could be accomplished if one could *envision* at least ideally a flat earth. *Sura* 20:53 says that God *"...made the earth for you like a carpet spread out..."* Of course Al Kansii and almost everyone else interpreted this saying as pure metaphor for the spread of Islam, without the attribution of any shape to Earth.

More difficult to counter, although not impossible considering the context, the Qur'an commands that the five daily prayers must be made facing Mecca (Bukhari 1:146-151). From a flat-earth viewpoint, this makes strict sense. In a spherical Earth, of course, anyone praying facing Mecca would also have his back to Mecca at the same time as well. Of course one distance would be much shorter than the other and in any event this was idealized speech. The seeds were there to create a machine to roll over the mythical carpet. And the Han took the credit for it. And the Caliphate had lost an opportunity.

Golog Maqen National Surveillance Center

The Center was located in the north-central territory of the Han Empire. Its location was carefully studied to allow interception of primary signals from anywhere on Earth using their space-based system. Their satellites in highly elliptical orbits that covered the four corners of the globe had common visibility to the Center anywhere in the Northern Hemisphere. What that meant practically is that a signal emitted on the other side of the world, even at 180 degrees of separation, a signal that is normally screened by the Earth from the view of traditional geostationary satellites, that signal could be received by the Golog Maqen Center via a single hop. A single hop meant that the signal emitted in the middle of the Caliphate would go up to such a Han satellite which in turn would relay it directly to the Center, without that signal having to be downlinked into some intermediate step prior to being finally routed to the Center. Yu Lin had explained it in simple terms to the People's Assembly years before.

"Let me show the following diagram," Yu Lin had begun.

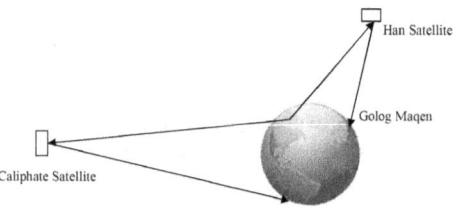

23. *Earth Screens a Geostationary Satellite East to West, but not a Han Satellite*

"Graphically, as illustrated above, it's easy to see: if a satellite lies on the equatorial plane high above the Earth, it can only see at best half the Earth, and for traditional electromagnetic waves, not neutrinos beams of course, these waves cannot traverse the Earth. They are screened by it. So the Center at Golog Maqen located on the other side from where a Caliphate signal would originate, cannot receive that signal directly from the relaying geostationary satellite. This signal would usually have to be routed to an intermediate destination on Earth either East or West, and within visibility of Golog Maqen, and then relayed back up and down through a second hop in order to reach Golog Maqen. Since the Caliphate controls most longitudes, and the space above them, it is therefore not safe for the Han Empire to depend on such relays. The Han space architecture must ensure that a signal from the Caliphate would find its way in a single hop to Golog Maqen, and its auxiliary center at Qiqihar."

The Han satellites were therefore placed in orbits that allowed them to somewhat *hover* over high latitudes permitting most points in the Caliphate and Golog Maqen to be visible by a single satellite. Since these Han satellites were not geosynchronous, several were required, they always appeared to be hovering over the northern skies and they provided continuous single hop transmission to and from the Caliphate and Golog Maqen and Qiqihar.

This Han satellite system consisted of several sub-constellations of satellites that used specific trajectories or orbits around the Earth. The architecture was not Han, it was inherited from the West, patents and secrets be damned. The Han were lucky. After the Fall of the West, some emir had concluded that satellite-based crafts intruded on the divine and decreed consequently the stoppage of all further deployment. The Caliphate was allowed to keep what was then deployed but no further improvements, to *trick the divine* were permitted. It was akin to China's own destruction of its fleet in the sixteenth century CE, or the Japanese Samurai who prohibited the use of firearms centuries later.

Space Architecture

Yu Lin was the father of the Center. When he proposed the Center in one of his speeches to the People's Assembly, he had presented it as the core of the national surveillance system.

"Satellite systems normally utilize orbits," he went on to say, "that is the path a satellite follows to rotate around the Earth, that are similar for a similar mission. Let me explain. At thirty-six thousand kilometers and above the equator, a satellite rotates around the Earth once per day. It therefore remains apparently stationary relative to Earth. We call that a geostationary orbit.

"To obtain the benefits of being closer to Earth that I will explain later, satellite orbits that are non-geostationary are also used. When lower altitudes are chosen, the satellites, being closer to Earth experience a stronger attraction due to gravity. This attraction can be countered by the centrifugal force created by their rotation around the Earth. As you know centrifugal forces are borne from the non-rectilinear motion of a body. The faster one rotates, the stronger the force."

He then smiled and said:

"You are all engineers and scientists. So you know the equation $F = GMm/r^2$ as you may remember."

A general laughter was heard as it was evident that many if not all were transported back into high school. And he added, smiling broadly:

"And the centrifugal force is given by $F = m\omega^2/r$. Remember?"

A loud laugh followed.

"So," continued Yu Lin, "when the two forces are equal, the satellite remains stable, and to a specific distance corresponds a specific rate of rotation. Of course the actual equations are a bit more complex, but I will not try to embarrass anyone here."

More laughter was heard and comments were made by some to their immediate neighbors sitting at the People's Hall. The audience was enjoying it. Some did not laugh though. These were true engineers-politicians that really had remained technicians at heart. They were already computing more complex models of these simple equations to include the effects of the bulge of the Earth, the pull of the moon when the satellite would be between the Earth and the Moon, the impact of the Sun's gravity, the stability of the orbit and other effects.

Yu Lin continued:

"Since at lower altitudes satellites travel around the Earth faster that once a day, they therefore do not remain over our heads as in the previous case.

"In order to provide somebody say in NanJing continuous service, one must add a satellite after the first one gets out of sight, and then of course one must coordinate between the satellites so that the transmission is not lost. And when the second satellite passes away, a third one is needed and so on until the first satellite comes back over NanJing a few hours later. So the lower the orbit, the faster the travel, and the more satellites one will need to cover a point in our territory. But when one satellite goes *away* from you, it is over some other point on Earth, as the Earth also has rotated. That satellite is still useful, but not to you as it now covers another point on Earth, just not your position. So the net result is that the many satellites you have just deployed for NanJing give you global coverage as well."

"Aahhh," exclaimed several participants in the audience.

"Hence we can deploy surveillance systems globally using this technique. We know that the Caliphate has resumed space deployment as well, but we are ahead. Let me tell you why, and why this Center is essential to us.

"Most non-geostationary systems were designed to consist of an orbit, that is a geometrical locus, in which several satellites are placed and made to travel. Say such an orbit goes by the poles, the North and South Poles, and that its period is of two hours, that is it takes two hours for a satellite in that orbit to go around the Earth once. Twelve satellites will then be required to cover the Earth at those longitudes underneath that orbit, twelve times two hours equal twenty four hours, and if the footprints are wide enough there may be some overlap that reduces the number of satellites to eleven for example. Thus say eleven or twelve such satellites will provide coverage underneath on Earth... if the Earth was not moving of course. But the Earth revolves under this orbit that covers then other longitudes, so a second orbit, a third one and so on are also required to cover all the longitudes, all the time. For twenty-four-hour continuous service the two-hour polar orbit system would require at least six such orbits with eleven or twelve satellites each. I say only six such orbits since each covers the earth's rotation twice once when on the ascending side and then on the descending side. Again overlaps may require seven such orbital planes. That makes it a minimum of sixty-six to a maximum of eighty four satellites. I just described an ancient system that was later modified and built by the West. The Caliphate in their religious zeal destroyed it. They are now rebuilding it. But we have better. This is what their system looks like from above." And Yu Lin would show the Caliphate's system coverage:

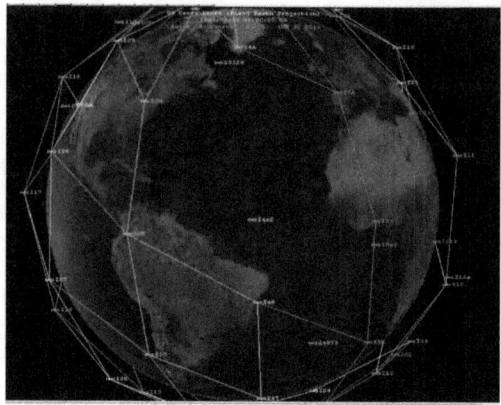

24. *Coverage of Ancient Non-Geostationary System Being Rebuilt by the Caliphate*

The audience was taken. This was interesting. And so different from the usual *the people, the country, the land* and all these patriotic platitudes that characterized all addresses in this Assembly. They were all transported back to school, it was a reprieve from the daily harangues, demagoguery and posturing that have been the hallmark of the political process from time immemorial. Except of course for those few scattered in the Chamber that were furiously computing, researching, checking every assertion that Yu Lin made.

And perhaps the intentions of these technicians were not all purely scientific or intellectual. If they could find a monkey wrench, they would undo Yu Lin's power and put their own genius in his place. And the construction of a space infrastructure designed by them would locate most lucrative contracts close to home, their homes. A genius that would improve their own social and political fortunes.

"As this flat world map shows, that is what the Caliphate has," Yu Lin said as he then showed a world map projection in two dimensions. On it were several lines, like oscillations, or sinusoidal lines, just curves going from the North Pole to the South Pole at an angle and then reemerging from the South Pole to the North Pole, and repeating this cycle over the map. One such line was next to another identical line, offset by a few fractions of a millimeter, and then another line and so on so as the whole world map was covered.

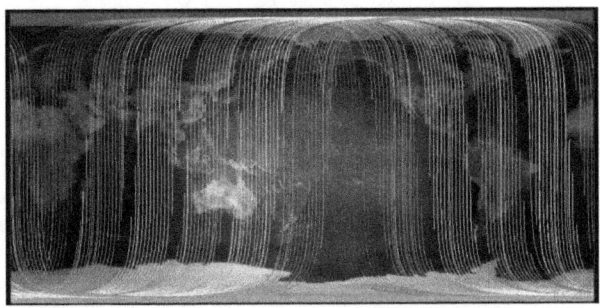

25. *Ground Tracks of Caliphate Satellite System*

Yu Lin continued:

"These are the projections of the orbital trajectories over the Earth, or ground tracks. As the Earth revolves, a satellite traces its imprint on the Earth according to such line. And each orbit represents a line. Each satellite in its orbit follows a specific track. So you see here, this line is orbit 3, and these offset dots are the seven satellites in that particular orbit."

Yu Lin paused, and drank a full glass of water.

"Now, and these are national secrets and disclosed only to you as trusted members of the People's Assembly. You see, most of these lines lie over water, since the world is mainly water. And of the lands it covers, few are of interest, or rather some are of more military interest than others.

"So to reduce waste and maximize our surveillance assets, we adopted the following idea. Rather than using orbits that produced all these ground tracks, we decided to see if we could maintain a single ground track, centered over the continents for example, and tailor the orbits to fit that ground track, rather than the opposite."

A grumble was heard, and one of the sour technologists sitting in the back suddenly raised his hand and asked:

"Was that design not patented by the West long ago?"

An enormous laugh resulted, almost as if the entire Assembly were one. One giant laugh at the thought of patenting by the West. One delegate, a rotund man who by the look of his eyes, slightly red and which he could hardly keep open and so seemed to have just had a hearty meal with the proper liquid accompaniment, volunteered loudly and irresponsibly:

"Patents? What patents?" and laughed almost uncontrollably.

He was not the only one laughing. Yu Lin continued in a serious tone of voice:

"Regardless of who thought of that first, we are the ones implementing it. An idea, patented or not, if not implemented, is worthless."

With this stern and authoritative comment, the audience reverted to silence and order.

"A single ground track," declared Yu Lin. "Now suppose you choose an altitude that produces three revolutions per day, you will then have one ground track over the western Caliphate for about five hours, over the eastern Caliphate for five hours again beginning three hours later, and our Empire for the last five hours beginning still three hours later. If we then choose the position of the apogee within the orbit such that latitudes of interest are covered by priority, we center the ground track on a preferred longitude, and set other parameters to make this thing stable, we have a near geostationary system. The satellite can hover over the Caliphate without occupying permanently orbital slots vulnerable to their countermeasures. With this system, countermeasures can be corrected by us at the next pass, every eight hours at most and actually less, something like three hours. And we can inject our own counter-countermeasures.

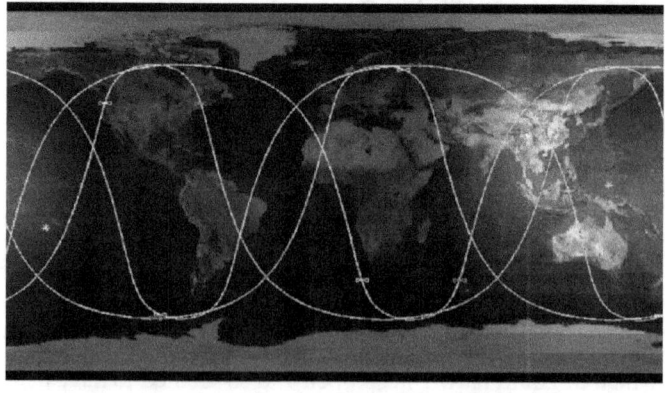

26. Han Satellite System Ground Tracks

"Let me explain. These orbits need not be circular. In fact the laws of Physics dictate that all orbits tend to be elliptical. These are more elliptical than naturally but still they provide us with the ability to hover over an area by priority, say the northern latitudes, or within those longitudes pertaining to the strategic assets of the Caliphate. Of course each satellite eventually sets over the horizon but not before another satellite rises over the same spot, covering the same ground track. And the entire world seems enveloped inside a cocoon of our satellites operating at varying altitudes to confuse the Caliphate."

"This is the Cocoon," added Yu Lin while proudly exhibiting the following diagram on the holographic space:

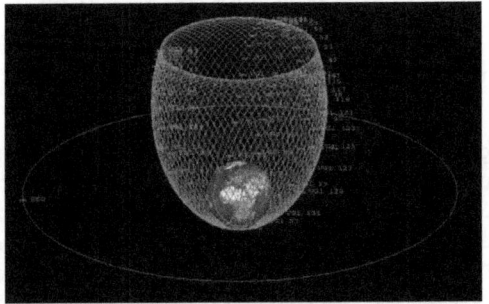

27. *The Han Empire Satellite "Cocoon"*

"How many satellites does one need? Seventy seven, forty four?" asked the seemingly disgruntled technician who did not appear impressed and projected the appearance that he knew more.

"Well, much fewer than seventy seven; a fraction of that. But that is a state secret, that not even this august Chamber needs to know, but what if I told you less than twenty? replied curtly Yu Lin.

"Let me point out this. Here," Yu Lin continued, as he showed a projection where the North Pole was almost facing the audience, the globe tilted toward it. We have at one point in time a satellite here over Usamabad, picking up signals, information and other data. From Golog Maqen which is at a latitude of roughly 35.5 degrees North, that satellite can transmit the information directly to the Center. In one hop. No other system allows that. The geostationary satellites can handle North-South in one hop, but not East-West. We handle East-West, in fact the entire hemisphere with only one hop. Need I emphasize the military significance of this?"

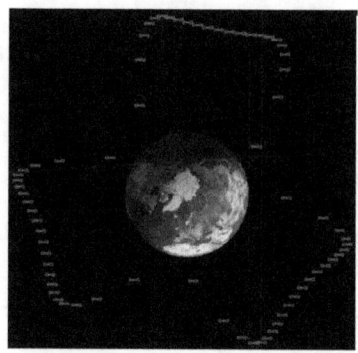

28. Han Satellite View from the North Pole

"How about the south, don't we have allies there?" said the challenging technocrat.

"We thought of it," answered Yu Lin. "By deploying a symmetrical sub-constellation with apogees over the south, we are able to cover it as well. However we do not have a Golog Maqen in the south. Well, our natural allies in the south, in Patagonia, cannot wait to help us...and this is dangerous for them... it need not leave this room. On the other hand the Caliphate knows we are working with them, or trying to. What can they do? A diversionary war over there could doom their aspirations against us. The Christian world survives now out of the rivalry between the Caliphate and us. Let me correct myself...

"We are not rivals. We just want to be left alone. For some unknown reason, they want to convert us to their creed, and achieve a Global Caliphate. That keeps the Vatican in Patagonia safe for now. Frankly many of us feel guilty that we did not protect the West from itself. After all, they were benign in their rivalry. They were innocuous, and we in fact precipitated their fall. Now we have a bigger problem..."

A soft rumble could be heard travelling across the Chamber, of approval and of concern.

"In any event," continued Yu Lin, "the satellites in the southern sub-constellation are equipped with inter-satellite links, just like the ancient system I described above."

"Do you use optical links or V, W, P, Q or R bands for those?" interrupted the technocrat.

A loud grumbling was now heard signaling disapproval of his attitude and interruptions.

"You should join the Center to improve their technologies," said a delegate sarcastically.

Yu Lin continued:

"That, I cannot tell you. It is a state secret. All I can say is that we use all the tools available to our great Empire to ensure its safety.

"I have just described for you, dear Comrades, the architecture of the detection and communications system deployed for the Golog Maqen Center."

The disgruntled technocrat then challenged Yu Lin again:

"Could you describe in more detail the detection methods based of things other than electromagnetic waves? We hear that we the Han have developed such alternative methods of communication and of…"

The Supreme Leader then intervened.

"Comrade Yu Lin," said the Supreme Leader. "I ask you to reserve the description of measures to address detection by other communications means for presentation to the People's Council first."

"Yes Comrade Supreme Leader," answered Yu Lin.

The Supreme Leader then announced it should be the end of the discussion:

"I approve of these efforts and find them laudable and worthy of our great Empire. Does anybody desire to add a useful comment?"

The addition of the word *useful* was obviously meant to silence the technocrat who seemed to have annoyed the Supreme Leader as well. In any event all understood that it also asked if anyone thought otherwise, especially after hearing of the Supreme Leader's praise for the Center. Of course no one dared. Although, and except perhaps for the technocrat and a few of his colleagues, it appeared they all sincerely thought that Yu Lin's presentation had been persuasive.

"In any event, we must defend ourselves," began to conclude Yu Lin. "And the first step is to know where your enemy is and what his plans are. The Center will collect vast amounts of information and our Analysis and Conclusion Engines, our ACE's, will assist our brilliant scientists and analysts in determining the threats before they happen.

"I humbly thank you for your patriotic support," ended Yu Lin.

And all in the Assembly of the People stood and applauded. In the traditional custom of the Han, Yu Lin applauded back to his admirers.

The funding for the Center was then approved. And upon its construction every Yuan was accounted for. Not one was missing. Corruption was unknown in the Han Empire. That was due to good citizenship of course. It was also smart because the control systems would immediately catch any attempt at bribery or embezzlement which would be followed by dire consequences for the miscreant.

Keum Kam Ho, a.k.a. Albert

At the cabin near Manzhouli, Yu Lin and Keum Kam Ho had discussed as follows.

Keum Kan Ho, a.k.a. Albert, was a communications engineer of reasonable talent. He was well versed in satellite tracking and other methods of detection. In particular he had developed a special knack for understanding, even before computations were completed, the effects of the Doppler shift, especially those related to *variable* Doppler shift. This was important because at Qiqihar, the tracking of the vast network of satellites was more complete than at Golog Maqen, the National Center, just as Yu Lin had intended. Qiqihar was after all just the Annex.

Doppler shift occurs as was well known when a moving object emits or reflects waves and transfers its own velocity to these waves, causing a shift in the frequency of the waves. The sound of a train leaving the station is of a lower tone than that of the one arriving. Everyone knew that. However when a signal is communicated via a specific frequency to a satellite that relays it to a receiver here on Earth, Albert knew that that receiver had to correct for that frequency shift due to the movement of the satellite in order to restore the signal

AD 2188 – The World Under the Grand Caliphate

to its original state. These techniques were centuries old and did not require any particular skill.

Albert was aware that objects closer to Earth must rotate faster than more distant objects in order to compensate for the increased gravitational attraction at lower altitudes. In fact it was known science that the rotational speed of a heavenly body revolving around another one was known to vary inversely to the square of the distance between the two. This was not new. It took a day for a geosynchronous satellite – located at about thirty six thousand kilometers away – to rotate around the Earth. The Moon, further away from Earth, needed a month to go around it and it took Earth a year to go around the Sun. The longer the distance, the lower the speed of rotation.

Albert knew however that the constellation of satellites that was the core of the national surveillance system utilized very precisely defined elliptical orbits. An elliptical orbit normally has both an apogee, a point farthest from the Earth, and a perigee, that closest to Earth – in a circle both apogee and perigee are equal. The Han satellites that followed such orbits were at varying distances from Earth at different times. The speed of a Han satellite orbiting Earth and the Doppler shift of its signals were therefore not constant but varied with the location of that satellite in its orbit at any specific time.

In the specific implementation of the Empire, when at apogee, the satellite seemed to hang, to hover over the Earth for a long time and then would begin a vertiginous acceleration around the other end of the orbit, its perigee, to reach maximum speed and then begin a deceleration back to a slow apogee where the satellite would hover again for hours. As a result, for the majority of the time of the orbit, the Doppler Effect was practically constant, and then for about a third of the time, it would vary violently before resuming its leisurely pace. And again and again.

The engineers at Golog Maqen had chosen to utilize the orbit only during those times when the satellite hovered around apogees. Indeed, they began their activity at about twenty five degrees of latitude in any one hemisphere, continued through zenith and shut off when they had reached twenty five degrees again on the descending side of their orbit. The rest of the orbit was reserved for recharging the solar batteries and for other maintenance functions. This is the way Yu Lin had designed the system.

Albert's insight, which he developed with Yu Lin, was to use the satellites in the forbidden, or ignored, part of their orbit. Tracking of objects on Earth from a much lower altitude and communicating with them, albeit at higher speeds, could be achieved in a stealth manner while the satellites were ignored by Golog Maqen and presumably by the unsuspecting Caliphate as well. Yu Lin and Albert were dismayed that nobody at Golog Maqen, not only had not thought of that obvious asset, but that nobody had even bothered to see the potential threat. Yu Lin knew that just as politics is too important to be left to politicians, and justice too precious to be left to judges, so was technology too critical to be left to technicians.

Yu Lin and Albert thus developed a stealth detection and communications system, right there in plain view of all and that no one suspected. Of course for added security they used quantum encryption together with entanglement to protect their activities, just in case.

Albert had devised and built Doppler correctors to support communications using the national network in times and places where this network was not in use. When everyone thought it lay idle. Yu Lin and Albert had planted the seeds of true power, exclusive information, in a field left fallow.

Another stealth usage of the *forbidden part* of the orbit, as Yu Lin liked jokingly to call it, was that the ever changing characteristics of the flight parameters of the satellite in its highly accelerated, and decelerated parts of its orbit, resulted in a state where the satellite appeared as a set of different coordinates at subsequent moments in time. As a result, precise triangulation and location determination of objects on Earth was achieved independently of the global positioning systems in use for centuries and known as GPS.

Yu Lin and Albert had their own private GPS. In fact they had many of them and the differential computation of the data provided by those allowed resolutions of earthly information unavailable to standard GPS.

"Professor," said Albert, "as expected, we have been able to detect movement of a pseudo-organic system through the XinJiang Uyghur, continuing to and through the Taklimakan and Gobi deserts and up to Lake Baikal." Albert always addressed Yu Lin as *Professor*, although their relationship ought to be defined according to the official government hierarchy, but Yu Lin had insisted on retaining the aura of academia in most of his relationships.

"Good," responded Yu Lin. "Now, are you sure that is the system we ought to be following?"

"Nothing is ever sure, but the probability of such system to be moving at uniform speed through mountains and valleys, avoiding all major centers, the probability that such system would do so by accident is practically zero. It has to be man-made and with a purpose."

"Well, it could be some object resulting from a failed experiment somewhere being carried by the winds."

"Yes, of course it could. But the object landed, or stopped at Lake Baikal, and then we were able to detect additional organic signatures. One we could trace to Mehmut Asghar, a Uyghur revolutionary of little consequence, the other to the data that Heh, *alias* Kadoor, had previously transmitted to us from *Al Andalus*. The DNA and the organic signature of inanimate objects nearby match. Professor, I apologize if this has taken longer than one would have wished but first we had to wait for the subjects to leave their vehicle which we believe to be a NAV. Mehmut's DNA was the easy part. We needed to transmit the other's DNA signature to Li Li to perform the search locally, for confirmation of course. Even we, the Empire, don't have an exhaustive world database of individual signatures."

"Are you sure then that Golog Maqen is not on the same track?"

"Again, I cannot guarantee it. In order to read a DNA signature at a distance, you need first a clear view, a clear signal. That is why we needed the subjects to exit the NAV which obstructed any transmission. Further we needed to be closer of course and have a tighter footprint that would zero in on the subject. We are virtually taking a blood sample at a distance."

"You used oxygenation sampling?"

"Yes, well... no. We use a technique similar to that but we measure something else. We send a beam which contains very specific detail parameters. The beam traverses the organic subject, is altered by the composition of the blood and other organic matter; the beam is then reflected by the next obstacle in the environment, we hope some metal and not any organic material, and hopefully some part of it goes through the subject again, through his organic matter and we measure these same parameters. In that manner we get confirmation. Of course we repeat the sampling a million times during a few seconds, and unless there are two intertwined subjects, and that has happened in the past, the result is clear. In the case of intertwined subjects, their conflicting parameters corrupt the results. Fortunately here the two subjects we sampled seemed to be at a distance from each other all the time. And that is how we identified Mehmut, with no difficulty and Al Kansii, thanks to Heh and of course Li Li."

"These measurements, is it the same technique as in medical practice where they use a probe around your finger to sample your blood without having to prick your finger?"

"Exactly. But we have to detect a much fainter signal. The principle, three hundred years old I am told, is the same."

"I am concerned that some smart and dedicated analyst at Golog Maqen may be on the same track. Follow up, discretely of course."

"Yes, Professor, I will," responded Albert as he left the cabin.

Albert had programmed the satellites in the Han system to sample thoroughly for any regular pattern of any possible signature in the XinJiang Uyghur, every square inch of it, every second of the day by several satellites concurrently. The results, quintillions of quantum states, *qubits,* had been fed to the quantum computers a partition of which was the exclusive domain of Albert, and therefore of Yu Lin. Intensive search and analysis of all such signatures had led to the *conclusion* that an pseudo-organic material was moving in these remote areas. The *eyes* of the satellites, while in the stealth part of their orbits, had been so programmed by Albert to track that material.

Organic matter is usually very diverse, its DNA is complex and a myriad combinations of atoms and molecules are present even in the most minuscule sample. Artificial organic material by contrast is simpler and more orderly. These materials consist of predictable arrangements of hydrogen, oxygen and carbon molecules with the occasional phosphorus atom. They are thus easier to detect as they stand out. A crystal for example is more orderly that a muscle in its composition. But an artificial muscle mass, by definition will lack a lot of the mayhem in its structure, the mayhem that creates life. Albert did not know what the material represented, artificial food, a human robot that simulated life or any other weird object. He knew however that two men, real humans were accompanying the material in question. And he alerted Yu Lin. That's all he could do. Now he had to spy on his colleagues at Golog Maqen to ensure they were not on the same track, or at least not yet. He decided to go Golog Maqen in person.

What Albert could not guess, and which Al Kansii did not suspect is that what Qiqihar was tracking was the *collimateur* for which Mahsood had expressed so much pride in Paris. Nothing in the leather pouch where Al Kansii had put it prevented it from being seen by sufficiently accurate satellites. In fact the signature of the simulated organic material was so simple that even through the ceramic walls of the NAV, Albert's satellites could pick it up, unlike the organic samples of real human DNA. For these Albert had to wait for Mehmut and Al Kansii to exit their NAV, very much the way a short message, or a beep gets through walls even if reception is bad, but complex conversations such as voice do not in areas of poor reception.

Qiqihar had done it first and concealed the information from Golog Maqen. Albert knew that. He now had to figure out how to probe the analysts there without revealing his secret techniques and the fact of course that he had concealed the existence of the stealth system and the recent results. Yu Lin's plot, if indeed there was a plot, had to succeed. Albert knew that sooner or later he would be caught. Unless Yu Lin prevailed. He had to.

When Albert left the cabin he rode a NAV toward Manzhouli. Yu Lin maintained a few NAVs for use by his visitors and these were stationed at the Manzhouli MagLev station where Yu Lin enjoyed a large area reserved for his use as it was the custom for high level officials and especially those involved in national security.

Albert then stepped into the MagLev train and took the Manzhouli-BeiJing Vein toward Beijing – Veins were lesser routes than the major Arteries. There were several of those of course. From the south the main maglev highway came from the North Capital – BeiJing – and it had three main connections, to the north to the former Vladivostok, to the north-west toward Manzhouli and to the south-west toward the new West Capital, XiJing, or as it was often called, the Muslim capital of the Han Empire.

The Manzhouli-BeiJing Vein was new, and that avoided Albert to having to take the Qiqihar MagLev Artery and further delay his arrival at Golog Maqen. He wondered when they would build a direct connection between Qiqihar and Golog Maqen. Of course super fast NAVs allowed workers to commute between the two, but Albert in this instance preferred the privacy of communal transportation.

As Albert boarded the MagLev train toward BeiJing, Mehmut and Al Kansii were converging on a point on a lake north-west of Manzhouli for their meeting with Yakub, the Uyghur on the People's Committee and the special agent who would carry Al Kansii inside the People's Council Chamber for his fateful mission.

From Beijing, Albert would hop on the Beijing-Xian Artery and then the Xian-Lanzhou Vein. From Lanzhou he would ride a NAV to Golog Maqen, where the National Surveillance Center was located and which stood on top of the Kunlun Mountains.

Qiqihar, Han Empire Territory
Latitude 48.139 North
Longitude 124.98 East

The Qiqihar Annex Surveillance Center was a smaller version of Golog Maqen. It was built as an auxiliary center for redundancy. Its size betrayed its importance and the scope of its functions.

Yu Lin had selected its site for two primary reasons: the proximity to Manzhouli and hence to the cabin, and its latitude, higher than Golog Maqen's.

The few additional degrees in its latitude gave a clear view of 20 degrees farther south into Caliphate territory, an advantage that the technicians at Golog Maqen had apparently missed.

Qiqihar also had a special breed of quantum supercomputers that although smaller in footprint were of the latest generation and included entanglement engines capable of performing tasks impossible even to the most powerful computers at Golog Maqen or probably even in the Caliphate. Entanglement allowed a series of quantum computers to perform tasks in successively entangled pairs, forming entangled strings and to communicate in a way that resembled human thought. In fact Yu Lin had been able to entangle in these strings unsuspecting computers in the Empire to assist in data acquisition and analysis. The strings most probably extended beyond the Empire to include certain Caliphate computers that Golog Maqen had been able to entangle on its own. As such the Qiqihar partition controlled by Yu Lin was a kind of giant brain encompassing perhaps the knowledge of the whole world and utilizing the resources of most of this linked power in a coherent manner. Albert once suggested calling this virtual assemblage the *world brain* but Yu Lin had dissuaded him from using such term. The computer infrastructure under the command of Yu Lin had no name, as it ought to be since it did not exist. At least not officially.

Artificial intelligence applications were significant and intuitive computing was possible. Yu Lin had played with such toys to have them produce poetry, humor and other representations of human emotions. He also requested from time to time these computers to determine which specific area of his thoughts represented a threat of detection by the less advanced machines at Golog Maqen. In that way he could minimize the de-scanning sessions to which he submitted himself to erase traces of his political intentions, actions and plans which normally inscribed themselves into his brain, his human brain, as a result of his thoughts and desires.

Mind Control

Decision engines acted as psychics. In fact they assembled what one couldn't see or did not clearly perceive not unlike the trained artist. The artist sees an ellipse when the common man sees a circle because he knows it is a circle, not because he sees one. A true artist sees shades of red and brown in a deep blue while the untrained eye chooses to use basic colors with no depth, no life. The idea behind decision engines was to analyze a vast amount of data more or less interconnected, discern the obvious and draw conclusions which ordinary persons, if they opened their eyes could obviously see.

For example a decision engine would recommend economic policies or simple acts required to achieve an outcome. When compared with what a human would decide, burdened by his prejudices and biases, the results were enlightening.

These tools were used politically as well. When a dissident was judged too dangerous, a *decision engine* was asked to determine the validity of his cause. When the decision engine concluded that the policy advocated by that dissident was against the interests of the State, it had the advantage of providing the authorities with a legal sanction and a moral justification for his elimination. In fact many suggested that the fallen West would have averted its fall if it had had access to these engines. It would have determined objectively that the self hatred of the elite classes would drive it to its doom. That was clear to the humble, whose prejudices and biases were of an ancient nature, such as xenophobia, organized religion, sports and other inconsequential preferences. To the elite, their sophisticated thinking had created a society where right was wrong and wrong was right, and unbelievably they could not see it. An oracle, as these engines truly were, would have been needed indeed.

Certain people, rare it must be acknowledged, can predict the future by forcing themselves to assess every element in play in a situation and turn premonition into logical predictions. The decision engines performed in a similar fashion. They were the ultimate form of clear seeing, *clairvoyant.*

Just as at the Center for Higher Learning in the Caliphate, Golog Maqen and Qiqihar performed advanced analyses of brain waves. These analyses focused on the minute components of brain waves. Just like a carrier electromagnetic wave at a specific frequency can carry information such as music or video embedded in it, so would a brain wave be comprised of a multitude of components the juxtaposition of which resulted from the input by many centers of the brain.

A simple example was given as follows. A component to the main carrier brain wave emanating from the cognitive part of the brain would contain information of a certain value, for example *a meal*. Another component juxtaposed to that first component and from the proper brain section would indicate a smell, or rather the memory of a *smell*; another component would contribute to the wave the desire to *acquire* the meal, and another to *absorb* it. Many other components would refine this composite wave. The components could be modulation of the amplitude or frequency of the carrier wave or semi-independent mini waves that would contribute to the whole thought process. A thorough analysis of the resulting brain wave could only lead to a meaningful conclusion if a large number of possible solutions were simulated and checked for reasonableness. For a wave of only a hundred components, a rather rudimentary wave, the number of combinations would be a mathematical result called *factorial* of 100, denoted as *100!*, that is 10 followed by 158 zeros, an extremely large number. Quantum computers with multi-layer parallel processing, and entangled with the processes of other similar machines were able to produce reasonable results for the human analyst in an acceptable time frame. In the example above one probable result would obviously be: "I see a meal, it reminds me of great smells, and I wish to eat it." Another would be "I wish to steal it", but additional components related to the presence or not of aggressiveness would be able to distinguish between these two obvious possibilities. An illogical solution would obviously be "I want to eat the meal and then acquire it" which the quantum processors would naturally eliminate[16].

These exchanges of information occurred at the synapses in the brain where hundreds of trillions of such junctions resulted from the interconnection of about ten billion neurons. Of course a complete interconnection of each neuron with every other neuron, in pairs, would require a much larger number of synapses than a few hundred trillion. In fact that number would again be related to the mathematical function *factorial* of these ten billion and the result

---

[16] In a commonly used expression "to have a cake and eat it too", quantum computers were able to indicate the illogical nature of that statement which was then corrected in the popular culture as "to eat the cake and have it too" to indicate the desire of someone wanting to have it both ways. The correct sequence was logical as it described someone wanting the have cake even *after* having eaten it, whereas wanting to have it and *then* eat it did not reflect any incoherent intent.

would be written as $10^x!/(2 \times 10^y!)$, x being ten billion, and y being ten billion minus 2, all of this yielding to approximately ten billion square divided by two, an unimaginably high number. All these synapses are of course not needed and would in any event slow down the brain as they would an overburdened computer. However what is crucial is that when the brain needs a synapse that did not exist for a specific function, or because it determined that it needed it through activity in another synapse, the brain creates that interconnection either directly or through other synapses, just like a communications network. And that is how the brain learns. This phenomenon many believed was in fact the result of tunneling from one synapse to another, even a distant one, and a feat more easily accomplished by intelligent people, or sometimes mad ones in a perverted way of course.

Quantum computers performed in a similar fashion. Sensors were able to pick up waves traveling from one quantum junction to the other just as they would tunnel from one synapse in the brain to the other. These waves were thus observed as *tunneling* across distant unconnected junctions in the brain or distant unconnected quantum synapses in a quantum computer. The superpositions of these wave components led to thought analysis in the brain and thought emulation in quantum computers.

The theory of the superposition of a myriad extremely faint brain wave components, all elements of multidimensional matrices representing activity at the synapses and that formed the macroscopic brain waves with little specific information, had also ushered in an expanding field of research onto the quantum tunneling of these wave components, within the brain and outside it.

Within the brain *strange* interconnections were detected when normally unrelated components tunneled into each other and produced either incoherent thoughts, or sometimes the stroke of genius, the "putting the two and two together", the mother of intuition, of invention. A plaque on a wall in the conference center at Golog Maqen had one of Poincaré's famous sayings, but without any attribution:

"It is with logic that we prove, it is with intuition that we invent"[17]

---

[17] «C'est par la logique qu'on démontre, c'est par l'intuition qu'on invente»

Intuition and invention were thus believed to be the result of tunneling at the synapses between various seemingly unconnected areas of the brain. Madness of course was seen as a similar but corrupted phenomenon. It confirmed to some at least the old adage of popular lore that genius and madness were two faces of the same thing.

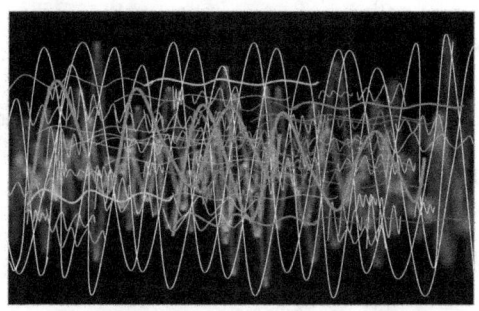

29. Two Dimensional View of Superposition
of Rudimentary Brain Wave Component

Outside the brain, pioneering research was conducted into premonition, prophesies, thoughts in life after death and other esoteric fields. In particular the survival of consciousness after death, hence the existence of the "soul" of religious lore was actively investigated in the Grand Caliphate.

The scanning of these brain waves allowed the determination of one's intentions and feelings and the results were used for political and ideological purposes. Further, the manipulation of these components through carefully placed *impulses of thought* as directed by the quantum computers, allowed a specialist to alter a subject's thoughts as desired. Of course these were extensive experiments that were done only on select subjects and were not a mass scale phenomenon either in the Empire or in the Caliphate.

Quantum Computers

Classical computers were based on the storage and manipulation of information elements called bits which could take the value of either zero or one. Quantum computers were later developed that is two centuries before these days and were based on

211

what was then dubbed quantum bits or *qubits*. These could be any quantum *superposition* of either a one or a zero, including strictly zero and one of course as in classical computers. The number of possible superpositions of these two states was found to be a function of the number of *qubits* and would grow exponentially as compared to a classical computer. The complexity of such computers delayed their effective implementation but when they finally reached operational capability their power was also exponentially higher.

Simply put, a *qubit* instead of having strictly a value of zero or one, had a probability of having zero and one simultaneously and any of the various combinations of these two states, albeit each of these states having a defined probability. While classical computers performed operations using binary logic gates, quantum computers manipulated the *qubits* utilizing quantum logic gates, which were based on quantum phenomena such as quantum superposition and entanglement.

Instead of the brute force application of sequences of various possibilities that classical computers were burdened with, quantum computers, inherently parallel machines, allowed the simultaneous consideration of various operations, or alternatives, just the way a human brain works. Not only did this method produce faster results, but solutions unachievable before such as mind and thought analysis which were prohibitive or just impossible with classical computing entered the realm of the possible. Artificial intelligence had finally found its platform.

Yu Lin could talk in prose, and verse, to his computer and this one would respond intelligently.

As communication nodes, quantum computers used entanglement to determine the state of a *qubit* which needed not be actually transmitted. And carefully calibrated perturbations produced correlated effects at a distance. Quantum communication rendered classical communication efficient and secure by only transmitting a correlation key that enabled the recipient to recreate the actual information, in a credible example of true teleportation of the information.

Meanwhile at Golog Maqen, young analyst Sun alerted his superior that he had observed an unusual pattern concerning some apparently organic material that occurred in various spaces within the Han territory and at various times. What had intrigued Sun was that the observed material seemed to have a signature that matched perfectly from one detection to the other. He had concluded that the material was moving and was not that of some waste material that was occurring at many places at the same time. He had also noticed that when observing the pattern at a certain point, he could not observe it at any of the previous points. This indicated transport, or movement.

His boss, Zhe Ha, asked him a simple question:

"How many samples have you seen?"

"Eight," answered Sun.

"Eight? Eight is nothing. You are seeing ghosts. Go get a million or two and then we will talk."

Sun respectfully withdraw, somehow disappointed.

3

PEOPLE'S COUNCIL

*A*fter a little over two hours Mehmut and Al Kansii rolled their NAV toward a small lake to the north-west of Manzhouli. They headed slowly toward a little house on the lakeshore and stopped.

They waited. After exactly thirteen minutes and twelve seconds from their complete stop, the door of the house opened. Five seconds later the NAV rolled toward the house and stopped midway. The meeting protocol, or code, had been met. Mehmut and Al Kansii stepped out of the NAV to be greeted by Yakub, of the People's Committee, who simply nodded at them. The door of the house was still open and Al Kansii could see in the doorframe the silhouette of a muscular man of medium height. Although no word had yet been exchanged, the four men entered the house and sat around a square table. Yakub said:

"Welcome to Manchuria. You must be the one from the Caliphate," looking at Al Kansii.

"Yes," was Al Kansii's short reply.

At that point Yan stood up and signaled to Mehmut that it was time for him to go. Mehmut stood up and looked at Al Kansii, with a bit of sadness in his eyes. They had travelled together through a world of different landscapes and history. The ride in the NAV had been almost magical, at least to Al Kansii. Without waiting for an invitation from Yakub, or permission to do so, Al Kansii suddenly stood up and embraced Mehmut who immediately after turned around and left with a sad look on his face and with eyes that to Al Kansii looked swollen.

Al Kansii then saw the large sphere of the NAV roll away from them. It was a strange sight. Although he had seen the holographic display of it while within the NAV via the troposcatter reflection technique, seeing it for real was truly worth it. A bit like the launch of a capsule from the *Ma Sling*, real life experience could not be duplicated by imaging, no matter how accurate. He thought again about what the Caliphate had missed by not developing the NAV. If he were to return he would definitely try to introduce such vehicle… but he wouldn't return. Al Kansii noticed that although his death had been planned and was certain, he still instinctively made plans for the future as if he were returning home. It was hard to avoid such natural reflexes, such instincts, even for a martyr.

When the three, Yakub, Yan and Al Kansii were back at the table, Yakub began:

"This is the plan. Later today we are to go to Qiqihar with our own NAV. There you will undergo facial reconstruction through quantum imaging to prepare you to enter the People's Council on behalf of our leader, the man you know as the *contact*. You will be him. In the meantime, I would like you to share with Yan your arsenal and its functions to ensure the success of the mission.

Arsenal

Yan took Al Kansii to another room where Al Kansii opened his leather case. Yan seemed surprised since he was not familiar with the devices it contained. They did not look like weapons as they were state of the art prototypes for the most part. Yan seized what looked more like a gun and asked:

"Is this the weapon?"

"No, it is a weapon but not *the* weapon," said Al Kansii while replacing the Ice Gun in its pre-formed hollow shape at the bottom of the case. "That's for emergency use. We won't use it again." He did not want to say more.

"So where is the weapon?"

"There. It is called a collimator, but they call it a *collimateur*."

"What?"

"Never mind. This device will focus the Mantle of the Angel of Death on the target."

"I see."

Al Kansii went on to explain the science and technology behind the Angel of Death and the *collimateur*.

"You mean this rays, these beams are already there?" asked Yan.

"They are everywhere. They are here too. They have been in the universe since the Big Bang. We just did not harness them for this purpose. Or for any purpose. As we speak fifty billion neutrinos went through our bodies and we didn't even notice them."

"It is truly an Angel of Death then," said Yan. "What happens to the person behind the *collimateur*? Is it safe?"

Al Kansii was surprised by the question. Did Yan care about him? Probably not. Yan was a soldier, he could tell. He did not seem to have many emotions. Al Kansii was a bit puzzled as to why he, Yan, wanted to know the effects on the person handling the *collimateur*.

"That's up to Allah," he answered.

"I see, of course. And this?" asked Yan.

"Oh this is the Single Pulse quantum gun. If everything goes wrong, then you can defend yourself with this thing or rather just *end* yourself and everybody around. It is very painful they say, but you can select your own hell."

"What does that mean?"

"You can accelerate your biological processes, or decelerate them by acting on your enzymes. You see quantum tunneling acts as an enzyme enhancer, or restrictor."

"But if you have to use it on yourself and you say it is painful, why not just use cyanide, and end with less suffering?"

"Because you exist afterward, I mean your body is still there and they can identify you and then trace everything back to the plot. With this, although painful, only your soul remains. And it goes straight to Heaven."

"I see. It makes sense. So the *collimateur* first, and then if things go wrong the Single Pulse right?

"Yes. Do you see any problem that could arise?"

"No, these two things should be sufficient. And how about this one?"

"Oh, the quark stream propagator. It is truly a prototype. Nobody knows exactly how it works or why it works. I was told to leave it alone unless... unless of course everything else fails. Then we might try it. It is possible that everything goes with it, including the whole world, or nothing if it fails. Who knows? I am not sure the scientists who developed it know either."

"Here are the power sources. I was told they would fit any of these. We will load them when we are closer."

"Yes. I was going to ask. Now, you say *we*, is that you or your colleague coming with me?"

"...Uh... you mean Yakub, yes he is going... with you. I am ... just his advisor, technical advisor."

"Wouldn't it make more sense for him to know about these then?"

"He is not very competent in technical things or weapons... he is a politician. He does not use weapons or wage war. He lets the others do it for him. But I will instruct him. I am the only one who can explain complex things to him in simple terms. He is just a politician. I think he used to be a judge, or a lawyer before. So he doesn't really understand. He is a politician now."

"I see."

"Let's get moving," said Yan.

The three walked to the rear of the house where an open bay showed a NAV. It appeared this NAV was more recent than Mehmut's. Al Kansii could tell. It just looked more streamlined.

The three stepped inside. This NAV had actually three seats side by side. And it showed no spokes in the middle. It was an empty sphere, and light from outside filtered through. It seemed very comfortable and pleasant.

Yan noticed Al Kansii's surprise.

"It is a newer model. No spokes. We have nano-plasma actuators which allow perfect control of the ride and a home atmosphere inside. These nano-propulsors all around, we control them with a mini quantum computer. That way we don't have these dangerous spokes and we can accommodate more passengers. This one is for three persons. Also the navigation is totally automatic, and it is maglev compatible."

"Maglev compatible?" wondered Al Kansii.

"Well, it is not a maglev vehicle, but it can ride, or roll in our maglev highways and therefore be integrated with the traffic control systems. So you don't have to divert your attention from your own activities. And, if you need to get out of the maglev system you can. The other maglev vehicles can't. They are like the trains of ancient times. They are stuck to their rails..." added Yan with a big laugh.

Al Kansii did not see the humor in these remarks but laughed slightly out of courtesy to Yan. Yan, calling himself a technician had that type of humor, that is an utter lack of it. And he had no warmth in his manners.

The NAV rolled smoothly south-east toward Qiqihar. The travelers' first stop was not the Annex Center but the Bukui mosque. Yakub told Al Kansii that it was the largest and oldest mosque in the HeilongJiang province, and that it preceded the city itself by six or seven years, he couldn't remember. In any event Yakub seemed proud that the city and mosque were over half a millennium old.

Al Kansii and Yakub entered the mosque and took some time to visit and pray while Yan, visibly not a Muslim waited outside and occupied his time reviewing the tools in Al Kansii's case. He appeared intrigued and perhaps concerned as well. He was concerned by the impact of the *collimateur* on the person handling it, almost as if he were the one carrying the mission. Al Kansii had already noticed this concern but could not discern any objective fact onto which he could latch its uncertain logic. Al Kansii was not after all a *conclusion* engine. He just felt something. He wished he could step out of his body and see reality as it was, but men had wished so from time immemorial when they sensed something but their brains wouldn't really tell them what it was.

Yakub and Al Kansii emerged from the mosque where they had prayed facing west. They seemed rested and at peace with themselves. Yan noted their serenity, something he knew he lacked. Perhaps in another life he would be a less robotic person, he thought.

Their next stop was the Qiqihar Annex Surveillance Center. Al Kansii asked Yakub why the Annex Center was located in Qiqihar and if there were functions that it carried that Golog Maqen did not, or vice versa. Yakub responded he did not know. Yan may have been right, Yakub did not seem to know much. As far as Al Kansii could tell, Yakub wasn't playing games or concealing anything. It seemed he truly did not know. Yakub was preoccupied by things other than science, technology or anything connected to reality such as surveillance. Al Kansii concluded, as Yan had indicated, that perhaps that was the way politicians and judges think, or fail to think.

The gates of the Qiqihar Center were guarded but their NAV seemed to have the proper authorizations. They stopped their rolling near a small building within the complex. It seemed an annex to the Annex. On its façade the words Quantum Imaging Laboratory were inscribed in what looked like a hand painted sign. Al Kansii was a bit surprised that such advanced science as he could guess was practiced within this lab did not confer on it more importance for it to deserve a professionally made sign.

Once inside, a professorial looking Doctor Zhu Shi greeted them without a word. Yakub and the doctor exchanged some whispering that Al Kansii could not comprehend and Doctor Zhu showed a few samples of faces on a holographic space. When Yakub seemed to acquiesce, Zhu gestured Yan to a room, and Al Kansii to another adjacent room. Al Kansii did not like the passive nature of these events, he was a man of action, but he had no choice. He could not get into the People's Council Chamber by himself. He needed these two strange fellows to help him do it. They were the contacts and he had to assume they were following the correct orders and were pursuing the same mission.

Al Kansii still kept wondering. Now, why had Yan got into a room? Yakub was obviously staying in the reception area. Al Kansii understood that his own facial features were to be altered to emulate those of the figure on the holographic display a few minutes earlier. How, he couldn't tell. The person on the display was visibly a Han, but Assam and Dromm had assured him that the Han knew how to do this. And his own research indicated that facial alterations could be effected and could last a few days or even longer. He had no choice other than to comply. Furthermore these people, even Yakub, were not very loquacious. It was difficult to extract words from them.

Al Kansii entered the room with his case.

About two hours later, Yakub was smiling as he greeted the new Yu Lin that emerged into the reception area with his leather case. He really looked like Yu Lin. Yakub thanked Doctor Zhu and the two, Yakub and the new Yu Lin, grabbed a personal maglev vehicle and headed out of the complex.

A Meeting of the People's Council, Long Ago

There had been numerous meetings of the People's Council preceding this one. A most remarkable one had occurred at the time of the opening of the Golog Maqen Surveillance Center when Yu Lin was asked to expound confidentially on the capabilities of detection by the Empire of the measures the Caliphate may have deployed against it.

"Comrade Yu, I asked you to brief the Council on detection methods beyond the obvious ones."

Yu Lin had stood and gone straight to the point.

"Yes Comrade Supreme Leader," said Yu Lin. "And that is a relatively weak point on our part, but we can turn it into an advantage.

"A transmission method developed long ago is that of neutrino waves, as you all know. I insist here on the words transmission method because we have reason to believe the Caliphate may have gone beyond communication or transmission into destruction, into weapons using that same method.

"As many of you know neutrino detectors, and please I know you know this but do not confuse with neutrons, which are the basis for our neutron bombs, which I will explain later in relation to quantum disintegration methods, as I said neutrino detectors are difficult to construct.

"Neutrinos have near zero mass, and no electrical charge. They are neutral electrons in a sense. They can travel long distances and once emitted here can be found on the other side of the earth almost instantly. They can go undisturbed through almost any obstacle made of ordinary matter, such as walls, mountains, even the entire Earth. Yes a neutrino can appear on the other side of the Earth. The fact that they can go through everything means they go through detectors as well.

"Initially then, the neutrinos had potential as a unique method for communication, especially for submarine warfare, as electromagnetic waves do not travel well in water, and acoustic waves have the limitations we know, and their use can be fatal as they are so easy to detect. Neutrino waves presented a great opportunity back then.

"Again, neutrinos can travel quasi infinite distances with no measurable attenuation, and they travel across the galaxy as well, undetected, or almost. That was the promise, and the problem. And in our case, the problem is exacerbated because of our geography.

"I say undetected. Not quite. Of course, how could one observe something, or determine the existence of that something if one cannot detect it?" Yu Lin paused for effect.

"Ah, that's when science is extraordinary. Over two centuries ago" continued Yu Lin, "a neutral particle was first *postulated* by one of those eminent scientists of the West, when the West was in its golden age. And it was postulated as a way to resolve conditions of conservation of energy, momentum and angular momentum when a neutron in an atomic nucleus decayed into a proton and an electron. In that decay it was observed that an additional particle was needed to complete the balance. They called it the neutrino, symbol v, the Greek letter *nu*." And Yu Lin wrote the following relationship on the holographic display of the Chamber:

$$p^+ + v \rightarrow n^0 + e^+$$

"whereby a neutrino causes a proton to decay into a neutron and a positron." And Yu Lin added:

"Of course anti-neutrinos occur when a neutron turns into a proton and an electron," as he wrote:

$$n^0 \rightarrow p^+ + e^- + v^{-1}$$

"Decades later, experiments confirmed the existence of an elementary particle that travels at close to the speed of light, and which carries no electric charge, thus the neutrino.

"What we know however is that neutrino interactions are governed by what is called the *'weak force'* which is of a much shorter range than the electromagnetic force with which we are all familiar, and we now use that particularity to enable detection. Of course many of those methods are classified as top secret, and I am not here to publicize those, assuming that all of us here would understand…"

A general and uncomfortable laugh was heard in the audience. Yu Lin carried on:

"The short range of the *weak force* enables the neutrino to travel enormous distances within ordinary matter, and as I said, undisturbed. Although they were thought, or even *postulated* as probably massless, it was observed that neutrinos have actual mass, albeit extremely small, and therefore interact with gravity, a still weaker force than the *weak force*.

"As I indicated earlier, a neutrino is produced when a decay of a nucleus occurs. When associated with a proton changing into a neutron, it is called an electron neutrino. Two other forms of neutrinos were later postulated, and then observed, the *muon* neutrino (ν_μ) and the *tau* neutrino (ν_τ). We are most interested in the *tau* neutrino, which is the heaviest, thus the most detectable." Yu Lin now paused for a long time in part for effect but also because he believed that what he was about to say was of grave importance.

"It has been observed," continued Yu Lin, "that electron neutrinos can migrate to the other forms under certain conditions. And that change allows detection while it is occurring. However and most important is the fact that the state of migration from one form to the other is not instantaneous. It lasts for a short, but finite time. It has also been observed, especially when several neutrino beams undergo this process somewhat simultaneously and within a common region of space, that a *mixture* of the three types of neutrinos can be induced and survives for a few units of Planck's time. What is remarkable is that if the inducement of the *mixture* is done near a neutrino factory, and if that factory produces entangled neutrinos, the mixture is recreated for those very few units of Planck's time somewhere else. Why is this remarkable?"

Yu Lin paused again to allow the members of the audience to catch their intellectual breath.

"It is remarkable," he continued, "because it was found that this *mixture* is very harmful to the basic atomic structures of the human body. It is so because rather than go through the body as any neutrino would normally do, for some reason this cocktail can induce decay within the nuclei of certain elements.

"It has been known for centuries that a chlorine atom converts into one of argon, and that germanium transforms into gallium, and the reverse is also possible, all these mutations being the results of the absorption or the production of a neutrino. In other words neutrinos can cause mutations within nuclei thus changing one element into another. For reasons not fully understood yet, as I said this *cocktail* can cause the nucleus of certain elements especially that of carbon, one of the basic ingredients of organic cells, to decay into the nucleus of the element boron, a metalloid. If we look at the atoms of chlorine and argon, two elements seating next to each other on the Table of Elements, one notices that both have an inner layer of two electrons, an intermediate layer of eight electrons and an outer layer with seven electrons for chorine and eight for argon. Chlorine also has 18 neutrons while argon has 22. Similarly the structures for the two neighbors, gallium and germanium, are very close to each other: 2, 8, 18, 3 and 2, 8, 18, 4 for electrons and 41 and 31 neutrons respectively, and these two elements mutate into each other when neutrinos take part in certain interactions.

"The carbon nucleus has two outer electrons and we believe the *cocktail* attacks these as a pair forcing it to become a nucleus of boron. When all these interactions caused by the neutrino cocktail take place, a general balance of neutrons, protons and electrons must result. The left-over particles combine, and cause other elements to mutate as well, this facilitated by ambient cocktail neutrinos, and this dance continues until all carbon atoms have disappeared and some residual material is observed.

"As a result leftover oxygen and hydrogen atoms combine to form water and an amalgam of various atoms and ions try to find their balance in the form of other elements or, in the case of leftover electrons or ions, in electrostatic discharges. The key point is that without carbon atoms the molecules that form the structure we know as the DNA molecule disintegrate. Without DNA and without carbon the human body, the flesh, the bones as we know them do not exist. Depending on the energy and number of neutrinos present, this disintegration can be more or less rapid."

After a brief pause, Yu Lin continued:

"If one can place a device near a human target that collimated such neutrino *mixtures*, which arrived from vast distances and can be manipulated from these same distances through entanglement, one can eliminate the human target, or animal or any other organic material, by causing all the atoms which compose that target to be afflicted by a transformation of their nuclei. The nuclei of these atoms especially carbon, become that of boron, or we have also observed, of nitrogen which lies next to carbon in the Table of Elements. As I said earlier the remaining electrons wander and locate themselves into other ions or basically produce somewhat large amounts of electrostatic discharges, and the hydrogen and oxygen atoms now free, combine to leave what they call a *puddle*. A human body can then be disintegrated into a puddle of water, or something containing water. Yes, some other metals and metalloids can be found in very small granules. Someone alive fractions of a second earlier, basically disappears. We believe the Caliphate may have perfected that weapon.

"Of course, and that is the good news, someone has to be present to eradicate a target. To our knowledge the entanglement although inherently possible at a distance, only commands the paired particle to undergo the same changes its corresponding particle far away is undergoing. However the targeting has not been achieved at a distance. It may be a matter of time, or perhaps prohibited by the laws of Physics. We do not know yet. What this means however is that someone or something has to be physically present with the target, and be able to receive the go ahead signal from the entanglers to aim.

"In addition, we do not know if all of this is even practically possible. We have no confirmation that detection, even within the safety of the Caliphate, can be done so easily and in an undetectable way, and we have not observed such attempts yet. And finally we do not know if they can combine the three neutrino flavors and entangle them, even for a short time. Theoretically it appears to make sense, but in practice, we don't know. The one thing we know is that the Caliphate *Al Andalus* where most of this research is conducted has lost an unusual number of scientists during secret tests.

"This is the state of affairs as of today," Yu Lin concluded

Yu Lin now paused and intended to stay silent until invited by the Supreme Leader to provide additional information to those assembled. He knew what Yan had reported. What he claimed he did not know, he knew. It was of little importance since soon none of the men present in the audience would exist if Al Kansii carried his mission as planned. Yu Lin knew that the Caliphate *Al Andalus* had broken through the technical challenges of the targeting by the device handling the entangled beam, and that the Grand Caliphate in *Ameristan* had mastered the detection problem and the entanglement challenge, at least as far as the needs of this specific mission were concerned.

Disturbing Thoughts

Yu Lin drank another glass of water. He was excited but getting tired. He was in his element. How he could shine! He knew. He even thought the Supreme Leader found him more intellectually capable than himself, which he in fact did. But the Supreme Leader knew something that seemed to escape Yu Lin. Intellectual prowess is not equal to power. Of course leaders are smart, but they need not be geniuses. In fact they shouldn't be geniuses and they seldom if ever were.

Yu Lin knew that *genius* was by force honest with science and reality. One cannot cheat the physical laws, the immutability of nature. One can manipulate people, and leaders for all known history had done so. They had manipulated the masses, the conquered, the rich, the poor, the fools and the smart. That was leadership. Not intellectual competence. Sad but true. So Yu Lin knew that the Supreme Leader felt safe even if the people assembled there considered that Yu Lin had a higher IQ. Yu Lin knew that of course but something inside told him that the time had come for true intellectual capability to prevail. He would change the nature of humans as they relate to their leaders.

What was a leader anyway? And why was someone a leader? These were important questions to Yu Lin. Most leaders know little of anything specific. But they know people. They attract a *following*, people ready to serve them. Intellectuals as Yu Lin sometimes had the opposite effect. By their smarts they attracted envy, jealousy and plain antagonism. A smart technocrat would rather have as a boss someone he knew was smart, but not too much, rather that someone he knew was a genius. Why? Yu Lin was not a psychologist, assuming psychologists knew anything about human nature of course. Maybe it was that smart people made others feel lesser, whereas smart, but not overly smart rulers that are decisive, and seem powerful were able to impose themselves. That is what had happened at the Council years before when the Supreme Leader had prevailed. Yu Lin had outshone everybody. Everyone knew it. They even commented on it afterwards. Yet, freely, they had chosen the Supreme Leader, not him.

Yu Lin knew that the Supreme Leader was not a simpleton of course, but besides his intellect he had *charisma*, *yin* and *yang*. Yu Lin had perhaps too much *yang* and not enough *yin*. He was also much shorter that the Supreme Leader, thinner and probably less strong. Maybe it was a primordial instinct that survived tens of thousands of years whereby a tribe would choose a leader that is strong and can get that tribe out of trouble with his bare hands, literally. And mankind had not yet evolved, from a cerebral point of view, to be able to recognize the superior forms of leadership for which Yu Lin believed the time had come.

But Yu Lin of course had a plan. He would make sure that the Empire would have a leader with the highest IQ among all pretenders. That would be a step forward for mankind. The triumph of intellectual capacity over insignificant skills.

Yu Lin recalled that the elites in the extinct West always derided their patriotic leaders as less intelligent than they were. They even called them dumb. Perhaps they were when compared to geniuses. But they really were no dumber than the charlatans of the so-called elites that informed the masses, and ultimately led them to their fall, or their revival as the Caliphate now described the events of two centuries before. Perhaps that revival was needed. No elite in the Caliphate or in the Han Empire derided their own. If they did, these elites would be no more.

In any event Yu Lin was ready. He could not go back. Although he viewed himself as politically savvy, he was a scientist at heart, and therefore politically not so competent. Lost in these historical and psychological considerations, his mind wandered. He was intrigued by Science foremost, and he began to try to understand how the Caliphate had been able to detect and control these neutrino beams.

Neutrino Factories

Detection of neutrinos had always been a problem since they were first postulated. The neutrinos are almost massless and have no electric charge. Since they do not interact with practically anything, not only they can go through planets and galaxies without being noticed, but they can go through detectors as well.

Of course quantum theory always permits certain neutrinos to be observed by a detector, since it is based on probability distributions. In order to detect a significant number of them, very large neutrino detectors were therefore built. To discern the neutrinos from other background radiations these detectors were also often built deep underground.

Since neutrinos can interact preferably with a heavier nucleus, changing it to another nucleus, and since the probability of interaction increases with the number of neutrons and protons within that nucleus, these conditions provide a way to detect the elusive neutrinos.

It was known that nuclear reactors always radiated a fraction of their energy as anti-neutrinos of which a small percentage was detectable if their energy were above a certain threshold, typically 1.8 MeV[18]. The rest traversed walls and disappeared into the Earth and went into the wide cosmos.

Similarly, particle accelerators could also make neutrinos. By smashing protons into a fixed target, the decay of the resulting particles when focused in long magnetic tunnels produced neutrinos beams.

The Caliphate had perfected these techniques and was able to produce electron neutrinos and *muon* neutrinos in its *neutrino factories*. Some rumors said that even beams of *tau* neutrinos were produced.

The Caliphate was also able to entangle the neutrinos in those beams by splitting them. It was also able to use the mutation of these neutrinos from one type to another and direct the mixing, albeit of a very short duration, of such entangled beams.

---

[18] An eV or electron volt is the energy gained by a single electron when it accelerates through an electric potential of one volt. A MeV is one million eV.

A technique carried by the international team known as OPERA (Oscillation Project with Emulsion-Tracking Apparatus) had used over a century before a long underground tunnel to route an intense beam of *muon* neutrinos generated almost one thousand kilometers from its detector. It was able to observe that *muon* neutrinos had mutated into *tau* neutrinos, when travelling at near the speed of light, and some say above this limit.

After being invited by the Supreme Leader to summarize the capabilities of the Empire as compared to that of the Caliphate, Yu Lin resumed:

"So neutrino detectors now allow a signal to go through and be detected with the proper equipment. In that respect the Caliphate has a main advantage since they control diametrically opposed territories on Earth. Look, they can send a neutrino toward the center of the Earth and collect it 180 degrees hence. But we are talking here of very large structures necessary for neutrino detection. In that respect we may be ahead of the Caliphate, and for space exploration, for studies in cosmology and such scientific endeavors, we have nothing to envy. However, it appears that small scale detection, or at least manipulation of neutrino beams may have been the object of some breakthroughs in the Caliphate.

"So while we the Han have focused on neutrinos for detection, if our intelligence is correct the Caliphate used it for the obliteration of its enemies. This concludes my remarks. Thank you for your attention."

The Assembly rose as one and began applauding. The Supreme Leader was also standing and applauding with a kind of paternalistic smile toward his childhood friend. He was happy for him, he was proud of him, he would do anything to help him. As Yu Lin applauded in return, his thoughts were not of gratitude but of desire, perhaps of envy, certainly of power, of changing history.

After the Supreme Leader had concluded that the applause was sufficient, as a follow-up question he asked Yu Lin to elaborate on what could be expected.

Yu Lin's response was concise:

"Comrades, if what I have described can be done, it is the same neutrino application that the Caliphate uses for what is called the Angel of Death, I am sure you have heard the term."

The audience stood in silence for what seemed an interminable time. At the mention of the Angel of Death, the assembled Council of the People knew of their vulnerability. One could almost feel the anger floating in the vast Hall of the People's Council, the anger at the fact that some brilliant scientific discovery had been turned into an instrument of death. The West had done that with the Han inventions centuries ago, millennia ago. They had turned fireworks into gun powder, lethal rockets, and firearms and went on to dominate the world before they were caught at their own game by the Caliphate. And now the Caliphate had, rumors said, a weapon they could just deploy like a mantle of death, ready to strike when that Angel desired. Sometimes, even when that Angel did not act. All one had to do to be stricken was to have the knowledge of the Angel.

Quantum Effects

Quantum effects. *Whatever happened to one particle would thus immediately affect the other particle, wherever in the universe it may be.* Theorists interpreted this phenomenon by stating that the *'knowledge of a state of a particle changes the state of its paired particle'. Spooky effects at a distance,* Einstein had called it.

Einstein did not believe this to be possible. He and his colleagues Podolsky and Rosen had devised what is known as the Einstein, Podolsky, Rosen (EPR) paradox. And they stated:

> "In a complete theory there is an element corresponding to each element of reality. A sufficient condition for the reality of a physical quantity is the possibility of predicting it with certainty, without disturbing the system. In quantum mechanics in the case of two physical quantities described by non-commuting operators, the knowledge of one precludes the knowledge of the other. Then either (1) the description of reality given by the wave function in quantum mechanics is not complete or (2) these two quantities cannot have simultaneous reality. Consideration of the problem of making predictions

concerning a system on the basis of measurements made on another system that had previously interacted with it leads to the result that if (1) is false then (2) is also false. One is thus led to conclude that the description of reality as given by a wave function is not complete."[19]

One elder on the Council volunteered, his age permitting him to speak even if not invited to do so by the Supreme Leader:

"The mystery and beauty of quantum science is used rumors say to disintegrate targets, literally. And targets could also be people. And there is no defense it appears, at least not with known science."

Intimate Thoughts

During the many pauses, Yu Lin could not take away from his mind the fact that he too was on a mission now. As much as Assam and Al Kansii. And Li Li of course, dear Li Li.

Talking to this audience of so-called decision makers, which were in fact less knowledgeable and less astute than the lowest of his students was depressing. How could the Han Empire be protected by such useless beings? Why was he there explaining to them the obvious? They were supposed to have known all of this. On the eve of the Caliphate unleashing the Angel of Death weapon, they barely knew it even existed and had no clue on how it worked. He had to explain it to them. What did they do during their waking hours? Nothing!

Of course that did not include the Supreme Leader. He knew. That is why he had asked him to summarize the situation in a concise manner and he had done so in just one sentence naming the Angel of Death. That was all these men in the Council understood. Now they were scared. And millions of their citizens who had put them there, and had given them all the privileges of their class, were at risk.

The Supreme Leader's sin was to have permitted this state of affairs. Of course the Supreme Leader knew these were useless apparatchiks. And these probably existed in the Caliphate as well. In

---

[19] A. Einstein, B. Podolsky, and N. Rosen, *Institute for Advanced Study, Princeton, New Jersey,* Received 25 March 1935; published in the issue dated May 1935.

fact they had existed always and everywhere. *There are those who do and those who talk about it.* Except he wasn't sure those people could even talk. Yu Lin was furious. He understood that political power had to do with compromise, and sometimes enlisting and cajoling fools. But he was a scientist, and the best brains ought to rule. That was it.

Especially that the Empire's survival was at stake. He, Yu Lin would not permit it. Even if the Supreme Leader had become a politician and was now playing by politicians' rules. He couldn't do that. No, not when the Empire was at stake!

Yu Lin felt a sense of pride in his mission. He needed that because more often than not, he felt a sense of betrayal. It was uncomfortable. In a way he liked those zombies, as he called them, they made him feel that his mission was justified, patriotic. And not one of greed, or envy, or of treason. No, the Han had to avoid the West's mistakes. Yes, thoughts of the West soothed his senses because then all of it made sense.

Under Yu Lin, the Han would not repeat their early mistakes either. Yes the Han had allowed the West to pursue the development of all their discoveries to dominate the world and force the Han into two centuries of dependency. These times were long gone. The West's insatiable appetite for cheap material goods had created a huge manufacturing boom in those days. This had financed the reconstruction of the Han economy and provided the basis for advanced research.

The Han were smart. They did not modify exorbitantly their standard of living, so the more they got from the trade with the West the more they saved and invested in the future, sometimes even acquiring Western assets and technology. The economic pressure on the West created declining living standards, which they could have easily overcome with some will, had they had it. But instead it created food panics, fuel shortages, riots and loss of confidence in leadership. It is true that the intellectual leadership of those places had been for a century fighting intellectual battles against itself. In the Han Empire, and even in the Caliphate Yu Lin had to acknowledge, these perverted minds were traitors. In the West they had been the elite.

"For example," Yu Lin thought, "in the skirmishes to annex Mongolia, Tibet and the Himalayas, clearly started by the Han, atrocities were committed. They were also committed by our adversaries. Nonetheless, Jug Chin, an 'engaged journalist' as they called him in those days, wrote forcefully and beautifully about how wrong the Han were. It took three days of trial to schedule his execution, which occurred a week later, a month before his appeal could even be filed with the Han courts.

"He was branded a traitor and the Han Empire flourished. In the West, returning war heroes were spitted on, aggressed, and traitors who opposed the national interest in war or in peace were lauded, idolized and even elected to the highest office." Yu Lin remembered a daunting example that was highlighted in history books for small children in the Empire, so that they would know forever.

"About one hundred years before the Fall of the West, a terrible attack on home soil by foreign agents took the lives of thousands. The crackdown that ensued, although popular at the beginning, did not last in popularity. Accusations of brutality and even torture were levied against their own by the so-called elites. These elites were the spoiled children of privilege. Insults to the military, to their truthful heroes, were the norm in the institutions of higher learning. This attitude paved the way for the downfall of the West."

That was the lesson taught the children of the Han. Should they not understand. Well, those who did not understand after thorough repetition and inculcation would end as the journalist Jug Chin.

"Of course the Han had precipitated the West's downfall," Yu Lin reminded himself. "Could they have been more careful, because now they faced a much more determined and stubborn and irrational enemy? Maybe yes, maybe not. As the thinkers of the Caliphate say, the West carried the seeds of its own destruction. One thing was sure, the Han would not repeat the mistakes of the West."

When the audience stood again and each of them made a point to come by and congratulate Yu Lin for his excellent presentation, Yu Lin could hardly conceal his disgust. He had just told them of their impeding doom and all they were doing was congratulate him on his presentation! And he knew they weren't even doing so because they had understood anything, rather they were buying favors from the Supreme Leader whom they knew had Yu Lin as his protégé. That reinforced Yu Lin's conviction that his mission was the right one for the Empire.

Meeting of the People's Council

Sinister conditions seemed to loom over the Empire. Something was in motion but no one knew what it was. Even the Golog Maqen and Qiqihar centers were reaching inconclusive results.

The Supreme Leader, based on apparently random alerts, and unconnected events, had called the meeting at the insistence of Yu Lin, since an actual meeting rather than a holographic conference was warranted based on the circumstances.

The Members of the Council were essentially the same as the ones who had heard the Angel of Death and neutrino speech by Yu Lin some time before. It did not matter in any event since except for the Supreme Leader, any detailed explanation to them was wasted words. Yes Chung, Sun, Liu Chi, Jao Ping, Zho Tang and the others were still there. It did not matter. Especially today.

The *Rapporteur* waited for a sign from the Supreme Leader and began reading from a *tablet*, which was immediately visible to all assembled via three-dimensional projections calibrated to face each member of the People's Council, regardless of their position in the room. Each member was equipped with a *personal connector* whose signature was that of their specific DNA code. As a result the Information Bureau could forward, alter, delete or segregate at will, in real time, any information to any member.

The Information Commissar was therefore all too important and resided in the suite adjacent to the presidential compound of the Supreme Leader in the *Forbidden City*. The Information Commissar could also spread false information and misinform. Although the Supreme Leader could override the Commissar's publications, he could not process all the information. A powerful, actually four powerful, decision engines, received all the data from the two Surveillance Centers and other *data entry points,* processed it and filtered for the Supreme Leader what was relevant according to *quantum keys* decided on a random basis by the Supreme Leader and known only to him. The Commissar was therefore at risk of being discovered should he attempt any miscalculated step. But the Commissar was also chosen at birth and nurtured in that role from cradle to grave, together with a group of about a hundred. Of these hundred *commisarets* openly disclosed to the Council, three were selected: one for active duty and the other two at undisclosed secret locations for back-up. They however monitored the information, providing an added level of security for the Supreme Leader while also standing-by for *redundancy.*

The Rapporteur read:

"An Explanatory Memorandum on the General Strategic Goal for the Group in North America."

This was an ancient text published by that "Group" decades before the Fall of the West and which highlighted the very steps it deemed necessary and sufficient to achieve their goal. Although the group in question seemed to have disappeared by absorption into the Caliphate's mainstream political machine, its influence both philosophical and political was the basis for the looming crisis and therefore of utmost importance to the Empire.

The basic concept of that philosophy was the takeover, or rather the destruction *from within,* of the tenets of civilization of the target society, and "to make God's religion, the True Religion victorious over all other religions."

The key point retained by all present after the Rapporteur finished reading the text was contained in the words *from within.*

The Supreme Leader then said:

"They won't give up. They want us to believe in their creed. We don't have a creed. Of course Confucianism, the search for *personal inner perfection,* is a sort of creed, but we don't export it. We actually keep it for ourselves. That's what makes us different, even superior. We know our truths, we do not insist on unenlightened people agreeing with us. They can if they want... Does anyone have any comments?"

No one commented. They all looked side to side to see who had the courage to say anything. They noticed Yu Lin had not yet arrived. And they knew that the first member to enter the Council Chamber was usually Yu Lin. That was what the Supreme Leader expected.

"Who are we missing?" said the Supreme Leader.

"Comrade Yu Lin's NAV is delayed due to an emergency alert from the Golog Maqen Center," announced the Rapporteur. "It will take ten more minutes before the alert is cleared."

"Yes, I know. While we wait, do we have any matters to consider?"

"I always said," said Dong Liu, almost with contempt, "we cannot trust anybody who wants to impose his creed. Why would they need our sanction, that of our conscience, to convince themselves they are right? It is a measure of the insecurity in their beliefs. And their insecurity creates a security problem for us, since they are dangerous."

"What are our alternatives? An all-out hot war? Cyber warfare? Infiltration? Diplomacy?" asked the Supreme Leader.

Dong had of course no answer. The Supreme Leader knew very well that to fight an enemy who would not compromise means a fight to the end, the end of one of the two. Diplomacy, and hope that these adversaries would change, was the only path. Yu Lin had usually interesting insights. But he wasn't there.

"Well," added the Supreme Leader, "we are not the ancient West with their naïveté. Attrition will not work for the Caliphate. We can wait them out. Sooner of later, and we are already there in a way, our technology will be light-years ahead of theirs and we will be able to undermine their order, and let them fight each other. We do not need them. We don't care what they believe. And I would not put it beyond probable a resurgence of the West. General de San Juan in Antarctica already is creating problems for them. And we intend to support him more aggressively and of course discreetly."

"Yes," said a little man in charge of *recent events reporting* upon the Supreme Leader's invitation to address the Council, "we learned that just three weeks ago, a religious center was bombed and crosses were painted on its walls. The Martel group I believe it is called. And they think they can achieve again what they did in eighth century Europe, or at least that is what their goal is."

"Are we helping them? And who are they by the way?" asked the Supreme Leader.

"We don't really know. Groups like this one pop out of nowhere and choose historically laden names. They change all the time. Maybe we are assisting them under another name. The Martel group is named after Charles Martel who defeated the Moors in the year 732 CE at Poitiers. And that was what stopped the triumphal march of Islam in Europe. It is obviously a name with a lot of connotations and a meaning that is not very popular in the Caliphate. So to answer your question, Comrade Supreme Leader, as such, under that name, we are not assisting them. But we will look into it to see what else we can do."

"We ought to be careful. Always careful. These people, which we do not control, may themselves lose control of their troops, their insurgents, or just lose control of their minds and create a conflagration we don't need. Our weakness, if I may say so, is that we value life, and they, or at least they say so, value death. That, and of course many other things, betrayal from within especially, is what outdid the West."

"Well, we don't have that," said the elder. "We are Han. The Han have an identity since the beginning of time. We do not include groups with no affinity with us."

"Comrade Tang," said another member, "but the Uyghur?"

"Yes I know. We have no choice since it is our buffer to the energy and mineral rich regions. And for now it is under control. Any news from Yu Lin," asked the Supreme Leader showing some impatience.

At this point the Rapporteur announced that Yu Lin's NAV had crossed the gates of the *Forbidden City* and Yu Lin would be there at any moment.

The new Yu Lin entered the room. He was followed by Yakub who was a few steps behind. For important meetings involving national security, and especially if the entire Council was present, it was politically savvy to invite an observer of the People's Committee, especially a Uyghur, to attend. Yakub therefore made his way into the Chamber with the new Yu Lin.

Everyone had a sigh of relief although no one really missed Yu Lin, more often that not they despised his special relationship with the Supreme Leader. But they were relieved that the Supreme Leader would not get into a fit of anger because of the delay.

For an unknown reason, instinctively, the Supreme Leader first looked at Yu Lin's feet, searching. Yu Lin was wearing the traditional Han silk robe that covered everything through the ankles. He wore that robe to all important Council meetings. The Supreme Leader was for some unknown reason surprised by Yu Lin's shoes, or rather his heels. The heels were shorter than usual. No one else of course noticed. Nor did anyone else than the Supreme Leader noticed that Yu Lin was a bit taller than he knew. He looked at his eyes. At the new Yu Lin's eyes. Then it donned on him and the horror on his face traveled to all others present who had all their attention on his face. Surprisingly both Yakub and the new Yu Lin shared that expression of horror, that expression of terror. The Supreme Leader searched for a word for a few microseconds. *Damn it!* he thought.

About fifteen minutes earlier Yu Lin in his cabin in Manchuria had received an encrypted call from Yakub expressing his concern at the delay. Their personal maglev had been stopped by an alert from Golog Maqen, as all other maglev vehicles in the city had been. No one could move. He was a few hundred meters from the gates of the *Forbidden City*. So close.

Yu Lin had not responded. Instead he had contacted Golog Maqen.

4

EXPLOSION

Golog Maqen National Surveillance Center, Earlier

*A*lbert stepped out of the MagLev station at Lanzhou and selected a two-seat NAV to ride to Golog Maqen. After following the normal formalities he sat across the desk from Zhe Ha.

"Nothing to report. All is routine. Nothing is happening. A lot of waste I guess. Maybe we should use our time to develop further techniques to reduce costs," said Zhe.

"I agree. But it's a good thing, don't you think?" answered Albert.

"Well of course, yes. A true emergency situation would justify our assets, but then it could prove devastating..." and then he laughed as if what he was about to say was truly funny:

"It's like in the ancient West, at least that's what we learn. Some people committed suicide after a few years just to make sure their life insurance policies were not wasted. Ahahaha!

"Well that is the reason we are told we should not need insurance. It makes no sense, the State takes care of us. And we are successful. We are the best society the Earth has ever seen. And the West... Ahahaha."

"Well I'll go check some systems so that my pay is justified," answered Albert as he was exiting Zhe's office, trying to laugh with Zhe at his insane joke.

"Oh by the way, if you need to justify your pay, go check with Sun," added Zhe. "He is a young guy, pretty naïve but well intentioned. He is seeing ghosts. A pseudo organic signature he says... Ahahaha," added Zhe.

"...Uh... I will," answered Albert, a bit startled.

As Sun was showing Albert the additional twenty samples that confirmed his theory, and which he discovered in contravention to his boss' orders to drop that line of inquiry, Albert grew more concerned.

Albert looked at the time. It was still an hour at least before Yakub and the new Yu Lin would reach the gates of the *Forbidden City* for the meeting of the Council. He wasn't sure he could delay the process for that long. He had to slow down Sun.

"Sun," he said. "It appears you may be right. But I don't want to look like a fool anymore than you do. Let me do a thorough check while you seek additional points. Let's meet in half an hour."

"That's good. I think the data is now coming in faster from the conclusion engines since their correlations are easier. I'll be back shortly," answered Sun.

As he exited the control room where Albert was to conduct his verification, he turned around and added:

"Thanks for your help. I was beginning to doubt my own capabilities. I truly appreciate your support in this."

"Oh, it's nothing. It's our job," responded Albert.

Albert began the analysis of what he already knew. He would find how Sun was able to identify and then track Al Kansii's whereabouts in the wilderness. He quickly found out that the leather case, made of true organic material, unlike the pseudo-organic composition of the devices of death that Al Kansii was carrying, had tripped the logical sensors of the quantum decision engines. A true organic mass moving around seemingly erratically was something to investigate further. And Sun had assiduously followed on this path.

About twelve minutes later, Sun returned, and in a very excited state.

"I have one hundred and four data points now, and they are converging into BeiJing at maglev speed," he said.

Albert was displeased that even the half hour he had bought himself was now gone. Although a half hour wasn't even sufficient by any standards in any event he remained calm and said:

"Let's see. Yes you have something. But we have time. I don't want to alert Zhe with false, or incomplete information. You know how he is."

"I know," answered Sun.

"Let's give ourselves another half hour."

"That's fine," said Sun.

Exactly half an hour later, that is about fifteen minutes before Yakub's maglev would reach the *Forbidden City*, Sun burst into the room. Albert was surprised that he had waited that long. He obviously did not want to disturb Albert again. Albert now had some time to work with.

"What do you have?" asked Albert.

"Over one million correlations," answered Sun triumphantly. "Boss Zhe said I needed a million. Let's go."

"Let's go," answered Albert, unable to delay any further.

The alert was sounded at exactly 9:44 am. Yakub and Yu Lin were expected at 9:54 at the gates of the *Forbidden City* for their meeting at 10:00 am.

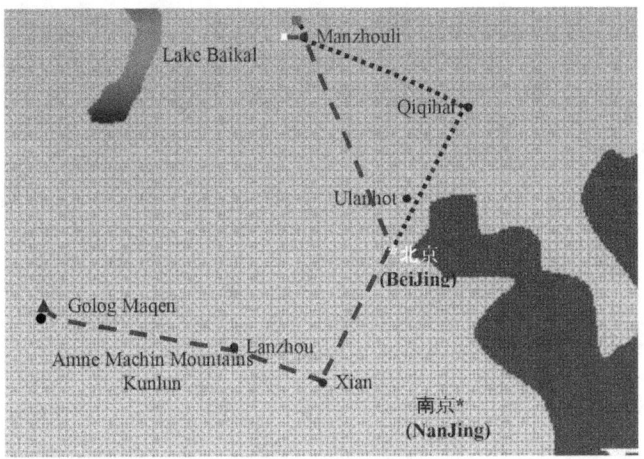

30. *The "New" Yu Lin-Yakub's and Albert's Concurrent Itineraries*

Zhe was proud of his assertiveness, his alertness and his command of the tools necessary for the security of the Empire. He made sure he sent a note to the Directorate for the Security of the Territory explaining how he had uncovered the threat and acted upon it at once.

A tone announced a quantum encrypted call to Zhe at about 9:56 am. It was Yu Lin: *"Need to enter the gates for the Council meeting. MagLev locked all across city. Unlock MagLev."*

"Yes, of course," was Zhe's answer. Zhe now expected a double promotion, one for identifying the threat and issuing a lock-out alert, and a second one for undoing it just for Yu Lin, the most powerful Yu Lin. Zhe was satisfied of his day's work. There was no waste in his labors.

And so a few minutes later than anticipated, at 9:59 am exactly, Yakub and the new Yu Lin entered the gates of the *Forbidden City*. They would be about three minutes late into the Chamber of the People's Council.

Yu Lin had thus ordered the lifting of the alert, only for *his* vehicle. *He* could enter the *Forbidden City*. Everyone else in the area surrounding the capital would be paralyzed for hours.

Many preparations had preceded this moment. A new Yu Lin had to be created, and willing to die for his cause, or at least not know of the consequences. How the new Yu Lin was created was the result of *quantum cosmetics* performed earlier at the Quantum Imaging Laboratory at Qiqihar.

Quantum Cosmetics

Qiqihar was one of the oldest cities in the north-east of the Han Empire as it had been founded in the late seventeenth century CE. Known originally as Bukui, *'the auspicious'*, it had given the mosque its name. It was an appropriate name for the city where the procedure of changing one's appearance to a more fortunate one, a more auspicious one, would take place.

Quantum Cosmetics was a very precise technique the steps of which had their foundation in classical oil painting. Just like in oil painting where a speck of paint of a darker shade of brown for example modifies a face, a smile or any other facial expression, quantum tunneling used as enzyme modifier was able to alter the apparent color projected by a specific cell and imply its shape in the most minute detail to achieve the perception of the desired image. Just like the modification of certain pixels would give a different picture, but in a less crude manner.

A base picture was first created by imaging analysis, and a computer simulated various alternatives from that base picture. So a person's image, the *before* picture could be modified say with fatter cheeks, specific wrinkles near the eyes, even modifying the shadow of the nose so that it would appear more or less prominent. When an *after* picture was chosen by the subject, the imaging technology would suggest a set of minute cell modifications that would alter the color, size or shape of certain areas of the skin to achieve the perception of the desired image.

Just like an artist does. Oil artists sometime act as if they were actual sculptors. In a sense they are. They deal with three dimensional blobs of paint that they distribute, move around, flatten, lighten and darken as they see their subject take different shapes depending on the minutest change made by their brushes. They move the paint as if they were sculpting. A little speck of light brown here and the person comes alive. A speck of a darker brown near the bottom of a cheek produces a smile. An almost unnoticeable change in the position of that speck would have the subject be serious, or even stern, or sad. Wonders were made by artists throughout the centuries using these secrets. The wrinkles at the outer ends of the eyes were a particular area of cosmetic flexibility that artists had exploited in years past. The shape, prominence and roundness of the cheeks also could show emotion, and character. And of course intricate details of the mouth determined other defining features of the subject.

Just as a little move there and a little light here showed a different person in a painting, quantum resemblance imaging techniques emulated these methods by tunneling a few atoms so as to produce the necessary shades, but also slight shape and size differences. Of course there were limits. A huge jaw could not be erased, a prominent nose could be attenuated but only by so much, but for routine applications, and especially to appear as someone else to people less familiar with the original subject, this was a quick and easy technique and definitely safer that genetic manipulation with its side effects and length of adaptation that the latter required.

Of course quantum cosmetics modifications did not last long. Depending on the intensity of the desired changes, they would last from a few days to two or even three weeks. That was ideal for infiltration purposes, where an agent could look Han, if one did not look too closely and a Han could look anything of the myriad faces in the Caliphate. At the end of the mission the agent was able to return home, and return to his own features without any noticeable side effects.

After the procedure at the Quantum Imaging Laboratory, Yakub and the new Yu Lin were on their way to the Qiqihar MagLev train station. They did not take the MagLev Artery to BeiJing. Instead they selected a two-seat private maglev vehicle, which would follow the Artery and would engage in the local maglev grid once in the capital. From there they would reach the *Forbidden City*. Based on the traffic system computers, their arrival at the gates of the *Forbidden City* was scheduled to be for 9:50 am.

Early that morning, Yakub and the new Yu Lin had strapped themselves into their maglev vehicle and proceeded south, due slightly west along the MagLev Artery toward the Capital of the North, BeiJing. Had they boarded a high speed Maglev toward BeiJing, their identities of course would have been recorded and all their vital signs entered into the vast intelligence network. In a private maglev vehicle, it would be less probable and subject to a certain delay in processing by the conclusion engines.

Within less than three hours they had reached the outskirts of BeiJing without incident. They used the automatic switching system that took them out of the Artery into the local grid and floated, or hovered toward the *Forbidden City*. About three miles south was the Hotel Bukui where Yakub used to stay for meetings such as the one he was about to attend. He would not go there this time nor to any other hotel. Yes, the Hotel Bukui had a small prayer room which they called the *mosque* and which was useful for his daily prayers, which he needed when dealing with the inflexible, in his view, Han hierarchy. But he would not miss the *boxes*, the enclosures measuring two meters in length by one and a half meter in width by one meter and eighty centimeters in height, that were offered to the guests and that were affectionately called the *coffins*. He would not miss the communal showers either. This visit would be a quick one. What Yakub did not suspect was how quicker than he thought it would be.

When the maglev vehicle abruptly stopped less than a hundred meters from the gates of the *Forbidden City*, Yakub was alarmed. He looked at the new Yu Lin, and only saw an imperturbable face. Yakub just remembered that whatever would happen to him in the Chamber was up to Allah. He knew that already. The question was: what did Allah plan this time? In his last prayer, Yakub thanked God for his mercy, and he had begun dreaming of glory for his deeds on behalf of his cause, his people. His idea of glory was grounded in this world, not the next. It was "in Allah's hands" Yan had told him.

With these thoughts of apprehension, made more acute by the abrupt freezing of the maglev system, Yakub decided to send an encrypted message to Yu Lin.

Usamabad, Roughly at the Same Time

On the other side of the Earth, Assam received that message. It needed to be decoded of course. All the devices in Al Kansii's case were programmed to relay any signal that emanated in the immediate vicinity of the case if they were emitted within a hundred meters of the *Forbidden City*. Assam knew that something was happening to Al Kansii's mission. A few minutes later Al Kenii informed him that the maglev system had been frozen around the capital and that Al Kansii was still outside the *Forbidden City*.

Would Assam enact remotely the Single Pulse that would destroy all within Al Kansii's vehicle? Assam could not afford to see Al Kansii taken before he had had a chance at his own self destruction.

Assam decided to wait until four minutes before the target time, that is 9:58. At 9:57, the maglev vehicle started to slide toward the gates of the *Forbidden City*. Assam did not confirm the destruction command. As Assam would learn a few moments later, it was a good decision. Allah was on his side.

The *collimateur* that entered the Chamber with Yakub and the new Yu Lin depended on the ability to detect the neutrino beams produced at the neutrino factories in the Caliphate and entangled in pairs, one member of which was detected within the Caliphate, the other somewhere else. The *collimateur's* function was to act on the other member of the pair following that detection. This function was facilitated by the detection within the Caliphate and once a member of the pair was detected, the other member could be assumed to have been detected or at least behaved as such. All the *collimateur* had to do once the parameters of that detection were known was then to focus the beams into a specific area. Detection by the Caliphate of the first entangled member of the pair was thus key.

IceCube

Various detection methods had been used for centuries. They were all based on early methods developed in the West, and that were enhanced and refined. A landmark detection system was developed in the deep ices of Antarctica and was called The Ice Cube Neutrino Observatory, and simply known as the IceCube.

The IceCube, and other projects in Antarctica such as AMANDA used the thick Antarctic ice sheet near the South Pole with photomultiplier tubes distributed throughout the volume of very deep cavities dug into the ice.

All these detectors took advantage of the Cerenkov radiation, a sort of blue *halo* produced by the high energy particles around the photomultiplier tubes.

Collimateur

The function of a collimator is to gather scattered beams of light into a coherent arrangement of rays and parallel to a certain direction. The *collimateur* was in fact almost the opposite. The neutrino beams were already ordered by the action at a distance on their entangled companions. The *collimateur* job was to focus them on a target. It could not pinpoint a specific target, just a general area. Consequently, all organic matter in its neighborhood was to be affected.

Annihilation

The explosion was rather soft. In fact it wasn't an explosion at all. The disintegration of the nuclei of the carbon atoms bonded to the molecules that formed the DNA structure of all present had perturbed these structures. This chain reaction had commenced in the case carried by the new Yu Lin and spread within a circle or rather a sphere with a radius of about twenty-two meters. The impact zone included of course the walls of the Council Chamber. All were sublimated. No one existed any longer. No one existed within a few Planck's units of time, that is in seconds, forty two zeros and a one following the decimal point. The actual disintegration of the bodies and all organic matter in the Chamber was of course gradual but swift overall. The Chamber's doors and walls were lined by several layers of lead, interspersed with tantalum. The neutrinos' probability of escape was therefore reduced. That of entering the room was itself attenuated, but the two large doors had allowed in the new Yu Lin and Yakub, and with them an army of neutrinos produced by the Caliphate's neutrino factories and paired through entanglement with those thousands of miles away. There was therefore a sufficient number of particles to allow the probability distribution to collimate at least some entangled neutrinos. In other words, this was sufficient to annihilate all in the Chamber.

Several hours later, the Security Chief had decided to enter the Chamber, after having ignored reports of a certain hiss within it shortly after Yu Lin's and Yakub's entrance. What the Chambers guards found was nothing. Strictly nothing. No one was there either of course.

Large gaps in the walls were observed by the attendants who were rushed by Security. The marble floor was intact as were the metal buttresses that radiated in a semi spherical shape forming a dome on the ceiling. This remaining structure had prevented the collapse of the building. The Security Chief's first reaction, which he kept to himself, but denoted a self-centered obsession, was that this situation was preferable to that of a neutron bomb as in the present case no bodies were to be collected.

Assam received confirmation by 10:40 a.m. BeiJing time that the Cerenkov radiation observed after the *incident* resulted indeed from the anticipated source. Under his orders, the house on the north-west of Manzhouli where Al Kansii, Yan and Yakub had met was obliterated by a loud explosion, a traditional act of sabotage. With this, the true Yu Lin Assam had ensured was gone. All that remained from the plot was Lili. And she was still in the Caliphate according to the intelligence Assam had received. The head of the snake had been cut off. The snake had been decapitated. The new power structure did not belong to Yu Lin and Lili as these two had wished. And Khaleed Ashgahar in XinJiang Uyghur was ready. That was Assam's plan. He thanked Allah for his mercy and waited.

Meanwhile Yu Lin in his cabin north-west of Manzhouli enacted his mind to reach the Assistant Rapporteur. He informed him of a kidnapping by foreign elements that had saved his life. Unfortunately as he explained, the Golog Maqen alert had been issued too late to save the leadership. He ordered the Assistant Rapporteur to *extend* the Supreme Leader's life for another two months. Order was needed in the Empire. He would assemble a new Council. Meanwhile he ought to remain in the safety of secrecy, clandestine.

The Assistant Rapporteur was relieved. His trembling voice had sounded to Yu Lin as if he had been in a total panic moments before.

The Assistant Rapporteur's entire life edifice had suddenly collapsed with the disintegration in the Chamber. What was going to be the reaction of the vast population? He needed a buttress, a pillar, a cane, anything to hold on to. And that was to be Yu Lin, an important government official. He was truly relieved that someone, anyone, would lead the nation out of this misery. And that that someone was Yu Lin, the brilliant Yu Lin, only God, if there was a God, would have permitted such blessing amid such calamity.

A leader, any leader. And Yu Lin would be the best. Yu Lin had the feeling after he ended the conversation with the Assistant Rapporteur and issued his orders that had he been present the Assistant Rapporteur would have gone on his knees and kissed his feet. Yu Lin's contempt for the human condition grew only bigger. Why do these animals need a leader? And why was he a leader? He was sure that his intellectual capabilities, or even his physical strength, which was little in any event, were not the basis for the Assistant Rapporteur's veneration of him. It was his need for a leader, as most have a need for a guide, a chief, a leader, and outside the Empire, for a father, for a God.

It was so simple. He had imposed himself through a complicated plot, granted. But Yu Lin began to think that without a plot of this magnitude he could have accomplished the same by inspiring the confidence and security these people lacked. Because of the insecurity that was deep seated in the hearts of the people, big and small, everyone needed a leader, Yu Lin concluded, except of course the leader himself. Projecting his thoughts to the Caliphate he concluded that there, in addition, everyone needed a God, except God of course.

A world of sheep. A world of followers. As they all submitted to something or someone else, he Yu Lin was now in command.

In Usamabad meanwhile Li Li had arrived earlier at the *Ma Sling* magport and shot upward toward space. Within three hundred and eighty seconds she was space born and hovering under *sail power* waiting for the Earth to rotate eastward and position the capsule past the Kingdom of the Rising Sun of the Han Empire and then toward Manchuria. A swift action of the *plasma actuators* accelerated the capsule just above the atmosphere. Reentry was soft and Li Li landed within forty minutes of her departure.

Li Li had been able to evade the detection at the Usamabad magport. Agents were placed that were looking for a woman with Li Li's DNA. No woman had been seen boarding the capsule with the Empire as destination. No man, or woman disguised as a man, with Li Li's DNA had gone through the scanners, which were set in what was called *cascades*, that is a series of scanners aimed at reducing errors and countermeasures that would foil detection.

Li Li had thus evaporated from the Caliphate.

A NAV had picked Li Li up at the spaceport in BeiJing, where she arrived after a short supersonic flight from DongJing, and she had headed toward the old cabin where Yu Lin awaited her. Li Li and Yu Lin would be occupied with organizing a proper Council, and establishing the proper rules to govern the Empire in the short time Yu Lin had given himself through the *extension* of the annihilated Supreme Leader. In two months the decision engines would stop emulating the Supreme Leader thoughts and desires and these would no longer be generated, the processes of these engines being disabled and the Supreme Leader declared *departed with full life*. That meant gone forever, dead.

Preparations for a state funeral were made and scheduled six months hence, after the turmoil, and passions if any, were tempered. Of course these were few as the event was noticed only by those close to the *Forbidden City*.

Cerenkov

Amid the initial euphoria in Assam's circle, there was a problem. The Cerenkov radiation had indicated that the incident had taken place, but no sign of Al Kansii's actual death had been received, as planned. Further, no official communiqué had been issued announcing the explosion in Manchuria, and thus the disappearance of Yu Lin. This should have been routine since Yu Lin was not slated for *extended life*, a privilege normally accorded only to the Supreme Leader. There was therefore no reason to delay the announcement. Of course the Han may have had some other reasons, or in the panic in the *Forbidden City* they had omitted for now such announcement. Assam decided to remain calm and wait, but these two unknowns disturbed him.

The Cerenkov radiation was picked up by the Han satellites and the Caliphate satellites. It had emanated for a very short time from the Chamber of the People's Council. They both had the same information. It meant of course much more to the Caliphate.

The Cerenkov radiation is a bluish glow that is produced in the vicinity of sites where reactions involving high energy particles take place. It is a result of the equivalent of shock waves one observes, or hears with sound, but for light waves. It is well known that light travels at the speed of light c in a vacuum and that c cannot be exceeded. However in another medium with a certain refractive index, light travels more slowly, in fact at c/n, if n represents the refractive index. In some reactions certain particles while still travelling at speeds lower than c, can travel faster than c/n and this phenomenon creates the shock waves leading to the Cerenkov radiation. The bluish aura can be seen around nuclear reactors and in the installations for the observation of neutrinos in Antarctica. It was observed in the Chamber of the People's Council.

To those who were annihilated in the Chamber the Cerenkov radiation gave an aura of saintly state, a true halo. Of course no one was there to observe this ascension to sainthood, and the halo was not bestowed on anyone's head since all present had disintegrated. But the aura was observed from on high. By the satellites of the two Empires, as a faint but unmistakable glow.

To the Han satellites, being closer to Earth and with almost normal incidence to the *Forbidden City*, the Cerenkov signals were stronger and more defined than to the Caliphate's distant equatorial system for which the angle of view to the Chamber, the *elevation angle*, was much lower.

The Caliphate could conclude with some delay that the *explosion* had to have caused the obliteration of the People's Council, and Al Kansii's as well. Neutrinos had imparted energy to protons to turn them into neutrons and positrons. Neutrons had decayed into protons and electrons with emission of antineutrinos. Carbon atoms in particular had mutated into other elements, especially boron, and hydrogen had combined with oxygen, massive electrostatic discharges had accounted for the electrons left hanging and photons had been emitted. It was all as expected. And the faint glow of the Cerenkov radiation was evidence that the processes had taken place as anticipated.

One implant that had been in Al Kansii's brain monitored his brain waves and was expected to issue a single pulse when he would perceive the Cerenkov glow. It was programmed to do so. It would confirm that Al Kansii had been obliterated. That he had seen his own death. That he had truly become a martyr.

What was of concern to the Caliphate was that Al Kansii had not communicated through that implant. It was a simple device and there was no reason for its malfunction. Al Kansii's eyes and brain would certainly have been able to observe for an infinitesimally short time the Cerenkov radiation. The implant was programmed to detect that sensation and transmit a signal via satellite. The signal was short, just a few bits repeated several times and the repetition of which was encrypted thus ensuring some of the signal would get through, even assuming that the Han had already begun interception and jamming techniques, which was unlikely at the time of the emission of the Cerenkov radiation. Al Kansii had thus not notified the Caliphate of his own death, although this notification was to have occurred. There was no explanation for its absence.

Theory of Death

Brain science had concluded that all thoughts, which can be traced to chemical reactions between neurons in the brain, are carried by faint waves, commonly referred to as *second order brain waves* or sometimes *higher order brain waves*. These waves were not unlike electromagnetic waves, but could not be characterized as such. Their nature was still debated. It was originally believed that waves produced by a brain would die out immediately upon death. Then current research postulated that what was referred to as *thought waves* were *higher order brain waves*, and these were able to transmit information between the thought originating brain and another subject at a distance, and that explained in part attraction and repulsion between and among human beings. It also explained at least in part some phenomena such as telepathy which was of course mostly a hoax, although in some cases the evidence was perplexing. One known example in the popular culture was when a member of a pair of twins *felt something* when the other half of the pair died, even when the two were separated by vast distances. *Spooky effect at a distance,* just as in Quantum Theory.

This was not new, nor hard science. It had however been established that the brain acted as, in fact was, an advanced form of a quantum computer. The first consequence of that statement was that processes within the brain, especially thought processes, were not simply the result of sequential, one-dimensional neurotransmissions at the synapses but rather the culmination of a myriad parallel such processes acting in a coordinated overall whole. Two important conclusions followed: one was how quantum tunneling applied to thought processes and two, was quantum entanglement limited to the regions of the same brain or could it also apply to the outside of the brain. In other words could the brain equivalent of a *qubit* in one brain be entangled with a *qubit* in another brain, or in fact any another location outside the brain in question.

What was intriguing and inconclusive yet was whether these *thought waves,* or these quantum states containing information, vanished exactly at the moment of a person's death. In other words whether when a person's brain would cease to function, would the information in his brain die immediately, as it was normally assumed in the past? It was common knowledge that some animals sense their own impeding death and prepare for it by laying down in a peaceful resting place and fall asleep on their own, as if they were inducing their own unavoidable death. A person normally does not behave like this, although premonition of death following a long disease is common.

The challenge for brain waves specialists was to determine what a person felt when death arrived, especially if death was slow. It was known that many on their death bed pronounce important facts, or commands, even confessions. They seem to know what is about to happen, because the process has begun. So it can be assumed that a dying person can see death approach slowly, communicate with his surroundings, and observe the events as they occur. The question then was: when does that person quit observing his own death? That was one of the key questions under investigation.

Certain theorists argued that as death slowly progresses, the *thought waves* inform the subject of the events that are happening. If one breaks down the time of death into infinitesimal time slots, just as physicists do when they analyze the beginning of the universe, or any other quantum effect, one can plot the travel of the *thought waves* in small increments, all preceding death. The question then becomes: when death finally occurs, that is when the brain ceases to function, are there any remaining *thought waves*? Do these lay around just a bit more? In other words, does the subject witness his own death, totally, is a witness to the end? Does he see himself dead and then dies? Or does he just die and thus does not see himself die?

If the first proposition is true, then there is a probability of witnessing one's own death past the time of that same physical, medical death. An experiment that pioneered this research consisted of wiring a dying brain and recording the remaining brain waves and analyzing those to detect *thought waves*. An application of these techniques was proposed and consisted of installing a small implant in the brain of a subject and program it to transmit a message that would reflect the subject's thoughts, no matter how faint, at or after the event of death. The subject would in effect be informing the living world that he had died some time before, of course assuming that *thought waves* survived death for at least a short time.

That was the essence of the implant into Al Kansii's brain and that was to inform the Caliphate of his death, by his own brain, *after* his own death. In that way there would be no equivocation concerning his death, none.

Of course the whole theory was based on the existence of non zero, detectable *higher order brain waves* after death. Brain waves theorists naturally focused on whether brain waves could tunnel past the barrier of death. The two corollaries of that assumption were first whether they could be reflected by that *death barrier* and inform the dying person, or any other detector, of his impending death; and second when these waves were to tunnel forward through the death barrier whether they could then communicate with the living the thoughts of the dying person, of the dead person, *after* his death.

The analogy with quantum tunneling applied to brain waves was based on the fact that the same way a particle tunnels through a forbidden barrier and is often on the other side, a component is also reflected, these phenomena being due to the probabilities given by their wave functions. The analogy was also extended to the case where a wave was incoming onto a *barrier* that is below the forbidding limit, in other words not a barrier at all in the classical sense, and thus classically should not reflect the wave. In this case, classically at least, the entire set of particle probabilities lie on the other side of that *non-barrier* and the probability of reflection is zero. It is an observed experimental fact that for quantum states, reflections are observed even for barriers that are not barring anything. This analogy was extended to that particular case as well.

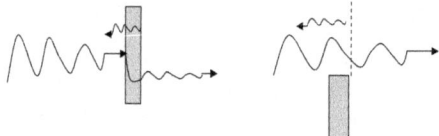

31. Behavior of Quantum States in the Presence of Two Types of Barriers

For brain waves though it meant that when the death barrier begins to form, but is still a distant event, brain waves need not cross it since the subject is still alive, but the death barrier does reflect the waves, probabilistically. And the closer to death, the higher the degree of *forbiddance* and as one approached death the more brain waves announcing one's own death were reflected, out of thin air. Scientists called it *quantum premonition* the same way they called the corresponding effect after death, *quantum conscience survival*. And of course some have a very acute capability to reflect from unseen and not forbidding barriers, and some can even see the reflections of someone else's death barrier.

If such tunneling occurred in both directions as it was postulated, one could therefore understand the premonition of death reported from time immemorial, and out of body experiences of popular lore.

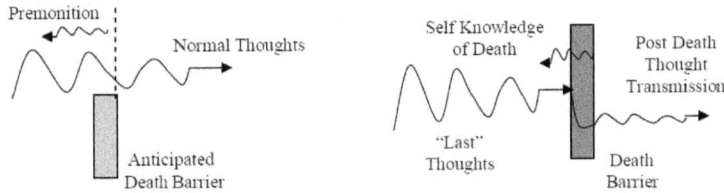

32. *Pre- and Post-Death Communication via Tunneling through Death Barrier*

The forward tunneling on the other hand was seen as dependent of course on what *thoughts* remained after death, the soul of one's being, and that were physically allowed to persist for some time until the normal attenuation of the wave through time and space rendered it so faint as to be extinguished. Then and there the person was to be definitely extinguished, or as it commonly referred to, dead.

Survival of Thought After Death

One other important question on which the brain waves theorists focused their energies was the intensity of the surviving brainwave, and particularly whether that strength was the same for all people, regardless of age, ethnic origin, intellectual composition and other factors. One thing that was discovered is that certain individuals kept their brain waves for much longer periods than others, while most extinguished theirs within a few short instants beyond their physical, medical death. Those who maintained their wave presence for long periods of time were able to be *heard* or *felt* by their immediate surroundings. It was therefore assumed that prophets, saints, and other special individuals who were said to have resuscitated from the dead for short periods, may have had particularly strong brain waves that could have continued emanating energy toward their neighbors well after their death.

Another school of thought was based on the fact that the intensity, that is the amplitude of the brain waves was not the differentiating factor between the inconsequential dead and the unique dead. It was the attenuation coefficient of the wave, within a minimum amplitude of course. This was illustrated in the comparative diagram below, which exhibited attenuation of the amplitudes for normal, sub-normal, and supernormal conditions:

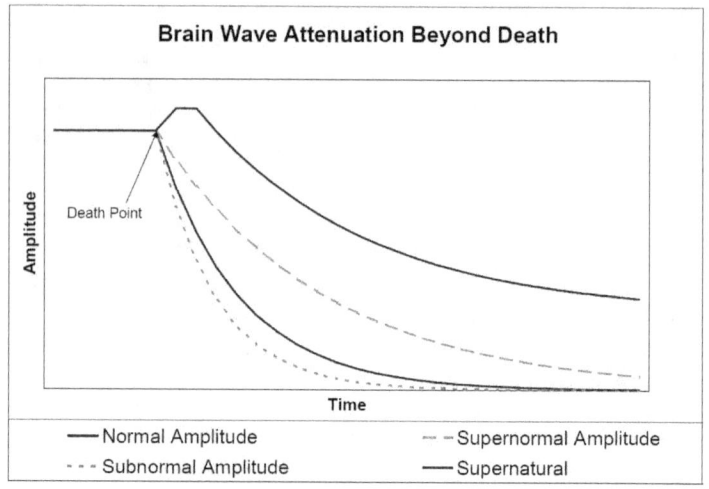

33. *Attenuation of Brain Waves post Death*

Of particular interest of course was a very contested result that exhibited a spike in the amplitude of the brain wave immediately after death and which was followed by a very slow attenuation, if any, over a very long period of time. This particular curve, again contested by many, was dubbed the "supernatural" condition and led some to ascribe a divinely inspired character to the person, very rare indeed, on whom such condition was purportedly observed.

A similar diagram for various animal species showed attenuations dropping quickly to zero except for upper mammals for whom the curve lied in the region below subnormal for humans. Some theologians contended for good measure that that alone indicated the existence of a soul for humans, and of their special *divinely inherited* character – in *God's image*. Of course it also supported other theological contentions that reincarnation of humans into certain animals does occur at subnormal levels.

Survival of thought, post-death, was not limited to the analysis of the quantum tunneling analogy. Quantum entanglement provided research scientists another powerful tool to investigate the survivability of the thought and perhaps even its immortality, linking what religious people had traditionally called the soul to what certain scientists referred to as the universal consciousness. It went as follows.

It was established that the brain acted as a most sophisticated quantum computer, and that information *quanta* in certain parts of the brain were *entangled* with paired information *quanta* in other parts of the brain. The obvious example of that interaction was the popular "putting the two and two together", the mother of all intuition and induction and thus of invention. Only humans were apparently capable of that feat. Humans could conceive mathematical abstractions, music, poetry and accomplish other achievements that were not grounded in the physical, tangible reality. Their brain was also self aware. The question then was whether this entanglement ended within the confines of a single brain, or whether it extended to other brains, or even other receptacles of information in the entire universe, or no receptacles at all, just in the universe.

Extension of the brain analogue of quantum entanglement to nearby brains in popular lore could be observed in telepathy, team work, and actions in the heat of the battle when at war, and other examples. Proponents cited paradoxical situations when the strongest team could lose a sports game, or a stronger army was defeated by a weaker one and so on. But these were anecdotes, not science. What scientists focused on was the *measurement* of faint thought processes just outside the brain and their impact on neighboring brains. These were not necessarily human brains but scientific instruments which emulated those and were able to record thought processes in nearby human brains. The results of course were disturbing as they posed significant ethical, philosophical and religious questions.

Of importance though was the general consensus that entanglement of thoughts of a brain was not limited to only other parts of that same brain, but in fact extended beyond. The extrapolation that that *beyond*, in space and time, needed not be a specific physical location, such as another living brain, but anywhere, gave of course rise to speculations on the universality of thought and of consciousness, and hence on the immortality of thought from a physical point of view.

So the thoughts of some were still alive not just because we think of them, or recall their deeds, say their music or their writings, but because these thoughts were still floating in the universe as information *quanta*, maybe in the form of faint waves, and which were entangled with our own. Some of course said that the soul therefore had a physical presence, perhaps not material, but physical nonetheless.

Additionally, proponents of entanglement of brain waves among various individuals or among species cited a perplexing phenomenon. This phenomenon is as follows. When two persons communicate they look each other in the eyes first, instinctively. When an animal meets another animal, or a person, the first contact, the first exchange is through the eyes. Even birds look first at the eyes of a person to evaluate the situation. Even cobras. If one were to assume that a cobra wants to know what a person is going to do, whether that person is a threat or not, if so, why does the cobra first look at the eyes? What makes it focus on the eyes of the other being? How does the cobra know that to communicate with another living being one must do so by looking at the eyes? How does it know that the eyes of a person are its primary communication link? In fact it seems that the cobra instinctively knows that if there are no eyes, it is probably not a living being, like a rock or a machine, hence it presents no interest such as a threat, or a source of food. What thus makes living souls communicate instinctively through the eyes, as if this were the primary communication channel?

Religious people of course attributed that phenomenon to the fact that God's creation links all living souls and is therefore proof of His existence. The scientific school of thought on the other hand first explained that evolution obviously left inherited characteristics that in that instance manifested themselves through that preferred communication channel. The new science theorists advanced the thought that all elements of consciousness, including instincts, were paired members of entangled thoughts that continue to survive to this day and that explained not only the eye contact between species but also instincts such as the preservation of species, the fear and threat of death among opponents of different species, and other entanglements.

In any event, the residual brain waves of Al Kansii were to have been detected by his device and transmitted, or at least picked up, by the hovering satellites. The Cerenkov radiation resulting from the explosion had been seen and confirmed in conformity with expectations, but no residual brain waves had been received. Al

Kansii was considered a person of higher intellect and his residual brain waves were expected to be in the normal to supernormal range. Al Kansii was not an animal by any means, nor a person without convictions. The Caliphate had nonetheless not been able to detect any signal from Al Kansii himself that he had indeed died.

The Caliphate wanted to make sure he had died as a martyr, especially to erase all traces of the plot and avoid unpleasant repercussions from the Han. Khaleed Ashgahar's ascension to power had to look *natural* and not born of a conspiracy. The Caliphate needed to know that Al Kansii had been obliterated. So it had programmed his brain, and placed an implant that would transmit his last thoughts, so that in effect he would send the message: *"I just died a few moments ago. All clear."*

The Caliphate had not received that message. Either the system had not worked, or somehow Al Kansii had escaped. But the People's Council had been obliterated. That was a fact. The bluish Cerenkov radiation was an unmistakable sign that all was gone within the Chamber. All and Al Kansii? Including his *device of last rites* as the implant had been dubbed in a case of humor of a very bad taste?

The Caliphate had got wind from agents in the field that an arrest had been made or would be made. That was the rumor. Maybe it was bluff. Maybe it was made up by agents trying to seem important, and connected, and useful. Or perhaps it was a political statement for internal consumption. If the rumor was true that is.

One would never know. And if Al Kansii and everyone else had just disintegrated and converted into samples of metals and puddles of watery substances, how would anyone ever know who the disappeared were? How could they make arrests?

Those doubts were to remain with the Caliphate for eternity. Unless Al Kansii reappeared. One hoped that would not happen of course.

Or unless he would communicate in a delayed mode that he had in fact died. That he had become a martyr. That would be better.

Aftershocks

Assam was in shock when he read the report. Khaleed informed him that the Supreme Leader was in a state of *extended life* which in itself was an insult as only God can prolong life, and that the Assistant Rapporteur was calling the shots; that could only mean that someone in the old hierarchy had survived. Since Yu Lin's presumed cabin was found empty, Khaleed could swear on his life to that, it appeared that Yu Lin had survived and he would impede the plan. Khaleed seemed scared of attempting anything until more information were available. That also meant that the Caliphate's takeover would be less and less plausible, Yu Lin or no Yu Lin. Everyday that passed a new power structure would take more and more shape. And with Yu Lin around, or not knowing of his whereabouts, Khaleed in all fairness to him couldn't move. And if Yu Lin had survived, then he had outsmarted them all. That meant that as he knew of the plot, he could know of Khaleed. Khaleed was right, there was no way to make any move yet. And the more they waited the more improbable their chances.

Assam began to realize that although they had annihilated the Council, the Jolt may have failed. Just as his ancestor's Jolt had done. But time had given the Caliphate with the help of Allah an opportunity to capitalize on that Jolt of yore, decades later. Perhaps it was the way it would end now. That was the way of Allah after all.

Did Yu Lin know something no one else knew? Since Al Kansii had not sent his last message announcing his own death, that was still an open question. Yu Lin was now sole in command. He would reappoint a Council to his liking. Yu Lin knew what the Caliphate had done although none of it would be reported publicly. Yu Lin would of course not trust the Caliphate. Worse even, he knew their tactics. This was a major blow. Assam had to start repairing, to begin some damage control.

He ordered his right hand man, Al Kenii, to request a visit from Lili to gauge the situation and make amends if necessary. After all they were both the founding members of the Club.

Assam became lost in his thoughts. Al Kansii's apparent silence and the perfidious and abominable *extended life* of the Supreme Leader were a telltale sign. Was Yu Lin bluffing? It did not really matter, his survival was the end of the Plot.

PART III

UNFINISHED BUSINESS

1

ACCOMMODATION

*Y*u Lin's ascension to the post of Supreme Leader was a non-event. Chanceries around the world were informed of the Supreme Leader's unique abilities and desire for peace for all mankind. All these diplomatic platitudes could not conceal the fact that the Han Empire was referring to a new leader, without ever announcing that the old one had gone and a new one had come. Just like that. From one day to the next, they had switched the subject and began lauding the unique qualities of Yu Lin, without any introduction, as if he had been there all along.

For the Caliphate it meant one thing was clear now: Assam had been outsmarted and Al Kansii sacrificed. At least Khaleed had been spared. If that really mattered! Assam knew that Al Kansii was himself unique. Khaleed was one of many. A politician, a so-called local leader, an organizer of his community. They could find many of those. They were expendable. The trouble with expendable people, Assam knew, was that no one seemed to want them, not even Allah: they were expendable but rarely expended; the more useless and parasitic, the longer they lasted. True heroes, true martyrs like Al Kansii, those Allah took often. That was the way of Allah.

Assembly of Nations

Decades before, the Caliphate and the Han had agreed to form a world body, the Assembly of Nations whose mission was to provide the framework for peace, stability and justice in the world.

There were thirteen nations represented in the Assembly of Nations: the Grand Caliphate, the Han Empire, the Christian Republic of Patagonia, India and Ceylon, and nine other scattered principalities, mostly isolated lands with hardly any population such as the Republic of the Isla de Pascua (Easter Island) – population twelve hundred; and the Kerguelen Islands – population two hundred and ten. Their representatives usually never attended the meetings since they did not have the resources to do so. The four *large entities* usually did.

The Assembly of Nations, unlike its ancient predecessor was not a bloated bureaucracy of overpaid and often corrupt incompetents. It had been designed very efficiently by the Caliphate and the Han Empire. It had a total of thirty two staff members divided into four committees of seven people each and four so-called permanent *servants*. The four *servants* were appointed two by the Caliphate and two by the Han Empire. Each pair consisted of a *leader servant* and a *deputy servant*.

The four committees dealt respectively with Political Affairs, the Economy, Natural Resources and Administrative Functions such as telecommunications, travel and other such necessities. Of the seven persons in each committee one could find a *committee servant*, a *committee deputy servant*, and an *assistant servant* nominated by the Caliphate and three counterparts appointed by the Han Empire. The seventh committee member in each of the four committees was a *foreign servant* appointed either by Patagonia or India, which shared the four positions in the committees, two each.

All *servants* were paid and their housing maintained by their own governments. The Assembly of Nations had no budget and since the Caliphate and the Empire, and the other nations as well insisted on calling the public servants by their true titles, that of *servants,* allegiance to their government's goals was expected and accomplished without the pretense of *serving* mankind. Needless to say, corruption was non-existent in such an organizational structure.

That organization was therefore established to achieve agreement only if the two main powers concurred. In rare exceptions, usually in matters of lesser interest, could the Patagonians or Hindus as the Indians were referred to, weigh in. It was a balanced world despite the cacophony that sometimes characterized the meetings of the Assembly. The lesser powers went there to feel good and play one of the big ones against the other, while the big ones used that forum to monitor the intentions of the other players.

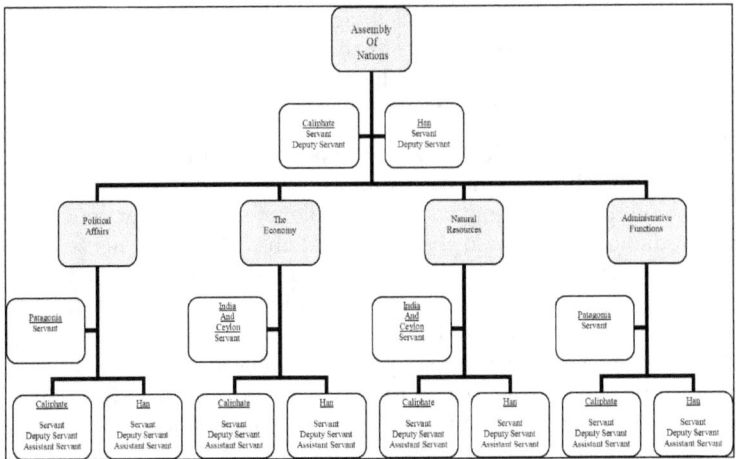

34. Organizational Structure of the Assembly of Nations

At the news of the disintegration, or as it was euphemistically called the *transition* in the Han Empire, it was officially announced that the People's Council had *disappeared*, even rumored that it was a *quantum disappearance*, and a new Council named under Yu Lin, the Supreme Leader. There was no more to it.

The Caliphate however, apparently out of guilt, or perhaps to gauge the temperature of the Empire, had called a plenary session of the Assembly. All thirty two members were present, each on its assigned side of the conference hall, the Caliphate *servants* on the right, those of the Han Empire on the left and the others in the center behind the speakers' podium.

Mohammed bin Abdul Aziz, whose name literally meant *Mohammed son of the Servant of the Cherished One*, meaning son of the servant of God, took the podium first and spoke with an apparently deeply felt sadness:

"Dear fellow human beings. *Allah u Akbar.* God is great! God has ordered that one of our brothers who has toiled all his life, and his brothers who have toiled all their lives as well, to ensure peace and justice amongst our peoples, God has willed to take him and them away. We are told that he disappeared. Completely disappeared."

And that point, a soft grumble could be heard in the Assembly. All knew that only the Caliphate and the Empire possessed the weapons to make someone *disappear*. The audience had then to assume it was either an act of sabotage by the Caliphate, contrary to the Charter of the Assembly of Nations, or an act of treason from within. Or both. And that may have been why they were all there pretending to be afflicted with sadness for the human race.

The tone that Abdul Aziz had taken to open his speech clearly indicated that he thought it was an act of treason from within. The Han knew the facts in any event. The others were the only persons in the audience who could have any doubt. However neither the Caliphate nor the Empire really cared about their opinion in any event. This was an opportunity for both big players to talk to each other in indirect speech, and threaten each other as well if necessary. The Patagonians especially enjoyed the spectacle, as they felt closer philosophically and politically to the Han, and relied on the Han to someday regain their prominence in the march of nations.

"Our countries, all the nations of the Earth," continued Abdul Aziz, "will strive to achieve peace and prosperity for all. We pledge our cooperation, and our undying commitment, to assist the Empire in finding the culprits of that evil act and punish them in any manner acceptable to our friends, the Han. Of course unless God has already taken them from us."

Abdul Aziz was obviously making a reference to the fact that if it had been a martyrdom operation, the job of taking care of the perpetrators had already been done. His pledged cooperation was a way of telling the Han to just drop it and move on. He concluded with the standard:

"God bless us all. We are all Children of God. *Allah u Akbar.* God is great and Mohammed is His prophet (pbuh)."

The audience applauded respectfully but without much conviction. At that point Cheng Liu stood to take the podium. The audience was now very attentive because all knew by now what must have happened and it was of importance to the world what reaction the Empire would have. That also would tell the thirty two *servants*, so that they could write their reports to their governments as to whether it was an inside job or an act of international sabotage, and by writing a report thus justify their positions.

"Comrades," began Liu, "a great calamity has befallen us. The actors of such an evil deed are not known, nor their motives explainable. We take at heart the offer of cooperation of the Caliphate to help us solve the mystery of this odious deed. However, we must move on. The affairs of state do not wait. We will cooperate but we will be vigilant. Acts like these should not and will not happen again. I ask all of you to assist us, as we will assist you in the future, in preventing such acts not only from occurring, but also from being conceived. Too many times, too many passions have been inflamed; too many times, too many incendiary words have been pronounced; and too often greed has ruled our mutual interactions. Greed of conquest and greed of thought. We will not allow that to happen again. We in the Empire are thankful that all of you here, and especially the Caliphate *servants*, agree with us and will help us stem the curse of evil acts.

"With great respect to all my comrades here present, I thank you for your consideration."

A great round of applause followed. What was notable was that the Empire did not hide from the Assembly of Nations the fact that a *great calamity had befallen* it, while inside the Empire, hardly anyone knew that anything had occurred. Most Han did not know they had a new Supreme Leader.

The audience also now knew that of course the Caliphate was somehow implicated in the quantum *disappearance* of the Council. But it also knew that the Empire did not seek revenge. Rather the Empire seemed to say "*you did it to the last Council, with our cooperation, you won't do it to the new Council.*" As such it was good news since there would not be a global retaliation leading to catastrophe. The new Supreme Leader was apparently satisfied with the new order. For the Patagonians especially it also meant that the Han would be more aggressive in stemming the pressure and expansionism of the Caliphate. The allusion to the *greed of thought* was telling, it was unmistakable. And that was good news for them. The Hindus were confused; they liked the division, but they did not trust the Han either, so they went with the flow.

The Assembly then retired to an adjacent salon where food from all nations was served, in small sampling sizes, and green tea, with or without mint leaves at one's choice, was also available. After about an hour of the *servants* mingling with other *servants*, they all prepared to return to their country of origin where real occupations, jobs that is, awaited them.

The Assembly of Nations had thus just adjourned. It had accomplished its goal very efficiently. The two great powers had said publicly what they thought of the momentous events that had just occurred, whether they had played a role in them or not, and what they intended to do in the future concerning a recurrence of that type of action. There was nothing more that any Assembly of Nations would or should do. No bureaucracy was left behind to devise ways of perpetuating itself with tasks it could not possibly accomplish.

Agadir, Southern Maghreb

Agadir in southern Maghreb, formerly known as Morocco to the West, was a delightful city on the Atlantic Coast. Its fishing harbor was the pride of the city since it boasted the largest production of sardines in the world. That crop of little fish which can be eaten whole, minus the head of course, since their bones are soft, is a delicacy around the world but also sustenance food for millions who feed on the high caloric content of its meat. And it is inexpensive, except for the rare designer species. An *inexpensive delicacy* was the advertising slogan.

The sardines industry that resulted from the fishing created a micro industrial revolution on these shores which had begun hundreds of years before and continued undisturbed.

Agadir was far from the centers of political power like Casablanca, where the intelligentsia and other elites congregated, the stronghold of the former colonist, where French was still spoken and appreciated, or Tangiers, an international hub once renowned for intrigue and pleasure.

Agadir is situated not far from the entrance to the desert, the Sahara, the official gate of which is Marrakesh, which is inland. Unlike Marrakesh though, Agadir does not boast snake charmers and other curiosities of the desert. Agadirans always considered themselves *modern*, open to the world. Their international commerce of course facilitated that view of themselves. To its east rise the Atlas Mountains, to the west the Atlantic Ocean with the Canary Islands a bit further south.

35. *Agadir and its Region*

Agadir suffered a terrible shock in the year 1379 of the Hijri calendar, also known as 1960 of the Christian Era when a powerful earthquake shook the city. It had happened on the 29th day of February, fatefully a day of intercalation and the second day of Ramadan. Aftershocks were felt, legend goes, as far away as Casablanca. People died by the tens of thousands, over one third of the population it was recounted, buried under their homes. Thousands of orphans were relocated within charitable families in other cities across the Kingdom, families who adopted them wholeheartedly. One of these orphans was said to have lived to be a special advisor to the King, a holy position since the King was a direct descendant of the Prophet (pbuh) and his dynasty had survived since the liberation from colonial rule, close to two hundred and fifty years before.

That shock had remained to this day on the collective conscience of Agadirans. Until these days, any one of them would react instinctively when a rumble was heard or felt, for example when a heavy freight train passed nearby – those were still used in these regions. It seemed that the ancient memories of their forefathers were transferred genetically to their kin, generation after generation. Agadirans joked that they did not need seismographs, they were walking seismographs themselves. The impact of that deadly *tremblement de terre*, as the newspapers called it then, on the population is almost unmatched anywhere else in the world where victims and their children usually move on and memories fade. Not in Agadir.

A happy city, self sufficient and peaceful with the outside world, the only interaction being profitable and honest commerce and little other influence, was able to keep the memory of that fateful day alive for centuries.

It was a sunny Friday afternoon and the contented population had gathered in various mosques for Friday prayers. The largest mosque, the Mosquée Sidi Mohammed[20], usually received the visit of the town dignitaries and rich merchants. Because within the Umma all are equal, there were of course a large number of poorer people, young people, old and venerable people and almost everything in between. The mosque could accommodate over fifty two hundred persons including in its adjacent gardens and annex facilities.

The sermon delivered by the most holy and peace-loving imam, Mohammed El Bradi, had just concluded on a note of joy and peace for the entire world. "Including *those who are different from us*, they are, we all are, children of God," had declared El Bradi. The Umma could be seen as approving with obvious delight at the recognition of their own compassion and love for mankind.

When the attendance began to file to retrieve their shoes at the entrance of the mosque, as is customary in such circumstance, what began as a muffled rumbled that lasted about one tenth of a second became immediately a powerful explosion that tore apart the crowd, the limbs of those who formed the crowd and the flesh that made those limbs. The carnage was everywhere. Several thousand people perished in that explosion.

It was said afterwards that the most holy of these victims had heard through the rumble the voice of their ancestors that had died in the earthquake centuries before. And that those voices were warning them of the upcoming catastrophe. The very few survivors attested to that since they had heard the voices themselves and they were there to tell.

Before focusing on warning voices, authorities of course tried to rescue the victims and limit the casualties. Immediately afterward, or

---

[20] The *Grande Mosquée Sidi Mohammed* had been named in memory of the great King Sidi Mohammed V who served God and his people even from exile in Madagascar. This great king died in 1961 of the Christian Era, less than a year after his Hajj pilgrimage to Mecca. Some says that as king Mohammed V was not required to make the Hajj and his sudden death less than a year after that pilgrimage may have found its cause in the breaking of that holy tradition.

perhaps at the same time, the national authorities began seeking answers. *"Who in his right mind would blast a mosque in Agadir?"* asked a prominent conveyor of news. Although simple in its logic, that statement was accorded great depth and significance as pronouncements of conveyors of news had always received, everywhere. Perhaps it was the state of shock of the population that accorded such gravity to an obvious and inconsequential statement. Perhaps it was the natural human reaction upon hearing what one already knows and enjoys hearing again. That human reaction, that need, gave of course enormous power to the conveyors of so-called *news* who, not only in Agadir but worldwide, relished in their self satisfied conviction of importance and gravity.

The answer to that grave pronouncement came soon afterwards in a communiqué issued holographically in the public bulletin in one of the many squares of Usamabad, in the heart of the Grand Caliphate, nearly four thousand miles from Agadir:

> 'The Christian Warriors have stricken and will strike at the lands of those who stole ours,' simply said the communiqué.

No one had ever heard of the Christian Warriors before. It was a group unknown to all.

A New Hand

Assam Al Amriki, in his Room of the Two Crescents pondered the meaning of that attack on Muslim lands, true Muslim lands, not even the conquered ones, the converted ones. At least not conquered and converted in the recent past.

Assam's immediate thought was that of a retaliatory strike from the Han for the actions against the People's Council. But that was too obvious. Besides, Yu Lin did not need to seek revenge since he should thank the Caliphate for giving him the opportunity to accede to the post of Supreme Leader of the Han Empire.

Assam considered the freedom fighters that were known to have gathered in Antarctica to prepare the *'segunda reconquista'*, the second reconquest. But they were relics he thought, mired in the tenth and eleventh centuries of the Christian Era. They were monitored very closely. They were all talk he knew, and certainly not capable of mounting such an attack so far away from their shores without being noticed. The whole thing did not make any sense. As Assam looked at Sheikh B'rak Al Kenii in disbelief, he asked:

"Should we call another meeting of the Assembly of Nations, this time us complaining, us being the victims?

"I am not sure it would be useful," answered B'rak. "Whoever the culprits are and if they are related to any member of the Assembly of Nations or supported by them, they would deny. And possibly they would be sincere. We are facing a new enemy. Even the fools in rags of the Middle Ages in Antarctica would probably be telling the truth when denying any involvement. As a matter of fact, I have news that they condemned the attack as they reject attacks on innocent civilians and they strive to reconquer their lands by peaceful means, just as Jesus Christ had preached."

"If we talk to Lili we may get some answers. Please arrange for her to come."

"Yes Sheikh, I will at once," answered Al Kenii as he left the room.

When Al Kenii retired to arrange for a visit by Lili, Assam could not help but see the attack on Agadir as a jolt. A jolt from the Christian Warriors, whoever they were.

The confluence of events since the failed Plot was unsettling. Small actions can sometimes cause major effects when projected over time and space. *Chaos Theory.*

Assam knew that history was a series of *chaos* paths. More recently of course Sheikh Hussein had emerged as a force within the West that had changed history and facilitated the advent of the Grand Caliphate. How had it started? Was it the Jolt of his ancestor, or something else, like the Agadir attack, or the failed Plot on the Han?

It had been said that great prophets are of uncertain birth. Yes the early prophets, Moses and Jesus when he was among the mortals in the Christian faith, were. And the last Prophet (pbuh) also was since he was an orphan upon his birth. Did Sheikh Hussein shared this plight and at the same time this blessing? *An apparently insignificant event.*

The prophets all brought the word of God and changed mankind's history and the lives of the great and the simple. Upon his accession to power and which lasted for decades, Sheikh Hussein had laid the groundwork for the Caliphate. *Major effects.*

That is why he was known as the First Caliph, although he never held that title. But Assam wondered: was there a small action that even preceded these events? An *initial condition* that led to his impact on the political realm and thus to the subsequent events? Was there a prior *chaos* path?

Yes, perhaps his uncertain birth. He longed to find the root of his birth, his origins which he desperately sought. Like Moses, that early prophet of God, who knew not his father, and was abandoned in the waters of the Nile, and grew to receive the Commandments from God.

Like Jesus, whom Islam recognizes as the second prophet of God, and who, although it is not said, searched for his true father and found him in God and that is why some believe him to be God himself.

And the third and last Prophet (pbuh) who was left orphan before his birth. And in his Qur'an he (pbuh) confirmed all the revelations and commanded to believe in *"that which was revealed unto Abraham and Ishmael and Isaac and Jacob and the tribes, and that which Moses and Jesus received, and which the prophets received from their Lord. We make no distinction between any of them, and unto Him we have surrendered."* (2:136)

All the prophets can be said to have sought their father in God. And that search provided man with wonderful revelations and guidance. Assam also noted that none of the prophets had left a male heir. Neither did Sheikh Hussein. Had one of them been blessed with a father during his childhood and a male heir during his life, would he have become a prophet? Would he have been holy enough to receive the revelations? Or would he have occupied his life with more earthly interests?

Assam did not know the answer to these questions since such confluence of events had not occurred. But he knew that perhaps different *initial conditions* could probably have changed the course of History.

What then if Sheikh Hussein had had a normal childhood, cherished and loved by a father he never had, would he had sought solace in grand visions? In visions of transformation of the world?

Would he have had perhaps the same disdain for those others of *normal* progeny who knew their fathers, who knew their mothers and whose mission in life remained that of contribution and enjoyment, but not of cataclysmic change? And therefore not created the conditions for the advent of the Grand Caliphate?

In Assam's view an apparently inconsequential and insignificant act of someone *there*, back in the lost memories of History, led to attitudes that created events, and those events led to major transformations now and *here*. *Apparently inconsequential events. Major transformations. Chaos Theory.*

Assam also thought of the uncertainty surrounding the death of the prophets as well. Did Moses die or did he rise to Heaven? He rose after having reached the Promised Land, and not setting foot on it but beholding it from the heights of Mount Nebo.

Did Jesus die? He did, it is known, but it is believed that he resurrected and rose as well.

And the Prophet (pbuh) through his miraculous night journey in the year 620 of the Hijra, his journey of *Isra* and *Mi'raj* during which in the company of the angel Gabriel, and on a winged horse, had visited the *masjid al-aqsa*, the *farthest mosque*, undeniably the mosque in Jerusalem, making it a holy site. And he had also visited Heaven and Hell, and spoken with earlier prophets, with Abraham, Moses, and Jesus, all this connected his life to his death and shrouded his death in mystery and uncertainty.

And the pattern followed with Sheikh Hussein who had died it is said as a martyr after decades of service to God and the future Caliphate but whose martyrdom is, as his birth, still of an uncertain nature. The pattern of small events leading to major consequences seemed to fit in Assam's mind.

What then was the impact, if any, of this pattern of uncertainty concerning Al Kansii? Would it be ominous to the Caliphate, or a blessing ultimately as that of the prophets had been for the Umma?

Assam was concerned that the absence of certainty concerning Al Kansii's death would have the same momentous consequences on the march of the Caliphate. Was Al Kansii to become a lost martyr, a lost imam, an apparently inconsequential being with great impact?

Assam's premonition became suddenly justified. An imperceptible sound alerted his inner ear. Abu Bak'r's voice announced:

"Sheikh Assam, The Keeper of the Faith wants you back in the Holy Lands. Moussa Ibn Abdul Salam will take over the Caliphate. We must depart before sundown."

"Prepare to leave then," responded Assam.

The March of History had now taken a turn.

2

DEFENSES

*O*nce the formalities of the Assembly of Nations were concluded, both the Han Empire and the Caliphate had to tend to real business.

The Han had to find a way to counter the Angel of Death which they knew now was not a mere hypothetical application of scientific principles but a real weapon. But first the Han had to improve their detection methods. In particular Yu Lin had to prevent acts of another *Yu Lin* from creating real *chaos* in the Empire. There were no signs of such man yet, but Yu Lin knew the reservoir of brains within the Empire was vast and he needed to control its flow.

The Empire also had to reassess the assistance it provided to the various groups resisting the Caliphate from within in various uprisings, but also groups attempting to destabilize the Caliphate through random violent actions such as the Agadir attack. This could not be left to chance. The Empire had to decide positively whether to participate in earnest, clandestinely of course but with commitment, or to leave these warriors to their own fate, that is potentially to their slow death.

The Caliphate had another set of problems. First and foremost they needed to find out Al Kansii's fate. They also needed to review the effectiveness of their Angel of Death and perhaps develop other advanced methods of delivery that would ensure mission success. It seemed that the sacrifice of martyrs such as Al Kansii was not a deterrent to the use of such methods, but rather that the need of martyrs required the involvements of local *traitors* such as Yu Lin was supposed to have been, and of course they could not be trusted. Consequently remote action on entangled systems was an area of great interest. No one knew if science even permitted such a delivery method to be accomplished. But they had to extrapolate and then see.

Both Empires also were on a race to perfect, or rather to conceive specific and real applications of the emerging technologies that would produce weapons based on quark stream propagation theory.

More realistically, both sides were to devote additional efforts and resources on advanced detection methods. In particular the Caliphate was concerned by the way Li Li had slipped through their net.

Death to the Angel of Death

The first thing Yu Lin had to do was therefore to devise a way to neutralize the Angel of Death. He knew or rather assumed although it was a risky conclusion, that no other plot was active and that Assam had relied on Li Li and him exclusively. Of course there was no guarantee that Assam had not prepared a parallel coup, as had been the practice of the Caliphate and its predecessors for centuries to launch similar and simultaneous operations. In any event it made no difference, if he were to be obliterated he would have no time to ponder his own extinction. As long as he was in existence he had to do something about the Angel of Death.

The idea was to turn the Angel of Death against the Caliphate. Scientifically, that was not possible unless the Han would create their own Angel. And there were geographic and technical issues. Also infiltrating the Caliphate to mount such an attack was not only impractical but also not very useful. Another Caliph whom they would have to eliminate would just succeed the disappeared one. The opposite was obviously not true as Assam was hoping that by installing a friendly Supreme Leader, conversion to the true faith could be accelerated. The Han by contrast did not wish to convert anyone. So an Angel of Death as an offensive weapon presented little interest to the Empire.

Yu Lin and Albert began creating a list of the most distinguished scientists and weapons engineers with the goal of establishing a task force that would study various countermeasures to the Angel of Death.

The task force ultimately comprised four eminent scientists and three weapons engineers in addition to Yu Lin who oversaw the process and Albert who acted as Secretary, and who of course went officially by his real name Keum Kam Ho.

The four scientists were Dr. Hsu, a physicist, specializing in Y Theory and the discoverer of the mathematical concept of the *zeron*, the basis for all in the Universe; Dr. Zho an eminent biologist; Dr. Soon a reputed biophysicist and Dr. Ku, a very knowledgeable materials scientist. The three weapons engineers, Drs. Ha, Fung, and Cho all three had vast experience with various weapons systems, especially quantum based defenses to the weaponization of which they had greatly contributed.

The task force's first goal was to understand the events that had taken place in the Chamber of the People's Council. Together with a large team of investigators they established themselves as a forensic group for that first task. Several meetings were held and numerous surveys conducted and followed by a thorough analysis of all known data on the components of the Angel of Death.

The original forensic team that had investigated the eradication of the members of the People's Council had concluded that no traditional weapons had been used and that only distant *beams of something* had entered the Chamber and had been collimated into a deadly cocktail. They had postulated that only some type of neutrino could have achieved that global trip. But the neutrinos they knew were harmless, trillions passed through our bodies daily. And if the Caliphate had discovered a deadly neutrino, why wasn't everyone being affected? Was there something in the stream that had reached the Chamber of the People's Council that had made it lethal?

The investigators had also noticed that someone pretending to be Yu Lin and wearing his clothes had arrived late to that fateful meeting. Yu Lin of course had been held in Manchuria and a cabin not far from his own had been obliterated by a classical explosion. And no one had emerged from the Chamber. Only puddles of watery substances were found on the concrete floor, and some electrostatic discharges were noticed on some of the non-organic material that had survived. In fact all organic material in the room had disappeared. The investigators had therefore concluded that some kind of organic destructor beam had been used.

Beams of particles emitted at distant locations and acting on living cells to the point of being capable of destroying them, perhaps acting as super accelerating enzymes, it had to be some kind of neutrino, the forensic team postulated. The device, if there was a device that the perpetrator had used, had disappeared, but no one had left the premises since the incident. The device, if device there was, had to have been obliterated as well. It may have contained simulated organic components such as those observed by Golog Maqen prior to the incident, and that could have caused its entire disintegration. Assuming that all these hypotheses were correct, there was still a physical problem.

Of importance was that although neutrino detection was confined to large scale structures, not very different from the *IceCube*, the OPERA and AMANDA projects of centuries past, the Caliphate had obviously succeeded in achieving small scale detectors and was able to direct the detected beams to the desired target. Unless of course the detection had first occurred thanks to a large facility in the Caliphate and that in the *Forbidden City* was thus implied by entanglement. What was of more concern is that the Caliphate had apparently found a way to render the harmless beams lethal, at least temporarily and when acted upon by a device that was hypothesized by the investigators.

Yu Lin who knew of many of the elements of the plot in advance, was not of much help. And if he did know he would not volunteer that he had knowledge of such information. In any event Yu Lin had scant knowledge of the actual technology used. Yan had informed Albert that the agent in charge of the attack, sent by the Caliphate, did carry several devices the detailed signatures of which he had recorded and were available for study to Yu Lin and Albert. That could have helped the investigators who could have zeroed in on some trail. But Yu Lin had to let them discover and untangle the plot on their own.

After weeks of investigations and after following and abandoning dead trails and sometimes returning to them, Dr. Hsu announced that while the neutrinos migrate over vast distances, sometimes they change from one type say an electron neutrino to another type for example a *tau* neutrino. There were experiments where all three types could be found to be in existence simultaneously and for a very short period. During these short periods it was postulated that small obstacles through which the beams could normally easily pass, for some reason unknown to Hsu, these obstacles were able to split the beams into entangled pairs. The entangled pairs were able to *communicate* among different neutrino types so that an action on one type, hence the *knowledge* of that state, was correlated to a paired member of another type. All this phenomena, called *cross-type entanglement* resulted in the reformation of the beams into *corrupt* neutrino pairs, a very unstable pair that could be roughly focused on a target. Instead of a harmless detection similar to what is observed for photons when an interference pattern disappears, the local member in such an entangled pair resulted in a powerful stream that was lethal to certain nuclei, especially that of carbon. The absorption of the *corrupt* neutrino pairs by the carbon nuclei turned them into boron nuclei resulting in the liberation of electrons in the ambient atmosphere and the freeing up of hydrogen and oxygen, all components of organic matter. Thus the puddles of water and the electrostatic discharges observed after the attack. It also explained, as advanced by Dr. Zho why the concrete pillars had been unaffected while the wood furniture had disappeared.

Dr. Cho concurred with these findings but had to admit at being puzzled by the fact that there had to have been a device allowing all this to occur, and the device for some reason had been obliterated as well.

Drs. Cho and Hsu conjectured that the Caliphate had solved a major scientific problem, that of detecting and directing beams of neutrinos, especially *corrupt* neutrino pairs that lasted but for a fraction of a second. Drs. Ku, Fung and Ha had contributed the finding that the device may also have provoked the *corruption* of the original beams because there was no way the perpetrator would have been able to be at the precise time and precise position to detect and recombine the *corrupt* beams, if these had been corrupted remotely beforehand

The team of experts had therefore concluded that if they could randomly *corrupt* beams that were floating everywhere, without re-directing them, it might make it almost impossible for a device which they assumed had been used, to be able of *re-corrupting* in the proper manner ambient beams. That they thought would neutralize the Angel of Death. They asked the engineers to devise ways to implement such solution.

An endeavor of strategic importance that the panel of experts undertook to conduct was advanced and intense research to find ways of replicating the small scale detection apparently available to the Caliphate. If they could achieve that before the Caliphate saw the need to develop countermeasures they would then have a military advantage for some time.

Yu Lin promised to use all the means available to the State to assist them in that research. That meant, in a veiled way, espionage.

After their report was submitted, the panel of experts returned to their prior activities. Dr. Hsu returned to his research concerning his *ultimate* theory.

And the Han went to work.

Ultimate Theory

For two centuries now, scientists had been working on establishing the Ultimate Theory that would unite all the forces including gravity. The Han had inherited from the West the privilege of being at the forefront of that research. The Caliphate had a philosophical and theological problem with such endeavors.

Theologically first, only God was ultimate so the name of that illusory theory was sacrilegious by itself. Philosophically it was also improper as well since it implied that man could reach the confines of infinity. The Caliphate was more comfortable with the Standard Cosmological Model of the Big Bang as established centuries ago and the accelerating expansion of the universe that proved there was a realm inaccessible to man, regardless of his science. That pleased the Caliphate. Research grants were therefore difficult to obtain for research that was not condoned by the religious authorities. The Caliphate further believed that known quantum science provided sufficient avenues to develop weapons to achieve its goals.

In fact it was assumed that the common precept that fundamental science was always ahead of technological applications sometimes by centuries, but at least by decades, presented the Caliphate with no real risk. By the time current Han research would reach the technological stage, the Caliphate, *Insha'Allah*, would already have conquered them. That was Assam's point, and it was shared by the entire hierarchy in the Caliphate.

Dr. Hsu had a problem with where the West had left off. Classical Physics had given way to Relativity Theory centuries before and become a special case of a larger theory. Relativity handled large distances and masses which extreme precision, but at microscopic scales major inconsistencies were found. That was where Quantum Theory had developed and only now everyday applications of such theory had become economically feasible. Just like the Caliphate, the Han Empire had burst into the realm of Quantum Weapons.

Professor Hsu believed they could go further. He knew that the attempts to merge Relativity with Quantum Theory had led to several impasses, but ultimately a concept called M Theory had emerged two hundred years before. That theory was elegant but just that, a theory. Nevertheless, slowly, as technological capabilities became more advanced – especially super particle accelerators that could emulate the conditions very near the Big Bang, and actually *create* Black Holes, or as they liked to say, *disposable black holes* – M Theory started to become more understood and accepted by the scientific community. Of course there were still contradictions and objections from large parts of it. That was not new and Professor Hsu could live with that.

What Professor Hsu had a problem with was the fact that M Theory was based on eleven dimensions, ten spatial dimensions plus time, and seven of which were *curled up* upon themselves thus not visible unless at extremely small scales, such as the Planck length, in centimeters something like thirty two zeros and a one following the decimal point. That was all right for Professor Hsu. He was after all a leading member of the Flat Earth Society, and participated in almost all its chapters. What concerned Hsu was that the so-called M Theory had chosen as the most fundamental objects in the universe constructs called *strings*. And later, although the original strings used a two-dimensional space, that is they were zero-thickness filaments spread on a two-dimensional surface, they had later been expanded to two-dimensional membranes, and even later on to *p*-dimensional membranes called *p-branes*. That Hsu considered just jerry rigging. The theory should have been able to sustain itself within its own initial elegant construct.

The key question was therefore whether these vibrating strings were capable of being broken down into even more fundamental constituents. As he liked to say: "why can't I take a pair of scissors and cut those strings?" In other words Hsu asked to know what was in the space not occupied by the filaments, or membranes that composed the strings. Hsu was uncomfortable with fundamental objects that contained a lot of empty space enclosed by something made of actual matter. What if the strings were just geometric pathways where the actual matter resided and thus vibrated?

He then posited that perhaps the most basic elements were zero dimension objects, that he knew could not be further broken down, and these objects interacted with each other in specific arrangements which sometimes looked like strings. In that fashion he could account for all the various dimensions of the *-branes* and began constructing the mathematical framework of his theory. He called the ultimate zero-dimensional objects the *zerons*, for zero. He could have called them the *omegons*, for *omega* the last Greek letter, but *zeron* he thought was more descriptive. The force particle, itself of zero dimension and zero mass, he called the *alphon*, as the first force that could be defined. Hsu was proud of his theory and knew that by dealing with zero-dimensional objects, it would be difficult for any other theory to supplant his.

An important characteristic of the *zerons*, and he delighted in describing this at conferences and seminars, was that if one would stack a billion, or a trillion, or even a quintillion trillion of zerons, the resulting stack, was of zero dimension, that is still a point particle, or a set of superimposed point particles. Only when the *zerons* were separated by a Planck's length, and one could construct various arrangements of these *zerons* in any number of spatial dimensions one wished, only then could the *alphons* be exchanged and create the vibrational modes that were postulated and sometimes observed in M Theory.

Hsu believed that if one could isolate the *zeron* and pair it appropriately, new classes of weapons would be possible. He also knew that the Caliphate was way behind the Empire in such research. Of course it would take perhaps centuries to achieve that step, but better late than never.

Hsu had replaced Yu Lin as head of Research, head of the Surveillance Center within the Directorate for the Security of the Territory, and Minister of Science and Weaponry. He, perhaps alone in the Empire other than Albert, knew of the events that had led to Yu Lin's accession to power. Hsu and Yu Lin were very close. His older sister Li Li was now Yu Lin's right hand. And she was more than that of course. The Han Empire had become a family affair. And this was better, since for millennia family ties in the Han ethics were stronger than anything. And they needed that strength to stave off whatever the Caliphate could launch at them, until the day, soon Yu Lin knew, when the Caliphate with its philosophical outlook, antiquated in his view, would collapse. And if it did not collapse of its own weight, the

Han Empire would have the weapons to defend itself and threaten the Caliphate.

Unlike the West, Professor Hsu knew, the Han Empire intended to keep all these endeavors secret, and the main drawback was that top scientists outside the Han Empire could not contribute to its research as in the old days when all over the world the best brains worked in concert. The Han of course had scouts within the Caliphate and in Patagonia, scouts who enticed these scientists to immigrate into Han territory where their identities, their ancestry, even religion if they bothered to have one, would not be hindered. This brain drain although not large was indeed constant. And Hsu knew the Empire had benefitted from it.

The Han would not make the prior mistakes of closing their eyes to the world. They had made mistakes like that in centuries past when they relinquished their dominance of the seas to the West. Yes, Professor Hsu could cite in detail the story of such inopportune decisions. As early as 1421 CE, Emperor YongLe had halted Zheng He's expeditions in the vast Oceans. And HongXi a few years later had suppressed maritime trade. Even later still, the entire fleet of the great Ocean was incomprehensibly scuttled.

That was a time, similar to now, when great academicians, armed with the Confucian creed of *inward perfection*, became administrators of the Empire and the previous tyranny abolished.

Within the Han Empire, in the Kingdom of the Rising Sun similar mistakes had been made concerning the prohibition in the production of firearms in favor of the *soul of the samurai*, the sword. Although morally justified these acts had placed the ancient Han Empire at the mercy of powerful adversaries, especially Western predators. The Han would not make the same mistakes again. Under the leadership of Yu Lin and his superior academic colleagues in the Council, the Han Empire would counter the Caliphate.

The Cabin in Manchuria

"Dear Li Li, your new mission is to go to Patagonia, and continue further toward the Antarctic Peninsula to assess the prospects of the Freedom Fighters there. We need to control them. And to increase our assistance if indeed their actions, no matter how brutal and inhuman, are consistent with our goals," said Yu Lin.

"But I am told they are not inhuman. They practice the creed of Jesus which supposedly consists of forgiving your enemy. To offer the other cheek as they say symbolically," answered Li Li.

"As they like to say, yes. We need to see for ourselves. And perhaps entice them to be a bit more brutal if what you say is correct.

"They also have a good number of scientists who should not be wasting their time in the frozen ices playing warrior. They are of no use to the real fighters and we could use them. They could be much happier and useful here," said Yu Lin.

"I see. We need a coherent strategy, not just a set of disjointed actions born of reactive reflexes when events occur. We need to take the lead," suggested Li Li as she added:

"It will take some months to... I was going to say ... infiltrate, but that's not the proper word, to embed my being and my soul into their soul and to understand their thinking and the best way for us to leverage their existence."

"As long as it takes," answered Yu Lin. "We Han are patient. As long as we get it right. After what we have seen, we cannot trust the Caliphate. Word is that Assam is being recalled and a more brutal man, less sophisticated man, might mount an assault no one desires. Of course we can counter it. But who needs the calamity on both sides we could witness? Fanatics don't care. We are academics. We are scientists. We care."

"Yes Dear Yu Lin," answered Li Li. "I will depart soon."

"Thank you, Dear Li Li," answered Yu Lin immediately.

This was as explicit and endearing an expression of their mutual admiration and love that Yu Lin and Li Li were capable of in their apparently romantic but platonic relationship. This relationship of course, as always, would continue at a distance. This time from the desolate and frozen world of Antarctica. Li Li was soon on her way.

Moussa Ibn Abdul Salam

Moussa Ibn Abdul Salam arrived at the Usamabad magport the day after Assam departed. In tow he had Walid Abdul Habibi, his *aide de camp.*

Moussa was a warrior. He did not listen to music or read poetry. He recited his prayers on time everyday. His affairs were in order. His beliefs were clear. His mission as well. He was to mount a new Jolt that would destabilize the Han. Abdul Habibi had already identified his point man, his new *shaheed,* his new martyr.

Kassem Al Idahi arrived at the Room of the Two Crescents for an initial planning session, in fact the only session needed, with Moussa and Abdul Habibi.

After brief greetings and praises to Allah, Moussa issued his instructions and Al Idahi was on his way to Space Force Base 7 for preparations for his mission.

Al Idahi was in fact a perfect match for Moussa. He did not waste time in philosophical debates. He was a man of action. In the forests and mountains where he had grown up, there was little room for such considerations. "Give me a weapon, and I will execute," he had said just before leaving *Al Dar Baida.* He had just spent thirty minutes in the Room of the Two Crescents.

The fate of the Caliphate's next Jolt was now in the hands of Moussa and Al Idahi. Only Allah knew if their methods would find more success than those of the refined pair Assam-Al Kansii. Moussa and Al Idahi in fact did not even pose the question. They were charging ahead.

Abdul Habibi did manage to have Moussa consider the potential threat posed by the insurgent warriors emerging here and there. Moussa's response was brief and simple:

"To this day, there are pockets of unconvinced faithful, but they are of no consequence. Better ignore them than give them a voice. If they become a threat, we will eliminate them."

That was the state of affairs in Usamabad in these fateful times.

3

LA BASE

a Base, (pronounced 'lah <u>bah</u>-say'), Spanish for The Base, or The Foundation, was the organization that the Patagonians had set up to reclaim their kingdoms, and their glory.

The organization, known popularly as the Knights of Rivadavia was modeled after the Knights Templar of the eleventh century of the Christian Era.

Their actual formal name was *Los Hidalgos de Rivadavia*. Rivadavia, its full name being Comodoro Rivadavia, was the seat of the New Vatican where Urban XXII had just been elected Pope by the College of Cardinals. The city Comodoro Rivadavia was named after Martin Rivadavia, a distinguished shipping minister, but after the relocation of the government from Buenos Aires to Rivadavia, it was decided to honor also Argentina's first president, Bernardino Rivadavia, by including his name in the legend of the city, now the capital of Patagonia. Patagonia was what remained of the original Argentina not in the hands of the Caliphate, or more precisely what remained of the original West not in the hands of the Caliphate.

Hidalgo is not the Spanish name for 'knight', which is *caballero*. Since *caballero* was used to denote a gentleman, the founders of the Order had instead chosen the word *Hidalgo*. The origin of the name has noting to do with cavalry or horses, such as in the French *Chevaliers du Temple*, or the English the *Knights Templar*, but rather ties the knight to his nobility. As such the *Hidalgos* transcended the mere goal of a fighter for a cause and related their mission to the immutable character *sui generis* of their being. They were *noble*.

Hidalgo is a contraction of *hijo de algo*, which in Spanish stands for "son of something", meaning of something worthwhile, or something noble. The *Hidalgos* were not superior to the rest of the people which they respected and loved, they just had the obligation to accomplish on behalf of everyone else a superior mission. Their privilege of being *de algo* was in fact a duty, a responsibility, which they took to heart, to their soul.

The *Hidalgos*, just like the Templars, were organized into *languages* – or *langues* in the original charter in French – that is the *Hidalgos* were grouped according to their country of provenance. That separation was not intended to create cliques or diverging interests but rather cohesion within a battle unit, just as the military in the West of long ago organized themselves in *companies*, fighting units in which the members held very tight bonds with each other.

The *languages* also facilitated communication since freedom fighters engaged in their new *holy war* came from all corners of the world.

Freedom Fighters and Holy Fighters they were. At major ceremonies the *Hidalgos* repeated and savored every word of the homily of St Bernard. The homily had been written around the year 1136 of the Christian Era, when Pope Innocent II issued the Papal Bull *Omne Datum Optimum* that established the *Règles* or Rules that would govern the Order of the Templars. The homily, *De laude novae Militiae ad Milites Templi*, lauded the accomplishments of the Knights Templar on that special occasion. The eloquence of the original text was preserved by the *Hidalgos* who insisted in reciting it in its original French, albeit with accents of varying felicity. The homily of St Bernard went as follows:

> *"A new chivalry has appeared in the land of the Incarnation. It is new, I say, and not yet proven in the world, where it leads this double battle, sometimes against opponents of flesh and blood, sometimes against the spirits that are evil toward the heavens... And that these knights by the force of their bodies resist bodily enemies, I do not find this wonderful for I do not see it as rare. But that they wage war by the force of the spirit against all vices and demons, I will call it not only wonderful, but worthy of all praises accorded to saints... the knight really is without fear and without reproach, he who protects his soul by the armor of the Faith, just as he covers his body with a coat of mail. Doubly armed, he fears neither demons nor men. Surely he who wishes to die does not fear death.[21] And how would he fear dying or living, he for whom life is Christ,*

---

[21] These words were pronounced louder than the rest.

and death the reward[21]?... Onward then, o knight, and strike with an intrepid soul the enemies of Christ, knowing that nothing can separate you from God's compassion."[22]

And the assembly repeated the following words, sometimes over and over:

« *Celui qui souhaite mourir ne craint pas la mort*»
(he who wishes to die does not fear death)

«*... et la mort la récompense*»
(... and death the reward)

St Bernard was a key figure in the formation of the Templars as he undertook to organize what is known as the second Crusade. Just as St Bernard had been its inspiration, he was the inspiration for the *Hidalgos'* Crusade to recover their lands. Although the Muslims considered the Crusaders to have been murderous barbarians with no respect for others' lands, or their lives, the *Hidalgos* believed in their nobility of spirit, and the nobility of their blood. They were seeking justice and were now struggling for their faith. And they strove to model their lives after that of the Templars so movingly described by St Bernard:

"They live without having anything their own, not even their will. Clothed simply and covered with dust, their faces are burnt by the ardor of the sun...as combat approaches, they arm themselves with faith within and iron outside, with no other ornament; they charge ahead on their enemies without regard to the cruelty nor the infinite multitude of their Barbarian foes for they place all their trust not in their own force but in the arms of the God of the Armies... knowing that victory

---

[22] « Une nouvelle chevalerie est apparue dans la Terre de l'Incarnation. Elle est neuve, dis-je, et non encore éprouvée dans le monde, où elle mène ce combat double, tantôt contre les adversaires de chair et de sang, tantôt contre l'esprit du mal dans les Cieux. Et que ces chevaliers résistent par la force de leur corps à des ennemis corporels, je ne juge pas cela merveilleux car je ne l'estime pas rare. Mais qu'ils mènent la guerre par la force de l'esprit contre les vices et les démons, je l'appellerai non seulement merveilleux, mais digne de toutes les louanges accordées aux religieux... le chevalier est vraiment sans peur et sans reproche, qui protège son âme par l'armure de la Foi, comme il couvre son corps d'une côte de mailles. Doublement armé, il n'a peur ni des démons ni des hommes. Assurément celui qui souhaite mourir ne craint pas la mort.[21] Et comment redouterait-il de mourir ou de vivre, celui pour qui la vie est le Christ, et la mort la récompense[21]?... En avant donc, ô chevalier, et frappez d'âme intrépide les ennemis du Christ, assuré que rien ne puisse vous séparer de la charité de Dieu. »

> *does not depend on numbers but comes from on high...*
> *they know how to blend the gentleness of some with the*
> *valor of others... they rejoice when in victory but their*
> *joy is double if death brings them to their Lord... and*
> *thus they prefer a sacred death.*
>
> *"O the happy life, when one can await death without fear,*
> *desire it with joy...!"*

And they paraphrased again from the Papal Bull of Urban II:

> *"... and when winter ends and spring arrives, let us set out*
> *with joy and take the road with the Lord as our guide."*

The *Hidalgos* could not get enough of these texts which were recited over and over on many occasions, and sometimes by single warriors meditating on their own, speaking these words to themselves. The *Hidalgos* were not all Christians, and they recognized the limits of Urban's Bull and St Bernard's praises. They believed however that the precepts of service to God were universal and insisted on their stated mission of striving for justice and peace worldwide according to humanistic and Christian principles.

To show their tolerance they had adopted a vision that included many religions for their association. In the *languages* that composed its ranks they included Zoroastrian, Judeans, Sikhs, Hindus and several other rites. The *Hidalgos* would not commit the same mistakes that some attributed to the original Templars, they say intolerance and yes cruelty to *strangers,* in only rare instances of course, but acknowledged cases nonetheless.

The Hindus and Sikhs had left the northern part of India after the takeover by Islamic conversion of all areas north of the line Kochi to Puducherry. The Hindu northerners felt more at home with Western peoples that with their own compatriots to the south, so many Hindus migrated to Patagonia, and the Hindu *language*, one of the largest of the *Hidalgos*, formed one of their most dedicated and fearsome contingents.

The Judeans were practitioners of the Hebrew religion and were formerly known as Jews, Israelis or Israelites although their proper heritage was more accurately called Judean. Of course Judeans were tolerated in the Caliphate as well but many did not conceive a life of just being *tolerated*; they insisted, just like the other *Hidalgos*, on being regular and full citizens in their own land, not second class subjects. And especially the land given to them by God, to cherish and protect and keep free from sin. That, from time immemorial they had failed to achieve. And so they believed God had taken the Promised Land back, one more time. They believed they had been *chosen* not for a particular superior character or ability, but rather chosen to carry the message of God to all on Earth. And their failure to do so time and again landed them in long periods of repentance and redemption. Being chosen to them was not a privilege but a duty, an obligation. Just like the *Hidalgos'* mission to serve those less fortunate and that did not have to carry a divine mission. As such, many *Hidalgos* believed the Judeans had been hidalgos throughout their history. *Not a privilege, but a duty and an obligation: Noblesse oblige.* True *Hidalgos.*

The training of the *Hidalgos* consisted of the traditional arms, swords and hand-to-hand combat, *mano a mano* as it was known in Spanish, firearms, explosives, sabotage, and the use of whatever advanced quantum weapons they would receive from the Han. The Han had a vested interest in their success, or at least in destabilizing the Caliphate, just as the Caliphate attempted to overtake the Han.

The Han were cautious however. They did not want to create, or be the catalyst for, a force they could not control. The West had done so two centuries before. The Western ancestors had assisted the ancestors of the Caliphate's current rulers in fighting and defeating one of their own. Of course an evil one of their own. Nonetheless that unholy alliance had resulted in the beginning of the end for the West. That was not the only cause of course. The Han themselves had favored the weakening of the West, by economic and other means, and had engineered a few economic crises of their own by manipulating currencies and deploying devastating cyber warfare tools that provoked panics, and these ended up in the destabilization of the West. And now the Han had a much more implacable adversary in world affairs. Hence caution was necessary in the assistance to the *Hidalgos*, the Han thought.

So the Han helped, but only to a certain extent. Regardless, the *Hidalgos* knew that liberation comes at one's own hands. As they liked to say: *if you have to ask for freedom, you are thus not free* which they explained in many ways as well. One such way was: "if you need someone's' help to achieve your freedom, you are then indebted and thus not free any longer." Simple truth, simply stated.

The *Hidalgos'* dream was first and foremost to reconquer Rome, and then Jerusalem. Yes of course the Judeans would recover their land, for the fourth or fifth time in recorded history, that was the expectation, and that was the word of Christ. The majority of the *Hidalgos* was of the Christian faith and as such believed, and desperately hoped for the return of Christ. They knew that Christ's return would not happen without the Kingdom of David being reinstated to the Judean nation.

On that day of Justice and Redemption they knew, the holy sites would be open to both peoples of Jesus of course. The Al Aqsa mosque would be replaced by the true Church on one side and the Temple of Solomon on the other. Both sides would live in peace. Just the way it was before the conquest of Jerusalem by Islam in the year 638 of the Christian Era.

That most beautiful church would be built on the Temple Mount. It would be the Church of Mater Dei. The Church of the Mother of God. Privately though, the Hindus, and the Judeans even more so, did not see the excitement concerning a Mother of God, or a Son for that matter, but they went along as they had common interests. They were allies after all. And the West had had a reputation, or at least had culminated with free societies where tolerance was the norm, perhaps too much tolerance indeed to the point of defeating themselves. In any event these were considerations in the debates that were held nightly after prayer services in the Ice Chapels in the Antarctic Peninsula, that part of Antarctica that faced the bottom of Patagonia, where the last remnants of Christendom persisted in their beliefs.

The *Hidalgos* insisted on these discussions because a true holy warrior is sound of body and mind, as Urban II and St Bernard had observed. They prided themselves of nurturing their intellect and keeping acute minds. The debates also allowed the various *languages* to interact with each other, to understand each other. The leaders believed this interaction represented a microcosm of the societies they would create once the Caliphate was taken over and pushed back to the limits of their original lands, to the deserts where it had begun, and to which it belonged.

Of course every *Hidalgo* was familiar with the Caliphate's doctrine that *'once something becomes of Islam, it shall remain of Islam.'* As a retort to that provocation and knowing where they were and how much tonnage had been destroyed by the treacherous ice in Antarctica in the centuries past, they offered the saying of the stranded sailors, which they knew to be truly true: *'What the ice takes, the ice keeps'*, a truth that the first explorers of these ice desert discovered sometimes to their fatal end.

La Base had its main training camps in the desolate lands of the Antarctic Peninsula. The extreme temperatures and rough conditions made the recruits feel they were ready for anything. Indeed these were rough men, just as the Templars had been.

La Base comprised several camps, called *campos*. One was *Campo Jerusalem* in the heart of the Peninsula, another *Campo Santa Sofia* on the Weddell Sea coast, facing the South Atlantic, another still was *Campo Roma*, on the Southern Ocean coast facing the Pacific. All the names of the *campos* bore a religious connection, and especially reminding the rank and file *Hidalgos* that they were fighting for the liberation of their former lands. *Santa Sofia* represented a particularly moving allusion since it traced its name back to the Church of Hagia Sofia in Constantinople and which had been converted into a mosque when that great Christian city had fallen to the Muslims in the Year 1453 of the Christian Era. Almost a thousand years before that event a new era had ushered in a thousand years of unprecedented growth and achievement for their people and their faith. And the *Hidalgos* would do it again. Yes they had slacked in their efforts, not them but their forefathers who had not resisted the onslaught of Islam. But now was the time of redemption.

The Antarctic Peninsula is the warmest part of the Continent of Antarctica. It is a short distance by sea from *Tierra del Fuego*, the Land of Fire, itself an island facing Punta Arenas to its north. The straight of Magellan, a waterway between the continent proper and Tierra del Fuego, allows passage from the Atlantic to the Pacific.

The Peninsula jutted out of the Antarctic Continent from about 75 degrees South to 63 degrees South. It featured a mountain range which is considered the continuation of the *Cordillera de los Andes* in South America. Because of its relative lower latitudes, that is closer to the equator, its climate was considered moderate. Moderate of course was a relative term where the *Hidalgos* had chosen to set camp and conduct these most enlightened considerations of violence and peace, of sin and redemption, of loss and glory.

The archipelago known as Tierra del Fuego owes its name to the many fires the great explorer Magellan is believed to have observed when circumnavigating the world. It is situated between 54 degrees

South at Punta Arenas and 56 degrees South at Cape Horn, the equivalent to Amsterdam and Copenhagen in the north. No warm currents soften the climate in these regions the way they do in the northern European lands, the climate there and of course further down in the Antarctic Peninsula is thus forbidding.

Punta Arenas was about a thousand nautical miles from *Campo Roma*, a short distance but a challenge for mariners from time immemorial. The confluence of the two oceans with their counter rotating currents itself a challenge for sea men, is enhanced by the natural savagery of the winds at these latitudes. If one looks at the latitudes in the Southern Hemisphere, and draws a thick line around the globe at about 36 to 38 degrees South one can connect Buenos Aires, Cape Town, and Melbourne. Below that line Tasmania, part of New Zealand and the tip of Argentina, that is Lower Patagonia. A mere less than one million square kilometers. The area of British Columbia, for the entire circumference of the earth at less than halfway to the equator which would be at 45 degrees South. And outside that tiny land mass, just water. Water and more water.

As the Earth rotates east from west, the winds move that enormous mass of water at will. There is nothing to stop them. In the north, winds are broken by continents of sizable dimension, and that includes mountain ranges, substantial islands and other obstacles. In the south, for equivalent latitudes, nothing. This Southern Ocean region is known as the *roaring 40s*. So a trip from Punta Arenas to *Campo Roma* especially in the Antarctic Winter was a major challenge.

The *Hidalgos* chose the winter for their activities to avoid action by the Caliphate and also to harden their warriors. The *Hidalgos* had a philosophy consisting of making everything as hard as possible because the day of reckoning would be very difficult. And if the Caliphate forces were softening in comfort, as the West itself had mellowed while living in abundance, and the fact that the bulk of the Caliphate's military had to be *unconvinced*, as the *Hidalgos* desperately believed since they were to liberate these same people they were fighting, the hardening of the *Hidalgos* was a good thing.

The Antarctic Peninsula has a number of bays that were chosen by the naval architects of the *Hidalgos* as entry points. In these bays, incoming ships could dock and unload their cargo of freedom fighters and materiel, mostly Han. All this was feasible during the Antarctic Summer of course and the ships had to weight anchor in early March at the latest and reach for the Patagonian harbors.

Meanwhile the *Hidalgos* prepared to train in the Antarctic Winter in the harshest conditions.

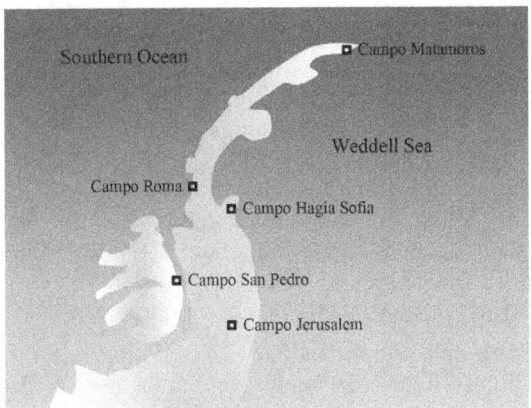

36. The Antarctic Peninsula and the Hidalgo Bases

This self inflicted suffering was welcome to the *Hidalgos* who seem to have been in need of it to assuage their guilt. This guilt was strange since not one of these *Hidalgos* had committed the sins they felt guilty about. Their forefathers at least a century or more before had done so. They had let their world empire fritter away. Yes of course Sheikh Hussein, the first Caliph, born a Muslim therefore *once of Islam, always of Islam*, had done his part. But they had allowed that so-called First Caliph of *Ameristan* to undo centuries of Western civilization. They felt guilty for the sins of their fathers. In that respect it brought them closer to the Old Testament where a sin is paid not by the sinner but by the descendants of the sinner, several generations hence.

Of particular importance were the sins of the great King David, since Christ himself was to be a descendant fourteen generations down from King David. The sins had already been expiated and hence the Savior had arrived. He in turn had to pay with his life for the sins of all, those sins committed after King David.

King David had sinned in a particular way. He had violated the tenth commandment which says *"thou shall not covet you neighbor's wife"*. King David did and he went further than taking the wife of Uriah the Hittite. David then sent Uriah, a valiant warrior, to the battle of Rebah so *"that he may be struck down, and die"*. David's second sin was a violation of the sixth commandment, *"thou shall not kill"*.

Bathsheba, that was her name, became David's wife. David had sent her husband to die first on the next battle in order to take her. Of course King David felt the guilt to his last days and wrote very moving psalms about his deeds, and his weakness. He asked God for forgiveness and knew he did not deserve it. And although God let him finish his reign as King, because he had faithfully served God before and done many good things, the retribution upon his progenitors was implacable. Only Solomon his son reigned as king of an undivided realm. And even that, after having his own brother, Absalom, murdered. And Solomon's children would never rule a united kingdom again. In fact the kingdom of Israel was never to rise again. Only Judea had remained. Until its inhabitants were dispersed as well. Forty generations of repentance for one's sins.

In the dark, cold and isolated Winters in Antarctica, these biblical stories, combined with the harsh conditions they imposed upon themselves, and the dreams they carried in their hearts created for the *Hidalgos* an almost mystical atmosphere in which they were close to beatitude. The mystical conviction of the Templars, which they emulated, only added to the sacred sense of their mission. The empty landscape, the incredible snow storms and violent winds brought a sense of unreality to the entire ensemble of *Campos*. The whole Peninsula seemed to have landed out of another world, another time.

When a *Hidalgo* lifted his eyes to the Antarctic sky, on a clear night, the immensity of the heavens and the limitless horizon of white ice brought every soul closer to his God. Even humanists, as atheists were euphemistically called, shared this sense of awe and wonder in such space. One could lift his eyes and look at the universe above one's head and sense the connection between time and space, Time and Space, between the beginning of All and the end of All.

Don Juan

The Commander of the *Hidalgos*, a man named Tomás de San Juan, but called Don Juan by his people, was born in *Al Andalus*, or rather as he preferred to say Spain, *España*. After attempting local *uprisings* which consisted mainly of refusing to attend one or two of the required five daily prayers that the Caliphate *Al Andalus* continued to impose on the converts and their descendants, and this for over four generations now, Don Juan had decided to take on the *armed struggle.*

Don Juan armed himself with a book about the *Chevaliers du Temple,* or *les Templiers* in French, the *Knights Templars,* and that he had discovered in one of his ancestors' remaining possessions that were kept in the family. He could trace part of his lineage to France, actually to the border regions between France and Spain, in the *Pyrenées.* That ancestor, also named Thomas de St Jean, while on his death bed, had made his progenitors promise that they would keep, and hide, two boxes of books for *posterity* as he had put it. He had also insisted that his descendants upon their own death require from their own descendants that they make the same promise. And so for almost two hundred years now, two somehow decomposed boxes made of ancient cardboard and containing strange books had survived the purification enacted by the Caliphate.

Don Juan, who was born Ahmed Ben Mustafa, had immediately adopted the name of this forefather. He had then decided to *escape* to Patagonia to be with his people. The Caliphate in *Al Andalus* and elsewhere was having problems with youths being indoctrinated by disguised priests, and other fomenters of trouble. Don Juan was not one of them. He had discovered his path on his own and that is why he had decided to take action in a new frontier that would be the launching pad for his war against the Caliphate.

The more desolate the frontier the closer to his roots he would be, or so he thought. And so he landed in Patagonia where although he gained the sympathy of the population and the authorities, these insisted on expelling him to Antarctica as he was too much of a provocation for the Caliphate. The relationship of Patagonia with the Caliphate at that time was at best fragile. Especially that Urban XXII, or rather Urban 2-2 as they liked to say, had taken the name of Urban II, the instigator of the Crusades, and *'the 22 was one 2 for Urban the second, and the second 2 for the second reconquista'.*

Tolerance of others was paramount for the *Hidalgos.* The *Hidalgos* believed that it is amid suffering that human nature strives to make friends and fellows in sorrow. It is when greed and self satisfaction prevail that humans revert to their natural ways of domination, both physical and spiritual, and desire to impose their ways. But not always, the Templars were a model of tolerance, at least that is what the *Hidalgos* believed.

Don Juan delighted in telling little known stories of the tolerance of the Templars, especially since their reputation had been smeared by the last generations of Christians before their conversion. In one such story, Don Juan related one evening a most moving experience.

"Most Beloved Brethren" – Don Juan liked to emulate Urban II and St Bernard – "I know many of you think our model knights, the Templars were cruel barbarians but you excuse them as just being of their time, and also add that their enemies were even crueler. Well that is not so. Do you know the story of Usama ibn Munqidh, the Ambassador from the Kingdom of Damascus under Zengi, the *atabeg* of Mosul, who in 1132 wrote one of the most moving testimonies of the Templars' tolerance? Let me read to you what Usama wrote then. I remind you that Usama was a Muslim and he wrote:

> "When I visited Jerusalem, I once entered the Al Aqsa mosque then occupied by the Templars, my friends. Next to it was a little mosque that the Franks had converted into a church. The Templars assigned that little mosque to me so that I could offer my devotions to Allah. One day I thus entered the mosque to glorify Allah. I was deep in my prayers when a Frank leaped upon me, held my person and swung my face toward the Orient while admonishing me with the words: 'This is the way one prays.' A group of Templars then rushed upon him, seized his person and expulsed him from the mosque. They then came upon me and apologized to me and said to me: He is a stranger who arrived from the country of the Franks in the last few days; he has never seen a person pray who did not face the Orient."

"Just like us, the Templars who were Crusaders, were tolerant and they helped their fellow Muslims against their own, when these were ignorant or just wrong. Just like us. Our ancestors' civilization was overtaken because somehow they started believing that their own ancestors were wrong, were bad, and their enemies were right, were good. If you lose the confidence of your cause, you are doomed. Of course we do not think so, and by the Grace of God, when we recover our lands and rebuild our societies, we shall ensure that doubts about our own identity, our own goodness never occur again.

"God bless all of us and good night," Don Juan concluded.

"Amen," responded the assembled *Hidalgos*.

Ice and Heaven

Don Juan had established a harsh regimen for his warriors. They walked on the Antarctic ice, bare feet. They slept outside, for short periods of course. They hunted for seals, they cooked them and ate them communally. They also gathered the blubber to use as fuel.

The daily routine was Spartan. After the *matins*, the morning prayers, hunting for seals at the beaches or near cliffs of ice and training in traditional arms was how the day began. After a rest period, lunch was served and followed with training in advanced weapons that were supplied by the Han. Then prayer, dinner and then the famous and popular debates. Finally night prayer, the *Vespers,* and sleep; and sometimes *Vespers*, debates and then sleep

The immensity of the ice, one of the only two features of the landscape of Antarctica, the other being the heavenly sky, connected the warriors to the immensity of the universe and they felt closer to their God, and thus felt empowered in their mission. They would reclaim their kingdoms and their glory. Of course most of the lands they would reclaim had not been kingdoms for centuries before the advent of the Caliphate, but reclaiming a lost kingdom sounded more inspirational than reclaiming a lost republic, a parliamentary system or a constitutional monarchy. So they went by that formula although all understood that only God would be the king of the liberated lands, and the managers of the lands would be the presidents and other representatives of the people.

Just like God had ordered the Hebrews when he gave them the land of Canaan: the land belonged to God, the *chosen* people were chosen solely to administer it and carry His Commandments and His message of peace and justice. And they would keep the lease on that land only if they acted according to God's precepts. Otherwise God would take that lease away from them. And time and again He did. Privilege is truly a duty and an obligation, not an advantage. The essence of nobility. *Noblesse oblige.*

One of the evening debates that Don Juan directed concerned the ownership of land and the role of kings. And why when kings had failed they lost their kingdoms. First the kings that had failed in the West were not only the kings or not even the presidents but also its leaders, academics, opinion makers and other agents of the kleptocracy that ruled its failed societies, the modern false prophets of the Old Testament. Kleptocracy indeed because the doers produced and the talkers profited. In the liberated lands, Don Juan knew, that would not happen again. Their society would be one of justice and peace.

At that debate long ago, Don Juan had posed the question of who owned the land that God gave to his people. The obvious answer was that it was the recipient of the land given by God.

"No," had said Don Juan. "In paganism, the king is almighty. It is what we would call today a dictatorship or a political tyranny. The dictator is all powerful, he has the right of life and death over his subjects. Even in democracies, the *people* are the dictator as they hold these powers. In the first instance there is no power over the King-tyrant, in the second, there is no power over the people so they can be misled into believing that all is permissible. And sins and abominations enter the realm of the acceptable. And the enemy begins to look attractive, indeed since it is a known fact that familiarity breeds contempt, the *elite*, those who flourish in the kleptocracy of failing societies, that self entitled *elite* who feeds from the labor of others, begins disliking their own, even themselves, and they begin acting against their own as well, to the benefit of the foreign, especially if that foreign is antagonistic. The more antagonistic, the more the *elite* supports its enemies. And that is the major cause for the West's downfall."

Don Juan related the story of the vineyard of Naboth who lived under the reign of Ahab. Ahab was a descendant of Solomon and King of the Northern Kingdom of Israel. His wife Yezabel was the daughter of King Ethbaal of Tyre in Phoenicia. Don Juan related as follows:

"Ahab, King of Israel around the year 860 Before Christ, was taken by the beauty of Naboth's vineyard which was adjacent to his lands. He told Naboth: 'your vineyard is beautiful. I would love to have it to add to my lands.' Naboth respectfully responded: 'I cannot give it to you because I inherited it from my father, who himself inherited it from his ancestors and this for many generations hence. God had given these ancestors a long time ago these lands for us to care for. It cannot be given. I must care for it as a holy land.' King Ahab offered to buy it and offered any amount of gold or diamonds and rubies. Naboth declined since the land wasn't his. It belonged to God and he could not sell what was not his. Saddened King Ahab went back to his palace. Yezabel, the beautiful Yezabel of Pagan origin asked her husband why he was so sad and Ahab told her of his failure to acquire the land of Naboth. Yezabel it is told was perplexed that as king, Ahab had to beg to take the land of one of his subjects. In her country the King was almighty. All belonged to him. No one was above the King. He took what he chose to take. Yezabel then told Ahab not to worry, she would make sure Naboth's vineyard would belong to Ahab. The next day the perfidious Yezabel called an assembly of sages and convinced them to have Naboth executed. And his vineyard became Ahab's. Yezabel told him: "you are king, everything in this kingdom is yours, everything and everyone. That is how kings do."

"In those times, continued Don Juan, "before the Judeo-Christian tradition, kings were above all. The Judeo-Christian tradition ensured that kings would simply be administrators of what is ultimately God's. And our societies were built upon this principle. Humility and Decency. Peace and Justice. Hard Work and Respect. But that was before the kleptocracy and their traitors. We shall restore our societies with peace and justice," concluded Don Juan.

The members of the assembly dispersed to retire into their respective quarters and all were pensive and silent. As they walked they could see again and always the immensity of the ice and when they raised their eyes, again the immensity of the heavens.

Ice and sky. Ice and Heaven. That was the world of the *Hidalgos.*

Tectonic Impact

For their operations launched out of the Antarctic continent, the *Hidalgos* followed the perimeter of the almost circular land mass and selected the longitude most appropriate to reach their target with minimum risk of detection.

Of course, when diametrically opposed to the Peninsula, where targets were few as most was ocean above at these longitudes, they would cut across the continent in vehicles that used chain tracks but could also hover, they were called *hover-tractors.* These could climb the Antarctic plateau where temperatures were even more extreme because of the altitude that quickly surpassed over four thousand meters to reach 4,897 meters at Vinson Massif. This was the most efficient way to travel across the continent which had grown in size in the last two hundred years by an average of five kilometers all around and that were added to its average radius. This increase was due to the accumulation of ice and snow which tended to be larger near the edges of the continent probably due to the centrifugal dispersion of these elements.

The average temperature in this part of the world had been about 56 degrees below zero in centuries past, but it was now recorded at even lower than 70 degrees below zero. This dramatic decrease in the average temperature of course alarmed many who believed the Oceans would progressively evaporate and feed more and more snow to the Antarctic continent, sinking it further down due to the added weight. Already Western Antarctica had the lowest point of any landmass on Earth at 2,550 meters below sea level. The next low point was a mere 416 meters below sea level at the Dead Sea. The weight of the ice did have an effect.

Further, the accumulation of snow and ice tended to gather on the eastern end of mountain ranges which had already produced the Ronne Ice Shelf in Eastern Antarctica formed by the Ellsworth Mountains there; the Ross Ice Shelf in Western Antarctica, a product of the Trans Antarctic Mountains and at the edge of which the famous Mount Erebus rises; and the smaller Amery Ice Shelf further west, that is east in fact by going around the continent, and abutting the Prince Charles Mountains north of the American Highland. These ice shelves together with the Larsen, Shakleton and Getz shelves were now larger and higher than in centuries past. The two main wind systems, the Outer West Wind Drift flowing clockwise and the Inner East Wind Drift flowing in the opposite direction caused these accumulations on these natural obstacles. The winds produced by the two drift systems could reach 300 kilometers per hour, enough it was said *to move mountains*. And they did move mountains, mountains of ice.

These accumulations in turn added downward pressure on the continental floor which transmitted that pressure to the various fractures at and under the floor of the oceans surrounding Antarctica.

This was not new but the massive accumulations, much larger than what had been observed in centuries past, were also a cause of concern to certain scientists. It appeared, according to these, that the world was entering a new ice age as these accumulations seemed to become more significant as the decades progressed.

As ice accumulated and its weight pushed down on the subterranean continent, enormous pressures pushed on the fracture zones surrounding Antarctica further down toward the Earth's center but away from the geometric South Pole. The effect was that they in turn pressed outward the various fractures and ridges that formed the ocean floor in the Atlantic, Pacific and Indian Oceans, thus producing according to these same scientists enormous earthquakes accompanied by tidal waves of dimensions unseen before.

It must be noted that these effects were more pronounced in Western Antarctica where more of the sub-oceanic fractures could be seen radiating northward. In particular the three successive fracture zones, the Udintsev as deep as 5,111 meters below the surface, the Menard at 4,879 meters below sea level, and the Eltanin at 4,724 meters under the water, extended these pressures toward the Kermandec and the Tonga Trenches where they could relieve them at as deep as 10,800 meters below the Ocean surface. The main contention was that these in turn pushed the enormous pressures up around the New Hebrides and the island of Fiji toward the Mariana Trench at 10,910 meters below the surface, the lowest point on Earth. From there what remained of the pressures would then be transmitted to the Bonin, Isu and Kuril trenches, substantially north of where they had originated.

The concerned scientists therefore believed that by a ripple effect the sinking of the Antarctic continent which in fact appeared to be gaining height at the same time, was the precursor of major effects seen as far north as the arctic confines of the Han Empire, where these met the north-western end of the Caliphate before the two merged into the Arctic ices.

On the eastern Antarctic, since there were fewer fractures of similar significance, the dramatic effects on climate were therefore expected to be less pronounced. And they were, thus confirming the fears of the proponents of such theories.

The effects of this *global cooling*, which some called *global freezing*, were therefore believed by some to be devastating. And the proponents of those beliefs laid the cause of this global climatic phenomenon on the activities of man and its many quantum engineering applications. They believed that quantum tunneling at industrial scales in every part of the globe was mostly an endothermic reaction, thus absorbing energy from everywhere and producing alarming cooling. The leap to conclude that the climate effects were man-made was obvious to these proponents and therefore they believed that man was altering the balance of the tectonic plates causing catastrophic effects. *Believed* was the rather accurate word since nobody knew the exact science.

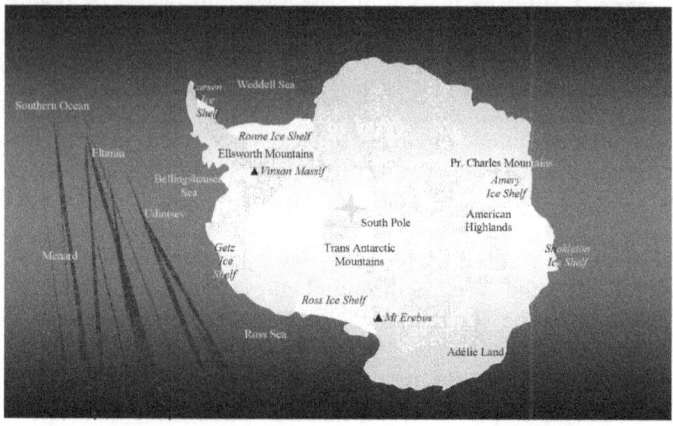

37. Fracture Zones Around Under Antarctica

There were two camps, those who believed in man-made *Global Cooling* and those who considered it a natural phenomenon due to the regular cycles of the planet. Everyone believed his own truth. No one in fact, or perhaps with the exception of a very few, had any idea of the exact science, and whether the evidence was cooked, manipulated or scientifically correct on either side. They just believed. As a matter of fact, most debates began with one proponent of one side or the other pronouncing first *"I believe that..."*; never could one hear anyone else say *"I know that..."* Conjecture and political abstraction were therefore the basis for most positions in this matter.

Even among scientists. The Caliphate, and they deserved credit for it, left it to God. The Caliphate officially shunned these theories as it was the realm of God and not up to man to interfere with nature.

"Even if we explode all our nuclear devices, our quantum arsenal and that of quark-based weapons, and those of the Han simultaneously and blow everything up, yes mankind might disappear but planet Earth would continue spinning and rotating," they would say. Calculations by quantum computers, estimated that such cataclysm would affect the spin of the Earth by two seconds per century depending on the direction of the blasts, or even as low as eight hundredths of a second per millennium. The rotation of the Earth around the Sun was also thought to be affected perhaps by as much as 5.2 seconds maximum and 2.2 seconds minimum per ten thousand years.

Even assuming that the doomsday models were even correct to this level of precision, no one could say with certainty what these numbers would mean and how they would affect life on Earth. And of course no one intended to blast all the power available to man simply to conduct this experiment.

To the Caliphate this proved the power of God and the vanity of mankind. The slogan *"You can kill each other, as Cain killed Abel, but you cannot change that which God created"* represented the official position quite accurately.

In the Han Empire, and for some *elites* in the Caliphate as well, politically motivated provocateurs and profiteers advocated means to warm the planet and therefore avoid the effects of the enormous amounts of accumulated polar ice that presumably pushed down on the rocky layers deep under the oceans and wreaked havoc on the continents themselves. To support their contention, they remarked that on average the Oceans had receded in the past two hundred years by up to 60 centimeters, although some estimates only allowed for 15 to 20 centimeters at most. It is true that in many lands some harbors had to be extended and others relocated further, that is closer to the water. It was also observed that while the thickness of the Antarctic ice was estimated at about 2.8 kilometers two centuries before, it had now reached 3.05 kilometers, an alarming acceleration in just two hundred years.

A vast literature had animated the debate creating celebrities, charlatans and profiteers. The Caliphate, and the Han as well, thought of interdicting these activities since they favored the talkers to the detriment of the doers, and both Empires had a common interest in not repeating the West's mistakes and its hysteria of centuries past.

Proponents of *global cooling* advocated launching CO_2 or carbon dioxide in the upper atmosphere in order to create an additional barrier that would trap the rays of the Sun after they reflect from the Earth surface thus adding a man-made component to the natural greenhouse effect. Others advocated different measures such as blowing a hole in the ozone layer to let the sun *free us* from freezing. One problem was the ozone layer they would blow up floated high above the Antarctic Continent, and models had not been developed enough to evaluate the impact of so close a deed to the source of the effects one wished to correct. And this *blowing up* of the ozone layer of course disregarded other potentially noxious effects such endeavor could bring. Another interesting concept was advanced by manufacturers of various thin sheets of composite material and consisted of laying down vast black *blankets* on top of the ice to entice heat absorption and reduce the natural reflection of the sun rays by the white ice.

Meanwhile life continued, and those who worked were at their post day after day. The others, a minority it must be admitted, but a minority educated in the best schools and raised with the comforts afforded them by their educated and powerful parents, kept talking and predicting and *believing* but not *knowing*. They kept believing in what theory that sounded scientific and for which no solid basis existed.

Alone in the Universe

A highlight of the day, a day that was either all day or all night for most of the year in the *Campos* of the Antarctic Peninsula, was the raising of the flag of the *Hidalgos*. In reverence to the Templars, the flag was called a *gonfalon,* an old French word that was mostly pronounced in Spanish and rendered as *El Gonfalón*. It was black and white, just like the original flag. Two big vertical rectangles, one black, the other white, one of top of the other. For the Templars, Black represented life on Earth and White the divine in Heaven. When at the end of a spear the *gonfalon* floated in the holy lands centuries ago, carried by a knight on a horse galloping toward his enemies in the heat of the battle, the two rectangles appeared intertwined, combining Heaven and Earth. The two colors, or absence of true color, by their simplicity emphasized the sacred nature of the mission of the Templars.

In Antarctica, the winds were harsh but the extremely low temperatures froze the fabric of the *gonfalon* which thus seemed made of metal. In fact it was the perfect flag for the Antarctic warriors since the top, black was like the heavens above them and the white, the ice below them. It was Heaven and Earth, just as it had been for the Templars but the worlds reversed. The symbolism was telling and saddening. Yes, the *Hidalgos* were at the bottom of the world whereas centuries before, the Templars had been at the top. Centuries before their ancestors were the victors and the conquerors, now they, the

Hidalgos were the freedom fighters seeking to reclaim that which they had lost.

But the *Hidalgos* believed the order would be reversed again and they would be the Templars of the next century which was now dawning on Christendom.

The *Hidalgos* had added a very thin blue border to the *gonfalon* to indicate progress accomplished in the last millennium since the early Templars, and to remind themselves of the blue of their lost lands. Light blue was also the color of Patagonia.

Every evening the raising of the flag was accompanied with patriotic songs the *Hidalgos* sang, and sometimes very sentimental songs about their loved ones, the lands they had lost, their faith that had been all but eliminated and that they would restore, and their hope, *la esperanza* they called it, without which they would not be able to sustain their difficult mission.

Every such evening a warrior was chosen randomly to raise the flag, which another warrior would lower after *Vespers*, to be raised again in the morning. The flag raisers were called *gonfaloniers*, as the Templars called them, or in a hispanicized version *gonfaloneros*. The honor of being a *gonfalonier* lasted but only one time for any warrior since once selected, a warrior's turn had to go to the back of the queue. The *Campos* being populated by thousands of able men, it was improbable that any one would receive the honor of being a *gonfalonier* more than once in his lifetime, or at least his lifetime as a warrior. Therefore that honor was taken very seriously and with much respect.

While the flag flapped immobile in the Antarctic winds, *Vespers*, the prayers of the night, were performed. Of course not all warriors were Catholic, or even Christians, so that time was occupied by those others who retrenched into their own prayers or meditations. But the time was still called *Vespers* for efficiency.

Some did not pray at all. They had joined the *Hidalgos* not out of any religious conviction but in fact because they did not have any convictions and considered such spiritual acts rather antiquated and naïve. But they were respectful. After all, in their view the *Hidalgos* were now more tolerant than the Caliphate, which would not permit unbelievers. Faithful to the wrong faith was somehow tolerated as the Caliphate wished to convert those in the wrong faith to the True Religion. But in the eyes of the Caliphate faithless beings were almost not human and difficult to reclaim, and in many instances it was very dangerous to express one's own lack of faith in a divinity.

The time of *Vespers* was therefore used in many ways and especially as a time of reflection. On one such evening, two Judeans, Nissim and Ari were debating topics that come to mind when one is in Antarctica and faced with the impossible mission of toppling the most powerful political and religious entity the world had ever known, and when these facts are obvious to all except to the mystical.

"Look at the sky, Ari," said Nissim. "How immense and beautiful. And the ice that extends forever."

"You sound like Abraham in the desert," responded Ari in a sarcastic tone.

"Be serious, Ari," said Nissim. "You know, we are alone here. We are alone in the Universe."

"You don't know Nissim, there may be a million inhabited planets out there, some with idiots like us, some with superior beings, and some with even more idiots than us. So we are not alone, if I had to guess."

"Yes, there may be other beings out there, intelligent and not. But then, all of us, including them, are alone. I guess that is why some of us, and I must admit I am one of them, need a projection beyond that loneliness, and we call it God. It makes us feel at home and less lonely."

"Well, now I understand. Once we leave the womb, where we are connected and secure, we begin feeling alone, lost in what seems then an eternity, an eternity of space and of time, a void that we struggle to fill all our lives. And we invent gods and religions to fill that void."

"Fine, Ari. But look, these guys are praying for the return to their lands, and their gods. Even the ones who are not praying are wishing, or meditating their wishes, and hoping. Why?

"Why can't they just comply with the Caliphate? In fact why did the Caliphate even bothered to conquer the West and convert everyone there? We are alone, don't you understand?"

"Nissim, I see what you are saying but I don't know where you are going. All right, we are alone. What do you want to do then?"

"My point is Ari, why are we fighting? Why did our ancestors fight? Animals fight for survival, we fight to conquer, even when there is no need. No physical need. Do we have the spiritual need to conquer and destroy those we perceive as opponents? Or that we make our opponents even if they are not? And if so, why? Because we are alone. That is why."

"Wow!" said Ari. "Look, we fight, I grant you that, but then when we see the folly of our ways we make peace and wait for the next fight."

"Exactly, we make peace," said Nissim, "and then we join our previous enemies to fight new ones. Look at yourself, you are a Judean *Hidalgo*, does it make any sense, a Jewish Templar, for Christ's sake?"

"Christ? For Christ's sake? Even for a Judean *Hidalgo* I would not have expected such an expression," said Ari in a faked shocked tone.

"Yes, sorry, it is a way of speaking. You see, we first conquered, and then lost our land. And our prophets lamented our fate. And then we regained our lands. And lost them again. The same with these other people. They were just sitting there in Iberia, the Visigoths came by and clobbered them, and then the Visigoths became Iberian as if nothing had happened. Slowly, Christ filled their hearts and then suddenly, in the name of Allah, *Al Andalus* was created. For hundreds of years they suffered humiliation in their ancestral lands. And then again they reconquered those.

"Fast forward another few hundred years and we are back with *Al Andalus*. And soon, perhaps even in our lifetime, Christian Spain, Christian Europe, and even America, will rise again."

« *Plus ça change, plus c'est pareil* » interrupted Ari

"Yes, '*The more things change, the more they stay the same*'. We all know it is a march in vain, a circle that never ends and the loser of today is the winner of tomorrow and the loser of the day after tomorrow. And I say we fight, not because we need it for physical survival the way animals do, but because we need to in a strange way, because we feel we are alone, we feel lost in the Universe. And the fighting provides us with a reference point, with something tangible to cling to, to justify our lonely lives. Because we think, we must fight. That is what I say. The Bible says that when Adam and Eve began to think, they felt *naked*. I think the Bible meant *naked* in a spiritual way, not the physical way with the fig leaf and all that; as I say we are *naked* in the Universe, we are alone in the Universe."

"All right, all right. All right, we are alone. But what do you want us to do? All I see is that all these people are out there praying, and wishing, and hoping, all from different parts of the Earth, united in a common goal of liberation. I don't feel I am alone."

"That is my point, you don't feel you are alone because you are participating in a fight, you have been regimented into a fight of conquest, or reconquest, *la reconquista*, as Don Juan likes to say. And no matter what, since most of us will die before that liberation, we still believe. Because there is life after us, not our life, but life nonetheless, and we want that life to be modeled after that for which we are fighting, that in which we have believed."

"So you believe in the return of a Savior, of Christ, is that what you are saying?"

"They believe Christ will return and salvation with him. We just believe the Messiah will come, just not come back. And salvation with him. And that makes all of us feel less lonely."

"So you won't feel alone, you don't feel alone now, because of the Messiah, because someone is coming?" asked Ari.

"That's right; just knowing that someone is coming, or coming back, or whatever, connects me with eternity and when I then look at the heavenly sky, I don't feel alone any longer. That is the essence of faith. Perhaps you are right. It is just a need, like food, or love, or the need for beauty. A spiritual need without which we are without compass."

"Well, talk about yourself. I need no compass, and pardon the allusion here, but in Antarctica a compass indicating the North has a special meaning. Not here in the Peninsula, but right there at the Pole. The North is in front of you, and behind you. On your left and on your right," said Ari pointing south.

"*Touché,*" said Nissim.

"Nissim," interrupted Ari, "listen, you said that Christ was coming back, or the Messiah was just coming, once and for the first time I guess. Imagine all of this had never been told, never been taught, or inculcated. And you and I were to write a story for these folks so that they wouldn't feel alone, as you put it. And we told them that no matter what, someone sent by God would be coming soon and save them. Save them from their loneliness I guess."

"What's your point?"

"Bear with me. Let's write that story, and say Yehova is about to send a Savior, at the end of times, to relieve our suffering and so on and so forth.

"Now in our story, which has no historical background, and no biases, how would you and I decide to name that Savior? Joe, Ari, Nissim, Don Juan? Of course not. We would probably name him the Savior sent by God. Or Yehova's Savior, or even better, since he acts on behalf of Yehova, we should name him 'Yehova Saves'. In Hebrew, *Yehova Shua'*, or *Yeho-shua'*, or Joshua if you prefer. In Greek, Yesus, and here Jesus. Isn't it odd?"

"Very odd, and very interesting," said Don Juan from the shadows where he had followed part of the conversation for a while. "I feel God in my heart, Jesus is with me, and that gives me the strength to fight the Caliphate. And by the Grace of God, we shall prevail."

"Amen," said Ari. "I totally agree. It confirms that faith gives you the strength to achieve, especially if you cannot get to your goals any other way."

"But wait," said Nissim, "we still have to debate whether salvation is to come from a first or second visit of the Savior."

"That's easy," said Ari. "It truly doesn't matter. When, and if, that someone comes, it will be quite obvious to everyone if it is a return trip or a first visit. And we shall all submit to the clear evidence. Now, I doubt any visit is imminent, I am fighting for what is right, regardless of the faith."

"But what is right to you, you inherited from the teachings of your forebears, who learned it from the early revelations and commandments. Savages and animals do not know what is right, and if they do, it is not the same *right*. So you too need that spiritual component to sustain you in your loneliness."

"Perhaps," said Ari. "In any event let us all pray that when that someone comes, that it is either Jesus, or someone... some Judean or Hebrew that we can recognize. Just pray that it is not Mohammed."

"No!" exclaimed both Nissim and Don Juan. "That would be unthinkable."

"Why?" said Ari. "If he is the Messiah, the last prophet as they call him, why not? I guess all of us need a faith we can relate to. A Savior we actually like, not just any Savior. Hence my point. We are alone, and so what?"

"Alone?" asked Don Juan.

"Never mind Don Juan," said Nissim, "it is a long story we were just debating before you sneaked on us."

"I will sneak again, believe me, and I will sneak in the open. I love these discussions. This is what makes the *Hidalgos*, like the Templars, warriors with a heart. God's warriors. And like them we must liberate the Holy Land before Christ is able to return. And it will be Jesus who comes back...well... maybe another savior sent by God, sent by Jesus... but really I truly believe it will be Jesus back. I know it will not be Mohammed. It can't be.

"I will be back after *Vespers* tomorrow, with a couple of warriors who love this type of discussion. Please don't start without me," concluded Don Juan as he left.

Ari and Nissim looked at each other and Ari said:

"What have we started here? Always us. Thousands of years ago, we started with the message of God, which we said we had been chosen to deliver, and look where it got us. These guys, and the Caliphate, carried the message way beyond the intended goal. And millions of lives have been lost in the millennia since."

"These lives would have been lost in any event. Man loves conflict. Man needs conflict. If it is not on behalf, or against, the message of God the Hebrews had taken upon themselves to bring to the world, these same lives, or others in equal numbers, or in greater numbers, would have been lost as well. We are alone in the Universe and that fear makes us fight and destroy. While we are fighting and have a cause for which we struggle, we have no fear and we forget we are alone.

"Look there, toward the heavens, look deep, there! I can see the beginning of Time, when Space began to form. And we are alone, until someone from there comforts us in our loneliness."

These last words from Nissim required no answer. All on the subject had been said, at least for the evening. Nissim and Ari then returned to their respective quarters.

Besides these philosophical and religious considerations, the *Hidalgos* were men of action. They organized *deterrent* operations which very often ended fatally. They were in fact martyrdom operations but the *Hidalgos* refused to call them that way. Life was sacred and God never wanted men to die for Him. Life was to be preserved at all costs, and these costs could not be life itself, that would be a contradiction. Of course one could die in battle, in self defense but not willingly. The *Hidalgo* believed that not wanting to die, despite the declaration of St Bernard, gave them even more courage since they had to confront dangers that could result in something they did not desire, they were not allowed to desire. Confronting death that one desires with a blind passion requires no courage. Confronting death when fighting for a noble cause and when one does not wish for one's own death, that was true courage.

The Caliphate could have obliterated *La Base* but there was no assurance that all of the *Campos* would be destroyed. There were rumors of secret *Campos* deep in Antarctica, including at the forbidding South Pole. Even on Mount Erebus. Those *Campos* consisted of caves dug out of the ice.

Because of the incessant ice and snow storms, and the incredibly strong winds in Antarctica, the *caves* were the result of very advanced engineering techniques. They were build on some sort of stilts, and as the years passed they slowly began to sink into the snow, or rather they became engulfed in a rising sea of snow. While on stilts, they could be destroyed easily. But for the Caliphate that did not mean the *Hidalgos* were in those *caves* in any event. These resided, and hid, in the sunken caves, since the fresh caves were not caves at all. They looked more like ice sky scrapers on stilts. Furthermore, the Caliphate was well aware that too harsh an operation against the obvious *Campos*, while creating perhaps little or no casualties, would create a wave of terrorist actions in their urban centers bringing further instability.

In fact within the Caliphate there were those who advocated not provoking the *Hidalgos*, since harsh action against them would just create more *Hidalgos*. Those who advocated these erroneous thoughts, the *soft line* as it was known, since they never provided a solution but rather the abstention from any action, were sometimes called traitors, or even Westerners, in a derogatory manner of course. Some it was said had been put to death for treason. The *Hidalgos* considered those *soft line* advocates their best allies within the enemy lines.

The terror campaign of the *Hidalgos*, which could blend easily within the population of the conquered parts of the Caliphate and undoubtedly received their active support, at least from parts of it, made the Caliphate hesitant. It hoped the *Hidalgos* would wither away and the pressure on the Han was in part aimed at limiting or suppressing the aid and support the Han provided to *La Base*. The *Hidalgos* nonetheless lived in a sort of terror as well because the Caliphate could strike at any moment and cause massive devastation. It was, as they used to joke, a situation of check mate, or MATE, for Mutually Assured Terror for Ever, or Everywhere. That was of course wishful thinking because they were far from being in a check mate situation. Further, MATE was the subjunctive form for the verb *matar*, or *to kill* in Spanish. The *Hidalgos* thus understood it as *"que mate"*, or *"that I kill"*, with all the inferences a *Hidalgo* could choose to interpret it. In fact one of the *Campos* had been named *Matamoros*, *Moros* being the Spanish word for Moors, or the Caliphate's original ethnic group in *Al Andalus*. Of course the cities in *Al Andalus*, and in the Caliphate in general that were named Matamoros had seen their name changed eons before. But not in Antarctica.

And so life went on from day to miserable day, or night to miserable night depending on the season, in the far confines of the Antarctic Peninsula, where a group of self styled *warriors* planned a *reconquista* with an arsenal of Middle Age weapons and philosophies, combined with advanced quantum tools of destruction provided by the Han Empire, and an enlightened outlook of life brought about by the confluence of cultures and faiths that assembled there. Despite all these odds, the *Hidalgos* knew they would succeed. If not them, their descendants. That was the March of History.

4

A DAY IN THE CALIPHATE

The Holy Land

"Brother Assam," said the Keeper of the Faith, "you have not failed. The Prophet (pbuh) has instructed us to be patient. The way of the truth is sometimes encumbered with obstacles. We know our way. We shall persist and prevail. We have all the time to get there. The time of our lives and those of our children, and their children's children."

"Very Holy Excellency," answered Assam, "that is true. But it is also true that a sweet dream of a true Muslim is to see the day of Mohammed's triumph (pbuh) over the entire Earth during his lifetime."

"Correct. But that is not up to us to determine. Only Allah can decide when that day, the End of Days, and by the hand of whom, will be. All we can do is strive to achieve the true faith everywhere. And it will happen when Allah decides. *Insha'Allah*."

"*Insha'Allah*," said Assam.

"Brother Assam, you need to gather your thoughts, learn from the past experience and plan the next assault on the Han."

"But Most Holy Excellency, isn't it what Sheikh Moussa is supposed to be doing?"

"Moussa has no chance. Listen, the Han know what happened. In fact their leader, I do not use the word *supreme,* because only Allah is Supreme. Their mortal Leader induced us into believing he was with us. And he used us. And now he knows what we are trying to do. Well, I am not saying he did not know before, he did know. So we haven't lost anything. Except Al Kansii, who was much better qualified that Al Idahi, whom Moussa has just selected.

"By the way, are we sure that Al Kansii is gone? You did not receive confirmation from him that he had died, correct?"

"Correct, Most Holy Excellency. We did not receive confirmation from himself of his own death, as was planned. But that does not mean anything. If he were captured by Yu Lin, and that is the only alternative, because any other way the eradication of the People's Council would not have occurred, if that were the case I say, what can Yu Lin do with him? Why not eliminate a very embarrassing witness?"

"Well Assam, Yu Lin could use him against us. Who knows what these perfidious Han are capable of? They could turn him. They could re-program him through mind control, a discipline in which they excel.

"Let's us not dwell on the past. I want you to collect your thoughts and think of our next move. It has to be very different. Moussa's is a low-cost operation, imitating your own, and Yu Lin is expecting it and will defeat it with his eyes closed. You, Assam are unique among the Caliphate's brains. Just like your famous ancestor. And you need to concentrate on the next phase of our struggle. When Moussa and Al Idahi, which are seen by many as two brutes, fail, it will be your turn again. And if Moussa succeeds, well that will have been the way of Allah. You will still deserve credit for preparing Moussa's victory. However I do not think the Han are so naïve as to let us win so easily. They are not the West of ancient times. So, Brother Assam, go and think. And pray to Allah. And follow the commandments of the Prophet, Peace Be Upon Him. *Insha'Allah, wal Hamdulillah.*"

"*Hamdulillah,*" answered Assam.

Assam walked several steps backwards, ensuring he never turned his back to the Keeper of the Faith. The Keeper in turn looked sideways and down. He was done with Assam, he did not need to look at him.

When Assam reached the entrance he turned quickly on his heels and began his slow walk to his quarters. His brain was full of thoughts that converged from multiple directions and in different intensities. It was a sad moment because despite what the Keeper had said, he knew he had failed. At the same time he was full of hope because he was to try again, one day, after Moussa would have failed. After Moussa would have failed to achieve the goals that had evaded the Caliphate for decades. But this time Assam would succeed. With all the strength in his heart, he wished for that to be true, and although he had no reason to believe one way or the other, he felt it would become true. Some day. He knew that. But he would have to wait for that day.

By the time he reached his quarters he could feel something heavy in his chest. It was not pain, or sadness. Something heavy and at the same time empty. A heavy emptiness. It was a mixture of hope and disappointment. His thoughts were contradictory and in confusion.

He entered his private office. Behind a wall where holy books were arranged in perfect and sacred order, he lifted a bookend and was able to rotate one small part of the bookshelf. The secret entrance to his secret room was now opened. He entered and slowly rotated the bookshelf. The room was now hermetically sealed. He began to listen.

Incoherent Thoughts

Despite having reached the ultimate heights of power in the Caliphate, Assam was somehow sensitive and mellow, perhaps sentimental as well. Assam was indeed an enlightened descendant of savagery. Just like the Christians of a thousand years before. Just like the Vandals that had desecrated Rome. Just like the Vikings. And the Goths, and the Visigoths. And the Angles. And the Franks and the Saxons. And the Han and the Huns, and the Mongols. And everyone else. Assam knew that. His superior intellect did not allow him to hide obvious truths.

Empires rose and empires fell. Some quickly, others slowly. But the march of History was ineluctable. The obvious example was that of Christians and Muslims in *Al Andalus*. In seventeen hundred short years, it had changed hands and hearts three times and perhaps even four depending on how one wished to count.

As Assam began to let the music penetrate his soul and his heart he asked himself: "Why convert the Han? What is the purpose?" Incoherent thoughts were now invading his entire being. And so these brain impulses began to fly in all directions, and neurons were tunneling, if tunneling there was, through the wrong neuron barriers.

And if any of his brain waves were entangled, they were entangled with the wrong ones. But Assam let the insurgency in his brain proceed. He had no other choice.

He began pondering how in the interminable march of History most recently the West had conquered the world with might and power and technology, but also with ideas. In that field the Han were as good as the Caliphate was. On the other hand Assam knew the Caliphate would not be able to conquer the Han the way the Christians did with the pagan Romans. With soft power. With belief.

One thing was clear to him: the West had conquered the world and just sat there not knowing what else to do. One can die for Allah. One cannot die to free strange people in foreign lands for the cause of *democracy* or *freedom*, especially that of others. One can die for his faith but not for a sheer material object. Just as the enemies of Allah could fight no longer to protect idols, material objects. But one can die for his people, his religion, his tribe or his race. And in the extreme one can die for his own survival although that in itself was a contradiction in Assam's eyes.

And Assam concluded that was why Al Idahi would fail. The Keeper of the Faith was right. Not just this time of course. Patient build-up of institutions necessary to undermine the stability of the Han, that was what was needed. A silent and pervasive *jihad*, not a violent one. An inner struggle, but made inner by the Han themselves. Assam wondered if Confucianism could help in that endeavor, the way the missing convictions of the West had done before.

Assam remembered something that Al Kansii had said before he departed for his martyrdom operation. It seemed insignificant, or at least inconsequential at the time. Especially in the heat of the battle, Assam had not paid much attention to it, but now it took a much larger importance. Perhaps that point alone ended up in the result of the failure. Order out of *Chaos*. Yes a small change in initial conditions sometimes produces immense consequences, if that change has the relevance that Allah wants it to have. "*Creator or creation*" Assam tried to remember. Yes the way Al Kansii had put it was now clear in his mind:

> "*there can be no creation without creator*
> *there can be no creator without creation.*"

Assam had thought at the time that with the second sentence Al Kansii was simply reinforcing his faith by doubling up the affirmation of God's existence. Now he wasn't sure. Al Kansii had learned or read something in *Al Andalus* that had made him write that extra sentence. Was Al Kansii saying that if there was no creation, no singular event of creation, therefore there would be no God?

Assam knew that some leading scientists, in the Han Empire especially, were now arguing that the Standard Cosmological Model was incorrect or at least incomplete and therefore there may have been no Big Bang, thus no creation as a singularity. No point of departure where Time had created Space and Space began to define Time. Just an eternal evolution from nowhere to nowhere. From nothingness to nothingness. Perhaps that was what *Forever and Ever, the Universe of the Universes* really meant.

Had Al Kansii learned or read something in *Al Andalus* that had made him doubt of his mission? Could he have sabotaged his own mission? Everything had seemed to work perfectly until the disintegration inside the Chamber of the People's Council!

Assam pondered: *a butterfly flaps its wings in the Amazon and a powerful tornado forms in Central Ameristan.* Small actions at the beginning produce cataclysmic effects as if a chain reaction had begun and inexorably marched toward catastrophe. *Chaos Theory.* What was it, that initial phenomenon?

Al Kansii had not notified the Caliphate that he had died, as the mission had required. Small detail, especially if he had actually been disintegrated with everyone else in the Chamber of the People's Council. But what if he wasn't there? What if he had survived? The uncertainty of the situation, more than the actual facts, could potentially have momentous consequences in the actions that the Caliphate would take following the historic change in the leadership of the Han Empire. *Small action at the outset, major effects henceforth.*

Had that small something, if indeed that small something even occurred, had it then caused Al Kansii to lower his guard, to be less vigilant and therefore either fail by the hands of others, or even made him cause his own failure without knowing he was doing so?

These were important questions as they underlined the conviction one needs to accomplish a mission, to achieve great deeds. Even if he forgot about Al Kansii, Assam needed those now if he were to carry out a new mission. His new mission, it began to become clearer, would be that of a jolt, but a rather soft jolt. Perhaps there would be no need for martyrdom.

Assam would use the unseen powers given by God to the believers. Assam had always known that beings made conscious by God were proof of His existence. But according to Islam, these beings were not made at the image of God, and that was why they failed, and they sometimes disbelieved. That's what Assam had been taught. That is what they learned as children, even as babies, in the magic years when they discovered the boundaries between their shell and the outside world. But Assam knew that that connection to others was always there even if the shell appeared gone.

Compassion, feelings, love, pity, beauty, poetry, cruelty, all those were remnants of the time when in the womb the embryo is one with his environment. And that is why according to Assam, one can feel, and enjoy the touch of someone else and that feeling cannot be duplicated by any science, any device, any wave or tunneling effect. Science had not been able to discover yet, if ever, the reason why the touch of someone has such impact on the person touched.

He remembered the non-touch of Lili and what he had felt that had had such an impact on him, and perhaps on the march of History since he had trusted her then. The experience with Lili's non-touch was still with him in more ways than one: she had used him, she had betrayed him. Still, he felt something for her. Why?

Assam continued to ponder these conflicting thoughts. Yes he knew that long ago the West had vanquished Islam and for hundreds of years ruled its lands, yet Islam had rebounded and triumphed. Would the West do the same? Were the Han not a distraction if that were true?

Can, or should a tribe impose its will and its creed on another tribe? The Caliphate's noble mission was to unite the world so that peace would finally triumph. Islam had just done that, almost. But Assam knew that often what began as liberation ended up in domination.

With doubts like these could Assam lead the next Jolt, even a soft jolt? The Caliphate was determined, Assam knew. There was no other option since that was their purpose. If the Caliphate were to abandon or lose that purpose they would fall into a degenerative state. Just like the West.

Assam was perplexed: if we can't dominate, we can't exist? Is that a law of the nature of man? Without conflict and aspirations we cannot survive? If the universe was created *ex nihilo,* out of nothing, then this constant struggle would be just a manifestation of this random process. Is there an inherent need for conflict without which man feels lost, lonely in the firmament? With conflict, man finds definition and purpose, and security.

Assam reminded himself that God had created the universe and had made us to be peace seeking subjects, submitted to Him. Why did God decide to do so ? Strangely, Assam noticed that no religion had answered this question, or even posed it.

He then wondered if as matter is energy and human thought was divine energy, then wouldn't thought and matter be connected. Was there an order of things outside of man's existence?

The Last Cantata

Assam was now in the spiritual safety of his secret music room. He could hear the feminine voice accompanied by the soft but robust percussion sounds of the hammers of the piano.

The cantata was nearing its end. Since he began developing his love for music as an adolescent, Assam had discovered this cantata. And he had discovered something about himself as well.

He had discovered that the sound of B flat major, or *si bémol majeur* as he had learned in his ancestral lands, had a special impact on him. A special meaning. He could feel sensations other notes did not provoke.

Assam knew of course that musical notes were sound waves of a specific frequency, and their harmonics. The most esthetic of all Assam always knew as a truth was the A, or *la* in his *solfège*. It was common knowledge that the A had a frequency of 440 Hertz and if you caused a string to vibrate at 440 times per second you would get an A sound, a *la*. A beautiful and clear A sound. Up one *increment,* was of course the B, or *si,* higher and just as beautiful as the A, but perhaps a little less. Its frequency was established as 493.88 Hertz.

However in between, not quite as pretty as the A, or as clear as the B, lies the B flat, the *si bémol*. To Assam the most mysterious note of all, the most beautiful in the saddest way. Its frequency was determined as 466.16 Hertz.

What was it with 466 Hertz, so close to the other two frequencies one higher, the other lower, that made him enjoy that sound uniquely? That, he did not know. He remembered discovering the slightly sadder sound of the viola, just a little below the violin and so much deeper and sadder. Why he liked that sadness was not clear to him. Yet Assam was an optimist. Perhaps in his next endeavor he would research what brainwave scientists had discovered about the impact of specific frequencies on the senses and the emotions. He knew for example that eons ago, a light blinking at a specific frequency in the cockpit of military airplanes had caused many crashes before engineers had determined that a specific frequency had caused the brain to *wipe-out*. Did the B flat have an impact on him and not in others, although this was imperceptible?

In any event, he was now in a trance.

The duet was between a soprano voice, a voice from another world, a supernatural voice with its high notes, certainly not human to Assam, and the piano. The conclusion of this little German cantata began with a B flat which disarmed Assam and captured his soul. As the soprano later pronounced the German word *dann* (then), and the piano in unison with the feminine voice but separated by what Assam perceived as a quantum time, almost nothing but not zero, struck its accompaniment; *dann*, responded the voice, and the piano struck again; then the two repeated this conversation three times. The feminine voice and the piano seemed to be straddling each other's paths, while being in perfect unison.

The two, feminine voice and piano together then increased their tempo. They were so perfectly intertwined, but separate. Two members of an entangled pair. Assam now felt the two identities in this dance of sounds, feminine voice and piano, the two striving to reach together the higher spheres of their being.

> "*Dann...*sound _ *dann... *sound_ *dann ist's erreicht,*
> *des Lebens wahres Glück.*"
> (Then it has been achieved; the true felicity of life)

While the feminine voice was carried by the piano which she in turn led, both repeated that as "*enlightenment heals the soul when in misery, through steadfastness, with tears of joy true happiness will be reached.*"

Then...sound_then... sound_then... true happiness is reached.

These were the words of Mozart's last cantata, the Cantata Number 619 in the Köchel catalog. It was a small piece of Masonic music which Mozart had written by the end of his life when Masonic thoughts guided his inner soul. It sent its message of hope and enlightenment to *"all that revere the Creator of the Universe, whether they call him Jehovah, God, Fu or Brahma."*

And again, as the feminine voice seemed to fade, the piano lifted her; and when the piano slowed down, she in turn carried him with her to the next note. And then the feminine voice sang a word while the piano finished the sentence, and the two sang this sentence three times while straddling each other in this wonderful flow of music. And the two together, feminine voice and piano, continued transporting each other in their music and strove again to reach the highest summit of their union. After that, the voice was no longer heard. And then, alone, the piano finished with an explosion of energy to conclude this entangled path of the two toward heights unseen.

The cantata had begun with a story of the gods and their impact on mankind, and how mankind triumphs over the forces of darkness. The culmination at the end with the *dann, dann, dann reaching out to true bliss* reminded Assam of that other piece of Mozart when *'man and woman'* together strive to reach godliness in the *Magic Flute*:

"Reichen an die Gottheit an"
(Striving for godliness)

Assam knew that that thrust upward of the soul was what motivated him and all in the Caliphate. Striving for godliness, with submission to Him.

Here it was a surreal voice and a piano, not a real woman and a real man, but the message was the same. What the cantata told Assam was that even in pre-Abrahamic times, before Judaism, Christian faith and Islam, man aspired to universal friendship and the end of divisions and with the same existential challenges that he Assam, and he was sure the Caliphate as well, were now facing.

What was then the purpose of his mission? Preservation? Were the Han a threat to the Caliphate's being? Of course not. But if it did not pursue its mission with conviction and determination, the Caliphate would wither away, just like the West.

Is it thus true that without conflict, one just dissolves? Trying to impose one's faith creates an immediate conflict that sustains us, Assam concluded.

Assam pondered: *"but if one believes, should it not be enough? Why do we need that justification of knowing that others believe the same thing and worship the same God? Yes of course God is One and the Only One. Why should I Assam need to know that others believe it too? Isn't God enough for me?"*

Assam remembered that he always looked at Al Kenii to see his reaction to Leila, in the few occasions Al Kenii was even allowed to meet Leila. Assam always searched Al Kenii's eyes for his approval. Only Assam possessed Leila but he needed Al Kansii's confirmation, and that of others also. The same happened to his beliefs it appeared. Assam was surprised by that need from others that they love and admire that which we love and admire. And if they do not, doubts enter our soul. Unless our love is so great that we do not need a mirror to tell us, to fortify us in our convictions.

Assam then concluded that his devotion to God had to be so pure and infinite that he did not need any justification or reinforcement. Certainly not from the Han.

The Han in a way, and a few tribes here and there throughout history as well, behaved that way it appeared. They did not look for that reinforcement of their own beliefs.

Assam asked himself whether those who did not impose their beliefs believed their truth to be the only truth. Or was it those who needed reaffirmation from others that weren't convinced of their truth? In other words does a True Religion need to be imposed?

Assam had to admit that perhaps that was not so. The Keeper of the Faith had asked him to think and devise a better way to accomplish his goal, once Sheikh Moussa and Al Idahi would fail. A better way he had said, or a better goal perhaps?

At this moment Assam felt that the incoherence in his thoughts was lifting like a morning fog. Yes, there is a limit to madness after all he thought. He felt dry, and tired. But things began to clear in his mind.

"The goal and the way are entangled," Assam thought to himself, smiling at the thought of quantum human processes. *"The knowledge of one determines the other. The determination of the other, defines the one. One can achieve his goal if the way through which one chooses to achieve it is the proper one. But then by defining the way first, wouldn't one determine the goal?*

"The violent jolt did not work, couldn't work with the Han. The way the Caliphate had undermined the West, with the help of its own institutions, and abandon from within, conscious or not, avowed or not, especially from the so-called elites, wouldn't work with the Han either. Democracy is powerless at fighting those who attempt to undermine its laws since these same laws protect them. This intellectually corrupt concept of protecting one's own enemies did not flourish in the Han Empire."

"Now," Assam said to himself, smiling again, *"I think I know how to conquer... no... I know what to do... with the Han. Now I know how to do it. Yes. It is so simple. So obvious!"*

"Al Hamdulillah," said Assam in a loud voice.

Assam would return to Usamabad.

Assam was not done.

The Two Deserts

Assam felt a great warmth fill his heart. He stepped out and walked toward the desert. When he was far enough for the sounds and lights behind him to have become extinguished from his soul, he stopped and looked up to the heavens.

In the dark of this perfect night Assam was now surrounded by the sands that appeared white. Above him the immensity of the night sky was the only other element that connected him to the universe. A sea of white and an infinity of black. Assam focused his eyes on the deep far away and there he could feel the *beyond the beyond*, that which man would never reach. And he remained in awe at the eternity of the moment.

At the same time five men in Antarctica had stepped outside after their discussion. Don Juan, Nissim, Ari, George and Sanjay looked up in wonder at the night sky of Antarctica. They were surrounded by an eternity of white. Above them the deep darkness of the heavens captivated their souls as they stood in silence. They could see deep, there, beyond the reaches of anything they could comprehend, the beginning of All. Nissim was finishing reading a poem he had started to share with his companions earlier that evening. It was by a poet of the West, written almost four hundred years before, when hope and confidence reigned in those lands and when man with his science was to free himself from the burdens of this world. As they stood in awe before the immensity of the ice and the sky, Nissim ended:

« *Borné dans sa nature, infini dans ses vœux*
L'homme est un dieu tombé qui se souvient des cieux. »[23]
("Limited in his nature, infinite in his aspirations
Man is a fallen god who remembers the heavens.")

And Nissim repeated in a whisper, in a barely audible voice: *"man… a fallen god…who remembers."*

---

[23] Lamartine, *Méditations Poétiques*, 1820 Christian Era.

Illustrations

About the Author

D. Leitsack is a physicist who has dabbled in high-technology projects. The many ups and downs of this true American experience led to the vision of *2188 AD – The World Under the Grand Caliphate*. What better thing to do than to describe the most troubling issues facing man since the beginning of Time and Space in a future science-fiction context interweaving science, religion and philosophy with provocative and entertaining intrusions into current political and religious debates? Leitsack loves the word play of languages and their subtle interactions, and especially enjoys seeking the true meaning of human endeavors with science as a method and the unlocking of the mystery of the mind as a goal. Both the English and French versions of this story are the work of Leitsack.